LIGHT ON THE SOUND

LIGHT ON THE SOUND

originally published by Pocket Books 1981
reprinted Bantam/ Spectra 1985
This Edition Diplodocus Press 2013
Revised Edition Diplodocus Press 2020

ISBN: 978-1940999-53-1 (hardcover)
978-1940999-54-8 (trade paperback)
978-1940999-55-5 (epub)

published by Diplodocus Press
Bangkok - Los Angeles
Main Office - 48 Sukhumvit Soi 33
Bangkok 10110, Thailand

for information about the author:
www.somtow.com
about this publisher
www.diplodocuspress.com

support S.P. Somtow by subscribing to
www.patreon.com/spsomtow

CHRONICLES OF THE HIGH INQUEST
Light on the Sound

by S.P. Somtow

introduction by Darrell Schweitzer
drawings by Mikey Jiraros

Diplodocus Press
Bangkok • Los Angeles

this one is for Mom and Dad

Spectacle!

a modest introduction

by Darrell Schweitzer

I have before me my copy of the first edition of this book. It is autographed, with an inscription that reads:

> *To Darrell,*
> *With Spectacle*
> > *Ludic*
> *Bhakti*
> *Bap*
> *and CounTERculture*
> > *Somtow.*

That takes a certain amount of explanation, but it does remind me that I have admired Somtow Sucharitkul (or. S.P. Somtow as he became known to the literary world) for somewhat over forty years now, which means we are both now vigorous and energetic seniors, whereas in the old days we were somewhat less senior, and Somtow at least seemed to be frantically energetic and creative.

I also have a copy of his first story collection, *Fire from the Wine Dark Sea,* which was published by the Donning Company in 1983. I was published by the Donning Company in 1983 too, so in this sense we were colleagues, although I think Somtow was more of their A-list author. The editor of the line was convinced he was a genius, and time has done nothing to erase that judgment.

My copy of *Fire from the Wine Dark Sea* is inscribed to me in the High Script of the Inquest. I have no idea what it says now. That may require a bit more explanation.

The Donning Company was something of a second-string outfit. It was impressive enough that I could get published by them (a story-cycle disguised as a novel and an actual novel), but they began with a short-story collection by Somtow because he was already a big name. He had won the John W. Campbell Award for best new writer. He already had two Hugo Award nominations.

So my primary publisher was his secondary publisher. His novels, starting with *Starship & Haiku* (1991), were published by Timescape, which, in those days Timescape was the flagship line for the science fiction field, the same imprint which brought Gene Wolfe's *The Book of the New Sun* out in mass-market paperback. It was the place to be noticed. David G. Hartwell, who has responsible for discovering and nurturing a substantial amount of the top science fiction talent was the editor there.

I first came to know Somtow because I was working as an editorial assistant for George Scithers on *Isaac*

Asimov's Science Fiction Magazine (a member of a team of several such, known collectively as "The Zoo"). By 1980 Somtow was a star contributor, one of the magazine's "big three," important new writers being heavily promoted by the magazine. (The other two were John M. Ford and Barry Longyear.) Somtow was always my favorite. I was amused and impressed by his "Mallworld" series, about a shopping mall in the outer solar system, where humans are overseen by the alien Selispridar, who have isolated the human race as unfit for galactic company, but have their own nasty foibles, such as that they eat millions of their own excess offspring like shrimp at a buffet as part of their normal life-cycle. *Mallworld* is full of great satire and humor, but also moments of pathos and real drama. It is not entirely silly. The silliness can ease you into much darker territory.

And now about "spectacle," "ludic," "bhakti," and "bap," which figure so prominently in that inscription cited above. These were some of the bywords of what can only be called Somtow Mania, a phenomenon quite evident in science fiction fan circles in the early 1980s. Think of the Beatles and the word "gear." Sort of like that. 1964 or 1965 was "a gear year." Remember that? You didn't necessarily know what it meant, but it got repeated. Somtow as a celebrity and personality was one of the most entertaining people in science fiction at the time, and what he said got repeated. A famous wit. He could draw a crowd at conventions simply of people who wanted to hear what he had to say or watch what he did, so they could tell a Somtow story later on. Harlan Ellison was like that too, although Harlan got into fights and controversies all the time. Somtow did not. Everybody liked Somtow.

Back in the days when desktop computers were still a novelty and if someone brought one to a convention it would draw its own audience, Somtow proudly demonstrated how he'd induced a music program on an early MacIntosh to clash with itself until he made it fart. The climax of such hijinks came with the Sucharitkul in 1980 campaign, in which he mockingly pretended to run for the John W. Campbell Award (for best new writer) as if it were a political election. There were bid parties. There were children wandering the corridors of convention hotels wearing sandwich-board signs saying "VOTE SUCHARITKUL IN '80." I still have my campaign button. Even more clever and witty than that was the fact that he admitted in an interview I did with him at the time that the "inner insidiousness" of the whole thing was that he did not expect to win, but the "joke" would get him attention. Then, he did not intend to campaign in 1981, his last year of eligibility, and therefore might win on the "pity vote." What was supremely clever was that this actually worked.

So, while Somtow established himself as a celebrity in science fiction, this frivolous and tacky exterior only semi-concealed and actually drew your attention to his greater depths. Even as those Mallworld stories were more than just jokes, Somtow has always been more than a jester. For one thing, he continues to have a significant musical career, as a composer and conductor. He has written operas. (He also wrote, at George Scithers's behest, "The Isaac Asimov's Science Fiction Magazine March.") But if you look at the Inquestor series, starting with the book you hold in your hands right now, you find something that is romantic and beautiful and strange, what Brian Aldiss once called "wide-screen baroque" science fiction, an imaginary universe of considerable complexity. Here we see a lot of characteristic Somtow touches. The heightened, poetic language. Sensitive, but not sentimental depictions of children characters. The theme of *Light on the Sound* is a discontent with the status quo which moves on to rebellion. His characters do the archetypal things that science fiction characters do, particularly young ones. They set out to discover how the universe really works, rather than just believe what their parents or tradition have told them. (Think of Arthur C. Clarke's *Against the Fall of Night*.)

We meet three such characters from three very different societies, none of whom are satisfied with their lot. One has a dull existence providing food for people of the "Dark Country" that he is not sure even exists. Another is a young girl who finds herself the only sighted and hearing person in the country of the blind and deaf. Her people live out their lives in darkness and in silence, their task being to kill and harvest "delphinoids," sort of air-whales that live in a vast, dark chasm, and produce songs and light-poems of such ineffable beauty that anyone who perceives them cannot return to being mere humans afterwards. The brains of the delphinoids make interstellar travel possible, which is the basis of the vast empire known as the Dispersal of Man. Incidentally, dead people from the Dark Country are recycled to feed the delphinoids. Overseeing all this is the ancient and all-powerful ruling caste of the Inquest, which as its stated mission seeks out and destroys utopias, since the whole setup depends on suffering. The third main character is one of the Inquestors, who also has come to question the traditional order of things and, after having disposed of twelve previous utopias, now may have found one he urgently wishes to preserve.

This is a more bizarre system than that of Frank Herbert's *Dune*. Imagine if David Lynch had filmed this instead.

Inevitably, probably because the ruling elite is called the Inquest, readers equate Somtow's universe with that of the SF master Cordwainer Smith, who wrote of the Instrumentality of Man and its Lords. In that same interview I did with him, Somtow expressed great admiration for Smith's work, but commented that his own universe is "less Oriental" than Smith's. Maybe so. Smith (real name Paul Linebarger) was a noted Asia scholar, a close confidant of Chiang Kai-shek, and the godson of Sun Yat-sen.

Somtow's universe is probably far more operatic than Smith's. I will let someone more musically literate than myself explore that. What his work has shown from the outset has been a genuinely different cultural perspective from that of most American science fiction writers. He was born in Bangkok, raised in several countries, educated in England (he went to Eton), and went back to Thailand early in his adulthood to learn the language and immerse himself in the culture. Thus he is able to write quite differently from someone who spent their whole life in a New Jersey suburb. His voice is distinctive. His imagination and talent are huge. His work is a genuine fusion of Asian and Western ideas.

It's great to see the Inquestor series re-issued, and to see Somtow writing more of these books.

You're going to like this series.

■ Darrell Schweitzer, April 30, 2020

LIGHT ON THE SOUND

Lady Varuneh

Book One

Out of the Dark Country

Zenz átheren a kéanis
áias tálassas
aiúd lukhs de' skaápnai
z líddar den ypnolan

On the sunless sound
On the sighing sea
Came light from the shapers
And songs from the dreamers

---Galléndaran folk song

One

The Overcosm

At the core of the curving of time and space, the overcosm coiled. A cosmic serpent. A monster of non-Euclidean paradoxes . . . beyond, between the dimensions of realspace that men perceive.

In the overcosm light went mad and battered the senses with music of color, and time became irrelevant.

Through the overcosm, pinholing from star to interstellar blacknesses to the hearts of dusty nebulae, ran hidden paths. Paths that could only be understood as abstruse equations in the memories of planet-sized thinkhives that stored all knowledge of the Dispersal of Man and wove perpetual patterns out of the chaos of data. Paths that could shorten the distances between the stars . . . if only someone could perceive them.

The paths are nothings now; they are power-paths that have rendered secure the power of the Inquest over the million known worlds, over the twenty millennia of the Dispersal of Man.

But once upon a time, there were travelers, traveling in the old way, searching for the paths: searching for centuries. sleeping mostly, awakening in new regions of spacetime, searching a little, then dying . . . and they found a planet. which they named, in the old hightongue that is still used by the Inquest, Gallendys.

What a strange planet it was!

On one of its continents, a volcanic crater stood, its walls a hundred klomets high, breaching the stratosphere; a thousand klomets wide. The walls rising pyramidally to an opening narrower than a single man. In the crater. no light fell. Not even starlight through the roofchink. For in the crater there survived a dense atmosphere, from a forgotten eon in the planet's past; and there was only darkness, and the churning winds howling like anguished animals over Keian zenzAtheren, the Sunless Sound.

Elsewhere the planet seemed human enough: here a desert, there a sea, here a valley for a Kingling's pleasure garden, here a mineful of precious ores fit tor a punitive colony.

But within the Sunless Sound, in the hidden country of darkness—

They found vast creatures, Windbringers, who swam through the thick air. With huge. formless brains, a hundred meters long. and borne aloft by a tang-scented light air they puffed into huge flapping sailsacs.

What a dull perceptual cosmos for them, if they had been built like men! There would have been nothing to see but the darkness, nothing to hear but the whistling of their self-made winds. But their minds were turned inward. They perceived the overcosm directly, that part of space that is at once the center and the farthest edge of spacetime.

In the darkness they soared up from Sound to ceiling, from wall's edge to wall's edge—

And they sang!

Imagesongs. Lightpoems that shattered the thick darkness. Harmonies that bounced and rebounded from the whispering walls, echoshifting, never quite dying, so that the whole enclosed world resounded with the weavings of their overcosmic visions. They sang and were at peace.

Until men came.

Men heard and saw the imagesongs. It was said that even the high warriors of the Dispersal wept, that even the stern Inquestors, Lords of the Dispersal, were so moved that their shimmercloaks glistened with tears.

The imagesongs were the key to the overcosm, to unravelling the quickpaths between the stars. They had to understand them! For they had a need to leap from star to star, to trade, fight, conquer, to stand on ever-new earths. . . .

But no. Those who experienced the imagesongs wept and were changed, and declared that they had seen perfect beauty and that the desires of men no longer touched them. The Inquest, as always, found a way.

Then more men came who could not weep at the imagesongs. And still the imagesongs burst and resounded over the darkness. But the men did not see or hear them.

They were blind and deaf: and the Inquest saw this as an act of compassion. Not knowing they could not see or hear. they were free men.

Or thought they were.

Two

The Shadow of Skywall

Great eyes of a young boy staring at the endless Skywall—

"Don't dawdle, Kelver!"

Kelver pressed another button. A bale of food vanished from the displacement plate. And then—

Skywall! They called a hundred-klomet-high mountain that penetrated the roof of the atmosphere, a mountain 3 thousand klomets long . . . to him it was Skywall, an utter blackness that halved the zenith, that divided the world into known and unknown. And behind it — the mythical Dark Country.

For a great distance the mountain was perpendicular and quite black; farther up it dissolved into a sheer mist flecked with greenery, and higher still, at the limits of perception, more blackness.

You could pretend the black was a giant holoscreen. You could project your fantasies on it, say it was the blackness of space and spatter it with stars and planets and hurl yourself into the thick of the overcosm wars.

Kelver had passed his third winter: fourteen years that was in the highspeech of the Inquestors. And when you were fourteen and stuck in a backvillage, with no clan name, and you'd never been so much as a step oil-planet, not even to the moons-what could you do? Dream. Make alien things in the Skywall that only you could see.

From the side of the Skywall mountain, perhaps a hundred meters up, the Cold River began, enclosed in its own metal wall and borne on pylons, dropping at a sharp angle until it reached ground level and stretching on forever away from the Skywall, impossibly straight.

Kelver pressed another button idly.

"Kelver—"

It was Uncle Aaye.

***

"It's pointless anyway," he said. "We're just pressing buttons and food is disappearing, and we always do this every week and it's a waste. . ."

He pressed a button. Another basket of fresh meat vanished. Uncle's voice: "You know as well as I do, Kevi. It's to feed the other people, the people in the Dark Country." As if anyone could live inside a mountain.

"Uncle, Uncle, this whole setup insults our intelligence! Why do we have to grow food for ten times the village population, and then sit here and watch it disappear?"

"Quiet!" Uncle Aaye said. "I'm ashamed of you!" He looked away as if terribly embarrassed.

I'll slip away, he said to himself suddenly. *Nobody will mind, really.*

So he did.

First he reached the edge of the village of porcelain houses, shunning the displacement plates that would have eased his feet. Then he passed the place where workmen tended the source of the Cold River. He started to run faster.

Got to get out of the shadow world—

Some days when the Skywall cast no shadow, when the suns were in opposition, you could hurl a ripe krellash at the wall and watch it sizzle and plummet, and you could run with the hot sour juice dribbling into you until you started to run into a country inside your head, a country of subtle shifting lights . . . but in the shadowtime you could freeze the same krellash against the wall, into an icecandy. In the shadowtime - and he had seen three of them - you couldn't run to the edge of the Skywall's shadow. Not in a day's running.

Run! Run!

He had to get away. And think. A strange anger drove him. He wasn't the thinking sort, so he couldn't define it. Like—an anger of wanting but not knowing what you wanted. He took it out on the hard earth, pounding the softness out of his fursoles, banging the rocksmooth ground.

He had to run anyway, for the cold. Shoveling food had warmed him for a while, but it was a deceiving warmth. He was wearing nothing but a small cloak of costly clingfire that his uncle had brought back from Effelkang, the great city. . . .

At the edge of shadow he braked himself.

A tongue of sweat licked at his hard little body, honed by the sandsharp winds from the badlands of

Zhnefftikak. He was lean, his muscles wound tight like the strings of a whisperlyre. Only his eyes showed any softness . . . they were green. Like the furgrass that dappled the walls of the Cold River, where moisture had condensed from the burning cold behind its crystal-clear, Inquest-built walls. It was along the Cold River that the earth was hospitable enough for villages.

He sprang out the cooldark shadowland—

Lightblaze. Twin suns white and blue.

The system of displacement plates had ended. Ahead of him lay a glarewavering carpet of chalksand.

It was a world of straight, ever-stretching lines for Kelver. The mathematical straightness of the Cold River, the sky-splitting straightness of Skywall, the far white horizon, razorstraight from eye's end to eye's end, and always the same. . . .

There was a world of curves out there. Far beyond the Zhnefftikak wasteland. A journey of maybe a hundred sunpassings. There was the Sea of Tulangdaror, the twin cities of Effelkang and Kallendrang, one hoverfloating over the sea, the other high in the sky. You could see it as a star sometimes—Kallendrang, that is—when the two sunpassings coincided and the bright side of Skywall became a flickerflecked darkness for a few hours. . . .

He longed for the world of curves. But he didn't really believe in it. He didn't believe anything his uncle told him, any more. Even though his uncle was Elder of the Foodmovers and an Interpreter and had a clan name too.

He looked up.

The blue eye danced with the white, in the dazzleglare of the sky, and—

A black bubble burst from between the suns. It fell. Grew. Kelver froze.

The bubble fell more, in a delicate spiral, and he couldn't tell how far it was or how big it was because everything was so featureless, so white. . . .

The silence was eerie.

It grew to fist size, then balloon size. then—

A hail of bubbles, popping from nowhere in midsky! Blotting out patches of the whiteness, cascading, dancing so slowly, so . . .

This is new. This has never happened.

He heard a sound then. His own heart, pounding. *It's something special! It's just for me!*

***

They were all growing now. One of them swooped above his head not twenty meters, and it was larger than a man, he saw, larger than several men. And then they all swung past his head, figure-eighted above each other, and there was a breeze, parch-hot, springing up in its wake—

Got to tell someone. Maybe it's important.

For a moment he panicked. He didn't want anyone to know about it, he wanted to clutch the secret to himself for a few moments—

He tensed for the sprint hack to the first displacement plate, stopped himself, turned. . . .

It *was* real.

He dashed into shadow. The shadow swallowed him. Almost as though the wall itself had eaten him.

***

He found them shoveling more food.

Behind him were the porcelain houses, box-shaped interchangeable-looking things, each box a solid glaze, blue, red, yellow, orange. Ahead a hundred meters loomed Skywall. The end of the world.

He flung himself through the crowd of workers, elbowing a woman aside. "Uncle Aaye!" he shouted.

The big displacement plate had been emptied. He saw his uncle's face mirrored in it, furrowed and unpleasant. The metal, curved a little, widened the face like a balloon. He crossed the plate and went to his uncle.

"How many times have I told you not to run over a displacement plate like that? Kevi, you could find yourself in the middle of Skywall, buried in solid rock under a hundred klomets of basalt!"

He looked up into his uncle's face. The scolding had been automatic; there was no heart in it.

No love passed between the two of them.

"I'm sorry, Uncle." Then, bursting with what he'd seen, "Uncle Aaye — if only you'd seen it! Outside, beyond shadow, today—"

"If only!" Uncle Aaye sighed. "You should have been shoveling food, but I know where you've been — staring at Skywall till your eyes popped out, dreaming about starships." To the workers, "Carry on. We've another load of food before the week's quota is done."

Kelver said, "I have to tell you this, Kaz Ashaki, Village Elder, Master Interpreter—"

His uncle stopped. "Formal, aren't you?"

Listen, will you!

"No," said Uncle Aaye, preoccupied again. "Not the grain, dolt! This is a meat bale! You want the people inside to get a vitamin deficiency or something?"

Pause.

Kelver watched them shovel. Watched the man at the console press the button. Watched the food disappear. What was it for?

In the ground, along the paths between houses, soft light . . . Kelver realized another winter, another shadowtime would come soon, when the dance of suns took them away from this part of the planet and the shadows became cold. People were testing the groundlights. . . .

He couldn't stand it any more. He just blurted out. "I saw black bubbles fall from the sky."

There was silence. He felt them watch him. He was the village liar and he knew it. . . .

"Inquestors!" someone shouted "It must be a coronation!"

"Bah," said Uncle Aaye. "Probably another tax assessment." He was trying very hard to act nonchalant, Kelver saw; but for a moment Kelver had seen the tears in his eyes. More kindly, his uncle said, "You all have leave to go and watch."

But he was talking to the air. They had all vanished, dashed down the path to the first displacement plate, out of sight.

Uncle Aaye looked at the boy distractedly. "So what did you see, really?"

Kelver sensed the old man's worry. But he was still burning with the excitement of it. It was the first new thing he'd seen since . . . since his father's corpse. He told him everything. . . .

"What are they, Uncle Aaye? What are they?"

"You haven't guessed?" His uncle looked at the boy for a moment. Kelver couldn't tell what he was thinking. Then he said, "You dreamer of starships, you . . . they were tachyon bubbles."

Kelver was afraid.

"They are bubbles of realspace," Uncle Aaye went on, "that are shot through the tachyon universe. They are used by the Inquest for instant travel between the stars. Some people say that whole suns die to fuel them. While other folk use the starships that sail the overcosm, and suffer from the disorientations of time dilation, the Inquestors can be anywhere at any time . . . someone in the universe is putting on a show of power, Kelver. A great deal of power . . ."

But Kelver wasn't listening any more. He was thinking, *At last, Gallendys, our own planet, is at the center of something important. Maybe even I can get involved—*

A crinkled hand on his shoulder. "The last time the Inquestors came was to command the razing of a city . . . and the decimating of the population. One in ten of our planet, Kevi, painlessly put to death . . . because some distant village had rebelled against the senseless task of feeding the mountain. They said if our planet had been less important they might have annihilated it."

"I'm sorry, Uncle! I shouldn't have seen them, maybe I'll be bad luck for all of us now!" said Kelver. That was when his father had been killed. He twisted free of his uncle, disliking the dry touch of his hand . . . and turned to watch Skywall, the unchanging blackness.

The blackness reached up to the end of the sky.

A whiff of raw meat for a moment, from the foodbales and then he kicked the bale over onto the plate pressed the stud, watched it fade away.

"I don't get it," he said. "I mean, Uncle, I mean — why are we doing this? Why is the Inquest so important?" There was no reply. He went on, more passionately now, "What gives them the right to do this to us?"

"I thought you wanted to rush out into space and fight the overcosm wars and work for the Inquest!" his uncle said harshly.

Kelver thought about it. His thoughts went round and round in circles. Something was wrong with the way things were and he didn't know what it was.

He sent another bale of food into the mountain. *I hope you enjoy it*, he thought at the people in the Dark Country. The people who didn't exist.

"Kevi—"

Kelver reached out and patted his uncle's hand. He was sorry for him sometimes . . . having an unwanted kid thrust on him like this. His uncle knew many true things, secrets; Kelver knew that they burdened him sometimes.

Kelver had told too many of the others about the starships that he saw in the Skywall. He'd never live it down now. They'd thrown him out of their circle.

But today he was something special. Even if it was only a bringer of bad tidings. He had been the first to see the rain of tachyon bubbles. And by nightfall everyone would be talking of nothing else.

They walked back to the house together.

In the atrium he saw his aunt Telzi. She and his uncle were two of a kind; tired, plodding people. She was beautiful though, even at fifty; she'd had a somatic renewal in Effelkang, at great expense . . . firm breasts strained against her polyrobe, bright hair flamed. But Kelver saw as he stood watching her come toward them. down the steep steps from their sleeping level, how they had been unable to change her eyes. From the angel's body, from the angel's face stared a hag's eyes. He hated her, hated them both; and now she ignored him.

To Ashaki she said Aaye, there's been a message over the holocom. A tachyon transmission relayed from Effelkang.

"The Kingling of Gallendys is dead. A new one has come, with an entourage, to be crowned by the end of the week. His name is Davaryush—"

He heard his uncle begin to shout, "So what difference does it make? They're all the same, one Lord of the Dispersal is just like another, they won't change anything—"

A slam. Darkness.

Uncle Aaye had blanked the lights, completely forgetting that Kelver was still in the atrium.

Kelver listened.

His aunt, quietly, from somewhere above: "And how did the food-moving go, dear, any hitches?"

A growl. Then, "Why did that boy have to be the first to see them?"

"It's not his fault. . ."

Kelver lay down on the floor: quickly it contoured itself to his body. The whispering upstairs began to crescendo. An argument was starting. "That boy, that boy . . ."

He'd gone to sleep to the sounds of this lullaby for years, almost as long as he could remember now. . . .

He tried to imagine the new Kingling. Davaryush. In the formal style that would be *Ton Davaryush z Galléndaran K'Ning, Inquestor and Kingling. . . .*

In the darkness he tried to picture the twin cities of Effelkang and Kallendrang: nothing came to mind. He knew of the towers built upon the towers of towers, but this was just a form of words, he thought. Once or twice he had seen holosculptures . . . but nothing whole, nothing to give an impression of the grandness of it. And descriptions from uncles and elders , . . wind from the desert.

So he closed his eyes and thought of starships. He flung them out into the blackness. zapped them in and out of the overcosm, and started to pound the floor as he lay, so fast it couldn't contour itself in time. . . .

Then he thought, *All the starships in the Dispersal of Man work because of the Inquest.*

The thought chilled him for a moment; but then he lay back and counted starships as they crossed the overcosm in his mind, counted them over and over until he was asleep from exhaustion.

Three
The Utopia Hunter

A room in Kallendrang. In the lowest tower of the towers that hung downward from the sky, almost kissing the pinnacle of the topmost tower of Effelkang. that tower built upon the towers of towers.

Invisible towers too: like the towers of force that kept the twin cities in this opposition, the one mirroring the other, suspended over it, the lower city Effelkang hovering over the Sea of Tulangdaror.

And round room like the deck of a starship. Like the towers, its walls were of force. Now they had been deopaqued to reveal the view.

The view: the Sea of Tulangdaror, pale-blue sparkletipped water from horizon to horizon. Water to the west: to the east—even at this distance and despite the curvature of the planet Gallendys—the tip of the Skywall mountain peered, an impossible perspective. A black wall leaping from its shroud of mist from a vague somewhere beyond the horizon. Impressive; there was no mountain like this known through the whole Dispersal of Man.

And below: spires of amethyst and chalcedony and azurite and rose quartz and olivine, skyscrapers of metals spattered with porcelain tiles' glass cathedrals sweeping in swooping curves, thin white streets that sutured the city.

And ahead. Hanging spires that echoed the leaping spires. Not a mirror exactly: they were not quite the same city. Here there were hanging ziggurats of stone, veined with vines from Vanjyvel and Ont, the Inquestral Palace. Here the streets were the tongues of windows, lancing the sky.

Kallendrang was all jeweled stalactites shrinking into the haze of mid-distance, arrowed by avenues, freckled with hovercars, glitter-rich with the dazzle of the blue and white suns.

And in the room, a man, alone, naked.

Waiting.

He was Ton Davaryush z Galléndaran K'Ning; for over three centuries an Inquestor, for two centuries a hunter of utopias, and now new Kingling of Callendys. He did not see the view: his eyes, heavy-lidded and heavier with sleeplessness, were closed.

His Inquestral shimmercloak lay dead on the floor beside him. It had been ritually stripped from him and sprinkled with prussic acid. An Inquestor and Kingling must discard his shimmercloak and take a new one to symbolize his role as an anointed ruler; his shimmercloak must be grown from a double-yolked egg.

Some hours before, he had stepped from the tachyon bubble into the room, dissolved the bubble with a subvocalized command. The room had been full then, Inquestors and the local nobility almost mingling. The Inquestors had included Exkandar, his contemporary in the seminary, Alkamathdes, a Grand Inquestor who had been his teacher, and others too: their shimmercloaks had swished and swept and glittered and sparkled in the huge chamber.

And then Alkamathdes had broken the egg over his head and they had left him alone, for the standard day before the coronation, to reflect, to let the new shimmercloak grow to maturity upon his body . . . a ritual, meaningless enough.

And tomorrow, more of the same. It would not be tomorrow on this planet, Davaryush remembered: here the days were strange and irregular, what with the complex dancing of the suns. But tomorrow he thought of it still—more meaninglessnesses. He would drift on a hoverfloat through cheering throngs and smile and cast an ember into the firefountain of Kenongtath that burned at the heart of Effelkang, in the Square of the Delphinoids; then ride the gilded elevator up the tallest of the towers, cross up to Kallendrang in a floater, traverse more cheering throngs, enter the Inquestral Palace, receive the iridium crown upon his head, be bathed in lustral water from the Sea of Tulangdaror, finally possess the multi-millennial seat of buttock-prickingly uncomfortable carved basalt from the mountain of the Dark Country, smile again—

All this didn't change the facts.

He was in disgrace.

He had been made Kingling simply to render him useless, by an Inquestral Convocation that had been too baffled to dispose of him.

He was a heretic!

It's strange, he thought, *how power moves in the world of the Inquestors. The people below, whose lives*

*are over in a flash, like daydream, like phantoms—they
always think we are power, all the power in the
Dispersal of Man. a pure quantity. Gods, almost. If they
only knew.*

Inquestors have all the answers. Davaryush opened
his eyes now, and watched the sea. The broken egg
trickled his head. . . . *Inquestors cannot argue amongst
themselves, can they? Being an Inquestor strips you of
your individuality. You become part of the unchanging
ideology, dogma, power. A truth symbol. A compassion
symbol. A symbol of unity.*

*For the universe of the Dispersal of Man is vast,
beautiful, terrible.*

But Davaryush knew also how lies had become
embedded in the image of shining truth . . . he himself
had dared to question some of these lies.

He was the most dangerous of all the types of
heretics. A heretic from within. And since an heretical
Inquestor was an unthinkable anomaly, they had
designed this elegant solution. To drown him with
glory. To imprison him with his own power.

To be a ruler. Not to think.

How many of the commonfolk knew that to be a
Kingling was the lowest of the low, the only point of
the Inquestral hierarchy that even touched the
commonworlds? As this room was the only room of the
city of Kallendrang within touching of the topmost
spire of Effelkang?

Davaryush relaxed as the threads of the
shimmeregg thrust out, intertwined, wove themselves.
Already there was a grid of strands crisscrossing his
body . . . he watched the city below. It seemed so
changeless. . . .

This prison was a subtle one indeed. For Gallendys was a world vital to the survival of the Inquest. And the human race. Here they built starships. Here the giant delphinoid shipminds, carcasses of creatures who were all brain, were soldered into the ships so they could navigate their way through the overcosm. And now men needed ships: for the Overcosm Wars, for the War Against the Whispershadows, aliens that had never been seen or heard except from under great billowing veils. . . .

And how could Davaryush do anything that would jeopardize the entire human race? The entire Dispersal with its more than a million worlds? He was a heretic, not a lunatic.

Davaryush admired the trap they had built for him.

And then he thought, desperately, a lonely thought: *But I do believe in utopia, still!*

For that was the nature of Davaryush's heresy.

***

Time passed: there was nothing but the tickling of the shimmerstrands as they inched across him, weaving, growing. Already the strands blushed pink against the blue, with new life, drawing some nutrients from his waste products and from the air. The growing of a new shimmercloak was a comforting sensation: four times he had felt it before, on reaching a different level of the Inquestral hierarchy. . . .

The first time, now. When he was twelve, an initiate. in a small room facing the power of the Inquest. . . .

You have compassion, Davaryush.

"Yes, Father." He had been a veteran of three wars even then. And now was alone, in a room with the

Grand Inquestor, whose eyes glared fire and millennial wisdom. Even after three centuries, the memory returned, vivid.

When you came to kill the condemned criminal, you did not torture him or play with him, as was your right, an essential part of the initiation. You killed him cleanly, in a matter of seconds, slicing him into two congruent parts with your energizer. It was artistically done. But why?

"Father, it was necessary to show skill, not cruelty. I have already killed many people." He feigned assurance; in truth, he needed desperately to relieve himself.

Very well. I name you to the clan of Ton.

Davaryush started, gasped audibly in spite of his knowledge of the proper conduct . . . he had come expecting to fail, to he returned to homeworld.

The clan of Ton . . . that would mean seminary, long years on harsh inhospitable planets, thankless labor for the sake of the Dispersal of Man. . . .

Loneliness.

"Father—"

You are unworthy. I know. Nevertheless the Inquest takes what it can get.

    ***

His first mission was the planet Gom, a hot planet of a blue-white star. The people lived in tall buildings, thousands to a building, fifteen billion to the planet. But they were happy. They were quite ignorant of their responsibilities as a fallen race: they relied on automata, they pursued their hedonistic existence without regard for their true natures. They suffered from the heresy of utopia.

Davaryush was a perceptive utopia hunter: he had found the flaw very easily. Every year, in a special ceremony marked by compulsive gratifications of the senses, all those over the age of fifty intoxicated themselves and then committed suicide, leaping by thousands into the lava lakes that boiled conveniently on every continent.

He'd saved those people. First he had whispered to only a few of them: *And what if you did not die?* He had created civil wars, unhappinesses, revolutions. People ran mad, setting fire to the machines that had succored them. Then the ships of the Inquest came, bringing comfort with them.

Comfort and truth.

But Davaryush had been tempted by happiness then. Alkamathdes, his mentor, said: *Remember, man is a fallen creature, Davaryush. Utopias exist only in the mind, a state to which it is given us to aspire. But to imagine that you have attained that state-that is to deny life. The breaking of joy is the beginning of wisdom.*

And after a while he had been no longer tempted. For he saw such as the planet Eldereldad, where the happy ones feasted on their own children, which they produced in great litters, by hormonal stimulation; and the planet Xurdeg, where the people smiled, constantly, irritatingly, showing no face except the face of ecstasy, until he had finally learnt that the penalty for grief was dismemberment to feed the hungry demands of the degenerating bodies of five-thousand-year-old patriarchs . . . yet when he asked one of those ancients what he most desired, he had replied: *To feel grief. But I am afraid to die for it.*

When he was a young boy facing his new destiny he had first learnt about lying. Alkamathdes had said: *Never forget the lie. This lie is the sacrifice that you must make, the little sin you will commit for the sake of saving countless millions. It is this—that the Inquest is seeking a perfect utopia. A planet that will be designated a Human Sanctuary, for the edification and glory of the Dispersal of Man. You will tell that always, and in your heart you will understand always that there will exist one fatal flaw.*

And always, after, the ships of the Inquest would follow him. In a year or so his subjects would awaken to their true natures. Then they would fight wars and exhibit pitilessness and avarice like everyone else. For man was a fallen being. For centuries he had never doubted this.

Until the thirteenth utopia.

Until he came to Shtoma in the cadent lightfall.

***

A brief night passed.

In the twin cities night and day were hinged to his whim, to his waking and sleeping. The dance of the twin suns had no provenance here; the shields that surrounded the cities could block out, could play holographic landscapes of their own choosing. . . .

When Davaryush woke, a gaudy dawn had dyed the Sea of Tulangdaror. Savage purple streaked the sea.

He woke with a start, rose from the floor. The floor flattened.

His shimmercloak was full-grown. The dark-blue fur blushed, shivers of pink rippling through the living material. He turned; the shimmercloak whipped around, echoing his movement.

Then he saw the dawn. They had sought to copy his homeworld, the lost planet he had not seen in three centuries. Did they think he would feel at home, more secure, then? But time dilation had stranded his homeworld in an unreachable past. Some time *between*, while he sat and watched the fire of the overcosm counting the years like seconds . . . they had obliterated his homeworld. There had been some war . . . well, that was what it was like, being an Inquestor. You got an overview. Lives flashed by like the lives of insects.

The dawn pained him, more than he thought it would. Was the Inquest playing a game with him, subjecting him to psychological tortures while he was caught in their trap?

He clapped his hands.

It was the Lady Varuneh who answered his call, materializing in the middle of the room. She came forward, stepped down from the displacement plate, slid gracefully into the required obeisance. . . .

"Lady Varuneh," he said, studying the face, "I want the dawn changed. I want the shields deopaqued so we can look at the real Gallendys all the time. I want to begin my reign honestly, if I can."

The shadow of a smile surfaced on the Lady's face and melded into the mask of humility. "I'll see to it," she said.

She looked about eighty—old for a woman not of the Inquest—and was severely clad in a black tunic with only a wisp of clingfire around her neck and waist.

Suddenly Davaryush thought. *Maybe she's a watchdog of the Inquest.* "Who ordered this dawn?" he said, selecting his coldest Inquestral voice.

"I did." Deceptively simple.

The woman looked straight at him. It was an ugly face, gray-streaked and lined and without cosmetics. Her hair was still black, but parched like a blasted field . . . her eyes were young, blue, powerful. Again the thought that she might be more than she seemed gnawed at him. "Discard the dawn, please."

The woman froze her features for a moment; presumably she had cyberinputs to the buildings themselves.

He remembered from his hypnobriefing who she was: a member of Gallendys's old aristocracy from pre-Inquestral times, now technically a planetary bureaucrat, directress of the shipyards—in practice a kind of court lackey, one who knew her way around the complexities of local protocol and could be expected to know many secrets of many Inquestral rulers.

He didn't like her.

I'll get rid of her as soon as I can, he thought. *Curse her for springing the dawn on me like that!*

Then came an image of his dead homeworld, of his dead parents. He was afraid of this woman too.

Abruptly he turned to look at the sea. The sky was shattered. Shards of the purple light broke off and faded in the painful brightness of the two suns. They had hardly moved, then, since the previous day.

And the towers glistened.

"Your Highness is ready for the official ceremonies of induction and coronation? Shall I inform the court?"

A little stiff, a little hurried, he thought, appraising her by instinct.

"Yes. Yes," he said absently, wishing she would leave.

"I'll inform them—"

What was she dawdling for? She must be a spy of
the Inquest, observing him, watching for a clue of
weakness so that they could close in on him and
punish him—

"You may leave."

She rushed toward him then. He put out a hand
quickly to ward her off. Then she knelt at his feet and
thrust something into his hand. Cool. Flat.

"Kill me if you have to!" she whispered fiercely.
"You must be the one!" Then she whirled around and
hurled herself onto the displacement plate and faded
away.

***

"What is this?" Davaryush cried. And then he stood
alone in the huge chamber. It had been an unnerving
experience; for a moment he had thought her an
assassin.

Then—

He saw that there was a message disk in his hand. It
was of the crystal parchment that scribes used. It was
written in the Inquestral highscript, with a fair, firm
hand, but it was not in the highspeech, it was the
tongue of Shtoma.

And he knew what it said.

The words were—

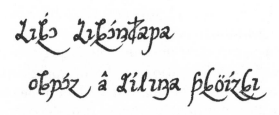

qíthe qithémbara

udrés a kílima shtoísti

"Soul, renounce suffering:
you have danced on the face of the sun."

Davarvush shook. Did the Inquest know then what
had happened on Shtoma? Were they only waiting for
him to reveal the canker-darkness in his heart?

Even now, Shtoma haunted him. Shtoma in the
cadent lightfall.

The planet where he had found his own heresy. . . .
Underneath the passage was a message in the
hightongue.

It was a different hand: nervous, spidery.

*We think you are the one who will change the way
things have been. To challenge the past. We think you
know that utopia may yet exist . . . on the tenth day of
the week, come stand by the firefountain of Kenongtath.
You will be contacted.*

Then the words dissolved. The ink had been timed,
giving him a chance to read it only once.

They were all waiting for him to catch the bait, to
show that he was still the heretic inside! Callendys was
a trap!

. . . Shtoma in the cadent lightfall . . .

Could it be that there were human beings
somewhere, waiting for him to come as a savior? Could
it be that the Lady Varuneh was not a spy, but simply
driven by desperation to reveal herself?

Davaryush knew how devious the Inquest could
be. . . . He filed the information carefully, suppressed it
with an effort, in case the Inquest had mindbearers
planted nearby. And turned his thoughts to the coming
ceremonies.

And looked out over the city. The spires, hanging down and pointed up, like the teeth of a monster ready to swallow him. A single false step . . .

The image of the homeworld dawn crept back into his thoughts for a moment. Then he knew that it had been no accident: it had been planned as a sign for him, to jolt him into an emotionally receptive state perhaps. There was no end to the Inquest's deviousness!

Selfishly, he wanted the mauve dawn back then. He wanted the sky streaked with half-remembered purples and the sea sparkling like liquid amethysts and the green grass tinted black by the sunrise. . . .

Tomorrow he would look into the history of the woman Varuneh. He would find out once and for all who it was who was trying to manipulate him, and why.

The ache of homeworld swelled in him. Outside, the city glittered.

The trap yawned, waiting.

mór ómbrel eyáh
dhánata ómbrel eyáh
chadáh y' ómbren evéndek
a témbris kíndaran éndek

The shadow is mother
The shadow is death
The shadow falls forever
On the children of darkness

—Text inscribed on all gateways
into the Dark Country

Four

The Dark Country

Girl-before-Naming wasn't human and she knew it. And she knew she could never tell anyone. She knew what would happen.

The Dark Country. That was what would happen.

She was a girl just past puberty and cursed with a gift that made her not human and she was terribly alone.

Like now. In the family catacomb, she was sitting with her arms folded, not touching the ground, and she *knew* where every object in the room was. Without feeling for the vibrations. Without tapping the floor with her fingers, easing along until they encountered an object, carefully identifying it by its texture, its smell, its taste.

She could feel with her eyes and ears.

Look! The others-before-naming in the room were playing ball. Sensing the caress of wind against their faces reaching out and catching, sometimes stumbling over stray rocks . . .

She felt the ball come to her with her eyes. She caught it with impossible accuracy. A boy tensed, feeling the sudden stillness of the air. Then he clambered toward her . . .

He grabbed her arm. *Cheat! Cheat!* he signed. his fingernails rasping her skin . . . she winced, moved away.

I'm not cheating, she signed.

All of them were around her, suffocating her, smelling her and each other to check who they were . . she felt everything press her in, she felt as though the far dark above would fall on her and crush her. . . .

Wildly she reached out to the first children within grasp and signed—each hand mirroring the other—*let me alone!* With her eyes she felt them pass the message down.

With her ears she felt them leave, through the circular machined opening in the rock. The curve-feel that meant *door.*

It always ended this way. Someone would start to get angry. to sign *cheat, cheat,* and then they would be signing it round and round and she could even feel them sign it with her eyes sometimes. she could make out the finger motions almost, she could almost figure out the code of the eye-feelings; sometimes it blurred for her. But there had to be something to it. . . .

I must be hallucinating, she would think sometimes. Logic said there couldn't be any senses apart from feel, smell, taste. And her eye and ear senses were feeble, shadowy senses, not like the real ones.

Sometimes they worked better than other times. It was in those rooms where a diffuse force flowed out of the walls themselves and widened the periphery of her feeling. She never could tell why this was, why some rooms accentuated her strange senses; for there seemed no source to the mysterious undarkness.

Now she pushed herself hard against the jagged wall of rock. Every well-memorized furrow grated on her back. Then she straightened her crotch-shield and tried to smooth down her new breasts, a little worried at them. With her eyes she paced the twelve paces to the other wall.

In a week she'd be normal. . . .

A presence by the round door. A boy-before-naming. Her touch-brother in fact.

He came toward her, inching with his toes, sensing her sweet young girl's smell. Then he sat down in front of her and reached for her arm. . . .

You're a strange girl, he signed. *With a twiddle of perplexity, a twist of anger. The ceremonies of adulthood coming up, so soon, and you still throwing balls with the other children.*

She signed, *I'm scared.*

Why? So they take out your eyes. Useless organs anyway. Nobody has ever figured out what they were ever meant for physically. So we consecrate them to the Windbringers, who are the source of everything. He was signing in neat mechanical strokes—Girl-before-Naming knew he must have just come from his instructor, that he had just memorized another sacred text.

It'll hurt. Of course she did not dare tell him what the eyes really meant to her . . . even now her eyes touched his face and she felt sweat there, almost as clearly as if she had wiped the wetness with her own hands. . . .

Oh, Girl-before-Naming, her touch-brother signed, *are you a coward even now? How much use will you be on the hunt? When we sail into the thick wind, with our snares laid and the Windbringer's breath flying over us and the windstorms churning?*

(More memorized texts, she thought.) *You know I'm not a coward,* she signed. But her fingers trembled on his palm.

Remember that we are touch-siblings. Our scent is one. We were so promised at birth. . . .

Somehow she knew that he was frightened too. So she drew him to her in the profane touch that is reserved only for touch-siblings, and they both drew an awkward comfort from each other. . .

Touch-siblings, she signed tenderly. *Our scent is one.* With her eyes she felt the face. With her ears she felt fear escape from his mouth, a windshape piercing the blur of air.

***

Girl-before-Naming reached the gatherchamher in time for a funeral. The Windriders had come home from the hunt, fifty sleeps long, and three were dead. The whole settlement came to touch the dark ones, some twenty catacombs.

She held hands with a stranger and they began the journey to darkness. The passage to the Dark Country where the dead went to join the angels . . . was only manwide, and dank-smelling. Girl-before-Naming was hemmed in by the closeness and the breathing of strangers with their unrecognized smells. Once the passageroof scraped her head. They inched their way to darkness

The dark! The ugliest sign in the language of her tribe.

To be *dark.* To reach out with your arms and touch nothing at all, to stretch out forever and still not reach the rockwall that meant you were still in a real place. . .

Dark is death. Death is dark.

They pressed on. *Slow down,* she signed weakly to the hand that clutched her in front.

A soft finger-pelting sign, repeated over and over in her hand, showed that the hand was the hand of a bereaved one...

—muscles twitching as someone stooped for a roofdip—

Then they filed past the bodies of the dark ones. Girl-before-Naming reached out to touch the cold, hard flesh that had become one with stone. The dank smell crammed her nostrils. She was shaking. And she felt the hand of the person in front tighten. The procession hurried on.

They reached the tunnels to the Dark Country. A man she could feel standing opposite her in the corridor handed her a glove-amp; she slipped it on and stood against the wall, waiting to feel the last rites.

It was Stonewise, her family elder, who signed first. She felt the glove holding her hand; it transcribed the sign into her palm accurately but emotionlessly, so she could not tell that he was thinking. . . .

We say farewell to these as they enter the darkness. We leave them in the Dark Country where the walls are further than an undark man can walk without going mad from lack of sensation. . . Angels will come out of the darkness and destroy their human forms. They will become one with the hearts of the Windbringers, they who gave their lives for the life of the Windbringer.

. . . Behind her was a child, breathing as if bored. In front the hand of the widow or widower gripped hers like a sandwich of stone slabs Girl-before-Naming had been to funerals before . . . but now that it was so near to her own rites of passage, she was tense. *This could happen to me,* she signed in her mind.

And then she thought of losing her eyes. With her eyes she strained to feel something, but that secret sense was dark for her. But with her ears she felt strange windshapes escaping the mouths of the others, stranglesounds that frightened her, that reminded her of the signs for terror and anguish—

O Windbringers, we thank you. For your first flight over the empty waters, when you made the humans and the corridors carved of stone. For your second flight over the waters, when you made the secret chambers where the food appears, so that your children would not die or perish into darkness.

From darkness we come; to darkness we return your children. May the angels you have made bear them home, to the chambers of cushioned rocks in the heart of your eternal darkness . . . .

With her hands the widow subbed, signing the grief-touch over and over.

Windbringers! Windbringers!

Girl-before-Naming lost interest in the ceremony. She began to think of the future. How she must soon sail into the void and help bring home a Windbringer. How she would get a piece of his windsac for a loinpiece and a cutting from his tailflap for a mattress to sleep on, to share with her touch-brother. There were only two types of people: hunters and waiters. And she already knew—even before the dream that she must have to confirm this—that she would be a hunter. Not for her the waiting at the foodgate for the bales of food that appeared as gifts from the Windbringers, a lifetime of waiting and cleaning the catacomb and being widowed perhaps, losing a touch-brother to the darkness.

Even as she knew this, she was afraid.

The ceremony was coming to an end. The elder Stonewise had pressed the stud that opened the gateway to darkness. Had placed the bodies on ceremonial mattresses woven from the headfeathers of the Windbringer. Had pressed the stud that tipped the bodies into the Dark Country. . . .

A strange thing happened then. She was nearer the gateway than she had ever been before at other funerals, through some chance of the order of the procession, and—

At the moment the gateway opened, a softness she could not touch flooded her eyes. With her eyes she could touch—

All the people! She touched them, flicking her eye from one to the other. She touched the knobbly ceiling that was hardly a handspan from her head. And then...

***

The chain was breaking now. A body or two squeezed past her, children ignoring the etiquette of processions in their rush to get home and eat—

Without warning, the hands that clutched her on both sides were gone. She stood alone for a distance of ten or fifteen paces in either direction, and this glowing softness from the open door bathed her, made her feel light-headed. It was an eerie thing, this softness.

She took a step toward the gateway. She could feel the whole circle of doorway with the eyes alone. She didn't have to inch along even though the corridor was alien to her.

She stepped out as though it were her own home.

She was at the circular doorway now. She felt with her eyes. . . .

Below—without the real senses she could not judge distance—were the three bodies.

How tiny they are! she thought. *Do people shrink so, when they come to darkness?* She reached out with her eyes. It was one of those caverns that glowed with the quiet, sourceless thing, that let her eyes reach farther. *Why is it,* she thought, *that I can feel so clearly in this darkness, touching nothing at all? Whys does it awaken the secret senses so strongly?*

It was still. No wind touched her face. She turned upward. With her eyes she touched—

Things. Alien. Huge, spidery, glinty-sharp. There was no ceiling it seemed: there her senses were truly dark. But the things up there in the height—

They were coming down toward the bodies!

They were growing bigger, bigger—

She closed her eyes, cursing the secret sense. Then she turned round and began to walk home. Even without touching the door she knew with her ears that it had made a wind of closing. *(It can't have been real, she thought. Maybe I dreamed the whole thing.)*

Abruptly the softness in her eyes subsided as the wind of closing finished. Things felt familiar again. She groped her way along the wall, reached the receptacle where she laid her discarded glove-amp. . . .

The dank smell came to her, mixed with the empty smell of being alone.

***

The floor of the preparation room had a cold wetness to it. A trace of the perfume of the

Windbringer circled in the still air. Drug-drenched steam caressed her face. Girl-before-Naming sat in the center of the room, the walls just out of arms' reach so that they were absorbed into darkness. The idea was to prepare you for the little darkness, the little death through which she must pass in her search for a name and a destiny.

She had been sitting for two sleeps, without food; her only sustenance was a sipper of water over her head. If she strained she could grip the dropnozzle with her lips and get water, a bitter water scented with Windbringer's blood.

She waited.

The steam was so strong that her secret sense was stifled. Her ear sense was muffled. Her eye sense found darkness as dark as the untouchable walls.

Time stretched. Her head was light. Still the dream eluded her. . .

She felt a hand on hers. The feeling was a blur, easing into focus . . . a name played on her hand, over and over.

Windstriker.

Father! she signed, only half-believing. *Why have you come?* Under the skinfolds she touched bone, sharp, old. She had not touched her father's hand since . . . thrice three hundred sleeps ago, when she had been consigned like all children to the preparation barracks.

Daughter, you were always special. I had to come. Though I've never come for any of my other children. . . .

She clutched him then, not signing but just letting his love flow into her like a warm wind from the Sound. Through the thick steam, her eyes touched a shadow that could have been his face. Where the eyes should have been, her eyes touched hollows, gouged out, smoothed by age. There was a fear suddenly. She gripped him harder, still not signing.

Not a word for your father?

Slowly she signed, *Love me, Windstriker. Give me strength.* And then he released her hand.

His touching vanished into the steam.

Hours . . . eons . . . later, in time beyond counting, another hand came and touched hers. Another old hand. This one felt like a cushion, the bones were deep and well padded.

Cold needles of terror—

Stonewise, she signed. Power Master, Elder, Interpreter of the Wind, she signed quickly, using all his titles.

Good, he signed. His fingers were cold. She waited for him to begin instruction.

He signed, *And do you know what you will become, Daughter?*

She signed, *I do not touch it clearly yet, Stonewise. When I reach out . . . it's like a crystal made of darkness.* She strained to touch him with her eyes but the steam was thicker now; they had intensified it, isolating her even more. There was nothing in her world but the cold floor and the cold hand and the cold, cold darkness.

How so? he signed. *You like paradoxes, then? You might become a power person, like I am, one day. . . .*

I cannot say.

I've fixed a place and a time for your initiation, he signed.

She waited.

Twelve klomets' walk from the farthest catacomb of our village in the direction of the village of the people-who-walk-sideways, there is a door that leads to a bluff that overhangs the great Sound. There you will sit in a darkness more profound even than this one. No hand will touch you. It will seem to you that you have died.

Then out of this darkness that is death but also is soul-hefore-birthing, out of this chaos of stillness.

Girl-before-Naming shuddered.

. . . Windbringer will call you. The scent of his spirit will touch your face. His wind will come rushing upon you even at the moment of utmost fear. For Windbringer is our protector, the bringer of life, the taker of life; we live in the touch of the shadow of Windbringer. . . .

She felt a slow trickling of sweat down the nape of her neck. She recoiled into herself. It's worse than being born, she thought. . . .

Power Master, she signed, *I'm afraid. Suppose his touch never comes to me?*

You'll die.

And she could smell his indifference. The steam grew stronger. Now she could taste the sour Windbringer blood.

And my touch-brother? she signed. *The one who is forever linked to me?*

He signed, *Both will die. You dream together, you die together.*

His hand jerked away from her, leaving her in the darkness. The steam grew hotter, draining the water from her. She reached up with her face and caught the water flow, but the water was sour and almost boiling-hot and did nothing for her thirst. She burned with thirst. The steam came in scalding waves purging her. . . .

My eyes! My eyes. . .

She thought of Windstriker. Why had he come? Why had he shown such an unnatural affection for her? Everyone knew that a father and a daughter must sign to each other only with the utmost formality, lest the intensity of respect boil over and embarrass them both. Suddenly she felt pride in her father. She felt he was different from the others—

Touch-brother was bound to her forever. They were one scent. They were permitted the most profane of liberties with each other's bodies.

But she could never tell him about the touching of eyes and ears. He would mock her forever and call her *Darktouch*, and shy away from her, and his lovemaking would become the caress of a cold machine. They would always be loyal to each other, because the tradition ran deep—soon they would dream together perhaps, perhaps even fall into darkness together.

But he would never understand her special senses.

Her father, though . . . *If I have to get help, I'll have to turn to him, she thought.*

And then, with a rush of despair—

There's no one else! No one!

She beat her fists against her eyes, pounding them, angry with them—

And felt another hand against her breasts.

Touch-sister, came the soft Sign, intimate and terribly distant.

Brother. Brother. Brother, she signed, but her mind was on the flight of the Windbringer over the vastness of darkness, on the pain of the ritual of the tearing of eyes, on the fear of never coming home.

setáliken feravó
et vashónuur
dáded:
hokhté, Enguéster,
mún verávis?
hokhté,
hos hyéma sta lávoryman shténjuu
dhandándah níkah?

l asked the starship if he felt pain.
He said:
You, O High Inquestor, you
ask me this, you
whose blood is distilled from the tears
of dying planets?

—from the *Songs of Sajit*

Five
Delphinoids

"To the mainland," Davaryush said.

The Lady Varuneh nodded. The floater soared out over the open sea. It was three standard days since the coronation; it was time to go to work. To inspect the domains of the Kingling.

In the distance behind him Davaryush saw the twin cities, two pyramids joined at the apexes, jewel-clear in the sun-light. He burned all over. The white sun had crossed the face of the blue, and even the waterglare hurt his eyes. . . .

He gave a command. A darkfield englobed them at once; a damp mist of water lightly spiked with the drug *f'ang* blew over the two of them. Through the darkfield the sea had a soft orange-brown luster, and the suns' glare fell to a whisper of light.

He watched the Lady Varuneh.

Her face, her movements, betrayed nothing of the strange scene that had passed between them three days before. Dignity stood between them like a forceshield.

"Lady Varuneh . . ."

"Yes, my Lord?"

"You are, theoretically at least, mistress of the shipyards, are you not?" He felt he had to break the silence, if only with repetitions of what he had already learnt. "You do much direct overseeing, then?"

"There's little enough to do." She smiled quickly, remembered her place. "The thinkhives govern everything, of course, Inquestor."

They flew on in silence, the Inquestor brooding, trying to puzzle out the woman. Who gave nothing away. She crouched in a bend of the floor of the floater. Today a scarlet sash, wound tight around the stalkthin waist, dazzled incongruously from the drab robe.

This was the woman who had only three days before placed herself in a position of certain execution.

And put *him* into an impasse: he did not know whether or not to acknowledge the message, whether or not to simply command her removal, whether or not to investigate further . . . .

After some fifty klomets flying over the open sea Davaryush spied land. It was ugly, brown land: only at the sea's edge was a there a fringe of green, startling in its way as the Lady Varuneh's sash.

"Ahead," said the Lady, "is the township of Un Angkier. My own estate is not far from the town center and I hope I may offer you some hospitality—humble as it is—for the midmeal. . . ."

"Where are the shipyards?"

But he saw them now, from the floaters vantage, a roofless labyrinth of low walls, chambers with the husks of klomet-long starships, beyond them a garage of tugs, fifty stories high, beyond them still a town of squat, unremarkable dwellings, mass-molded and repetitive. And specks of people, tiny insects crawling over the high-hulking sunglittering ships . . .

. . .and the river, enclosed with crystal walls, that ran from the center of the labyrinth and turned sharply in the mid distance and stretched to the limits of his vision—

In the mid distance, too, at the corner where the river angled out to infinity, began the flat and featureless white clay that was the wasteland of Zhnefftikak.

"Bring down the floater."

They came down, the labyrinth raced toward him and expanded into—

Great walls of stone and steel, five meters tall, and topped with lethal field generators that rotated, winking in the sunlight—

The two of them stepped down from the floater.

"There is no reception committee," the Lady Varuneh said as they dismissed the floater and he watched it rise and wait above then heads, making a little shade from the brightness. "I understood you might perhaps want to view the shipyards. . . incognito."

Davaryush looked around. This chamber of the the shipyard was at least a klomet square: its walls were low lines, distant.

Against a far wall a hull was being erected. No one had observed them: or if they had, had thought nothing of it. . . .

"Look," he said, "No one is watching. What was the meaning of the message?" He saw Varuneh blanch, recover control.

"What do you mean, my Lord?" she said. Then, under her breath: "Just do as it says!"

"You dare command me?" He turned on her, angry.

"I don't presume . . . ." she began. Then she said, "If you would care to progress to the next displacement plate. . . ."

They stepped onto the plate and rematerialized—

And he was face-to-face with a delphinoid shipbrain.

It stretched to left and right for fifty meters and towered high over Davaryush, an ashgray ovoid shape, wrinkle-furrowed, quivering a little. Overhead, huge rotating jets sloshed nutrients over the mass of flesh. . .
.

He was not prepared for the wetness of it. Or the slow quivering. He had always known how a starship worked—how there was a delphinoid shipmind that saw through the overcosm, under the control of an astrogator who mindlinked with the ship and became one with it. . . . But he always imagined a starship as machinery. Not as a living thing.

He moved nearer. Wondering, he put out his hand and touched—

Slippery. His finger traced a line in the flesh, the line sealed itself up. . . .

He walked the distance of several city streets and came to where a team of workmen on a scaffold were leaning against the brain working with solder and blowtorch.

"Does it not feel pain?" he said, disturbed.

"How can we know?" the Lady Varuneh said. "How can we dare to know? If they did feel pain, would we halt the advance of the Dispersal of Man, just to assuage the anguish of aliens?" She spoke too quickly, as though making a jest of it . . but Davaryush caught the twinge of bitterness in her voice. He decided to drop the subject.

"You have many shipyards, Lady Varuneh?"

"From the world inside the mountain issue perhaps twenty-five of the cold rivers, leading to twenty-five shipyards across the continent. Each shipyard is serviced by perhaps a hundred tribes of the people in the Dark Country, the hunters . . . but the Inquest has not told us who those people are, and why they remain in the mountain. . . ."

"It's not for you to question the Inquest," he said automatically, gazing up at the workmen. They were singing as they drilled passages into the brain and reeled in electrode gables from a crane-held dispenser.

He caught fragments of the words, sung over and over again to a pentatonic melody, hypnotic and sad:

> zenzÁtheren a Kéanis
> aias Tálassas
> aíud lúlkhs de' skáapnai
> z líddar den ypnolan . . .

They were words in the common form of the hightongue, not in the dialect spoken around Effelklang, not in the shadow-speech of the outlying villages. . .

"The song they're singing," he said, turning to the Lady Varuneh.

"Ah," she said. "I doubt whether the workers themselves know what they are singing. It's only an old folk song, perhaps as old as when the first Inquestors came to the planet. . ."

The song went on. The workers hove a big drill into place and then began to unreel more cable, chanting the same strange words. . . .

"*On the Sunless Sound,*" Davaryush translated to himself. "*On the Sighing Sea . . came light from the Shapers . . . and songs from the Dreamers. . . .* What does it mean, Varuneh?"

"How should I know?" she said, twisting away from his gaze.

I shall never understand her, he thought. *Here I'm asking a perfectly innocent question, and—*

He stepped into the shadow of the brain again. Out of the burning into the damp and cool. He looked up, the delphinoid brain curved, the grayness deepened near the top. It was like . . . a sand dune in the desert. A sand dune that breathed.

When they had finished connecting up all the nerves, they would begin to build the ship. Then they would tow it out into orbit; an astrogator, of clan Kail or Harren, probably, would come and link with it and they would burst into the overcosm, where time stood still and ran faster than itself and lights danced maddeningly . . . hundreds of ships a year.

And those hundreds not nearly enough, were it not for the additional power the Inquest could exert through its control of the tachyon bubble, the Dispersal of Man could hardly be the unit that it was.

And this planet, and these strange people in the mountains, the only way. The brains emerging into the cold rivers, liquid nitrogen encased in a stasis shield that let nothing out, floating slowly toward the shipyards.

There were mysteries here. And Davaryush hungered for knowledge. It was this hunger that had led him into the most powerful clan in the known galaxy.

"Perhaps," the Lady Varuneh said, breaking into his thoughts, "we should break for a midmeal now, my Lord?"

***

The atrium of the Varuneh mansion was at first sight blatantly barren—almost self-consciously impoverished.

Davaryush followed the woman and they reclined on the floor. To his astonishment, it did not contour to receive his body.

"Malfunction of the floor mechanism?" he said. "You should have someone from the palace come over and see to it."

"No . . . it's just a personal idiosyncrasy of mine," Lady Varuneh said. "But the floor fabric is silk and stuffed with *kyllap* leaves—not uncomfortable when you're used to it."

Davaryush settled himself uneasily. They did not speak for a while. He saw that there was a kind of opulence here, much different from the dazzle-richness affected by the Inquestors in their dwellings. . . .

The atrium walls—which mimicked the ubiquitous white plastic of poor men's dwellings—were actually Ontian marble, etchveined by the firesnows of that violent planet. The cost—

In the center of the atrium a low firefountain played, a liquid rainbow flicker spurting from a base of iridium set with intagliate mandalas highlighted with diamantine crystals.

And above them the sky, filtered and made bearable by a soft darkfield. The glow was almost like . . .

He flicked aside an image of Shtoma in the cadent lightfall.

Soon there were serfs bringing trays and goblets of sweet zul. Davaryush watched Varuneh eat, very fastidiously, carefully crossing her silver skewers from left to right. . . . She had once been beautiful. Not a doubt of it.

"And do you like our world?" Lady Varuneh said. She managed to slip a note of innocuous mockery into the platitude. . . .

"I am perplexed," he said. "I don't understand you. I don't know what is going on. I should sit back and let the thinkhives govern, and send in my starship consignments according to the instructions of the Inquest, and be at peace here . . . but I can't. Someone, something is trying to disturb my peace."

He had spoken tactlessly. He should not have dropped his guard in front of this woman, who was perhaps a spy of the Inquest. . . . *Perhaps, when she reports this, they'll think I am on to their game. Whatever it is.*

"Isn't that as it should be?" Lady Varuneh said lightly. "*An Inquestor can never rest from thinking; for an Inquestor stands at the center, suffering the necessity of thought for the sake of the salvation of the Dispersal of Man.*"

"You know the Inquestral texts!" he cried, startled.

"I have known a great deal in my time. Ton Davaryush z Galléndaran K'Ning," she said.

Davaryush ate. . . .

"And the previous Inquestor who ruled here," he said. "Was he a fair Kingling? Did he oppress the people too much?"

"I was his mistress."

Davaryush watched as she plucked the feathers of a roast jangyll, and laid them one by one in a neat pattern on the tray . . . and offered him the dusky meat, perfectly skewered.

***

As the floater swung upward toward the sunlight, and the twin cities rose into view like crystal stalagmites from the water and jewel stalactites from the roof of the sky. Davaryush remembered Shtoma . . .

He came to Shtoma in the cadent lightfall, his tachyon bubble breaching the gilt-fringed incandescent clouds like a dark meteor.

... the thrill of a virgin utopia, ripe for the unmasking of its purifying flaw...

He was two hundred and thirteen years old then, and at the height of his analytic powers. With the destruction of twelve deceptive utopias, experience had banished misgivings . . . he knew that every utopia must have its flaws.

He remembered.

Shimmering cloudbanks. An extravagant landscape growing as he fell, sharp-angled trees like giant pink spiders, with then ferric-based photosynthesizing pigment . . .

Whimsical spiral dwellings of transparent plastic, jutting up at irregular intervals from the blanket of dense vegetation, crimsons and vermillions.

The wind thrashing his translucent sphere as it adjusted to the gravity, cushioning his fall to Shtoma. . . .

What he had been told of Shtoma. How they had fallen into a pattern of ecological stasis, from which he must release them, whatever the cost. And this was no backward, back-to-nature, primitivistic planet, but a world whose technical sophistication rivaled his own homeworld's. Exceeded it, even: for Shtoma alone, of all the planets in the Dispersal of Man, understood the secret of gravity control. For which they had no use, except for the manufacture of toys. And which they guarded with such miserliness and irrational fervor as to belie their much-vaunted saintliness, their notorious lack of greed and every other *human* quality. . . .

And the rumor that it was a utopia was more than could be tolerated.

If it was a utopia, it could be destroyed. He was a master iconoclast, a utopia hunter. *And every utopia has its flaw.* Otherwise, why was the Inquest necessary?

. . . His bubble slowed itself, brought him down upon the field of rust-colored grass. An alien song-snatch haunted his ears. With a mindflick he deactivated the bubble.

And an old man sang to him—

qíthe qithémbara
udrés a kílima shtoísti

"Soul, renounce suffering; you have danced on the face of the sun ..." Strange words, with opaque and patently sinful meaning. He said to the stranger, disregarding the greeting: "I am from another world. Who is it that addresses me?"

The alien's gaze chilled him. "You are Inquestor Davaryush of the clan of Ton. Welcome." Abruptly he beamed and stretched out his arms to embrace Davaryush. The Inquestor yielded ungracefully. This was no peasant then; he had misjudged. . . .

"I come to investigate Shtoma's utopian possibilities, so that it may be considered for the honor of being named a Human Sanctuary," the utopia hunter said. He did not blush at the lie: it came easily to him by now.

"So! How delightful . . ." The old man laughed; his eyes broke into a hatchwork of wrinkles. "I am Ernad, your host. You must be weary. Come."

A man—poorly dressed and without a single attendant—had dared to address a Master Inquestor by name! The alienness of the world unnerved him.

The clouds had parted to reveal the white dwarf sun, unnaturally close. The rough wind tousled the grass, blood-red and tall. Everything was wrong with this planet—it hugged its primary impossibly close yet had a standard atmosphere, its characteristics violated all possibility—Davaryush started to answer the man, but he had turned, expecting him to follow.

A stony path led to the first recognizable artifact: a displacement plate, incongruous metal in the red field. It was no primitive world! Despite the absence of war or slavery . . .

And the house.

He reeled from the vertigo of it—the crazy spiralings and swirlings of transparent walls, the cacophony of chiming and chirping that bombarded his senses. How could they live amid such a wilderness of sensual stimuli? Where was their discipline, their culture?

Children and young people sauntered by. They showed no respect. They shouted at him—*qíthe qithémbara!*—without respect.

"You must forgive them," Emad said, interrupting his dismay "You are an offworlder, and . . . well, it is an especially exciting time for them now. It's nearly time for the festival of initiation, and anything can spark their enthusiasm." He spoke with no trace of criticism in his voice. How alien!

"Your attendants?" Surely someone this important . . .

"No, neighbors, friends, relatives. Our houses are open, Davaryush."

What of the initiation ceremony? Davaryush thought. *Perhaps there's some unspeakable rite here, perhaps that's the flaw in the utopia.* "I must rest now," he said. "But after, I would see everything in your world: your games, your pleasures, your prisons, your criminals, your asylums, your places of execution. "

Ernad paused, as though he were translating something to himself. . . . "Ah yes. I have heard of madmen and criminals. I am not uneducated, Ton Dayarvush. . . ."

They turned down a corridor of glass that swerved upward into the air, and Davaryush felt a sudden dislocation, as though he had changed weight and *down* had become *sideways*, and he found they were walking upside down on the ceiling. "What is happening?"

Ernad laughed mildly, "It's" the same principle, you know, as the varigrav coasters. You must have seen them, our principal export—"

"But why fool around with gravity inside your dwellings?"

"Why not? Would *you* not be bored if all direc tions remained constantly the same . . . ?"

And the room.

A large chamber perched on the point of a translucent pyramid in the sky.

Davaryush saw on the far wall a huge capelike sheet of some sheer material, the room's one adornment. Like a rainbow sail rippling: with in the room's ventilating breeze. It was beautiful, he conceded, but bewilderingly complex, undisciplined, uncivilized.

"This cape? What is it for?"

"Oh. My wings," Ernad said.

Davaryush knew then how addicted they must be to the varigrav coasters, those "toys" they had inflicted on the rest of the galaxy. . . he looked at the old man. Was his sincerity merely stupidity, and not deviousness?

For there was such a toy, hanging on the wall, as though it were a god.

Davaryush felt sad already. After twelve successful missions he found himself still vulnerable to pity.

For he was nothing if not compassionate.
***

"I know you are thinking of Shtoma," Lady Varuneh said.

Davarvush was startled from his reverie. A light wind, salt-scented and damp, had permeated the darkfield and played with a few strands of Varuneh's hair, white-streaked and flax-textured . . . . ahead was the gate to Kallendrang, a diamond-shaped barrier set into the invisible forceshields. And behind, still distance-misted, the twin cities. The sky-foundations of Kallendrang disappearing into wisps of cloud, Mirrorspeckle windows twinkling like tiny stars.

In her way, the Lady Varuneh was still beautiful. A woman weathered and worn smooth by time. . . .

Slowly he said, "If you wish, you can restore the programming of the city's forceshield, have it replay the dawn from my homeworld, mornings." Vaguely he sensed that she had won some kind of victory. They were playing a colossal game of *makrúgh*, the Inquestral game of strategy and control; and the mysterious woman was gaining ground . . . he watched her.

The woman had no right to know so much about his past. She must be an enemy. And yet he found himself drawn to her, as an insect of the night toward the flame.

***

The false dawn pleased his eyes that morning. He breakfasted alone; then went to the audience chamber and issued some harmless routine decrees. He requisitioned a certain percentage of starships for the planet Keima—it seemed to be at the forefront of a new war. War was a game the Inquestors played at constantly; for most could not be satisfied with the *makrúgh* of computers and boards and metal tokens. And of course, war honed the human animal for the good things of life. So it was prescribed in the Inquestors' ideology: and so he had always believed, until Shtoma.

Davaryush found the city's thinkhive in a small chamber of the Palace that had no windows. It was a room without curves, perfectly cubical, and walled with mirror metal. He entered, seeking answers—

"What," he said, "is the real reason for this planet's existence?"

To serve the Inquest. The voice echoed in his head. The thinkhive had access to all knowledge on the planet. But one must ask the right questions, for it was as wily as an Inquestor, and yielded nothing until it had judged the questioner thoroughly.

"Why is it that the people on this planet—with the exception of the twin cities' population, who are all civil servants and bound to the Inquest—are in such a state of technological backwardness? Beyond the shipyards of Un Angkier, the displacement plates come to an end. There are villages, each one stranded in the shadow of the dark mountain—"

Come, come, Davaryush! What are you driving at? You know as well as I do that it is to the Inquest's advantage for planets of such critical importance as this one to be kept in ignorance. How would it be, if one world could hold an entire Galactic community to ransom?

"Tell me then why so little is known about the way the delphinoid shipminds are harvested and brought into the shipyards."

Everything is known, Davaryush. You haven't asked, that's all.

"So tell me."

In the mountains there is a culture of blind and deaf people, so mutated by the Inquest at the beginning of the period of Inquestral power. They hunt the delphinoids: thrust the brains into the cold rivers . . . their whole culture, their whole mythos, was manufactured by the Inquest. Their lives center around the capture of delphinoids; they have no time even for foodgathering. Nor can food grow in the emptiness of the Dark Country. So the Inquest created villages of feeders who supply them with food. But in the mythos of the Dark Country, it is the gods, the delphinoids, who supply everything. . . .

"But why are they deaf and blind?"

It is not in your interest for me to supply this information. Davaryush felt cold fear then. He gathered his shimmercloak about his shoulders, even though the cold came from the inside and not from the perfectly controlled weathermakers of the cities. A thinkhive could not contradict an Inquestor, not unless . . . there was a truth here that gnawed at the very roots of the way things were. . . .

But it's all very clever, Davaryush. For instance . . . just in case there are genetic throwbacks, the mythos contains a puberty ceremony that involves eye-gouging. No sighted person could possibly remain. . . .

"And if—" Davaryush stopped to frame his question carefully. "And if one of the people in the Dark Country should escape?"

It's impossible.

"All right. I know that between here and the Dark Country there is an impassable desert. I know it's populated with al'ksigarkar, fanged creatures who eat flesh. I know there are stone-age men in the wasteland, too, planted there for the sake of separating the civilized cities from the rest of the planet. But also we've had no contact with the people of the Dark Country for twenty thousand years, isn't that so? Couldn't some development occur—"

Darnryush, Davaryush. Do you think I don't see into the very heart of the Dark Country? That the Inquest did not provide me with eyes and ears even over the winds of Keian zenzAtheren?

"I suppose so." Davaryush said.

And besides—the voice of the thinkhive continued—*there are other built-in safety measures. For example: in the caverns where the dark people dispose of their dead, set into the cavern roofs, are robot drones. Their function is mainly to clean and vaporize the bodies and dispose of the organic slush. which sluices into the Sound and becomes part of the amino-acid soup which the delphinoids eat. . . . These drones have another function also, one that has not been exercised in twenty thousand years.*

"And that is . . . ?"

If someone should escape from the Dark Country, the drones will follow, hunt down, kill.

"The Inquest is very thorough," said Davaryush, admiration tempering his distaste.

I am very thorough, the thinkhive corrected. *Although the instructions of the Inquest left little room for error.*

For instance . . . I was entrusted with the creation of the dark people's sign language. I was very clever with it. Do you know what word I use for the drones who come and dispose of the dead, the drones who would chase and terminate any escapers?

"I couldn't guess." Davaryush said. He started to leave.

The thinkhive said: *The drones are called . . . it translates as "angels," I suppose. Isn't that funny? In a sardonic sort of way. I mean. Oh yes, the Inquest gave me quite an appreciation for semantic niceties.*

Six
To Touch the Lonely Wind

Still fog. Hot damp gusts of aloneness. And darkness, except for the patch of floor that Girl-belore-Naming sat on . .

After a time she could not estimate, Stonewise touched her lightly, waking her from the light trance. He held her hand as she rose, giddy with the intoxicating scent of steam laced with Windbringer's gall. . . . *Quick, quick,* he signed.

What is it? Should I go over to the bluff now? she signed feebly.

No. Come with me. They are sending Windbringer home. Girl-before-Naming crept after the old one, her hand resting lightly on his back. Her eyes had crusted with the chemicals in the steam; they could not touch through the darkness. And her ears were clogged.

After a while she felt the fog disperse. Now they were in a narrow corridor, her fingertips brushed against slickwet walls, grainy basalt. It was a passageway not often trod: for even after all the years the tribe had lived in this section of the caverns, the floor was rough and rubbed against the calluses of her feet.

Please wait for me, she signed on the old man's back. The skin felt like old leather from a Windbringer's hide . . . they said the old man slept on hide ten Windbringers thick, he was so wise and so old.

They took many turns. The corridor twisted like the tail of a Windbringer when it is first struck by the stunspears. . . .

And then she smelled wide space, and she knew by the gentle touch of a wind that she was in a vast chamber. And her ears, with the liquid drying from them, began to touch brittle windshapes that echoed round and round, as though rocks were falling far away. Her eyes were still crusted, though; so she could not touch with them the gathering of people whose many odors she could smell on the soft wind. Many strangers. Young people, by the scent: other children-before-naming, soon to be initiated and to learn their identities and the paths of their future.

Suddenly a hand behind her crotch-shield, stroking her in a profane place. A throb shook her—

Touch-brother's fingers laughed against her skin. Dry fingers slipping on her steamslicked back. She reached behind and smiled on his chest with the palm of her hand. His scent touched her nostrils, sweet and familiar.

Glove-amps were being handed out.

Then, the tickling touch of Stonewise as he addressed them all through the glove-amp's circuitry. . . .

Before Windbringer returns to the fragrant places above the darkness, and reaches the home whence he sprung, we will touch him—

Through her filmed eyes, Girl-before-Naming touched a shadowvast touchshape. Stretching on either side further than eye could feel. And when she raised her head she could feel no end to it.

It quivered slowly as her eyes touched it, although the wind was subdued and could not have caused the quivering. It was alive. It was the brain of the Windbringer, half a Hornet long, shorn from its sailsacs, plunged into the hunters' forcenets, returning to its high home beyond the darkness—

We will touch him, all together. You will all gain strength from this, for your respective trials, for the seekings after true dreams. . . .

(So the chamber must indeed be huge, she thought. To contain Windbringer himself, to be a way station on its journey to the land of angels. Awe crept over her like a child's fear of the dark, of not-feeling.)

"Now I activate all the glove-amps, not just in the direction of teaching, but in the direction of communion. And you must know that when you are people-with-names, and have truly become part of the living, you will return here often, and draw spiritual strength from the Windbringer who is at the root of our being—"

She felt Touch-brother's hand tighten on hers. (Yes, she thought, it's clear that *I'm* going to he the hunter of us two. He's more afraid than I am, more fit to wait and gather the food that appears out of the empty air, than to swoop through darkness in a little airboat. . . .) She clutched him. (I must be strong.)

—Now reach out—

Hesitantly she released Touch-brother's hand and stretched out to touch the flesh of Windbringer. . . .

And flinched at the unexpected heat. Then reached out again—

Explored a furrow in the softness—warm, warm—a home-warmth almost, a—love—

Then the touchings of the others invaded the feeling in her hands.

A hundred crevasses of warmth. A hundred touching hands, linked together, together, caressing the soft warm, and there was no darkness here at all but touching everyone everywhere, the surface of Windbringer a warmth dispelling darkness—

And with her ears she felt ecstatic windshapes that flew from the lips of the others-before-naming—

They were warm together, warm as love is warm, warm as the touching of touch-siblings is the ultimate warmth--

—*Retract!*—

It broke. There was an ache, as dead and dark as the communion had been. One glove-amp fell from her hand. She reached out for someone, anyone. And caught her touch-brother, trembling . . . groping, she found the glove-amp.

Through it she felt Stonewise's hand on the cool stud in the wall that would send Windbringer home.

And then her eyes touched emptiness. She could not believe that her secret sense had lied, so she flailed the empty air with her hands. Empty, empty, empty . . . Windbringer had returned to his home in glory, in warmth, in the fragrance of angels.

Go, said Stonewise. *In a few sleeps you will all go out to touch the lonely wind. And you will dream or die.*

Girl-before-Naming found herself—without quite knowing how she'd gotten there—in a corridor she had not trodden since little-girlhood, years before her womanblood had flowed for the first time. It was the way to her parents' private catacomb, only a little distance from her own but separated by tradition and the need for high respect. . . she knew she should not go, not but a few sleeps from her destiny, but she could not help herself. She remembered it as a warm dry place and indeed it still was. The walls were close together, so that she could tap them both by spreading her elbows a little. Her elbows remembered furrows in the rock where before she had had to stand arms outstretched to touch them. And now the roof brushed her hair sometimes, making her bob her head. She loved the smell of this corridor more than anything. It was the earliest smell she could remember. . .

And reached out to touch the arms of Windstriker.

Father, Father, she signed, an intimate touch that defied convention, so that he recoiled for a moment. Then—his emotions overcoming his regard for custom, he embraced her, and neither of them was embarrassed, both clung with a hunger uncommon in a father and daughter.

She thought: Since Mother died he has been like this. It isn't good for two touch-siblings both to be hunters. It isn't natural. My parents were strange ones. . . .

She broke away from him. With her eyes she touched the walls of the small chamber. Her father lived here alone now. He gathered his own food. And he still went on the hunt, and still maintained an airboat, ready for the Windbringers. He was a true brave one, that man; on the death of his touch-sister he had pledged himself to die in the arms of Windbringer. He would hunt with a divine fury, he would vent his sorrow on the wind over the Sound. She admired him. And now she felt a surge of love for him. But she did not dare touch him again, after the moment of unforeseen intimacy, because she had overstepped the bounds of proper respect. . . .

Why have you come, Tickle? he asked her as though she were a child.

She felt no anger at this. Then she signed, slyly, *You came to see me too, Windstriker, when I was in the preparation room. I didn't expect that.*

Yes, he signed, with a twinge of ambiguity.

Father, I'm afraid! she signed. There I go again, she thought, uttering the word *father, father* as though it were not too sacred a bond to utter so lightly—

He touched her face. For a moment she thought he would embrace her again. But she knew better, in time; for his hand drifted to her own hand, to a distance proper for two people bound by such a wonder, by birth and by death. *Everyone goes through it,* he signed.

And then he lifted her hands and placed them over the sockets of his eyes, and she felt the emptiness and the roughness of scar tissue, but before that she had already touched his eyes with her eyes and touched the touchless holes that marked his mastery of childhood —

If I should somehow . . . do something different. Father (his hand flinched as she signed the word again, but came back at once, to reassure and warm her), *if I should not find what I'm supposed to find . . . you have to help me. That's why I'm here.*

You have your touch-sibling. She felt the regret in his signing, and knew that he still remembered his touch-sibling and still yearned for her. . . .

Father—Windstriker—my touch-brother is bound to me by scent and loyalty. But we are bound by birth and death. You are the only person I love, Windstriker. (Shall I tell him now? Shall I . . .)

Her eyes touched the body of Windstriker. Hard. Lean. Smooth as though the wind from the Sound had worn it down. And then he took her hand and signed. *You're a strange girl. If you need me, I'll be here.*

Abruptly she turned around and groped for the entrance. For she knew that if she stayed for another moment, she could not refrain from throwing herself at him again. It was unseemly for a girl past her first blood, on the brink of becoming a woman, on the brink of bringing her eyes to the Windbringer, perhaps on the brink of death. She knew that a good father must not seem to grieve for a daughter about to brave the lonely wind. As she stood at the entrance, back turned to him, his fragrance, an oily mansmell, touched her and she breathed it deeply, feeling not shame but pride, that a man with a hundred hunts behind him—a man pledged to die in the hunt, a man practically an angel—could still find it in him to touch his daughter. And to care for her. He did not need to carry himself arrogantly like a boy who has returned from a single hunt. He knew who he was.

The pride lifted her up like a buoy in the wind currents, rising in the Windbringer's wake. . . .

For a few more steps.

***

She had not gone twenty meters when she collided with some young children. . . .

Play ball? one of them signed.

She reached out and felt matted hair, soft face speckled with grimecrusts . . . it was her own brother, a boy hundreds of sleeps-before-naming.

All right, she signed. A twinge of longing for lost childhood—

You'll cheat.

No. No.

They squatted in the corridor that had opened out a little and he handed her the ball, a dry leathery thing patched together from scraps of Windbringer hide. She threw it to him. He waited for the ball's windtouch, then snatched it skillfully out of the darkness. Then she felt the wind change, felt him throw it to some other child.

—Ball, rushing toward the touch of her eyes—

She caught it. At once they were clustered around her. *How did you do that? How?*

I touched it beyond the darkness, she signed angrily.

Hah! Darktoucher! Liar! No one can do that. . . .

(Not again, Girl-before-Naming thought.) Rubbing her hands on her face in exasperation, she got up and left the children. (Anyway, she thought, I'm too old for that now. Too old . . .)

She made her way toward the preparation chamber.
***

From the sayings of Stonewise, who heard them from the signs of his grandfathers and down from the earliest men, and from dreams and portents brought him by the lonely wind—

Our darkness is not really darkness. When the angels have carried us home we will perceive as one with the Windbringers.

The world is the belly of a cosmic Windbringer that courses through an infinite darkness. Who knows? In the vastness outside there may be other Windbringers carrying little worlds of their own, with their own special fragrances, their own textures, their own warmths. . . .

This is how the world was created. First the Sound was distilled out of the darkness. So wet and dry were the first sensations to be distinguished. There was not even warm or cold then. These things were dark to the touch. Then the first Windbringer rose from the Sound. He hovered over the waters, and when he moved the wind sprang up. And then the Windbringer immolated himself. This is the supreme mystery of nature, the act of love that unlocked the universe. His body shattered and the shards that were flung the farthest became hard walls of rock. His bursting breath became the warmth that burned and boiled the water of the Sound; and his blood mingled with the water, and the warmth of his breath incubated the blood and water as a mother's womb a little child unborn.

And so men and women rose from the water. There was a terrible darkness and they were afraid. But the force of Wind-bringers bursting blew them onto the rocks and then they touched cold as well as warmth, and knew the difference between life and death. And out of the same substance were born the Windbringer's children who fly the thick winds over the Sound. Who make the food appear on the floors of metal. Man and Windbringer are as touch-sibling and touch-sibling, then. . . .

And the wings of Windbringer became the angels.
***

For seven long sleeps she sat in the chamber, the damp ground the only respite from darkness. For seven sleeps the gall-soaked steam penetrated her pores and drew the sweat from her, and she did not eat. She went beyond the dull ache of hunger into a kind of euphoria. She sat and her fingers danced laughter on the hard ground.

They came for her. Her eyes were crusted over. Her ears too. Her lips were crusted and parched in spite of the steam and sweat. Giddy, she rose and followed the one they had sent for her, a stranger cloaked completely in Windbringer's hide so that she could not identify him, so that where the scent of a human should come there was yet more darkness. She followed him quickly. The feel of the hide instead of flesh on the stranger's back filled her with heartpounding unease. She signed nothing, but followed. Her eyes could not touch beyond the crusts.

Quick, the stranger signed with a gloved hand. The signing was cold, emotionless.

She followed him out of the preparation chamber. They took a turning she did not recall having felt before. She stumbled. The stranger's pace didn't slacken. *Quick, quick*, he signed, and thrust farther into darkness.

I don't— Dizziness. Faintness. She felt her legs could hardly carry her. Still he hastened her. Her fingers barely skimmed the coarse leather before he moved on. (He knows this way thoroughly, she thought. Why have I never seen it?) It was a path riddled with pocks and stones that stung her feet. She smarted and moved on. This passage must be used very rarely if the floor could still hurt so much.

Another chamber. And she was released into the arms of her touch-brother.

Tired . . .

Be still, be still, he signed. *We have to make ourselves still inside.* He hugged her close. Then he drew soft circles on her palms with his fingertips. Then he touched her breasts, but without urgency. She felt an involuntary lifting in them, but her mind was elsewhere.

The dream, she signed. So he would stop. *This isn't the time.*

Yes. We go.

The stranger seized them roughly by their wrists. *You will walk on this path,* he signed. *For some distance yet. You will walk separately, without touching. When you reach the appointed ledge overhanging the Sound they will prepare you. Now find yourselves. If within three sleeps you do not return we will mourn for you, but we will also rejoice with you for your return to the home of Windbringer—*

The hand broke away quickly.

They walked on. She might as well have been alone. Her feet touched sharpness, stumble-stones, teeth jutting from rock. She walked on. Her feet bled.

She collided with him at one point. Quickly she made a sign of aversion, but not before he had signed sadly. *You are dark to the touch, Touch-sister.* She walked on. Her feet glued themselves to the rock, the blood and sweat were like glue, she had to drug herself onward. Hunger ate away at her innards. How long now? She trudged, throwing aside the hunger and pain. . . .

And presently the hunger subsided. The pain became more like joy. The pain itself became warm. She marveled at this, but she was too tired to think for long. And presently—

Her ears picked up a windshape in the distance. A windshape of anguish, of a distant seething—

The big wind hit her all at once.

She was on the ledge now. Her eyes were clearing, and with them she touched her touch-brother standing a few meters away. And now she set her face against the wind.

The wind pinned her against the wall. She resisted. She thrashed, hard, against it, but it pushed her relentlessly. And the windshape rose and fell like the windshapes that escaped the lips of the dying—

Be strong, be strong, she signed against her body, and she could hardly move her arms to sign against the windtide—

Darkness itself was alive! She tried to break free. To brave the lonely wind, to run farther out on the ledge—

And pried herself from the wall! And now she stepped out, and the wind battered her from all sides and the howling windshapes came like ghosts of the dead crowding her, breathing on her, and she took another step and she was cut loose from all the hardness except for the patch of hard rock that she stood on and all around the darkness raged howlshape after howlshape the hairstream slapping her cheeks—

Another step—

(I am alone here. I will touch with the hands of my mind now. I will touch with the hands of my heart, through the barrier of wind and darkness.)

Howlshapes gathered hurricane-eyed tempested stormed—

(I will send out the hands of my heart and they will touch the truth.)

More steps now. Each step prouder. For she was the daughter of Windstriker who had braved the wind a hundred times and wrested the heart of Windbringer from the heart of darkness.

(I will know who I am.)

And in the wind at fragrance, the fragrance of a distant Windbringer. She knew it not from experience of wild Windbringers but as though from a memory implanted in her before birth. A womb-memory—

She breasted the big wind.

Her feet were her only contact with her past. And when she lifted one foot the wind soared burned past tore her along like a dustspeck—

(Reach! Reach!) And her hands stretched out like one-who-walks-when-sleeping.

Now her secret senses became dark, even though the crusts were long blown from her eyes. Only her ears registered the windshape that roared in anger and terrible anguish—

In her mind she stretched her arm out to the heart of the world the center above the Sound and further and further and still her mind reached no wall on the other side and still the wind battered her and still she walked out, tottering but still erect—

A vibration in her mind now, like a divine word-signing

LIFT UP YOUR HEAD

It was a touch from within. Almost as though another person was there with her. The sting-tang streamed over her eyes. She had to close them, they smarted, the wind was pushing at them, she had to —

LIFT UP YOUR HEAD

and then she forced them open and sent the touching of her eyes far far far out into the ends of darkness and then they touched

An *undark*.

For a moment it seemed that the wind had become frozen. Beyond darkness her eyes had touched a new thing.

An *undark*.

(How? she thought wildly. How can the darkness part so, and this pattern of undark-that-I-have-no-name-for play over the darkness like a mother warming a newborn child?)

And then she knew that she had perceived something that had never been perceived before. There was no answer in the words of the old myths or the fingerchants. Or in the truth-telling dreams that visited Stonewise the knower.

And she had done it with her eyes.

In the impossible distance the undark played. The undark glimmered like a memory that surfaces and is gone before it can be recalled. . . .

And then she knew that a terrible thing had happened. Because of this she must not lose her eyes. The gift that she had was not a useless aberration that let her catch balls from gullible children and let her pick the pebbles out of her path before they bit into her foot. The gift—

(But will they understand? No! They'll throw me into the Dark Country and the angels will get me before my time—)

And then she remembered the glinty-sharp things that had fallen upon the corpses and devoured them . . . *they* were the angels. They were *machines*.

And the undark came again this time with a different—scent? texture? what was the name for the textures of undarkness?

And her heart was stopped with the beauty of it.

Though it was but the edge of some greater beauty beyond her grasp.

Then the darkness swallowed the undark. The winds seemed to return. But she did not fear them now. She had touched beyond the wind.

(I'm not a girl any more. And I must have a name.)

Then she felt the touches of the children in her mind saying *cheater darktoucher liar* laughing at her mocking at her claims—

(I am a woman. The daughter of great hunters. I will never run away. Even Windbringer will not make me flee.)

—windroar—

(I will embrace the name of cheat! I will he named *Darktouch!*)

Then Darktouch wiped the water from her eyes and turned her back, rebuffing the big wind, and her hands laughed at the hungry spirits of the dead that hovered in the wind to suck away the spirits of those who cannot dream. . . .

Darktouch! she signed on her body. And surrounded the sign with a circle of bitterness and a skinrasping square of scorn.

The wind blew her into the wall. She groped her way along it until she found her touch-brother sitting patiently braving the wind. She touched him gently.

Are you the dream? he signed. *Are you the thing I'm seeking?*

There is no dream, she signed. *What I have found is beyond all dreaming.* And then she started to tell him of the undark and of her name and of her power to touch through darkness.

He shook with fear. Then he signed, *You can't do this to me! The darkness has driven you crazy!*

Then she knew how terrible this thing was. Even her touch-sibling could not understand. How could he under-stand that she must never lose her eyes? How could he understand that this was not shirking adulthood, but embracing it in a new dark way?

(I know who I must go to now, she thought then.)

As the lonely wind touched her she thought of Windstriker. He was the only person she could turn to. . . .

At least he knows who he is!

The lonely wind beat at them as a mother beats her breasts when she has lost all her children to the wrath of Windbringer. But Darktouch was too tired for fear now, and too tired to feel compassion for Touch-brother, for Boy-before-Naming whom she had left behind.

Darktouch dashed panting till she found the old corridors with the old panging scents that signed her dead childhood to her mind—

Father! Father!

He recoiled from her. To ward oil the darkness that still must cling to her, after the long touching of the lonely wind.

(She thought: We should not sign to each other at all, not until eight sleeps have passed. I am untouchable. . . .)

Father!

She smelled touched sweat, a blood vessel pulsing between his thumb and forefinger, the hand trying to be firm.

Then, strong and compassionate: *Has the darkness driven you mad, Daughter? Will you go to die now, to join with Windbringer in eternity?*

She felt him become very still. His hand had become dead. Whether from astonishment or repugnance she could not tell. Was he steeling himself to reject her, so that he would feel no pain when they cast her into the Dark Country?

I have a new name now, she signed softly. *I am Darktouch.* His fingers rasped her skin. *This is a cruel jest!*

No, Windstriker. Her signing had switched to the formal mode and she no longer called him Father. She did not wish to pain him by reminding him of a relationship which he must perhaps repudiate. . . .

Windstriker. I have dreamed a dream. In the dream was a truth that Stonewise even doesn't know. There is a thing undark, that lives behind the wind.

Darktouch—he scrawled the unfamiliar name slowly. But she felt a wary exultation, that he had recognized her right to hear the name, no matter how strange. She was proud of her father, breaker of tradition, no matter what.

Touch, Windstriker. At the edge of the reach of my eyes, I touched the dark and there was the shadow of an undark. There is a new Great Mystery, maybe greater than Wind-bringer himself. There's power in my eyes.

Windstriker! And a purpose too. Maybe a power we could all have or all have had once. I hate to keep my eyes, Windstriker! Perhaps I will have to lead our people toward the undark. Perhaps there must be a changing of the way things are. . . .

I don't understand, signed Windstriker.

A pause.

Then with a strong motion he clasped her to him, almost crushed her, and she felt his sweat all warm against her and still he was dark to the touch, immeasurably dark, and then he signed against her, cradling her still, *Darkness has driven you mad, you poor child.*

No! No! She touched him with her eyes then. She touched the holes where his torn eyes had been, touched the old scars. And she imagined she saw tears, wrenched from the old sockets, like a baby's. . . . (He loves me, she thought. I can still get through to him.) She broke free from him and backed slowly away, still keeping her hands clasped in his.

Then she wriggled them loose, bent over, touched the floor with her eyes, picked up a small flat stone.

She pressed it into his hands.

I want you, she signed, *to walk away from me in a dark direction, calling no windshapes with your feet. I want you to throw the stone. . . .*

Puzzled, he went.

With her eyes she touched the hard rock, her ears caught the zing of the windshape slicing the airstream —

She reached out and caught the stone.

I have caught it. With my ears and eyes alone. She signed the words to him slowly, so that he would know precisely what she meant, the words that seemed to make no sense. . . .

You're my daughter, he signed at last. The words rasped harshly, they had been wrung from him. *I must accept this thing, because my own hands have felt it. I must believe that my own offspring—is something not quite human!*

You must see now, Windstriker, you must protect me! She had thrown all caution aside and was touching him all over now, his hands, his sweat-drenched chest where her eyes touched tufts of curly hair. *We're linked by birth and death, not just by scent and loyalty! Remember your touch-sister, my mother, who died for what she was!*

He signed nothing for a long time. Then: *It seems that I am to be the first that you will lead beyond darkness.*

But his saying was dark to the touch. She waited for him to go on.

You have done a terrible thing, he signed, *to remind me of your mother. Remember that for her sake I have vowed to die in the arms of the wind. . . .*

Darktouch embraced her father. She felt sadness shake him, and felt pride in him, that he had expressed emotion and not hidden under a mask of traditions. (Yes, she thought: Windstriker knows who he is. . . .)

You'll protect my eyes?

I'll do the only thing I can, he signed resolutely. *Once they find you gone from the ledge, they will assume that you have failed the test of the lonely wind. Then they will send you to the Dark Country. So you must come with me now.*

Father, where?

He stiffened. The signing came slowly: *Another great hunt is beginning. I will take you with me in my airboat. You've broken so many traditions already, maybe your eyes can come in useful. Maybe you will touch the Windbringer before even our sensors can.*

Darktouch signed, *And then they will assume I'm lost, by the time the expedition returns, and then we can slip away to another village, perhaps, begin anew—*

I have made my vow to the Windbringer, her father signed coldly. *As you have found the way you must follow, whatever the cost, so also I. You and I are alike in this . . . more alike, at times, than I would have wished, strange daughter . . . it seems that your path leads to banishment, to strange new perceptions. Perhaps they are hallucinations, perhaps something real and important. I have a path too—and it leads only to one thing: to the arms of Windbringer, to the fragrance of eternity.*

Then Windstriker shook his hands away from hers, so that she was isolated from him, in her own private darkness. (Why can't I be a girlchild again? Why can't I be a girl-before-naming? she thought.)

She dried her tears with her long hair, knowing that it was no longer proper to behave like a young girl who did not know who she was. For she had a name now, and a proud father who bore his name meaningfully, so that it was no mere arbitrary twiddle of fingernail upon palm. . . .

She wanted to reach out to him. She wanted him to touch her and stroke her cheek and call her his Tickle. But she had no right to inflict her childish tears upon him. He had dedicated himself to the wind, and had become more important than any new-named girl's private anguish. He was almost already a whisper of wind, an arm of the tempest.

Stonewise had said: *The wind touches everything, but the love of the wind is like fire, like acid, consuming everything but the soul.*

She flicked her head around, maintaining the touch through her eyes. Without feeling him, she knew—

Windstriker had bent over, squatted by the wall, felt for the stud that opened the stone larder . . . and taken out four or live sheets of dried meat, two round loaves of bread fresh from the materializing room. Then he reached for the larder spigot and filled two nippleflasks with water that was mixed with essence of Windbringer fragrance. Without signing, to her he handed her the food. Then he placed her hand on his so she could feel what he was doing. She shook him off. He signed, dejectedly, *Whatever. If you claim to perceive without touching.*

He wrapped up half the food in a kerchief of woven Windbringer bark; she copied his movements. He motioned her to follow him, his hand just grazing hers. His emotions were dark now. She knew they were focused on the hunt. The hunt was everything now. The rhythms of children's fingerchants pounded in her mind . . . she knew that to interfere would break his concentration, shatter the power inside him. The power to face the big darkness, alone, in a precarious airboat, isolated from all the others, navigating by the windtouch and the patterns of fragrances. . . .

Come.

He had pressed a stud. She felt a vibrating against her feet. She cast her eyes down and touched an opening. And a shadow of undark, a vague reflection of the thing she had touched in her dreaming.

Put one foot in front of the other. Slowly. He signed without any emotion. She might have been any apprentice hunter, fresh from the dreamseeking. . . .

(The thought of Touch-sibling crossed her mind. He must still be out there. Waiting for what could only be half a dream. She imagined the big wind on him, tormenting him, and knew he did not have the strength to rebuff it alone. . . .)

(*But I must be what I am,* she told herself fiercely. She etched the words again and again on her arms, and they stung long after her nails had ceased their raking.)

In the dim undark her eyes touched steps.

Her father's body had already shortened, and he stepped into the descending passageway. She followed dumbly. The way was quite new to her.

The steps steepened, then ended. Her hand skimmed the passage walls. Smooth, unearthly smooth. Stealing the warmth from her fingertips. They were metal, then, not man-made, not hollowed from rock as man-made corridors were; these walls had been there since the world began. Her hand flinched away. But the chill stung them still, and she knew it for a chill of the heart. This passageway was sacred, and for the touch of hunters only, and a girl with her eyes intact should not, could not—it was violation of the worst kind—

Her mind touched the wind that waited at the end of the passageway.

Darktouch, quick! urgent fingers dancing bony on her.

The corridor, still no more than man high, widened. Every fifty paces or so there were globes of the muted undark, and they threw circles of undark onto the blackness. It was strange and regular, too regular to be human. So she knew this was the work of the first Windbringer.

As they crossed the pools of undark, Darktouch found her eye-touching clearer than ever. Her father stood out as a mass of many textures, coiling and uncoiling, and cut by knife-sharp shadows.

(Why are these pools built into the old passageways, destined or permanence? she thought. Then she thought: Perhaps the early people needed them. Perhaps they shared my secret sense. Perhaps it is a lost talent. . . .)

A room. No undark here.

In midroom the floor gave way to a nothingness. Something was moored there, to a stake, with a thick rope. She felt the coils, tough, skin-chafing. Her ears touched a whisper of a wind . . . .

We are on the edge of the wind, Darktouch, Windstriker signed. *This is the private mooring room of . . . your mother and me, Darktouch. She who was given to the wind. It is my love for you, strange daughter, that brings you here, breaking all propriety.*

Our airskiff floats here, over the void, he went on. *When we unmoor it, the gates will open and we will be in utter darkness, save for the wind's big arms. Are you afraid? Shall I leave you here, have you take your chances?*

Timidly she signed, *I am afraid. But I will go.*

He touched her mechanically, masking his emotions. *When we push off,* he signed, *the wind will hit you, hard. But perhaps you'll learn to love it, I mean the big loneliness.*

He cradled her in his arms and lifted her on to the airskiff. A wind brushed her; she felt it bob up and down, buoyed by the heavy air.

He put his hand on hers and placed it on a flat panel. It was soft, leather-skinned. When she skimmed it she felt sharp blips. *The other ships,* he signed. *Remember their signs, their patterns. There*—he guided her hand—*those are the underfleet. They will sweep underneath us always, weaving the patterns of force. They have no stuncannon, but their positions, perfectly synchronized, generate a forceshield into which the Windbringer will fall stunned.*

We, Daughter, and the other stunhunters . . . are the ones who will bring him down.

Blip. Blip. They pricked her palms, the little pulses that were airskiffs. She cast her eyes around her to see what they could touch. The glint of metal there was in the vague undark; airskiffs, the passagewalls, the angels, all belonged to the old things that came with the creation.

He signed that she should stash their food in a little panel under the floor which was a metal frame covered with hide. She learned how the wings were raised and lowered

These—he pushed her hand against cold metal, sharp-edged against the wings—*are propellers. Don't touch them once we are in flight. You'll lose your hand. Then you'll be silent forever.*

She sat retracted into herself, and it was very cold. *And now, before we go,* he signed. . .

As she felt with her hand, he drew out a flask from the floor panel. Of course, the scent-dousing. Without the delicate directional scents of the various skiff-types wafting in the wind, many of the hunters would lose direction.

Windstriker unstoppered the flask. Heavy fumes. Nausea. *If you must vomit, do so now!*

She retched over the side. Her throat felt raw. Nothing came.

She remembered her lessons now, and breathed in deeply, remembering the smell. The pungent, acrid scent penetrated her, made her guts miserable—and then she smelled another odor through it: a sweet afterfragrance. Windstriker began to sprinkle the boat with it, splashing the liquid over every thing, over their hands too; there was grease in it, and something else, lighter than that; several immiscible fluids. He pressed a stud and sent the odor waiting outward, away from them.

For the sake of Windbringer—her father scratched the words hard against her palms—both hands in mirror fashion, almost drawing blood—*this is the smell of a stunhunter.*

I know, Father. I've taken the lessons. I know I may only have my nose to guide me, if the skiff's data panel should fail.

Now I'm setting the homing device, he signed.

(I'm still his Tickle, his little daughter, Darktouch thought impatientlv. But with a twinge of love for him. . . .)

Darktouch knew, of course, from the models in the teaching room that every child fingered and handled with such longing, how an airskiff worked. She knew there was a starting mechanism, propellers operated by a strange force called electricity, for which power boxes were delivered in the places where the food materialized. That the mugs could be retracted, angled, halved, extended in whatever way necessary for the fleet to maintain its position. That the skill had a thinker inside it that was set for home, and could be set for other directions, so that it could fly without a flier, if its owner were killed. . . .

She wasn't prepared for its smallness. Its precariousness. Why, she could stretch out her arms and she was touching either side of it.

Her father showed her where the safety belts were. Then he turned round to warm the engine and to feel the gauges for fuel and power. Fuel was another thing that came by the miracle of Windbringer's bounty. Then he cut the engine and Darktouch felt the floor tremble, a soft purring like a mother's touch. . . .

Windstriker—

Afraid?

No It's just that . . . well, I've been selfish, haven't I? And foolish too. I didn't think about you at all when I ran away to you. I've just realized—I've doomed us both, haven't I?

No matter. We'll find another village. But his touch felt clammy and false.

Then he touched her all over and signed, *You're not properly covered, girl!*

It was true. Her crotch-shield had been lost in the panic. *Well, Daughter, cover yourself!* he signed gruffly, throwing her a rag. *This is serious, sacred work were doing, bringing the Windbringer home. If you die, do you want to meet him naked?*

I've brought about your downfall! she signed hysterically. Then, hesitantly, she signed, *Father, Father.*

No matter.

That was how much he respected the bond of birth and death, Darktouch thought wonderingly. He could sign "no matter" when at best they would be driven out, become pariahs in another village, not knowing the signs they used, learning a new language, gathering food instead of hunting . . or at worst, the Dark Country. To meet the angels in the flesh.

She wanted to tell him how much she loved him. The feeling welled up in her but she could signal nothing. But she was about to mention some mindless triviality, to cover up her emotions, when—

The gate flipped open!

All at once the wind caught them like a toy and darkness enveloped her, and they were flung into the howling of the windshapes, into the ghosts that flapped against them with signs of anguish—

The wind pinned her down. A shape of terror escaped her throat, a hoarse breathing exploded from her mouth, her eyes touched nothing, her ears touched a thousand screamshapes echobounding crashing around her—

Windstriker caught her in his arms, pried her from the flooring, made sure her belt was secure. Now her head protruded above the skiffwall and she felt her hair stream behind her. . . .

From a distance, the wind carried the smell of the other stunhunters and she could pick out their positions. She could almost have scratched the formation on the floor beneath her. At this distance the smell was sweet. Only the strange, almost cloying afterfragrance came wafting toward her, not the pungent concentrate.

After a while the wind abated a little. Or she became used to it. Darkness was everywhere. They sliced through the darkness smoothly, like a knife through water. There was an exaltation now. As though the wind were burning all feeling from her, leaving only the movement itself, the arc of flight. After a time her body fell into tune with the humming vibration of the skiff's engine. She and the skiff were one giant instrument, one fingerchant, one rhythm.

Now she understood why both of her parents had to become hunters. How could anyone stay home and gather food, when they could fly in the wind like this?

(I'll never fear the dark again, she thought fiercely.)

There was no undark to awaken her eyes, only the howling windshapes rang in her ears. They ploughed through wind that seemed to know no ending.

Seven
The Shadow Falls Forever

Kelver was a celebrity—for four or five days at least. The village buzzed for that long with the news of the tachyon bubbles and with speculation about what the new Inquestor would do. But since no one had seen an Inquestor, and nothing changed in the village . . .

There were more pressing problems. A pride of al'ksigarkar had been seen, skirting the Gold River. And meat was vanishing from the nutrient tanks faster than it could he recloned. They would not reach their quota for the week, and the tenth day of the week, the shoveling day, was approaching. And then something else happened—

In the field that hugged the Cold River. Adults were huddled around something. Grainstalks lay trampled as though a war party had swept through the fields . . . they stood under the staring sun. Kelver and some other children had come to see what was wrong, but they couldn't see through the elders that had clumped together.

Kelver pushed some boys aside—all smaller than he was—and strode toward where his uncle stood. Here the Cold River reared up on pylons for a few klomets where the land dipped a little. Rust-earth showed through the patches of green.

"What's happened, what's happened?" he exclaimed. They ignored him, and he heard snatches of their quick intense whisperings. . . .

. . . It's a violation . . .

. . . They're too bold, do something . . .

. . . a posse, we have to round them up and eliminate them, vermin, vermin, vermin . . .

Kelver couldn't make much sense of it. He stepped hack to where a pylon's shadow barred the burning ground and sat down on the green. He got up at once, plucked some stalks and tried to wipe off the gooey mess. Now he knew that an al'ksigark had been here. This near to the village. He was angry. But he also wanted to take a weapon and join the hunt. So he sprang up and went to the group of elders again, trying to become a part of them.

A child smiled at him and he elbowed him out of his way. "Uncle, I've found its spoor."

The group fell silent. Uncle Aaye pushed his way out of the huddle and Kelver showed him the stains on his tunic from where he had tried to sit down. He turned and ran to the spot. The elders followed, stumbling and puffing, and Kelver suppressed an urge to laugh at them.

There was a patch of greenish, slimy fluid there, under the shadowbar of the pylon. Uncle Aaye ignored Kelver at once and the group started to buzz again, pushing him out. Kelver spun round and—

Suddenly he saw what the elders had been standing around before. It was more interesting than a puddle of congealing body fluids. So he sprinted over. Some kids were already prodding the body with grainstalks then retreating.

"It's a dead one!" someone yelled. "I want the skin!"

"There's two of them!" someone else was shouting. Kelver reached the spot pushed the other children aside easily—they were too scared to get near it anyway —and then saw them.

Green-stained tin with those tiny spiderfast legs, muscular and mammallike, but too many and too small, a body of globs and light-sensitive patches that served as eyes, and that gaping, orcine mouth crowned by the huge rheumy nostrils where eyes would be on a man's face . . . two al'ksigarkar. One of them had his mantle partially protruded. It was perhaps a couple of square meters at the moment, sprouting out from an orifice in the head, bright green and veined in black . . . this one had eaten well, then.

In the badlands they lived in herds, thousands of them. They spread their mantles—often amounting collectively to many square kilometers—and photosynthesized, and never moved at all. But . . . if a living prey came by, they could become carnivorous. They could switch over to hunting functions. Then the dormant jaws and the layers of razor fangs and the swift spider feet and the rasping claws would come into use. And there were rogues. A lone al'ksigark breaking from the herd and becoming a full carnivore, eating, eating . . . until it died. These had come far and were reduced to eating plants. Somewhere nearby there must be a herd. The pact had been violated.

For the al'ksigarkar were, in a manner of speaking, sentient. Although their predominant urges were hunger and revenge. They possessed a kind of language, of perhaps two hundred different cries, produced by making their teeth chatter and rubbing their legs together. . . . There had been a pact. They were not to come near the Cold River. These two had died for it.

Everyone in the village hated them more than anything. Because the al'ksigarkar, whenever they could, ate people. Not, of course, the civilized ones of the village, unless they wandered out too far from a displacement plate . . . but there were the ghost people in the desert, a stone-age culture that one never saw or thought about much, except when one came stumbling into the village, his arm bitten off at the shoulder, once in a decade or so. . . .

Only an Inquestral summons—and that once in a very long time—could take you safely to Effelkang. They could send an airfloater for you that would cover the distance in less than a day. Only Uncle Aaye had ever done that. . . .

Kelver looked at the corpses—in the heat they had already begun to decompose, and the stench was staggering—and listened to the buzz of the elders as they discussed plans for a punitive search and the buzz of small insects that hovered over the dead al'ksigarkar. "Disgusting," he said to himself.

Behind him, all the kids were screaming, "Let's have a hunt! A hunt!"

"Want to play, Kevi?" A shy girl's voice. It was two-winter-old Haller who had always had a secret crush on him.

"I'm too old—" Kelver saw the imploring look. "All right." "You can be the alksigark!" a fat boy shouted. "You're the biggest and baddest!"

"Ha!" Kelver cried out scornfully, running for the nearest displacement plate.

Kelver stepped from behind the blue house. The blue glaze on the porcelain scattered the diffuse groundlight and the shadow blued his tunic a little. . . .

Where the shadow crossed the shadow of a yellow house there was a triangle of green-tinged darkness. Just beyond it, the displacement plate.

Damn children! he thought. *But I'll make it so they can't find me. They're all out there jumping from plate to plate, the lazy monsters!*

He picked a path between plates, shuttled from shadow to shadow, and soon he found he had crept all the way to the side of the Cold River. He could see where it entered the mountain.

—shrieks—

They'll never look for me here. They'll think I've plated all the way over to the very edge of the village. Children think very obviously.

—shrieks fading now, tickling the silence—

Picking a direction at random, Kelver found himself following the river. A coolness came from it. Once or twice he stopped to lick the dew that always settled on its walls, collected into pockets crevassed by the way the moss grew . . . he found himself staring at the Skywall. He found he could see no sky at all, almost as though it were winter and the suns had gone to sleep.

At the base of the river walls, a faint blue light showed him the way. He hadn't come to this part of the Skywall before: it rose straight up here. Usually if they were playing, they would run to a part within sight of the village, where some of the pylons to the Cold River had steplike holds and you could balance atop the river's walls. One day on a dare he had even perched on an impossible ledge and launched three stones at his uncle's house with a slingshot.

(He also remembered the beating. They'd had to reglaze the roof. . . .)

He stared at the wall and . . .

I don't want to fight for the Inquest any more, when I grow older, he decided, remembering the to-do after the tachyon bubbles, and finally forcing himself to remember his father's corpse. It came as a cold memory—he could not stand to color it with emotion. *But if I don't become a soldier, he thought, how will I ever touch the stars?*

A grief touched him. He didn't understand it; he didn't want it, but he couldn't dismiss it with just a shrug.

"There he is, ambling along like he doesn't know what's coming to him!" A shrill voice piercing his thoughts.

Ah well, they've found me. I was beginning to feel lonely.

Other children charging at him—

He did a passable al'ksigark screech and a girl looked pale and stopped in midrun for a moment—

He turned and sprinted toward the mountain.

An idea. He reached one of the pylons that supported the Cold River, about eighty meters above his head now, and climbed it quickly. Then he grasped a vine that hung from the river wall and shinnied up with a bloodcurdling yell. The cold burned his stomach so he unflattened himself and held on with his elbows

and knees. They were little points of cold knifing into
him—

"He's going to climb up there, the devilish
al'ksigark!"

He stood on the wall, and underneath him the
crowd of children were hooting and booing. "I'm sick
of this game!" he shouted down.

"Al'ksigark! Al'ksigark!"

"Go catch a real one!"

Nimbly he ran along the wall—it was perhaps a half
meter wide—without so much as looking at the Cold
River rushing below, soundless under its protective
forcefield and shooting out tendrils of cloud as it
hurtled toward a place far away.

The river ran into solid rock. *Now what?*

"Quick!" A little voice. "This way!"

"Huh . . . ? Haller!" He gasped. "You're supposed to
be chasing me. . . ."

"I know a place they'll never find you—" He saw her
now, lit in the riverglow from below, upside-down the
shadows of her face. "Here." She flattened herself on
the ridge and inched onto a ledge of the black rock,
and Kelver saw a fissure. With a faint light coming
from deep within. They crouched at the jagged
opening.

"It's okay." said Haller. She touched him and he
shied away. "I come here all the time. I hate my
parents, and I come here to get mad all by myself."

"Why, do they beat you or something?"

"No. It's not that simple," she said. "Come." She
began to lower herself into the rock. Her head sank
and the hair glowed a little golden, like ripe grain. . . .

A room.

"Do you hear the other kids yelling?" she said. "They'll never find us, not until we're ready—"

A shy smile.

The room . . . a cavern, rather, with rock walls that shimmered with a cold phosphorescence. Kelver took a few steps. There didn't seem to be an end to the room . . . .

"I didn't know there were any passages inside the Skywall," he said softly, wondering.

Above, the ceiling glittered like a starlit winter night when the suns slept, silverglitter of far stars, of far worlds . . . a longing tugged at him. He didn't look at Haller. Although he suddenly suspected that she had maneuvered him into coming here. . . .

All right," she said, reading his mind. "I was hiding, here, waiting, hoping you'd show up. You know I've got this helpless crush on you. You tell stories about things you've never seen. You don't just sit there jabbering about al'ksigark hunts and boasting of how you can fight. Although I know you can beat up any kid in the village. And a lot of the adults too."

"Hey," he said.

"Want to play sex?"

Kelver walked on a little.

"Kevi?"

"Oh, Halli," he said without looking back at her. "You're just a kid." He looked steadily ahead, to veil his insecurity: adolescence was not sitting too comfortably on him either. . .

He heard her babble on "D'ye remember, Kevi, these hundred sunpassings past, the day we played by ourselves among the grainbales and no one was looking, and we showed each other things . . . ?"

Above, a vague screaming—

"Shit." Kelver stopped dead. "They've found us." He darted farther into the cavern. A passageway suddenly opened where he thought was a mere crack in the rock. . . .

Another cave now.

And silence.

For a moment he almost wanted Haller with him. But she was doubtless still out there, timidly awaiting his return.

"Powers of powers," he whispered "It's *artificial*."

Walls here, metallic silver-gleaming walls that curved up in a majestic sweep to twine in a spiraling roof shrinking to infinity, whether mirrors or reality he couldn't think. . . .

A hum, fainter than a heartbeat. Machinery.

Crystals set into the walls. Studs, patterned lights, twinkling.

There were curves here. An orgy of curves, sinuous, sensuous to his eyes that were from a world bound by straight edges . . . mirror curves. Soft twisting metal, like waves of a girl's hair in the wind, but frozen. . . .

"Why is it always I who make the discoveries in this village?" he said. The echo came back from behind him, louder than his own voice, and softedged like a shape in dawnmist. . . .

Slowly he crossed the room.

The spiral ceiling turned with him, a giant corkscrew of a mirror. Footsteps, loud, harsh. His own. He stopped, whirled round, before he realized he was alone here. Sighed relief. Strode across the room now, pretending confidence.

Then he found the round door. It was twice manhigh, set into the wall, an ordinary enough doorway; and at its side an ordinary doorstud.

He deliberated for a while, then thought: *Let the children worry!*

He shrugged and pressed the stud. The door dissolved and—

Thunder crashed in the distance! A crazy labyrinth of passageways twisting, forking, weaving, warping—

The wind hit him.

He stood his ground for a few moments, stunned. The wind rushed at him, gusted over him, his hair flew and his tunic flapped, there was no wind like this in the world, vehement, pungent, alive—

On the wind he smelled . . . a fragrance he couldn't recognize. A scent that stirred excitement and rage and desire, all at once, as the warm wind battered him and shook him into shivering—

After a few moments the wind subsided a little. And then the song came. Just an echo of an echo of an echo of a songsnatch, caressing his ears so that he almost yelped with the joy of it, and then it was gone and a grief came on him, a tragedy he couldn't understand....

Got to close the door! I can't stand it—

Palm slammed on stud.

Cold metal biting him.

The door resolved again.

Silence.

And then he saw the words that were written on the door, written in the Inquestral highscript that he had learned—with many beatings—from his uncle, in an ancient hand, etched onto the metal with a quill dipped in acid, no doubt:

THE SHADOW IS MOTHER
THE SHADOW IS DEATH
THE SHADOW FALLS FOREVER

ON THE CHILDREN OF DARKNESS

and then he knew that this was the gateway to the Dark Country.

As he turned his back on the door, dread breathed on his neck, like an al'ksigark ready to pounce.

Somehow he felt he must be in trouble. *I'll never tell Uncle! Never!*

He heard his own breathing reecho from behind like the breathing of a giant creature. . . .

Run! Run!

The fragrance lingered beneath the surface of his mind. There was a new longing there, quickly repressed. It was more urgent than the scent of a girl, even. . . .

Quick! Back into the passageway, out into the cavern, don't look at anything.

Footsteps, patter, patter, patter

You don't see the machines—

patter patter

You don't see the walls that curve and curl and swirl like dreams of girls. You don't smell the fragrance.

patter

He scooted into the passageway. Rock rubbed against his shin. He cried out, giving himself away.

You don't hear the song.

He emerged. They ambushed him.

"Ha, ha, al'ksigark, the village sleeps safe tonight—"

"Hey, let me breathe!"

With a sigh he gave himself up to their gleeful vengeance. But his mind was somewhere else.

Eight
Light on the Sound

Loneliness. The wild windstream, like a firetouch. The airskiff ploughing, rocking a little . . . and the darkness stretching for ever. Darktouch with her hands on the pulsescreen, measuring, the patterns of airskiffs, crosshatching, shifting, coalescing somewhere beneath them. When she nosed her head her eyes touched nothing. But here and there she would smell a soft odor of bittersweet or peardrop, as skiffs of the appropriate scent class settled into position.

Windstriker moved around, setting controls and sniffing the air for his directions, relying more on scent than on the datascreens. Sometimes he would hand hex a ruddertip to hold fast against the wind. Sometimes she would be ordered to heave her weight against one of the levers that lifted the wingflaps. The

shift would shudder for a moment, ease into a new
direction on the windcurrent, and then the shuddering
would smooth out and they would sail as in a dream.

She slept a while. She dreamt of pincers gouging her
eyes out and the blood-trickle congealing on her face.
She woke with a start. A whole sleep had passed. They
soared now, they and the other stunhunters, she could
smell them through the smothering blanket of
darkness.

More time passed. But there was no touching to
mark time.

Her father's hand, suddenly, tense: *Sniff!*

—the scent of the preparation room, the steam
drenched with the gall of the Windbringer, the sweet
fragrance in the hot mist—

Windbringer, she signed. *He's near.*

Yes, her father's hand signed, a quick tick of
contact. Still her eyes touched nothing. Only her nose
sensed it, the shadow of an awesome thing. . . .

The wind was wrong. There was a pocket in the
wind ... ahead, a hollow of calm. The wind dividing,
shearing, off in two directions; skirting a vast
emptiness. *Windbringer.*

Quick, Father signed. An object in her hand, round,
knobbly. A grenade. The stunners would be separating
now, soaring above Windbringer, seeking to drug him
with high-velocity opiate pellets from their stunguns
and with burrowing grenades. She knew what to do.
When it struck the lining skin, it would start to
burrow, claws would gouge out scraps of flesh, needles
would inject paralysis gases stored inside at
tremendous pressure. It was beautiful, how
Windbringer fashioned his own homecoming.

The object gave off a glint of undark. She knew it for one of the old things. She knew it must cause pain, like the rituals of adulthood: but this was part of the order of the cosmos. Gingerly she put it down, fearful. She did not want it to be triggered off by her body warmth.

Windstriker placed her hands on the mechanism for tiring the stuncannons too. He let her waste a volley into darkness, to make sure she had gotten it right.

Then they soared!

Darktouch touched the pounding of her heart. Wind churned against their passage, The airskiff soared up glided propellers roared wings lifted rudders turned hair flapped forward backward sideways wrapped itself around her face—

The tang came from beneath now. She hurled the burrower and her ears touched a dead abrupt windshape and she knew she'd hit. Wind thrashed crazily around, echoed the Windbringers thrashing, still darkness and wind and the sweet intoxicating smell—

Good, Windstriker signed, his fingers touching the databoard. He fired the cannon and

—fingers of undark lightning flashing, a moment of undark, a shadow a huge sailsac, throbbing vast darkness—

Windstriker! Her lingers danced. *He's moving, I feel it with my eyes, I feel it on the wind!*

Above them another vessel spewed sparks of undark and her eyes touched hugeness, glitterstippled, wet flesh at the limits of eyetouching—

She was hurling grenades now more in terror than anything, her eyes had touched the living Windbringer and all she could do was throw frantically, windshapes of terror bursting from her lips—

We're too close! Windstriker signed, his fingers grating on her back. *More power, got to more up more into the wind-drift—*

(Don't be too brave Father don't dare too much now Father she signed in her mind crying out. . . .)

The skiff bucked, a flash of undark from another skiff above—

—sailsac lashing toward them for a split second—

Then the windwave exploded, grenades flew, struck her face, she flung herself on the skiff floor and—

She reached out to her father. He stood breasting the strong wind, emotionless.

And then she knew that her father's great moment had come. He had vowed to be taken by Windbringer in the most blessed of deaths. He had shown daring beyond all daring since her mother's death, in his search for a glorious end.

Her father signed against her neck. *Good-bye . . . Daughter.*

No! No! Another flash of undark and—

The great sailsac whipped forward. Darktouch clutched the boat hard and her eyes touched her father still standing arm: outstretched as though to embrace the wind—

Then Father falling toward the quivering flesh so graceful in the wind—

Sailsac flailing the boat, the skiff skimming the skin, slipping, catching the wind, soaring, out of reach, and

Dead pocket of Windbringer plummeting.

The airskiff spinning crazily, slowing down, easing.

Like a Sleepwalker she righted the controls and set the homing pattern. Touching the message panel, her hands read the signs that told of victory. Darkness had come again, and her eyes did not touch the last of her father, nor did her ears touch the windshape of crashing, hitting.

(I may as well jump in after him, she thought. His life is fulfilled now. They'll make a beautiful fingerchant about Windstriker, bravest of the brave, and children will chant it till their fingers are sore. But no one will remember *me*, the freak, the failure—)

The convoy was drifting homeward. Below her, she knew, Windbringer lay immobile, trapped in the meshing forceshields, the life bleeding away from him.

And then—

Then came the Windbringer's last song. . . .

***

Gallendys Thinkhive Memory

SECRET: RETRIEVAL ONLY ON GRAND INQUESTRAL OVERRIDE

Report on the Gallendys Exploration Mission

COUNCILLOR TON GADREZ ASH UKANDERRAKH: What do you mean, Kaz Errekath, you cannot describe the imagesongs you allegedly saw on this planet of yours?

KAZ ERREKATH (Expedition Leader): . . . Lord Inquestor, they were songs of utter beauty, utter joy. We can never disturb the delphinoids, sir. Otherwise—

COUNCILLOR GADREZ: You presume to command the Inquest?

KAZ EKREKATH: Slow bands of light, sir. Each band a stardust-speckled rainbow. Troughs of lights in pastels, crossing the far walls of basalt, the crystal dust in the rock catching the glitterfire and sparkling fiercely, dying . . . lightforms undulating . . . and the music! Slow, stately music. They should have music like this to accompany the movements of the stars . . . oh, powers of powers I can't go on, I've been touched, I've been changed . . . Mother! Father!

COUNCILLOR CADREZ: Remand him and the others in the custody of Huriel of the clan of Healers. Erase their memories. Even the memory of the Inquestor who traveled with them.

Thinkhive's addendum: The new identities were found unsuccessful upon reexamination twelve standard years later. None ever recovered their senses, so the Inquest compassionately devived them.

First came the undark. Warm to the touch, warming her eyes. New textures of warmths, new scents of undark plaved with her eyes. And a quiet throb of windshape, a slow pulse like a heartbeat but lower, deeper, that plucked her body like a string, so that she vibrated with it. . . .

In the undark, slowly, the Windbringer flailed against the wind, she felt the wind curve and part on either side of the skiff.

The undark rose slowly. More undark than ever her eyes had touched. It was like—

Embrace of an ancient mother wind coming to life with motes of undark, soft quiet glitter like the whispertouches of a mother on a newborn baby, wombwarmth of an eyetouching . . . and a fingerchanting of windshapes, the air dancing on her ears like risen angels. . . .

Then strands of undark, another shade, weaving like the fingers of touch-siblings who have begun to explore each other's bodies for the first time, meshing, breaking away, points of undark that broke free from the strands in time with the fingerchanting of the dancing wind. . . .

(Father's dead, she thought wonderingly. But she was distanced from that thought; she felt no grief yet. Only the immense warmth of undark on her eyes.)

Then explosion of undark! Stinging her eyes, burning them! Sudden searing warmth, the blur of tears concealing every-thing, pellets of windshape caressing her ears! A thousand fires bursting, her eyes stretching to unthinkable limits and touching far walls that trembled with the touching! Grenades of undark imploding in her guts!

And then a quiet glow of undark that quelled the howling with its soft-whistling windshapes, that calmed the nightmare like the slow fingerchant of a mother shushing her child. . . .

Through the blur her eyes found faint webs of undark.

It was the edge of a terrible beauty. And anguish too. As if the pain of the Windbringer in his death throes were being transformed by sheer will into patterns of warmth, of comfort. She stood for a very long time. The firetouch washed over her like clear fragrant water.

The imagesong played on her eyes and ears, and finally became—

A raging tornado with herself as its eye, patterns upon patterns, levels upon levels of undark and windshapes—

None of the others perceive this! she signed to herself. *Now I understand what my special gift is for!*

The undark sang to her of beauty mercilessly slaughtered, of a dream shattered before the end of the dreaming—

And we are the murderers! Because all the others are dark to the Windbringer's song! We're all butchers! There's a terrible terrible injustice in our universe and only I can touch it!

The imagesong was faint now. Through the parting dark she touched reflections within reflections, echoes within echoes. Then the windshapes rebounded from the far walls and piled harmony upon harmony and shade upon shade of the undarkness, until the whole universe seemed to be one song, one living thing, and she an alien openmouthed in wonder, being drawn into it, her body humming with the hymn of all creation. . . .

The song subsided

If Windstriker had known this—

She found anger in herself at last.

—he'd never have been a hunter! He'd never have been a murderer of beauty!

The airskiff splintered the shards of undark, scattering them into chaos as it flew homeward.

And the song was over.

And then she knew that she would run and run until she found an answer. She would force open the chambers of the dead if need be. She would thrust into the caverns where the cold angels waited for the dead. *Someone must know the truth!* Someone must he able to convince her that she wasn't crazy, that this special gift wasn't a terrible delusion.

I'm not human and I know it, she thought. *My eyes are my special thing.* She couldn't go back and lose them. Now that she had touched the undark behind the darkness. Perhaps the Dark Country of the dead was the only place for her now. She didn't belong anywhere.

Her fingers drummed the old chant:

Jumper jumping
In the wind

Only the memory of the undark was alive, burned into her soul, as the airskiff sped on its pre-programmed journey back to the walls of the world, in a darkness heavy with loss.

She didn't notice the churning wind as it gathered up the skiff and plunged it homeward. Nor the messages pinging on the databoard, pricking her fingers and telling of joy and victory. She stood in the wind like one already dead. Part of her had gone with the Windhringer. Forever.

***

Running. Running.

The door to the land of the dead.

Then a familiar touch. *Get away!* she lashed out *Don't touch me!* Her touch-brother was pressed against the door, his arm covering the stud.

She touched him, but the song of the undark was singing inside her, its touch was more vivid than the touch of Boy-belore-Naming—in the diffuse undark she noticed the blood on her touch-brother's eyes. *You did this to yourself!* she signed softly. He didn't react, but seemed to withdraw further, but never moving from the doorway.

Go away, Girl-before-Naming! I've been shamed!

My name is Darktouch!

A fine name, that . . . I should let you walk in there, into the Dark Country—to die!

She hugged him, then. Deep inside him there was a little warmth. How wan compared to the singing warmth of the whole cosmos . . . . *What use was mutilating yourself?* she signed sadly. *Now you'll run away, I suppose, and live in another village as an outsider. They'll never make you one of them, and you'll never find another touch-sibling . . . . For the sake of Windbringer! We are bound by scent and touch, Boy-before-Naming.*

He pulled away, backing further into the door. She grasped his arm firmly. *Don't run from me! I've been on the hunt of the Windbringers, and I've touched a new, terrible truth! The legends lie, Boy-before-Naming!*

You're only lying so you can get away with never growing up, her touch-brother signed. *You've hurt me, you've played with my life as though we weren't bound at all. Don't presume on our bond!*

No, no, she signed hysterically. *There is a great mystery, a beautiful undark that comes from Windbringers. And we're all guilty of murdering it! I've got a power, an overtouch, and I know my eyes have touched the truth!*

He was still now, his body straining to catch her words. Softly a wind touched them, driving his familiar scent into her nostrils and making her ache with her love for him. But even this love was a darkness compared to the haunting thing that lived in her heart. She touched him all over. He was less real than the big undark. Even though she could feel how his arms were scoured rough with the wind-dust of the lonely wind.

I'm going away, Touch-brother. I don't know where. But first I must go through the caverns where the Dark Country begins and where the angels live. There must be another world somewhere—even if it's beyond the deathland! Where they know the answers. Why do I possess this overtouching? Why has our past lied to us? I've got to find out why they've caused us to murder the songs for so long! Then I can come back and stop everything!

Tenderly she touched his face. The eyes were congealing, sticky. She smelled hot blood. He must hurt terribly.

Whats the use? Touch-brother signed wearily. *We're bound by scent and loyalty. You're a power woman, even though it may be power for evil. I've got to come with you. All we have is each other. Until we die.*

He stepped aside.

Elation surged in Darktouch. The memory of the imagesong sang in her. She pressed the stud, seized her touch-brother's hand, and raced for the opening that appeared in the wall—

They were at the beginning of the Dark Country.

They took a wary step.

An angel swooped with a screeching windshape, gleaming harshly—

Nine
Below the Water,
Above the Wind

The floater came to rest on a floaterdais overlooking
the Square of the Delphinoids, where the firefountain
of Kenongtath surged from the city's center, a pale
flamespurt against the spire-streaked sky. Davaryush
stepped down. He was alone and his shimmercloak was
covered with an overgarment of somber brown. It was a
poor disguise, not a disguise at all, really: but he knew
he could not appear as himself, ruler of Gallendys.

He took an airtube to the ground. Mosaics
sundialed from the fountain, scenes from the history of
the Dispersal of Man. The first Dispersal from
legendary Old Earth. The early wars between the
stellar nations. The ships of the Inquest transsecting
the silent starfields. Tachyon bubbles bursting from
the sky.

Why have I come here? he asked himself for the
hundredth time. He cursed the thing that drove him

always to ask questions. The thing that the long years of seminary had never destroyed in him.

When he reached the Square, the mosaics no longer made sense. They were random concatenations of colored stones, some from the nearby quarries, some which had traveled a thousand parsecs to lie alongside the others. It was a wilderness when you did not look down on the Square from a great height.

So, too, thought Davaryush, *is the Dispersal of Man. Only the Inquestors, detached from all of it, living in their world where time dilation could be averted by tachyon travel and a man could truly rule a thousand worlds—only the Inquestors see reality. They are the ones who look from above. But perhaps—*

Perhaps we see only what we want to see. Perhaps we have become so isolated that we are blinded, blinded like the poor people behind the mountain wall who work for a purpose they cannot even conceive.

The Square—open to the populace only on days of feasting or coronations or the weddings of Princelings —was desolate in the sunlight. Davaryush walked to the firefountain, about three hundred meters from where the airtube reached the ground.

Mosaic stones clashed and flashed, catching the slow dance of suns' light. He waited until the suns had crossed behind the tallest of the far spires and were hidden in the umbrella of Kallendrang, mushrooming out from the spire's apex. . . .

Then there was another shadow. But he heard no one breathing, even though the shadow of a man had crossed his face. He turned slowly. His eyes met the amber eyes of a young man, eyes that focused on nothing. He wore a plain gray tunic and moved stiffly. He pushed a message disk into Davaryush's hands.

Davaryush snatched his hand back. The stranger's hand had been like ice.

Follow this messenger. The letters danced across the plastic. *He won't talk. He's dead. He will lead you. Qithe qithémbara. Follow him. He cannot talk.*

So that's why he isn't breathing. Davaryush had never come so close to a servocorpse before; they were used on some planets, and were as commonplace to some as robots or slaves might be . . . but they had none on his homeworld, nor on the seminary planet where he had learned to be an Inquestor.

The dead man waited, unnaturally still.

"I'm ready," Davaryush said.

The corpse beckoned him to follow. It moved silently over the mosaic stones, never pausing. After a while Davaryush followed, his nervous footsteps echoing imperfectly the even shuffle of dead feet.

They passed the firefountain. They were in an area of mosaic that depicted—Davaryush k n e w t h i s from seeing it from above, for he would not have recognized the picture so close up—the first landing of Kaz Errekath on Gallendys. They crossed a wide swath of faceted blue stones, the Sea of Tulangdaror no doubt: about ten meters later, harsh browns represented the desert of Zhnefftikak. And then a striation of blackness.

The dead man stamped three times on the black stones.

Suddenly Davaryush realized that they were sinking into the ground, he and the servocorpse; that a portion of the tile floor was easing into the ground. He panicked for a moment. The corpse touched him, steadying him. The chill of the corpse's hand bit into his shoulder and crawled down his spine. Darkness closed over him and still they fell. Then he sniffed fumes.

They're killing me! he thought wildly.

An image of dawn on homeworld wavered, magenta light and a wind in the tall black grass—

The corpse held him in an unbreakable grip. The deathchill spread through him, burning.

Curse my curiosity! Curse it!

Sleep took him in the darkness.

***

He woke standing in a ripple-swept pool of light. They must be underwater, in the network of forcebubbles that formed the float-foundations of the City of Effelkang.

Lines of half-dark moved across the dead man's face. The dead man released Davaryush.

Davaryush saw another person. An Inquestral shimmercloak. It blushed even in the darkness . . . already he could almost recognize the person—

Yes. Waterlight on the graystreaked highlights of the black hair. "Varuneh!"

"I am," Lady Varuneh said, "Ton Varushkadan el'Kalar Dath, Grand Inquestor, Princeling, Hunter of Utopias."

She came toward him, unsmiling. "Our other friends," she said, gesturing. He heard cloaks stirring and knew that he must be in a huge bubblechamber under the Sea of Tulangdaror. "There was a city here before Effelkang, " said Varuneh. "Here, in the sea. Isn't it beautiful?" She took his hand then. Cold. And under the cold—

Desire stirred in him, incongruously. What game was she playing now? Did she suspect, did she *know*, about his fascination with her?

"Lady Varuneh—Grand Inquestor Varushkadan—we learned at the Seminary on Uran s'Varek, that you were dead."

"Daavye, Daavye," she mocked him gently, "you still believe everything they tell you, you still toe the line, then? Haven't you learned anything?"

Davaryush knew about Ton Varushkadan—Grand Inquestor a century before his boyhood—he'd heard the tales. How she'd crushed a far rebellion by stealing a Princeling's heart; how she'd hollowed out a planet for a pleasure dome, and exploded a star for the pretty lights. . . .

"So why are you here, posing as a traitor, risking our lives?" he asked her.

Her hand clutched his harder. There was tremendous power here. He'd bluffed this game of *makrúgh* too far. He was outclassed.

"Many years ago," Varuneh said, "I disappeared. I was in disgrace and should have been deprived of my rank . . . but it's a large galaxy. This is my secret realm now. Galaxies no more. I was a perfect Inquestor once. I killed completely when I killed, and with utter compassion for my victims. I destroyed a hundred utopias for the sake of the human condition. . .

"Then you *are* a spy of the Inquest!" said Davaryush. "And you found a flaw in my ideology, and now you must destroy me!"

The dead man stirred. Varuneh beckoned him away. "How I hate these servocorpses!" she muttered. "But what is one to do? They are the only servants one can trust completely. The only servants with no souls."

"You're toying with me!" Davaryush said.

"I'm not of the Inquest," said Varuneh simply. "I was destroyed . . . by Shtoma!"

At last Davaryush understood. He embraced the strange old woman, who crumpled into his arms like an armful of old rags, and wept.

Through the forceshield that prevented them from drowning, water churned, lanced by the stinging light of the high far suns. . . .

He heard Varuneh's voice, soft, bitter: "The Inquest has stifled the human race. Davaryush! It has squeezed the laughter from children by sending them to wars and death. It has frozen the old into loveless icicles . . . you and I were sent to Shtoma to crush it because it might have been a utopia. You remember, don't you, how Shtoma changed us? We went there, mocking their lack of greed and every other human quality, suspicious of everything they said and did . . . laughing at them because they rode the klomet-high varigrav coasters instead of using their knowledge of gravity control for something useful. And then we learned that their sun *udára* had come to life, that every few years they danced in the sun's gravity fields and were purged by their sun's limitless love. And then we didn't believe in the Inquest any more, not entirely. We didn't trust its high tenets, Daavye. We thought, *Perhaps man isn't a fallen being. Perhaps he has a right to be happy.*"

Her face was aglow now even in the half-dark. Davaryush loved her then, for they had been through it together—fallen into the sun of Shtoma, been touched by its voice, become nothings touched by love.

He remembered the endless light. . . .

No heat, no crush of gravity, because the sentient sun held them in its embrace and had mastered the environment by an act of will.

Varuneh smiled for the first time since they had met that day. "You did a foolish thing, Daavye, returning to Uran s'Varek and trying to bluff it out. You should never have faced the Inquest again. I knew that. I disappeared ... found a new identity. The galaxy is large, Daavye, and the Inquest only imagines it controls everything.

Davaryush waited.

"Now there's only one thing I want," she said. "I want the end of the Inquest."

Powers of powers! Davaryush thought. *At last, I've finally heard the unutterable thing . . . uttered. I've had so many doubts, but I've never conceived of the destruction of the web that binds the Dispersal. . . .* "No!" he cried out.

"Look around you," said Varuneh. "I am not alone."

She clapped her hands for light, and Davaryush saw that the room was crowded. Some of the people wore the shimmercloaks of the Inquest even—but the cloaks were mostly threadbare, dying ones. Among them was Ton Exkandar, the most loyal Inquestor he could have imagined. And ordinary folk too: slavechildren with Chrysanthemum brands on their foreheads, young soldiers of the Overcosm Wars in their clan uniforms, Princelings in their peacock-rainbow robes. All hushed and waiting. Here and there, dead men stood stiffly, ready to he commanded.

Davaryush thought: *If they really are committed to the end of the Inquest, they're doomed. How appropriate that they must use the dead as their slaves.* Aloud, he said: "This assembly is unsuitable! There are people who must not stand in the presence of high clans, yet they're all mingled without order—

"Oh, Daavye." said Varuneh, "the Inquest created the order for its own ends. This isn't the Inquest!"

Davaryush saw then the joy in all their faces. It was as though they were at the beginning of a great new journey. Here under the sea he had found people with a strange new hope. "I should have you all executed," he said, his tone playing him false. "You have no way of defeating the Inquest—and for my own sake I should not let any of you survive!"

"We have a plan." said Varuneh, "to cripple the Inquest. We need your help. To curtail the production of starships, we must control starship production if we are to bring down thousands of years of control . . . blow up the Skywall mountain. Cut down the Inquest at its most fragile point. And then the way will be open . . . for a real utopia."

"You're mad!" Davaryush cried. "You can't expect me to cooperate. Only I can requisition power enough to blow away this much of a planet — and only by subverting the thinkhives and lying to the Inquest. We don't indulge in wanton destruction, you know that, Varuneh—"

"Oh, really?" The voice was hard.

"You want to destroy this mountain, when there is a race of people who live in the darkness of Skywall, who harvest the brains of the delphinoids for the starships, who would perish? You want an act of violence to be the fanfare for your utopia?"

"Remember Shtoma, Davaryush. Shtoma in the cadent lightfall."

The trap was closing in on him, the trap that had been set at the very beginning, when he had first set foot in the twin cities—

"We're all puppets, Daavye." said Varuneh. "Like . . . this servocorpse." She mindflicked at the dead man. The corpse began to dance, a slow elegant sinuous dance . . . the dead eves hypnotized Davaryush. "That's all the Dispersal of Man is, Daavye! A cosmic corpse that twitches to the mindflicks of an Inquest crazed with power!"

"No!" cried Dayaryush, grasping at all he had been taught—'The Inquest miscalculated. As they will again. They wanted to make you perfectly loyal by making you indispensable to the human race's stability. But didn't they teach you once that change is good, that utopias imply stagnation? Doesn't that lesson tell you that the Inquest must fall . . . that this is implicit in its very ideology? Ha! I've played the game of *makrúgh* longer than any living Inquestor. I can call their bluff. I've been in Shtoma, and they haven't. I'm changed, and they aren't."

"But not changed enough," Davaryush said, surprised by his own bitterness. "You're an Inquestor through and through. Especially if you would destroy a people for the sake of saving another."

He saw her pale at this. This, then, was the chink in her armor, the flaw in her great stratagem. If this were *makrúgh*, he should be elated at his victory. But he was not. He was only tired. Behind their struggle, he sensed a kinship. That they had shared the experience of Shtoma, yes; that they had doubted the Inquest together, and we're now considering its downfall, yes. But there was a deeper kinship, too, an attraction. . . .

Then Varuneh said, very tired, "We're not playing any more, are we? Well, let me tell you another thing, something you must have seen through already. I love you."

Then she tottered into the crowd, never once looking back at the man with the power of life and death over her, over the whole planet.

And Davaryush knew that she had played *makrúgh* with consummate mastery. By playing the final card, the one that said *I am not playing makrúgh with you.* She was all Inquestor, that woman. He knew that she knew his every weakness. He'd been indecisive, he'd procrastinated, not wanting to face the canker in himself. The last remark had gone in like a twisted laserknife, a masterstroke of *makrúgh.* No matter what side she was on, she was of the clan of Ton. A master Inquestor.

I'll cooperate, he thought.

He forced himself to forget about the people behind the Skywall, the people of eternal darkness.

The harshness of the undersea lighting brought tears to his eyes. Across the floor, the dead man was still dancing, for the Lady Varuneh had not yet rescinded her command.

***

It was morning in Kallendrang. False mauve-tinged light from a long-dead planet tinted the glittering spires. Davaryush stood before the thinkhive. . . .

Something has happened, said the thinkhive. *There are two persons in the corridors that lead out of the Dark Country, where my angels rend the dead for return to the water of the Sunless Sound. But they're not dead. I think they're trying to escape.*

"Aren't you going to do something?" Davaryush said curtly. *They won't get far. They're deaf and blind. Even if they crawl out of the mountain, my searcher drones will eventually be activated. The angels will follow them wherever they go. The machinery's a little creaky—it's never been activated, after all—but it's there.*

What could a man do, a man who had to protect the unity of the galaxy, a *heretic*? The Inquest was bursting at the seams. "But why," Davaryush shouted into the empty room, "why the secrecy? Why must they all be deaf and blind?"

Sorry, but you are not of sufficient rank to he informed. This is all I can divulge: that the motive is compassion.

Davaryush stormed from the room.

He found the elevator tube to the summit of Kallendrang, many klomets above the sea. In the airtube the wind rushed against him, a clean, powerful feeling. He reached the dais at the high summit, the point from which the city's protective domeshield was generated. Here, shards of the true dazzling sky of Gallendys splintered the purple dawn. There was a turret that led outside, a hundred steps of curving metal. . . .

Now he was outside the field. Below the cities sparkled. Two suns glared, but it was cold because of the elevation, and a thin wind whistled about the deck. And then he saw the sea beneath, fiercely reflecting back the suns' light. It stretched to the far horizons and blended with the shimmering haze-hung sky—

From one edge of the horizon, the black edge of Skywall, peering from the water and distorting the perspectives.

From behind the Skywall mountain would come an answer? And someone was trying to escape from there, even now.

Why? It was hopeless. But he must talk to that person. Find out what the thinkhive would not reveal. He shivered in the high wind.

And then another thought—

The dead man twitching in parody of a dancer, in the room under the city.

It's true! he thought bitterly. *We are all dead people! But somehow I think I am being readied for something. I'm never going to be a dancing servocorpse. I've been changed—by knowledge. The whole universe is changing, and the Inquest is playing* makrúgh *with forces even it cannot handle. The old things must crumble . . . like timed ink on an old message disk.*

And now someone's trying to get out of the mountain. It's a sign! I wish him well. His people are doomed. But we must all burst free now—from the cage of the Inquest, from the prisons we have built around our own hearts.

"I'm free!" he shouted into the howling wind. "I'm free! I'm free!"

He felt no joy in it at all. Only pain. His old teacher Ton Alkamathdes had been right. *The breaking of joy is the beginning of wisdom,* he had said. It was the central tenet of the utopia hunter. . . .

He saw the dream of utopia that Varuneh and the others had. It was a beautiful thing. But the beauty was an ache, an emptiness, a terrible hunger. And Varuneh's way of achieving it—through violence—was not perfect. But he could see no other way!

But the dream . . . the dream . . .

He remembered Varuneh then, sleeping softly in the dawnlight of a dead world. They'd found each other, but time was already running out. No wonder they slept together in the light of an annihilated planet. They were committed; they had already chosen death. It was strange, how much more alive one became, when one had something to believe in.

The time had come to throw away the past. To be a heretic in deed as well as in thought. He'd found himself—with a vengeance. Under his terrible exhaustion, Davaryush found a wary elation, almost . . . a peace. For he had come to Shtoma in the cadent lightfall, and he had danced on the face of the sun.

Ten

From Darkness to Darkness

Quick! Dodge it now! Darktouch signed, throwing herself and her touch-brother to one side—

—cold metal of the angel scraping skin, sharp pain, warm blood trickling—

(Got to keep moving! she told herself.) Touch-brother signed, *Faster, faster,* but her body was solid rock, rooted like the rock of the world itself. Farther down the pathway they stumbled. She turned and touched the metal angel with her eyes. In the diffuse undark it glowed, splinters of flashing warmth rippling down its body. It was burrowing into the floor where it had landed, where they'd been standing.

Harsh thudding windshapes as it scratched at the bare stone. Rock shards spattering the smooth surface of the angel. Whoosh of the closing door, change in the wind's direction.

It's eating us up, it thinks! she signed. *It doesn't know we're alive, we can move . . . if we stay moving, if we're cautious, we can make it!*

The stud to reopen the door was blocked by the spidery angel. They were trapped. They could only go onward. *Quick!*

Above, here and there, her eyes touched glinting metal creatures. Ominously they moved, scanning from the ceiling with swift crisscrossing lances of undark. The shafts moved in a slow fingerchant. Against her body she felt Touch-brother's pounding heart. He didn't know the place and he had no eyes to guide him,

Slowly, easing down from the vague height—

The angels were descending!

Run! her fingers rasped. *The angels are coming down. I touch them with my eyes!*

They moved with a clanging, jarring windshape, spider arms stretched out and catching the filaments of undark that rippled in the heavy air—

She ran, her hands just touching her touch-brother, her only contact with the old world. Her hand on him; *Hold me! Don't let go or you'll be lost!*

I can't run! I don't know this place, there's nothing to memorize, there's too much for my feet to understand all at once—

Trust me, it's not dark to me—

I can't. I—

Pebbles biting her feet. Now and then a vertebra crunching. Now the squish of a fresh dead man. She stumbled over a skull, lost contact with Touch-brother, turned, touched a whiff of fear, eyes touched him flailing the emptiness, scratching despairing wordshapes on the heedless air. Her hand seized his arm. *Don't let go!* They'd been still for several moments and now an angel had scanned them and was plummeting, so gracefully, so deadly—

They're not made to catch the living! she signed as they dodged it. *If you stop they'll think you're a corpse, then they'll devour you*—

The angel crashed on to rock, began to pound the hard basalt, sending sharp windshapes into Darktouch's ears. She whirled and eyes touched Touchbrother being mauled by a glistening claw, she pulled, wrenched him loose, he was like a sack of old Windbringer entrails, there was no life in him at all, must keep running, she thought, never mind the blood —

Touch-brother weakening in her grip.

Cold metal jabbed at her back. In the distance her eyes touched water. She couldn't tell how deep. Angels on ground level were scooping the pulped bodies into the water. It must he the duct that led the nutrient soup down into the Sound, there to mingle with the big water that no man had ever touched . . . she had been told of the big Sound and the churning waters that seethed and steamed from the pressure of Windbringer's breath, the big Windbringer, that is, in whose belly the whole world lay. . . . A sweet smell came from the water, and her ears touched the ear-tickling windshape of its constant running.

Beyond the singing water, a round thing with a stud, set into the wall—a door, shrunk by distance! She didn't know whether it was a *real* door, surely the shrinking of distance could not make something man-high into something the size of a child's fist. But perhaps—

Got to keep moving, she signed grimly. Water washed her foot.

I'm going crazy! her touch-brother signed weakly. *It's all dark to me, there's nothing to recognize, nothing to touch but things that always change—*

Be brave. She dodged an angel. She was getting good at it now, sidestepping it and observing it pummel the stone relentlessly as though it were a corpse.

They were waist-high in thick, flesh-sodden water. Touch-brother was still, giving up in confusion, and she was gripping him hard and supporting his dead weight.

Her feet were sinking into slush. There was no way of telling how deep the slush went, and whether there would be room to stand. *We have to push on,* she sighed, *through this water. . . .*

On impulse she began to thrash at the water wildly with her arms and legs. The water was buoyant. Perhaps she could float toward the ever-growing circle of door . . . no. A current was pushing her inexorably away from it. She thrashed harder, battling the stinking water, while her touch-brother clung like a leaden thing. *Only a little way—*

A final shove, and her feet left the bottom and she found herself thrusting toward the metal circle ahead. Then dryness.

They rested a while. Here the floor was metal. Across the water—Darktouch had never touched so much water before in her life, could not conceive of such a thing, for she had known only jars and pots of the liquid—the angels scurried, mincing bodies and ignoring them.

I think we're safe, she signed. He didn't answer.

What's wrong, Boy-before-Naming, Touch-brother mine?

And then she realized how important her special gift was to both of them. Things she had taken for granted were dark to him. He was moving in utter darkness, with nothing to cling to except his strange touch-sibling who wasn't quite human. . . .

The angels made no move toward them. This was clearly not somewhere they were trained to scan. Resolutely she turned her back on the cavern of the angels and the dead bodies, and made for the door, scrabbling at the metal stud and—

They were through!

The door clanged! Quickly she had pulled Touch-brother through. A curious, hollow gasping windshape escaped his lips, now and then, and he lay in the stillness. For now it was perfectly still, as though—

Yes. There was no wind here at all. The air was still and lifeless.

I must be dead, Darktouch thought. *This must be a dead land, truly.*

She cast her eyes about her, and they met strangeness. There was a chamber that seemed to have no ending. The floor was featureless metal. It was not designed for humans, obviously—there were none of the crannies and bumps that told your feet where to go. There were no guidewalls to touch, so you could know where you were. A soft undark, warmer than in the cavern of corpses, glowed from the very walls.

She was hungry and had to relieve herself too. And the windlessness was more frightening than anything else she'd ever known.

Why did I do this? she signed in the deathly stillness. *Why?*

And then she remembered how the imagesongs had moved across the big darkness. She remembered how her whole soul had sung with the Windbringer—it all lived still, deep inside her, a slow burning. *I came to find an answer,* she signed to herself.

Eye-images danced inside her: the angels with their pincers outstretched, her father plummeting, fulfilling his pact with the Windbringer, his own life's dream—

Music of undark, warming her, stilling the terror.

The imagesongs haunted her now. Even as the horrors of the flight through the dead land were fading from her memory a little. She stood a while, waiting. Her eyes became used to the new undark. She could distinguish no distances, for the walls were far and untouchable. There were wild spirals of rock far above and metalfaced machinery that whispered and thrummed in her ears. . . .

But Boy-before-Naming never moved.

Brother, brother . . .

There was no answer from him at first. Then faintly he scrawled on her arm, *Darkness . . . darkness . . . nothing to touch going . . . crazy . . .* His body began to twitch like a newborn baby's. She tried to calm him, touching him all over, covering him with her warm body. He didn't react.

Of course, she thought. *All he can touch is the ground, and that has nothing to remember. It is quite dark, all of it. He is starved for sensations. Slowly, the darkness is driving him mad, and there's nothing I can do!*

Please communicate with me, she signed, *please. . . . Sign anything at all, even a children's fingerchant, just so I know you're alive, if you won't you'll die—*

And then, slowly, he began to drum slowly into her hand, the old fingerchant which all children learned in the nursery, which taught the basic shapes for the words without the squiggles of tense and case and the curves of emotion, love, hate, anxiety. . . .

Jumper, jumper,
Lost his name,
Jumper jumping
In the wind

Bringer, bringer
Run to kiss him
Jumper, nameless.
Bringer, fall,

Stunner, topple,
Scent of bringer
Jumper jumping
In the wind

Bringer come! Bringer go!
Catch my soul
Fly, jump, fly, jump,
Belly, beast, mother, death,
Warm, soul, fly, go.

Darktouch remembered the words of Stonewise: that this fingerchant had most likely been the gift of the first Winbringer of all, since the shapes had been found magically chiseled into the walls of the chamber where the knowers knew and the dreamers dreamed their wisdom.

Now she signed, encouragingly, *Good, little brother. Let's do it over and over now so you'll get it right*, and he was scratching all higgledy-piggledy like a young child learning to sign, and she chanted it with him, in firm strokes, in the big room built for other than humans—

Jumper jumping
In the wind

(and she remembered Father falling, falling into the arms of Windbringer, dying in a blaze of glory . . .)

Bringer come! Bringer go!
Catch my soul!

(she signed harder, drawing blood, and Touchbrother's touch weakened further on her arm, and Father fell over and over . . .)

Belly, beat, mother, death,
Warm, soul, fly, go. . . .

(and the undark rippling in the huge darkness, and the tingling windshapes, and the nightmare fading into quiet joy, firetouching the distant water below, and the windghosts blazing . . .)

The tears were streaming, hot, stinging her parched lips. And now her touch-brother was still.

Come on! she signed, forcing gaiety from her fingertips. *Come on, kid, fly, jump, fly, jump* . . . Then she clawed him, trying to drive all the warmth of her into his body. But he was cold, and growing colder.

I'm alone, she thought. She covered her eyes, yearning for ignorance: but even in the self-made darkness the Windbringer's song haunted her memory.

Touch-brother was dead. He could not cope with the sensory vacuum of the enormous chamber, the metal floor, after the nightmare of the flight through the Dark Country. He had died rather than face the new world.

The angels did not come for him. There seemed to be none here. At least he would not he mangled and turned into soup for the strange moving water, she thought, more in hope than certainty.

Then she turned her back on the body and the door that led back to the country she had known all her life, and began to walk steadily toward the unknown.

***

Kelver was in trouble, as usual, and for dreaming too much, as usual . . . and so he came to the secret cavern again. He usually came every day now. Sometimes he would just sit there and make the vast chamber into an imaginary helm of a starship or a Lordling's hall of audience. Other times—when he felt braver—he would go to the door into the Dark Country, and carefully touch the stud (as gingerly as though it were a dormant al'ksigark in the desert) and feel the strange-scented wind on him. Sometimes it would bring odors of putrefaction, other times bittersweet fragrances that stirred him and shook him and made him uncomfortable. But he always came back.

And now a girl was walking toward him out of the Dark Country.

He watched her for a while, stunned and unmoving.
The girl did not walk like people. Her head was trained
straight ahead as though she were blind, and yet she
seemed to be able to see. She walked stiffly, her feet
reaching, toeing the metal floor very carefully to test
for strange objects. She didn't look down. He held his
breath, waiting. . . .

She stood still, about twenty meters away from him.
She was whiter than the chalksands of Zhnefftikak. As
though the suns had never touched her at all. Kelver
marveled at that. She wore nothing but a loinshield of
some indeterminate skin, and her hair fell, black as the
Skywall mountain, all the way down to her waist. He
saw that she was looking at him. He saw her lip quiver
a little. He didn't know if it was fear or some other
emotion. Her face showed nothing at all. It was almost
as though she did not know how to show emotion with
her face; it was a mask, lineless, perfectly composed.

"Who are you?" he said, wondering.

She showed no reaction. Around them the secret
world hummed. Lights twinkleflashing, whorls of
metal shimmering . . . the girl. "Why are you here?" he
cried out. And then he felt a strange kinship with her.

Something flashed in her eyes: guilt, laughter,
recognition, he couldn't tell. "You've never been in the
sun, have you?" he said. "You're from the Dark Country.
You've run away . . ." *Like me*, his mind finished. They
were both misfits, escapers:

*First I saw the tachyon bubbles. Then I found the
spoor of the al'ksigark. I'm a finder, aren't I? Now this.
This is so much more important! This is something . . .
the Inquest has to know.*

He thought of the inquest. Then of his father's
corpse, a distant memory, hazy as mist on a chilled

crystal goblet, and cold. Then, vividly, his father's smile flashing, then the stone-dead face—*I wish you were here!* his mind cried out. "Can't you talk?"

Suddenly she rushed toward him and—

***

—seized the strange boy's hand and signed to him, the signs rushing thick and quick from her fingernails, *Oh please please person from the end of the world, I've run away out of the whole world and I've touched the songs of the Windbringer with my eyes and ears and everything has fallen apart, and I need answers, I have to know why they've all lied to us and why they've denied us the power to perceive the Windbringer's songs*

—

There was no answer. Instead, a stream of windshapes issued from his mouth. They seemed almost purposeful, almost meaningful, very alien compared to the involuntary windshapes of babies or of those in anguish. He didn't even understand her signings!

Give me an answer! she signed with her last strength. *Give me*—

***

He held the girl to him, even as she was raking contorted scratchings into his arms. He knew somehow that she did not mean to hurt him by it. But exhaustion took her and her finger movements became feeble. He had blood on both arms. He held her tight, soothing her like a wild animal. . . .

"It's all right, there's nothing to fear, nothing to fear. . . He walked her a few steps, toward the entrance of the secret cavern.

The girl made a strange noise in the back of her throat— "There's nothing to fear. . . ."

"Fear." It was a distinct word.

"Oh, so you *can* talk," he said. They had reached the entrance and he showed her how to crawl through into the natural part of the cave. She was more at ease as soon as they reached the smaller rooms. With their pocked floors. He didn't have to hold her now; she followed him, her hand resting lightly on his back, not looking to right or left. Just like a blind person.

"Don't worry." he said. "Uncle will take care of you: he's a good man, even if he's too tired to really pay me much attention, too wrapped up—"

"Fear." The word reechoed.

"Don't keep saying . . . oh, it's all you can say, isn't it? Did you just copy that from what I was saying? Don't they speak the Inquestral tongue in your country? Or it's a different dialect, I guess, like the ghost people from Zhnefftikak—"

They reached the cave mouth. It was broad daylight. Kelver stepped out of the cave. Ahead, the Cold River stretched on its pylons, angling down to ground level for about fifty meters and then running on to infinity. Above them the mountain loomed. The suns were one behind the other, unbearably brilliant, and the rocks burned even Kelver's callused feet. The girl stood in the cave month's shadow and tor the first time she moved her head from side to side, and fear seemed to fleck her eyes. She darted back into the cavern, he ran in to seize her and bring her out again, and they stood there, he clasping her tightly and the girl shielding her eyes with her hands. (Carefully Kelver pried them away and then pointed ahead to the bright porcelain cubes in the mid distance that were the village, and she shook her head wildly and then looked out, finally, and then she murmured. "Fear. Fear. Fear. Fear."

And he knew now that she did not know what it meant but had just managed to mimic one of his words; but then he thought of the implications of what had just happened—how he, a mere boy from a back village in a backwater planet in a backward solar system, had stumbled on something that no one in his whole cosmos knew existed, something so important that perhaps even the Inquest itself would be dragged in—when he thought about all this he felt fear too.

"First things first," he whispered. "We'll go back to the village and we'll teach you to talk our language, and find out why you're here . . . then we'll see if we must tell the Inquest. . ."

But he already knew that he was at the beginning of a journey to unknown places and among people of power. Kelver was different from the other people of his village, after all. He could see beyond. He could imagine starships streaking through space, in the black emptiness that was Skywall. But seeing did not make him any less afraid.

"Fear! Fear!" the girl cried out.

There was much that Kelver could not yet see. How, half a continent away, the planet's thinkhive was buzzing, activating dormant robot drones from the heart of the Dark Country, breathing life into never-used circuitry, issuing commands to secret machines of death. The girl should already have been dead—but a vast instrument of death that had not wakened in twenty thousand years could not be bestirred in a few seconds.

There was still time: how much time, not even the planetary thinkhive knew for certain.

Darktouch

Book Two

Out of the Burning
Wasteland

mi' brendéh aíros
chom z'hartnen Zhénveren
min verdens aíroten
chom z'hartnen a ómbrel ayán

Love burns me like the wasteland of Zhnefftikak
Love freezes me like wasteland under the shadow

—Galléndaran children's love song

Eleven
Windshapes

There was a room where the floor was almost liquid; it flowed around you, comfortable and yet disquieting because it couldn't be remembered like a real floor. There were circles of undark in the sky your eyes couldn't even hear to touch. Most of all, there was a hugeness—the air and the rooms and the floors went on and on and people never even noticed that the world was not walled into easy segments. She had been in the strange world for two sleeps now, and she understood nothing at all. So she had abandoned herself to the world, drinking it in moment by moment, not questioning it. It was a good world: people were kind to her, feeding her and always uttering the windshapes that she now knew must be somehow full of meaning. For one thing she had noticed, almost from the start: they were not a touching people. They communicated some other way: perhaps by the endless variety of ear-touches they could make with their mouths, perhaps even with their minds. She was sure they were not a cold people, that they did not stand so distant from each other out of hatred or unease. It was puzzling.

Darktouch woke in the room, the atrium of the old man's house. The old man and the young woman with the tortured-looking eyes seemed to have some relationship to the boy who had found her at the door to Windbringer's world. But he did not treat them with the same diffidence and circumspection with which a well-bred Boy-before-Naming should treat his parents. Her own relationship with Windstriker had been special and at times almost improper, but she had never carried on this way, arguing sometimes, impetuously showing affection sometimes—it was something else to puzzle over.

She woke. The soft floor startled her as ever, shifting when she shifted. A flood of undark burst in on her. Unlike in the Windbringer's world, this undark had definite sources: glowing globes, set into the room's walls, which surrounded her well out of touching range.

The boy was touching her. His mouth curved broadly to show flashing teeth. Perhaps this facial grimace was some kind of ritual. The touch she understood, though, even though it had no pattern. She read curiosity in it, a little concern too; for the boy had no art to his touch, and could not hide his emotions.

Her eyes met his: she realized that he was touching her all over with his eyes. It warmed her, that he shared her gift. But then all of them shared it in this strange country. . . .

She belonged here. That she knew.

Now the boy pointed to himself and made a clear windshape. "Kelver."

Was this a name, perhaps? Was he trying to teach her their form of communication? She struggled with new muscles in her throat and only came out with "K . . . k . . ." Then she repeated the one windshape she knew she could make. "Fear." By now she knew that it meant something undesirable. The people she had met always seemed to recoil at it. They would turn away the touchings of their eyes.

"Kelver," the boy repeated. If it was his name— But how could he have a name? A boy who still kept his eyes must surely be a boy-before-naming. This was a topsy-turvy world, without any logic to it, except that somehow she knew it was more real than her own world had been . . . she remembered the other boy-before-naming, the one with whom she had shared the profane touchings, even. And then she forced herself to remember Windstriker, too, falling into the abyss . . . and the beauty and terror of the great undark. She tried to make the windshape again, and seemed to come closer, perhaps: the boy curved his mouth again, and then a silversteel explosive windshape, a ha-ha-ha, burst from his lips. It did not seem unfriendly, though, and it was easy to produce, just a burst of breath over the wide-open mouth. like so—

They held hands. Intuitively she knew that they had exchanged something very much like laughter, or what passed for it in their world. It was a pleasant— windshape—she groped for a different concept-name on which to peg this new meaning, but in vain. She laughed again. They both laughed, holding each other close, and she realized that the boy's closeness was arousing her a little. She flinched, ashamed suddenly. He is not my touch-brother! she told herself sternly. I've got to control myself, observe all decorum. . . .

And then she took his arm, and very deliberately, avoiding all emotional inflections, keeping to the most angular of children's sign-forms, she signed her name.

Darktouch. Darktouch.

An expression of. . . puzzlement? . . . stole over the boy's face. He jerked his hand away, and seemed lost in thought, almost ignoring her.

And then he seized her hands and repeated the signs for her name, perfectly, without a single error.

Darktouch was trembling.

You understand, she signed, without being taught at all, Boy-before-Naming, how is this possible?

But he didn't understand her. Again, he signed the word Darktouch.

Then he rose abruptly and left the room, excited over something or other. Darktouch was perplexed more than anything: but she did not get up to follow him. She settled down on the warm floor, letting it flow around her, emoting its warmth. Even the arms of Windstriker were not like this, accommodating her every movement. This was indeed a strange world, where floors changed their shapes and left nothing in the memory to remind the feet which way they had gone. A world of shape-shifters. A world that did not value permanance. Where even the floors were vague as dreams, and where darks and undarks could be snapped on and off with a flick of the head or hand. . . .

When, she wondered, will they tell me about the Windbringers? For she had not forgotten the thing that had driven her to throw aside everything she had loved and believed. And if they would not answer her

soon she would surely have to flee again, to some yet
stranger country. . . .
***

"Uncle Aaye. listen to me—"

Kelver stopped dead, realizing it was a bad time. His
uncle and aunt were half-standing, half-reclining in
the conversation pit on the upper level of the house,
where the floor dipped and was even softer and furrier.
But they were on opposite sides of the pit as if in a
formal argument.

"Yes, what is it, Kevi?" said his uncle. "The girl?"

"As I was saying, Aaye," Aunt Telzi continued,
ignoring the boy, "you really must report that girl to
the City. Someone must take her away. Its upsetting to
the villagers. . . ."

They know? Aaye seemed angry.

"A girl, Haller I think, was here this lightsend, and . .
." Kelver looked from one to the other. "I want her to
stay here," he said decisively.

"You and your father," Telzi said, looking away from
him. "But," said Kelver earnestly, "she proves that we
aren't doing all this for nothing, doesnt she? I mean
the food growing and the button pushing. I think she
should stay."

"She may not be from the Dark Country," Uncle
Aaye said, "but from another village, or from
Zhnefftikak."

"You know that's not true." Impulsively, Kelver dived
into the conversation pit and seized his uncle's arm.
"Look, can you understand this" and he scrawled
characters on the arm, in bold hard strokes.

"It's highspeech. Témberash. It means dark touch.
What's that to me?"

"It's her name, Uncle Aaye!" His new discovery came bursting out. "They use touch-signs for a language, Uncle, touch-signs that spell words in good Inquestral highscript . . . and they have other things we don't understand, squiggles for moods and shortcut signs and circles and squares for emotions—"

Uncle Aaye shook the boy away. Kelver caught the look of dismay, quickly camouflaged. "Uncle, what's the matter, what's wrong?" He saw Aunt Telzi's face go white.

Then Uncle Aaye said, *"Chadah y'ómbren evéndek a témbris kíndaran éndek.* The shadow falls forever . . ."

" . . . on the children of darkness," Kelver finished. "Oh, Uncle, you knew all the time. We have to help her!"

"She should have been deaf and blind," his uncle said wonderingly.   "I wonder how she was spared. In the Dark Country they are all deaf and blind, you know. I've been Village Elder for a long time and you pick up a little here and there when you must travel to Effelkang once in a while. But there's no question about it . . . she must be given to the Inquest."

"We can shelter her here for the winter, can't we?"

"I'm not looking forward to the Inquestral commission that is bound to want to investigate everything," his uncle said. "I think we can safely wait until the annual trading caravan from Effelkang, and send her along with them."

"That's only thirty sleeps from now! And she can't talk yet!"

"Who's to say she'll ever be able to talk?" Uncle Aaye grated. Kelver sensed a bitterness in him that went much deeper than the immediate problem. Could it be that even his uncle, the Inquest's servant, who was never heard to criticize the way things were in the universe, resented them sometimes? The Inquest was so high, though. To see an Inquestor must be like staring straight into the sun. Then his uncle turned to Aunt Telzi and said gently, "Let's have yunáki stew tonight, shall we? A little treat. And bring the girl."

Kelver knew that his uncle was trying—in his own way—to make peace. The yunáki had been his father's favorite dish. He wondered if the thought of his Father pained Aaye as much as it did him. It had always been hard for Aaye to express affection, picking a dish for dinner was about as far as he'd ever go.

Kelver wondered, too, if his uncle had taken any risks by not reporting the discovery of the girl from the Dark Country at once. And if so, whether it was from love for his nephew, or from fear of the Inquest, or . . . it was hard to understand old people.

Presently his aunt and uncle began to talk of their domestic problems, and Kelver wanting to avoid being drawn into this conversation, slipped away quietly and went down to find the girl Darktouch.

She was sitting where he had left her, on the contour-floor of the atrium. She looked up at him; he was certain now that what she saw she was trying to interpret in some alien, ungraspable way. When he came close to her he could smell an unfamiliar fragrance, as though the Dark Country still clung to her.

"Let's teach you how to talk then," he said. sitting beside her. He took her arm and scratched the word home, and said the word, and pointed all around them. With his free hand. He used the highspeech, not the lowspeech. After all, her signings seemed to be in that tongue. Also, selfishly, he didn't want anyone else in the village to be able to talk to her. "Home," he said "Kézeh, home."

"H—home." He was stunned for a moment, and then smiled. And then he saw that she, too, was struggling to make a smile, forcing the muscles of her face into the uncomfortable, unfamiliar posture.

It was a strained grimace, and then, miraculously—

"You're smiling!" Kelver whispered. The smile faded abruptly. "Home," he said in the highspeech, echoing her.

"You're smiling," said the girl, mimicking his awed whisper. He could hardly contain himself now. He reached out to touch her cheek—

She flinched, pushed him away. I have to draw her out of where she is, thought Kelver. It's as if she's still trapped inside a little bubble of the Dark Country, like a tachyon bubble. . . .

Later they would call her Girl-who-burns, because she picked up every sound that was thrown to her, highspeech and lowspeech, she was consumed by the need to know speech and to communicate. . . .

But Kelver could not yet tell what it was that had driven her out into the alien world. For now he was content to teach her, to bask in her presence. When the thirty days were up he would find a way of keeping her. He would go with her to the Inquestors, if this was what was decided. After that he would be noticed and he would go off and fly the overcosm. She was his ticket to making his childish dreams come true. She was his.

He was in love, after all.

Twelve
Compassion

I hate this room, Davaryush thought. It glitters with malice. . . .

He stepped forward into the wombroom. He felt the mirror walls hemming him in. As he glanced around, he saw himselves distorted over and over in the curving mirror wall, a grotesque old man hiding behind the blur of a shimmercloak. As he moved, the thousand other shimmercloaks swirled with him.

Back so soon, said the thinkhive, Ton Davaryush z Galléndaran K'Ning? Davaryush thought he could hear a note of contempt in the thinkhive's voice. But that was impossible. He must not let the situation drive him paranoid, not now when he most needed to think clearly.

A charming conceit, said the thinkhive, to ban all servocorpses from the twin cities . . . what arcane

symbolism is this? Or is it that you have become
terrified of death lately, you who are so ready to inflict
death? I fancy you are making ready for a game of
makrúgh. Davaryush, in which millions will be
compassionately devived . . . am I not right,
Davaryush?

"Impertinence?" Davaryush cried. He never wanted
to look at a servocorpse again, because . . . he would
see himself, dancing to the Inquest's whim. "I want you
to tell me about the persons who have escaped from
the mountain."

Very right and proper, Davaryush. We must make
sure they're dead, now, mustn't we? We can't leave any
loose ends, not if we're going to embark on something
as huge as a game of makrúgh . . . directed from here, a
world central to the Inquest's power. I can smell your
strategies from klomets away, Davaryush.

Panic hit him for a moment. Could the thinkhive
know? "What of the escapers?"

Isn't it true, said the thinkhive, evading the issue,
that you're throwing a tremendous reception soon,
culminating in a cloud concert and the music of the
famous Shen Sajit, and that you've invited several
Inquestors to this planet, including no less a person
than Ton Ynyoldeh the Deadly, the Queen of Daggers,
Grand Inquestor of Warfare? The Inquestors who
made me made me well, Davaryush. I, too, see with the
eyes of the Inquest . . . and I see beneath your
shimmercloak, down to your very heart . . . . I see
makrúgh, Davaryush, a dangerous, powerful makrúgh
that even you may not be equipped to play. Is that not
so?

"It's cold here."

The temperature rose a notch, but Davaryush felt no warmer. Planetary thinkhives were wily things, programmed at the very beginning of the Inquest's power. In a way the thinkhive of Gallendys was a more fearsome opponent than even the Lady Varuneh would have been. . . .

Thinkhives were driven only to know. They did not have compassion, Davaryush thought, even though they could understand it in their masters. They played makrúgh for knowledge alone, deriving no power, no satisfaction, no joy in the game well played. "Answer my question," said Davaryush coldly, concealing his emotions behind the Inquestral impassiveness; for one learned soon enough on Uran s'Varek to concede nothing at all to a thinkhive.

I should think you would he too busy, said the thinkhive, what with your present worries, to spend your time down here, trying to trick me into revealing the secrets of this planet.

"I rule here," said Davaryush, allowing his voice to reveal just the right shade of anger.

Puppet! the machine said.

"What has happened to the escapers?" Davaryush said steadily.

Do you sleep with the Lady Varuneh?

"Inquestral override!" Davaryush rasped.

Attá heng, said the machine sarcastically. It was the formula for admitting defeat in a game of makrúgh. Then the thinkhive said, A body was found at the entrance to the Dark Country. Davaryush.

"So the threat is over."

Not quite. I said one body. The angels have taken care of the body; it has been pulped and returned to the Dark Country. But there were two, weren't there? I shall have to mobilize the Skywall's hidden resources against them . . . it may take a while. My nerves, which cover the whole planet like the roots of a monstrous grass plant, my nerves are twenty thousand years old, Davaryush! They are rotting . . . give me time, give me time. They will be destroyed.

So the machine had guessed nothing. Carefully Davaryush concealed the relief from his features. "How will you find the other one?"

I will follow the refugee with angels that rain fire from the sky. What does not burn the al'ksigarkar will devour, and the ghost people will hunt the al'ksigarkar in turn and grind them for bread.

"Very beautiful," Davaryush said bitterly. "I commend your taste."

Powers of powers, man! the thinkhive said reprovingly. Can you not swallow your compassion, but must you show it even in front of a mere machine like me?

"I respect them," Davaryunsh said. Perhaps they were trying to tell me something.

Unlikely.

"I—"

Oh, Daavye, Daavye. Will it make you feel better to pound me with your fists . . .? Believe me, I understand you, better than yourself even. You must feel for the unfortunate, for the destitute, for the despairing . . . that is your nature, that is why they made you an Inquestor. Now, shall I order the angels from their hiding places?

Powers of powers, Davaryush thought, if I don't let them die the thinkhive will suspect me, and I wanted them both to live so much, so that there would at least be something left of the Dark Country— Then he said firmly, "Of course, thinkhive, you must do whatever is necessary to preserve the integrity of the Inquest."

And of the human race, the thinkhive added.

"And of the human race."

And now, for the preparations for your grand cloud concert—

Ladv Varuneh's floater drifted toward him as he watched the cities from the parapet of his palace. The city simulated night; a night of jeweled moons stitched into sable tapestries, an illusion shattered only by seams of brilliant light where the bright day outside shone in. It was a complex night, compounded of many planets' nights: the moons of Ménjifarn and Angred, the silk-sheened star-wreath of the galactic arm, like the neckpiece of a dead queen, imitating the night sky of Arrendarran, homeworld of many Princelings. The city slept; the towers of Kallendrang, upturned pagodas hanging from the caveroof the night, glimmered. The floater came to rest on the parapet. Davaryush hastened to the railings, and they embraced.

"Daavye." The furrows were gone from her face; it was taut now, almost young. "Are you sure that we must involve Ynyoldeh in this?"

"We have to," Davaryush said. "This project must seem at first to be an accident, against the backdrop of a distant and far-reaching game of *makrúgh*. Otherwise—"

"We'll be caught before we can cripple the Inquest. The Inquest has to turn its back." With a wave Varuneh dismissed her floater. It soared up into the blackness, vanishing against the pearly neckerchief of the Milky

Way. They crossed to the palace on a bridge of forceshields, seeming to stand on the empty air; beneath them, the cone of Effelkang twinkled with a million lights that mimicked the stars above that mimicked the stars of distant worlds. . . .

Suspended over the emptiness, Davaryush said, "You should not have said love, that day you said you loved me, Vara. You should not have done that. How can I think clearly if I must love? I am an Inquestor—"

"Who can't feel love, but only greater love, compassion for the whole of humanity? Is that what you mean?"

"Thus my teacher Alkamathdes told me—"

"And thus I taught him, half a millennium ago! But now I know that if we do not love, we have no right to rule," said Varuneh fiercely. They walked on in silence until they reached the palace's first balcony, where dark vines slithered over bricks that glinted copper and silver in the half-dark. They held hands but did nothing more, in case they should be seen. And Davaryush would never dare to do more than look at Varuneh, without her bidding: for always he knew how much older she was, that she was like a mountain to a flower. Their love, whatever Varuneh claimed, could never be like the love of the short-lived. They had come too far for that; they had left innocence behind, in that place where go the high voices of young boys and the fragrances of dead flowers. . . .

"I feel—" As they neared the palace Davaryush could not talk any more. The Inquest might be listening, with its mindhearers or its secret eyes and ears whose clutch tentacled from the thinkhives of Uran s'Varek itself. "No more speaking," he said.

"Yes. Daavye." Three moonshafts striped her face, her hair, highlighting the gray. He knew now that she had made herself more beautiful for him, some cosmetics, some touches of a renewer's art. Stepping into the palace, she said, "Remember only Shtoma, and know that what you do is right."

"But I feel so bounded—so used! It's not fair for me not to be free, free as the lowest of the clanless—"

"Shush, shush, Daavye, Daavye," Varuneh whispered, "free means nothing. You? Free? An Inquestor and Kingling?" And she laughed, a laugh that was not meant to hurt him and yet did, a laugh both bitter and sympathetic. Dayaryush stepped through the barrier of nothingness into his private chamber. The darkness was complete, oppressive.

"Lights!" he called out. "Music, color!"

At once the walls were bright with shimmerblurring whorls of light, and music erupted, a jangle of broken whisperlyres and untuned waterflutes—

"Let the attendants sleep," Varuneh said. "You don't want all this pageantry now. You need . . . something else." And she embraced him, leading him on . . . with a wave she silenced the unseen slaves who minded the machines that minded the Kingling's whims. There was darkness again, warm this time. Distantly. Dayaryush felt desire stir in him. He felt the floor soften beneath his feet, he felt himself lose his balance, fall into the arms of the old woman—

"Forget Ynyoldeh now! Remember only Shtoma!" Varuneh whispered.

Davaryush mindflicked, dismissing the shimmercloak. It flowed away from him, huddling in a hollow of the floor. The woman waited; she was naked now, but clothed still more than ever in her immense age, her knowledge, her power. He fell toward her, he felt the falling like—

—a varigrav coaster! When Davaryush was nine years old, celebrating the end of his first war—

They had come to Alykh, the pleasure planet, he and Tymyon and Ayulla and Kyg and the other companions, losing themselves in the cacophony of crowds. . . .

"Wait until you see this!" Kyg shouted, and she leaped onto the plate like a cat. They disappeared—

And Daavye saw it. A topless tower of brick and stone and concrete and plastic and sparkling amethysts, studding the walls like jeweled knuckle-dusters. "What is it?"

"Daavye, don't you know anything?" Tymyon, cackling offensively.

Kyg, with mock primness: "It's a . . . VARIGRAV COASTER!"

The tower glinted oddly, catching the sunset. "Look," Kyg said, "you dive off the top, see, and it sets into action a series of random gravity-field interferences, and you plummet like a hawk and you float upward and you swing dangerously and you curve and then you land where you started, like a feather. . ."

("It's beautiful," whispered Ayulla the silent.)

"Well, let's *go!*" Tymyon and Kyg raced each other to the tower, and everywhere were the crowds—aliens, childwarriors brandishing their weapons, pimps, crusader-flagellants, Inquestors and their retinues, slave hunters, veiled whisper-shadows from the far borders of the Dispersal, dirty children strumming on dreamharps: dissonant alien musics, an itinerant space opera howling and screeching through full-blast ampli-jewels, and Davaryush was standing spellbound unmoving. He had never . . .

The tower held him, though. And the little specks that were people, dust-motes in the violent sunset.

"Aren't you coming?" Ayulla's voice, almost lost in the confusion.

"No." He was petrified!

"Come on! They're all the rage now, they're all the way from Shtoma, don't you know, from the far borders of the Dispersal—"

"No! No!" (It was said that the greatest thrill, when you fell, was the very certainty of deaths suddenly averted by a twist of the field. At the moment of inevitable doom, it was said, you felt so alive.)

Ayulla was laughing at him. "How many people have you killed. Daavye? How can you be so scared of life?"

. . . but now I am Ton Davaryush z Galléndaran K'Ning, and the Whispershadows whom no one has seen are at war with the Inquest, somewhere unthinkable parsecs away from here, the heart of the Dispersal . . . and those childwarriors who I fought with where are they now? The children laughing scornfully as their laser-irises sliced the enemy, dying suddenly in terrible pain that lasted but a nanosecond, living too fast to understand the reasons for their lives, living only for laughter and killing and the oblivion of the varigrav coasters . . . I'm an Inquestor. And they're dead. With all the time dilation I have been through, they are less than dust by now, they are atoms in the air, particles in space, less than vacuums. . . .

Davaryush awoke just in time to force the tears back into his eyes. Varuneh was looking at him and combing her hair; the air-comb ruffled the scraggly strands and then smoothed them out. "You call that lovemaking, Daavye, when you fall asleep in midembrace . . .?"

"You've known the greatest lovers in the universe. I suppose, and they're all dust now." Davaryush said, hiding his discomfort in an easy riposte. Then he summoned his shimmercloak to him and rose, "Give me the real dawn," he said imperiously to the waiting walls. "No fakery today."

All at once the night lifted, shifted, silted in pieces of broken daylight until they could feel the two suns hugging each other close, shimmerdazzling the cities into a blinding smear of light. . . . "Darkfield!" Davaryush called out, and the light was tempered a notch, soothing the smart in his eyes. Attendants with trays of morning viands were materializing one by one on the displacement plate of the chamber; now they advanced toward the two, making formal obeisance and presenting the breakfast. Davaryush picked a skewer of sourmeat and brandished it like a dagger for a moment, the two laughed nervously. "The Lady Ynyoldeh is here?" he asked one of the pages.

The boy clambered forward; he had not expected to be addressed by the Inquestor himself. "Lord Inquestor, her palace is in orbit, maintaining its position directly above the pinnacle of Kallendrang," he said.

As he spoke there was a sudden swift darkness. "Look!" Varuneh said, pointing to where a shadowshape blotted out the sun. "Like a hawk, like a bird of prey—"

Theu stood up and rushed to the deopaqued walls. When Davaryush looked down he saw the wobbly shadow flitting over the City, a moving blob of blackness. The attendants clustered around, not wanting to miss one of' the Kingling's whims. Then Davaryush looked up at the sky and saw, where the suns had shone a moment before—

Great silver wings, spread out and motionless, a hawk with a starship's span, slicing the blue-white sky —

"It's Ynyoldeh," Varuneh said. "She has style, certainly." "Quick!" Davaryush shouted. "Prepare to receive her! Get a clearance for the palace to land at once!" But he continued to stare at the monstrous bird . . . now it seemed to swerve, playing the wind. Now it overtook the sun, freeing a shaft of light to burn Davaryush's eyes. Now it turned quick somersaults in the air, now it retracted and flapped its wings with a thunderpeal . . . Davaryush tried to remember Ynyoldeh.

Once they had been young together on Uran s'Varek. They had been Inquestors-to-be, learning the mysteries of compassion from the Grand Inquestor Ton Alkamathdes, who had hunted a hundred utopias. She had always been cruel, even then . . . he had always wondered why the Inquest in its wisdom had use for such a person. But the Inquest was wise—

Uran s'Varek of the endless pearly daylight . . .

Memories, a plain unbroken, furred with green and speckled with blood-red flowers . . . a city like a smudge of mist, hugging the horizon that smeared into the luminous sky . . . and the girl.

Coming toward him. Deliberately, her eyes never leaving his. Her hair, grass-green and wild, streaming in a man-made wind, a luxuriant gesture for the chill stillness of the air. The shimmercloak carelessly slitted and knotted at the waist, to show the curve of incipient breasts, just a hint of them . . . the slow, graceful walk, like a willow bent by wind.

And now she faced him and her eyes were level with his, and yet she had never seemed to stop moving. Angrily, he was saying, "What are you doing here, in my assigned territory?"

"I am Ynyeh. Are you Daavye?"

He nodded. "You shouldn't be here. I've been given a year's solitude, you shouldn't have blundered here..." But what harm could she cause? She must be fresh out of puberty, freshly named Inquestor. He was sorry for her. Gently he said. "Ynveh, where are you from? Shall I conduct you back to the seminary city?"

"No ... look!" She clapped her hands and a shtézhnat board appeared between them, a holo-sculpture; then she said, "Make the first move!" They sat on the grass and moved the pieces idly, not caring who won or lost, even cheating at times. And then—

The board was snatched out of the air. There was Alkamathdes, the Grand Inquestor, glowering, his sunken eyes onyx-bright.

"Davaryush. Ynyoldeh." He never spoke above a whisper, for this was his way of commanding absolute concentration in his pupils. "Know that for each piece you played and lost, a city, somewhere in the Dispersal, has fallen and its millions killed, dispossessed, maimed, widowed. For each starship you slaughtered a starship has died. Know this always! There is no move an Inquestor can make without wielding life and death!"

Daavye, shaking, trembling, protesting, "I don't want to kill anyone! I used to kill when I was a soldier child, I killed and killed and I never want to kill again —"

But Ynyoldeh had said nothing. Her face, absolutely beautiful, utterly remorseless, did not change.

Shrugging, Alkamathdes said, "It's just an allegory," and vanished.

Had he been real, or just a projection of the thinkhives? On Uran s'Varek they taught that the central truth was what mattered, not the reality—and the world was a flux of apparitions, shifting and twisting around the truth.

"Only an allegory," Daavye whispered. Then he said, bitterly, "Must they always watch us? Wasn't I supposed to be alone for this year, the only year of my whole life when I need not feel weighed down by compassion?"

A clenched look crossed Ynyoldeh's face, then cleared. Davaryush recognized the look with a shock "You wanted them to die!" he said. "You don't want it to have been an allegory!"

But she only smiled a coquettish smile, and invited him to play at sex; they played for a while, and Davaryush found that he could no longer enjoy such games . . . that already, while he was barely in his teens, he suffered from the continual anguish of Inquestorhood, the need to think and reflect and contemplate and build enormous labyrinths of thought, not to see things simply . . . Ynyoldeh had not come by chance. The Inquestors left nothing to chance; if you did not learn this in your first few hours on Uran s'Varek, your life was in danger, compassion or no compassion.

On the topmost parapet the great bird perched, its silvery claws clutching two twisted spires, its mirror eyes sparkling in the twin sunlight.

So this was what she did now. Davaryush thought, this woman whom the inquest has given power over the weaponry of a whole quadrant, this Queen of Daggers . . . little Ynyeh. He mounted the steps, each step a different marble laced with lapis. His shimmercloak flapped behind him in the wind of the city's highest level. Behind him came the people of the court: squires, lords, jesters, musicians with twangish lyres of steel and trumpets of gilded conch, making a raucous ceremonial music of welcome   . . . there was Varuneh too, her shimmercloak put aside and replaced with the sable robe and clingfire sash of a woman of rank. The crowd murmured: Davaryush sensed their uneasiness. He waved for silence. It fell, like a cloak falling over the corpse of a fallen warrior.

Then he spoke: "I greet you, Lady Ynyoldeh. Welcome to this poor planet of mine, you who dominate a thousand planets."

The bird seemed to open its beak and utter a bloodcurdling screech. And out of the screech, like an afterecho, came the silvery laughter of a young girl. He remembered the voice, and froze.

The voice—unchanged after all these centuries? Davaryush approached the mechanical avian. Its wings flapped once, with a ghostly rasping sound—an ancient flier with its joints unoiled? an old afflicted man moaning his death-cry?—and then came the girl's voice again: "There is history, and there is no history."

They were ritual words in the game of makrúgh. Davarvush did not want to be rushed like this, but he could not help but respond: "All things must change, yet all is encompassed in the greater Stasis. We are one, our eyes are illuminated by the one Compassion; we are of the Inquest."

"History there is. and yet no history." The crowd of courtiers was still hushed. Then another peal of girlish laughter rent the air, and a ripple of nervous chatter swept through the gathering.

"Ah, Ton Davaryush z Galléndaran K'Ning!" the girl's voice saidm still half chuckling. "I give you the freedom of my flying palace, the freedom of my domain."

The belly of the silverbird burst open, and disgorged a railinged floater englobed in a darkfield. It came down noiselessly, landing at Davaryush's feet. I'm in danger, Davaryush thought. She's been here for thirty seconds and already she's used the Ritual. The exchange had been in the hightongue, of course, so many of the courtiers would not have understood any of it. Shrugging, Davaryush climbed onto the floater, nodded once, swayed for a second as the floater whirred to life. In a moment he was high above the crowd, whose welcoming music lost its harshness in the distance and became gentle as shimmerviols. . . .

In the bird-palace's belly was a navel-portal that irised open to admit him. He was in a huge antechamber, it was carpeted with fur that imitated the texture and color of a shimmercloak. Ruby carbuncles infested the Ontian marble of its walls.

Davaryush began to walk ahead of him, when—

Blocking his path was a mechanical: a hulking, three-meter-tall, pithecine man-mimic of dull metal, with a square head and four crude hinged arms. But nestled in those arms, like a baby in the arms of a mother, was—

Davaryush felt surprise rush to his face. Cursing himself silently, he put himself on guard. He hoped that his face had not colored even for a moment; for he knew that every trace of emotion was being monitored.

In the arms of the robot was a young girl in a shimmercloak. Unchanged. How? How could you forget the grass-green hair that billowed in the artwind like wind-tousled fields of grain? And yet those eyes . . . blank as the mirror eyes of the hawk that was her palace. . .

"Ynyeh—"

"Pretty, no, Daavye?" It was the same small voice with just a twist of mercilessness in it. "I'm still in orbit around your world, you know. This hawk-palace has a nest-palace, not built for atmospheric journeys. I'm not here in person because . . . I like to keep the odds in my favor. I thought the choice of soma would tickle your fancy, you sentimental old fool."

Davarvush waited. To speak now would be to lose ground. Clearly Ynyeh had embarked on the *shénjesh*, or formal exposition, in the game of *makrúgh*.

"Tongue tied, Daavye?" The blank-eyed girl laughed snuggled into the mechanical's metallic embrace. You're wondering about this body aren't you?" She reached her hand out, tantalizing him. "Here, hold my hand."

He touched it for a moment, snatched it back—
"You're—"

The girl laughed again. "You're wondering where I get them aren't you? Oh, Daavye, Daavye, how I hate to be old! I clone them silly. Then I devive them, just before puberty . . . compassionately of course, compassionately!" she added. "Pretty, no?"

"You cannot play makrúgh by proxy! I'll not come to terms with a—"

"You can't say it, can you? Oh yes, I heard of your decree banning them from the city of Effelkang. But you can't have a personal meeting. Although you must admit that this is all very sophisticated—I mean, the technology that allows this thing to speak, to move, as gracefully as I once did. . . ." She flashed her eyes at him a grotesque parody of an erotic look. But it's so chillingly appropriate!"

"I suppose so."

"I take great care in my selection of proxies, you know. They are what the world sees, after all. Even if they are only corpses."

Thirteen
Colors

Touch-brother!

She woke, signing it on the soft alien floor. Already
the boy was there. He seemed to fall into Touch-
brother's place so naturally, but yet . . . she could not
quite repress the knowledge that to feel love for him
would be unspeakable. The boy was there and there
was light here, and she saw him. She saw him with the
touching of her eyes.

His own eyes first, not blood-gouged and empty, but
shining, like undark over moving water.

"Have you had a bad dream?" Kelver said. She
scratched the windshapes on her arms, making sure of
what he had said. Then she replied, carefully forming
the windshapes, "Touch-brother." She coined the word
easily out of the words she had learnt to build from
windshapes.

In the light—it burst down from the deopaqued
ceiling, almost painfully—she saw how his hair was like

fire almost, shifting from dark to undark in unpredictable patterns when he moved his head. He was so beautiful to her . . . more beautiful even than the angels of the blind, the angels of the childish fingerchants that had proved so alien to the truth. "You are thinking about the boy you lost, in the Dark Country?"

She said, "Dead." But what she meant was dead without shame, for he had not been consigned to the angels. And she needed to do that for Touch-brother, because he had belonged to her people in a way she had never belonged, and she wanted him to have the respect of a real death.

She closed her eyes and thought of him, squeezing the light tight out. And now she was in the Dark Country and had no word for seeing and he was touching her in her profane places, and his touch was a slow smile. But the undark was bursting behind and forcing her to see—

"I don't want to see!" she cried out, lacing her words with the new rasp of bitterness.

"Do you want to go back," said Kelver, "and take care of the body?"

"It's been many sleeps, I don't know. . . "

"The body will be rotten by now."

Darktouch didn't understand this. Bodies were bodies, surely, until the angels gorged on them and returned them to the Sound."

"You still know so little about our world," Kelver said. "We've tried to keep you away from the village, in the house, until you could cope. But we love our dead too. We'll slip away for a few hours, Darktouch, while Uncle Aaye is busy. . . ."

I wish I could love you, Darktouch thought. For as the boy rose and walked to the atrium entrance she saw how he moved like water, like the wind itself, careless of caution. He has something of Windbringer about him, even, she thought. A flash of firefur at the entrance . . . then she saw he was gone, and her eyes touched the empty space that meant door. She got up to follow him.

Was it possible to forge a touch-bond even here, to love a boy not linked to her at birth by touch and smell? She did not want to dwell on the thought. Disquieted, shuddering as the floor wriggled under her footfalls like a live Windbringer, she began to go where he had gone. She tried to mimic his carefree gait, not to heed where her feet went, trusting her eye-touch alone . . . it was awkward. But she remembered Touch-brother in the cold and dark, and she went on.

   ***

"Don't be frightened, Darkt—" Kelver saw the girl walk round and round the burnish-bright displacement plate, as if it were an al'ksigark's corpse. "It's just a displacement plate. Look." He seized her arm and pushed her onto the metal, subvoked the commands, and laughed as the scenery shifted. . . .

"Our house." He pointed behind them. The houses clustered, unnaturally bright cubes of emerald, chrome yellow, turquoise, lavender, scarlet. . . . "See? Which is your favorite color?"

"Color?" They jumped again, and the Skywall came nearer. Kelver stopped short. The girl looked at him, not understanding.

"You don't know about color?" She shook her head.

"Color is—color   is—" Words dried up suddenly. He was silent as they shifted again. . . .

Quickly now, as a crew of workers sauntered past hoisting their hunked meat from the clonebaths, ready for shipment into the Dark Country—

"What is color?" said Darktouch in her newfound voice. It scared him, how her inflections echoed his so precisely, like a voice copier from the city. He didn't know how to answer, so he just said, "Like scent. Like texture. Color. "

Then they were running the last hundred meters or so from the last plate to the junction of the Cold River and the mountain. They were in shadow now, shivering. She was as fast as he was. They reached the last pylon. "Come up quickly!" he said. He mounted the toeholds easily, hardly thinking about it because he knew the place so well now. I'd better slow down for her! But when he looked down she was clawing at his heels, not using her eyes at all but clambering nimbly by feel alone. They ran along the river wall to the ledge where the cavern was that led to the Dark Country—

Kelver looked back for a moment. A curtain of cold cloud-tendrils blocked the view beyond the shadow of the mountain. "Uncle Will be back soon . . . we don't have time. . . ." For a moment he remembered the girl Haller who had led him there, he remembered the silly sex games they'd played, and wondered whether Darktouch would—but   no. She had flinched away from him as if burned, when he'd even tried to caress her cheek.

There was the fissure with the faint light, eerie in the Skywall's shadow-darkness. "Are you sure you want to go back there?" Kelver had not returned to his private place in all these sleeps, not with Darktouch to worry about.

Darktouch said, "Yes." Kelver dropped lightly down the shaft. It was even colder now. He put out his arm to catch Darktouch.

"Ha!" A shrill voice sundered the silence. "I knew it!" Kelver whipped around to glimpse a streak of gold hair vanishing behind a stalagmite.

"Haller!"

The girl came out Kelver had not seen her for a long time, not since she had shown him the secret cavern. Her tunic was torn, and she seemed hysterical. "I showed you this place," she shouted, "and you used it to find another girl, a child of darkness, a witch-child! What they said was true, there was a girl from nowhere staying at your uncle's house. . . "

"She's come through hell to find us," Kelver said evenly. "She's suffered a lot. I don't know why she's come, but we have to help her."

"I showed you this place so we'd have a hideaway to run to, to play sex in . . . you betrayed me." She glared at Darktouch, who backed away into the phosphor-glittering stone. "Who are you, anyway?"

"I am Darktouch," Darktouch said.

"An ill-omened sort of name! You must be from the ghost people out in the desert."

"I'm from the Dark Country."

"Let her be, Halli!" Kelver cried. "She's come to find her dead brother's body!"

"The entrance, Kelver," Darktouch said. "Where is it?" "Come." Kelver led her past a corridor that twisted like a thin snake. The walls were moist, slimy against his bare arms. Haller was tagging behind still, complaining.

"I've been waiting for you for weeks here," she was saying, "you have no right to fool with this girl—"

"Be quiet!"

"I wanted you to like me!" Kelver felt a stab of pity for the girl, then repressed it as she followed him too close behind. He touched the familiar stud and—

Humming. Mirror metal floor. Lights that swirled like galaxies gone mad. And now he saw Darktouch running ahead, toward the far door with the inscribed words of doom. He caught up with her.

"Here. The body was here." She pointed.

There was a stain, dried-brown, boy-shaped, on the mirror metal of the floor. Darktouch fell on the cold metal, signing furiously, desperately, against its unscratchable surface. . . . "What's happening to me?" she said at last, jabbing hard at her eyes.

"You're crying, Darktouch, crying. . ." Kelver bent down to comfort her.

"Why? Why?"

"Don't they cry in the Dark Country? No. they don't have eyes, do they? It's grief, Darktouch, grief—"

Haller stood over the two of them, shaking, mouth agape. She was klomets out of her depth now. Then she said, "I'm sorry! I'm sorry! I didn't steal the body, honestly!" and turned away not wanting to see the strange girl's grief. Kelver heard her begin to cry, dry coughing sobs that were twisted into throbs by the eerie echo of the hall. And he touched her gently and tried to comfort her. What could he do?

To Darktouch he said, "What happens to people when they die, in your Dark Country?"

She said, "The angels come for them. As they have come for him. Now I know, Kelver, that the angels power stretches out even into your domain . . .

"Who are the angels? said Kelver.

They are spiders of metal who rend the bodies and return them to the waters of the Sound. . . ."

Kelver could not understand her. "I know," he said, "what an angel is; it's a thing of beauty, of dream, You just described a meat-render, like we have to mince the products of our clonebath meat products"."

"No," she said, signing on her arms as she spoke, as though she were translating some text word for word, "the world is one, the belly of a cosmic Windbringer, and we come from him and return to him, and all is beautiful—"

"Darktouch," said Kelver, "angels are like pteratygers, like lighthawks. They don't come down and slice up slabs of fresh killed meat—"

And Darktouch was in tears again. He would never understand her. "You know," he said, "that something's wrong with your world . . . or else why did you come here? Why would you risk everything If you didn't know what the others couldn't know, if you couldn't see or hear something that made you reject everything you'd ever lived by? Oh, Darktouch . . . what was it you saw in the Dark Country?"

"I saw . . . I saw . . ." Kelver saw her close her eyes, remembering. For a moment her features were frozen in a terrible peace, like a dead man's face.

Then Haller said, "I don't understand any of this, Kevi. But I've liked you ever since we were kids. I guess you haven't noticed that I'm a woman now. You'll never notice, now that she's . . ." She seemed about to cry, but blinked back her tears. "Kevi, let me help you, let me at least be near you. I—"

Kelver silenced her with a touch. He pitied her. But more than that, he wanted to know what it was that

Darktouch had seen. She could not talk about it yet, perhaps she needed to learn more of the nuances of speech, perhaps she would never be able to talk about it. And then there was the Inquest. Perhaps it was that important.

And for a moment, in the back of his mind, great starships crossed the whirling madness of the overcosm, the starships of a young boy's dreams. "Perhaps," he whispered, "perhaps if we all went to Effelkang together. . .

They walked back toward the opening of the cavern.
***

Touch-brother! Darktouch signed in her mind. She had touched the stain of his body with her eyes and she knew that the angels had come. And that the others did not really believe or understand.

Slowly she followed them to the cavern mouth, carefully she wriggled out onto the ledge in view of the Cold River. For a moment all three stood silent, thinking their own thoughts. And then, with her sensitive hearing, she caught a whoosh of a windshape arcing high above, and pointed—

Angels! They were coming out of a point high above the Cold River, like silver drops squirting out of the Skywall, each sounding a strident buzz, and—

"The village!" Haller was shouting. Explosions rent the air in quick succession, and then, where the village should have been, flamebursts, eye-burning undarks, a thunder-roaring peppered with death-shrieks—

"Hide! Behind the rocks!" Kelver screamed. Darktouch took shelter reaching for the rocks without her eyes and ears. The three piled on top of each other
—

—huge shapes of undark shifted in the sky and Darktouch understood them suddenly to be colors, textures and fragrances of the light, and a moment of delight broke through her anguish, so she screamed out, "Color, Kelver, I understand color now—" before terror silenced her—

Haller was saving, over and over, "They're all being killed," disbelieving. In her emotion Darktouch scarcely made out the windshapes that were words, and in her heart she knew that the angels wanted her alone, because she belonged to the Dark Country, because she had dared to defy them . . . impulsively she ran out of the hiding place, signing on the empty air, I'm here, don't kill the others, I'm waiting for you—

It was Haller who pulled her back and clutched her arm and made sure she couldn't be seen. She tried to speak to Haller, to break her grip, but the windshape-words were swallowed up in the hiss of the spurting flames and the crash of explosions. And then—

The angels soared upward, ignoring them, they flocked together and burst into a curve that streamed up, up, melting into the mountainside immeasurably high above, and Kelver was saving, "How can we find the Inquestors? How can we tell them what injustice has been done, so that they can come and make everything well again?" and Darktouch felt, in Heller's grip, the terror and incomprehension, even without the words of signing, and she turned to see the flames flip-dance like a wounded Windbringer—

It was color, then, that I saw, she thought, making the windshapes in her mind for the first time, forcing herself to think in the alien way. Color in the songs of the Windbringers. And music of the ear. And for a second she mistook the death-flames for the light on the Sound. . . .

Memories stormed in her mind like the high wind over the Sound.

Windstriker—

"Windstriker!" she cried out in the strange language of windshapes, knowing that in this utterance of her inmost yearnings she had stepped irrevocably into the world beyond the Dark Country—

"Windstriker!" she screamed, and grief taloned at her guts like a hungry hawk.

Fourteen
Windstriker

Falling open-armed, into the embrace of death—

He felt the Sound pulling him. Fragrances of different airskiffs kaleidoscoped in his nostrils. All was as it should be, the grand moment, the Windbringer calling, and now only the empty air, almost dark to the touch, even the memory of the wayward daughter fading like the smell of lovemaking after a long sleep. . . .

But then . . . . there was no ending, no cessation of being. He floated in the darkness, no glimmer of touching on his fingertips. Slowly he came to the realization that—

Somewhere beneath, beyond touching, a thing worked furiously to sustain him in the thick air. And when he reached something tangible finally, it was cushion-soft, moist, redolent of Windbringer, and it moved ponderously in the windstream. Windbringer!

His fingers worked the warm surface; the surface creased about his fingers, and an oily ooze squirted from it. He couldn't believe it. Windbringer had broken his fall. He was not dead. Upon the air he signed an anguish-song, making the words in jagged strokes that left no trace.

And finally, a deep shudder of a touching seemed to stir in his mind. But no hand signed against his hand. Only in his head, the beginnings of alien thoughts, as though something were seeking to learn his language.

Mindtouch? He had heard of power men who had claimed to touch the very thoughts of Windbringers, but he had always dismissed them. He had always been a realist, exult-ing in the physical sensations of the hunt, and not the mystical ones.

I am Windstriker, he signed finally, tentatively.

And the ghost touching signed, feathersoft, Help— me—

And Windstriker was awed by this. Help you? he signed on the leathery surface. I'm only—

The killing—end—not what it seems—a wrongness —a wrongness—

Haven't I returned to you, haven't I fulfilled my oath? he signed humbly.

For a moment the ghost-touches swarmed, indecipherable. He drifted between life and death, wondering what purpose Windbringer had had in mind, breaking his fall, obstructing the natural cycle of birth and death.

Out the ghost-touching crystallized more words: Change the order—you not—understand yet—

The spectral hands groped in his brain, searching out memories. Your daughter—your daughter—has touched the—truth—

Windstriker felt the slap of the sailsac vibrate through his weak body. (What kind of crazy dream is this? he thought. My daughter, how could Windbringer know of my daughter?) And then he signed, What is it that my daughter's eyes have touched?

As she to you—so we to her—we touch beyond even time and space—as she touches—the undark—you not understand?—we not gods, we—a wrongness here a wrongness—help, prevent—killing—

And Windstriker knew that he had come to the end of being Windstriker, that he had truly fulfilled his vow. He had broken through to a new world, where the rules were not the same. He felt ravenous suddenly.

Eat—my flesh— came the signing. He dug out a small piece of the Windbringer; it was succulent brain meat. He had eaten of the living Windbringer now. Truly he must he invincible.

Let me know how I can help you! he signed vigorously.

Stay with us—become one with us—mindlink with us- came the reply. A faint joy stirred in him, somehow a nerve in his brain was being goaded to pleasure. Then Windbringer signed, You are the first—we have caught—let us understand you—let us read your soul —we do not understand the wrongness—you will teach us—

How can I . . . .?

Then came other sensations, scents that could not exist, impossible textures that tantalized his fingertips, tastes that mingled gall with sweetness, and then . . . confusion swept through him as he sensed silky smells and touched sour tastes and touched signings without meanings, and he thought, This must be death at last, the Windbringer's final vision.

Yes! he signed through the welter of sensation. I will help you, Windbringer, if I can, and then tiredness came over him and he touched a darkness tinged with warmth and found it welcome.

The sailsacs filled quickly. With stunning grace the Wind-bringer plunged into an air current and soared aloft, bisecting the heavy air, looking for a place too far for the hunters.

Fifteen
Makrúgh

For a few hours Davaryush rested from the tedious minutiae of ruling a planet that ran itself. Ynyoldeh was installed in her palace perched in the sky; other Inquestors were guests of the palace. Davaryush had time yet before lightsend and the grand entertainment. He took his floater and crossed over the twin cities, over Tulangdaror a little way, to where workmen were towing in the clouds for the concert. He watched them drift in slowly, perfectly formed holosculptures of fleece and mist. He stepped from the floater: a cushion of force stopped his fall, for here in the sky was the great arena of Kallendrang, englobed in a darkfield for a dozen square klomets or more, lighted by a false sun, a pale blue one from an uninhabitable world. The clouds came streaming about his feet, curling and swirling over the invisible floor beneath which he could see the steeple-stippled sea.

In the distance a single tower pierced the clouds, a facet-sparkling spear of a million hues. Now Davaryush began to walk toward it, for he knew that it housed the Inquestral Seat. He did not summon his floater or his attendants to escort him, but walked by himself, enjoying his aloneness. Mist came, sweeping his face. There was no moisture to it, no dryness even, no sensation at all. It was an illusion. It was all illusion, all insubstantial, less real to him than a dream. Like the Inquest! Davaryush thought angrily. He walked on. Glancing behind he could see them shaping the twisted towers of cloud, he could see the rainbow fliers, like insects in the distance, painting the spectral outlines of people or animals against the backdrop of cloud . . . the rainbow fabric shimmered briefly and dissolved, and the rainbow fliers would return, tracing the outlines over and over in a strange ballet: perhaps they were mimicking the courtship dances of alien birds, perhaps the patterns were random, out of a thinkhive, perhaps a member of his artistic staff had spent a lifetime perfecting it . . . Davaryush could not know. An Inquestor had no time for art, not for the deeper aspects of it. It was for the short-lived ones, the ones who lived with such incomprehensible intensity, to experience the beautiful . . . sadly, Davaryush moved toward the glittering steeple. It was a low tower, he saw now, ringed with guards and with a single entrance. Like a single man, the guards came forward and bowed obeisance. The foyer was cool, a round chamber seamlessly paneled with white rock. Davaryush stepped onto the displacement plate at the center of the chamber—

***

A burst of noise, a thousand chattering voices, burbling into silence.

A balcony overlooking the field of cloud, on their couches of clingfire and shimmerfabric and still-living silk, arrayed in tiers that centered in a half-circle on the Inquestral Seat, were courtiers. Shimmerviols played softly: it was an overture music, designed to fill the time before the Kingling's arrival. And now a thousand pairs of eyes turned to him, a thousand voices murmured their obeisances in highspeech and a dozen different lowspeeches. Four guards, tall women with their magenta hair piled like exotic seashells, rushed to escort him to the Seat. His feet touched carpeting that contoured to caress his every footfall. Here and there a suppliant would stretch himself out on the steps; compassionately, Davaryush stepped gingerly over them, not wishing to hurt them. He knew what Ynyoldeh would have done. Today, he thought grimly, I will hurt no one! Thrusting through the aisle as quickly as he could with the crush of courtiers, Davaryush reached the throne. As he sat down and the guards dispersed to the four corners of the thronedais, the raucous ceremonial music piped up as it had earlier in the day.

"I'm heartily tired of this noise!" he murmured. A lackey dashed into the crowd. The music metamorphosed in mid-phrase, into the quiet music of shimmerviols; they had begun the overture again. He relaxed a little. Four Inquestors had arrived, he saw; they had come on hoverthrones that were parked helter-skelter at the foot of his own Seat. There was the young one named Elloran, who must be watched very carefully, they said. There were the Inquestors Siembre and Kiembre, clonetwins joined back to back and

enveloped in a single shapeless shimmercloak . . .
Davaryush remembered them from Uran s'Varek.. And
another . . .

"Daavye!" A chillingly familiar voice. "Shall we
begin?" He looked behind. The tall mechanical
lurched forward, clutching the Ynyoldeh clone-corpse
like a frail doll, tender and grotesque—

"I hate this official music," said Davaryush, avoiding
Ynyoldeh's eyes. "We came to hear the songs of the
great Shen Sajit, not some mindless gut-turning
fanfares. Official music is so soulless."

"Ah yes, Davaryush," said Ynyoldeh, "insulting me
already. " The robot moved closer; if Ynyoldeh had
been there in the flesh he would have felt her
breathing down his neck. He shuddered.

"Your paranoia is refreshing," he said

"As befits my position. Now treat me well, or I won't
let you win your game of *makrúgh.*" The little girl-
corpse waved languorously. "Gifts!" she said. "I have
gifts for all of you!"

Inching through the crowd was a palanquin borne
aloft by more mechanicals. It came to the foot of the
Seat, the curtains were drawn back at a superb gesture
from Ynyoldeh—

There were three children. They were completely
motionless, hunched on all fours in an almost foetal
position. They were naked, and very beautiful. "I don't
like servocorpses!" Davaryush rasped.

"No, no, nom how can you be so naïve?" Ynyoldeh
said. "They're not at all dead, just in stasis. You see, I
had a war last year and several worlds were
dispossessed. We sent the people out—in your
compassion—in people bins, stasis-stacked by the
hundreds of thousands, the usual thing you know, and

one of the bins aborted. There's no way of reversing the stasis shields on them. But they're so conveniently crouched, and they're so stunningly pretty—at least, the ones I picked as presents for the three of you— sorry, Kiembre and Siembre, for thinking of you as one person, it's so hard not to sometimes—and they make wonderful footstools, or little tables for wine, or what have you . . . in my palace above, I use them as stands for vases. I do so love flowers. I love beautiful things, you know, especially morbid ones."

Davaryush swallowed, and then said with icy grace, "I thank you, Ynyoldeh, for your thoughtful gift." Inwardly he was trying to figure out the riddle she surely meant to convey. Was Ynyoldeh really so callous as to allow herself to be surrounded by such reminders of the Inquest's necessary cruelty? People bins, with which wasted planets could be repopulated, traversed the overcosm constantly, towed by convoys of delphinoid shipminds . . . he had never heard of one's stasis devices aborting. Perhaps this was some dreadful idea of a joke. Ynyoldeh was certainly capable of such jokes. He would have to plan his countergift well. His *makrúgh* must hinge on this one thing. . . .

"How long before the concert?" he turned to ask a servant. "Some moments yet, Lord Inquestor."

It was best to acknowledge the presence of the other Inquestors then. "Take away those . . . tables." he ordered. The palanquin of living dead was hustled away. He saw it disappearing into the back of the balcony, bobbing up and down among scintillating hairdos and palatial headdresses, and then he interrupted the Inquestors who were talking in low voices among themselves as their hoverthrones darted around him.

". . . I've just been hunting this utopia." Kiembre or Siembre was murmuring to the Inquestor he did not know, "where the flaw was—I couldn't believe it!—overeating! Crime and madness had been replaced by incredible orgies of stomach-stuffing. I saw the patriarch of the world must have weighed five hundred kilos, who spent his whole life in a private hoverpool, too fat to move . . ."

"History," Davaryush said. The short form of the Ritual.

Startled, the Siamese twins wrenched their whole throne to stare at him. "My, you seem anxious," they said simultaneously. "History!" they added maliciously.

The unknown Inquestor said nothing. "He's in training," Ton Elloran said, bringing his throne closer to the Seat. Elloran was a young man, with clear emotionless gray eyes and savage hair. "History."

They picked sectors—distant ones—and began to plan their game. *Makrúgh* was like the child's game *shtezhnat*, only its rules were limitless and its rulings lethal . . . though usually not to the Inquestors themselves. *Makrúgh* took place not on a board but in the mind; it was played with power and destruction as goals, and yet its purpose was intended to be compassionate, for even Davaryush was forced to accept that war was a necessity in the Dispersal of Man, honing the human mind and keeping it at an intensity that belittled its greatness.

And, as a fringe benefit, made the power of the Inquest unassailable.

Where would man he without the compassion of the Inquest? Davaryush found his mind wandering, as he thought deeply about the new Dispersal he wanted to create, the Dispersal without the Inquest . . . what

would replace compassion as the ruling order of
things? He felt like . . one of the people of the Dark
Country, like one who had had sight and sound
described to him but could not imagine how they
really felt. More than ever he hated what he must do. . .
.

"Ha, Daavye!" said the twins. "You take no joy in
this game? Has becoming a heretic lessened your
much-vaunted powers?"

He turned to them, smiled a little. "I concede the
sector," he bluffed. The hard part of the game was to
come, prying the weaponry loose from Ynyoldeh and
incidentally demanding the power-satellites necessary
to destroy the hub of Gallendys itself, without ever
once seeming to . . . why had she given the three of
them that grisly gift? It was a riddle, he knew. Ynyoldeh
was a *makrúgh* player of great deviousness, and he
could divine without much thought that the whole key
to getting something out of her lay in that gift and its
meaning. He rose from his throne and started to
approach Ynyoldeh, wanting to get it over with.

The Inquestor he had not recognized said, "Ton
Davaryush, your move is unconventional; one rarely
gets up and leaves when a world is at stake; it shows a
singular lack of compassion."

He whipped round. "Who are you?"

The young Inquestor Elloran spoke. "His name is
Sajit. He's not an Inquestor at all, but the artist who
will perform for us soon."

"Outrageous—"

"No, not really. Sajit and I have shared many secrets.
Ever since we found the mad Inquestor Alkamathdes
and dethroned him—"

Davaryush was in confusion. "Alkamathdes? My old teacher? Dethroned? He was at my coronation not thirty sleeps ago—"

Ynyoldeh, who had overheard, said sharply, "A servocorpse, Davaryush! It was me all the time. We didn't want you to know, we didn't want to know ourselves—"

"Sajit and I were boys together, stranded on the planet that Alkamathdes rules. He had created a utopia, peopled entirely with the living dead. Corpses," said Elloran.

The image of the dancing servocorpse twitched in Davaryush's mind—

"No!" he cried out, sinking into his throne. The revelations had been perfectly timed. He was too flustered to think. *"Atta héng,"* he whispered, conceding the round gracelessly. "Sajit, get ready for the concert," Elloran said. The stranger stripped off the shimmercloak and left it lying on the floor. Beneath it he wore the kaleidokilt of the clan of Shen. Quickly he jostled through the throng until Davaryush could no longer see him. Elloran had seized the moment to confer with the Siamese twins. Clearly Davaryush would have no allies at all in the game. But he did not mind. It was better, even.

He and Ynyoldeh were alone together, caged in their own little silence amidst the cacophony of the crowd. "Ynyeh—"

"I can spare you a moment or two, Daavye, I think." she said in her dainty, corpse-cold voice. "But only that. After all, I don't want to miss a second of Shen Sajit's song. And by the way, the soma you're talking to is a pretty sophisticated device; I want you to know that I'm listening to the other little monsters, too, as they plot your destruction . . . maybe I even have a mindhearing implant. Would you believe that?"

"No." Slowly he was recovering his composure. He thought she was bluffing there; mindhearing in *makrúgh* was definitely unethical. Even if it was an imperfect technique that often yielded fantasies or irrelevances. Ynyoldeh would not go so far as to break a rule so deeply ingrained. . . .

"I want—" he began. He looked away from her, concentrated his gaze on a fantastical spiral of matched cumulonimbus clouds that sent out darts of fiery cirrus clouds, a catherine wheel in white, probably a klomet in diameter, a shunning designer's trick. The catherine wheel turned slowly, twisting as it turned. "I want twelve delphinoid ships, fully equipped."

"Fine."

"I want six people bins: three for the space around Fenjidarengith, two for the vicinity of Andrell, one free-floating. I want armies: child-soldier armies without planetary affiliations. I want power satellites: sixteen hundred of them, half at the main tachyon nexus that interjoins with the disputed areas, half in orbit around Gallendys."

"Around Gallendys?" Had Davaryush said too much? It was these that mattered! They were all that mattered! Planets could burn uncounted parsecs away at his command, but he needed those power satellites, and around Gallendys! Carefully he kept his eyes averted, waiting for the response. Presently Ynyoldeh said, "Why around Gallendys?"

"I want," Davaryush said very carefully, "to threaten to destroy this planet. I think it would be a clever bluff."

The little girl laughed, a hideous, old woman's cackle. "That's the most inventive strategic stroke I've ever heard of!" For a moment Davaryush felt hope surge up. Could it really be this easy? "No," said Ynyoldeh, and the mechanical staggered forward so that the girlcorpse's face almost collided with his own. He flinched involuntarily.

"In the first place," the corpse said. and it made Davaryush uneasy that no breath came from her mouth as she spoke, "who could take such a bluff seriously? Do you imagine for a moment that anyone would seriously jeopardize the human race, the Inquest, everything we stand for? It would be an empty, expensive gesture, Daavye. Besides—" As she spoke the cloud-catherine wheel suddenly began ejecting cirrus darts in a wild flurry, and they flew over the audience and exploded in noiseless fluffy fireworks, and released a fine mist of *f'ang* scented with exotic perfumes, eliciting a throaty roar from the crowd, then half-inebriated applause. "Besides," Ynyoldeh said, "you might just do it. You are a heretic after all"

"If you thought I would do it, why was I placed in command here?"

"I do not judge these things. I only hand out plastic darts for your children to hurl at one another. . . ."

"Ynyoldeh—" He could not press too hard. She would suspect. If she truly suspected, he would be relieved of rule here, perhaps even devived. Killed, he thought, forcing him-self to shatter the Inquestral euphemism.

"No," Ynyoldeh said. If he could only solve the riddle of the gift—

And then, flung out over the arena in a simulholosculpture two klomets tall, was Shen Sajit. He had nothing but a whisperlyre, a child's toy instrument, and he began by singing an old song, a haunting song about utopias—

eíh! asheverain
am-plánzhet ka dhand-erúden
eíh! eskrendaí
pú eyáh chítarans hyémadh . . .

Dayaryush translated it to himself, in the lowspeech of his boyhood on a planet long since annihilated: "Ai! At the Dispersal of Man we wept for the dead earth, we cried out, "Where is the homeworld of the heart?"

"Where indeed?" Ynyoldeh said, startling him. He had been drawn to the simplicity of Sajit's performance; he did not embellish the ancient melody at all, but sang it rather as a child might, wondering to himself why the universe was such an ugly place, such an unjust place . . . "No wonder." said Ynyoldeh, "they need utopias. The poor, poor people ."

Sajit's face rippled as the clouds were towed slowly across the simulated sky. Was Ynyoldeh really compassionate beneath the image of brutality she promoted? Or else why would she have been chosen to be Inquestor?

"I know what you're thinking," Ynyoldeh said. "Daavye dear. You think I'm softening, don't you? Well, compassion rules all my thoughts—" (Quickly Davaryush stifled all his thoughts, reminding himself of the Queen of Daggers' threat that the servocorpse incorporated a mindhearing device.) "And the answer is still no. Although I give you the option of lying to the others' if you like, and going through with your bluff anyway. But if that is what you intended, you would not have needed to ask me for the weapons around

Gallendys . . . I'm warning you, Ton Davaryush z Galléndaran K'Ning! The Inquest does not trust you!"

All for nothing, Davaryush thought. He pretended to be listening to the music. After a while the *f'ang* vapor and the music itself drove him into a stupor of self-pity, carefully masked.

***

During the intermission he fled to the chamber of the thinkhive, thinking: Perhaps I can clear my mind, sparring with a thing without a soul. He stood in the half-dark, not knowing what to ask . . . or, rather, knowing but not wanting to give away too much.

The thinkhive did not acknowledge his presence for a time. And then: *Remarkable, Davaryush! Such an incredible risk. Win or lose, your reputation as a* makrúgh *player has risen considerably. Up there they are talking of nothing else.*

"You're listening to the conversations in the view-balcony of the cloud concert? You heard everything that transpired?"

Enough.

Then he asked: "The escapers?" He made his tone brusque to disguise his concern.

You're a very diligent Inquestor, Ton Davaryush z Galléndaran K'Ning. Know, then, that the village is burned down, and that there's not a soul left alive there. I had to make sure.

"Good." He looked away, even though he knew his face could betray nothing.

But— The thinkhive paused impressively. Davaryush wondered whether it was programmed to toy with him. He could well imagine this being done, a part of his punishment, perhaps for deviating: from the correct ideological stance on utopias. . . . *But,* said the thinkhive, *I do not find, among the wreckage, traces of organic matter whose genetic structure corresponds with that of one of the persons whose blood I detected.*

"It's your business to detect such details, not mine!"

It's possible that one of them is still at large. The body counts don't match. The discrepancy is perhaps inevitable when examining the situation from so many klomets' distance, and yet it feels significant.

"What does it matter? Halt the search. It is a tiresome game."

I must regretfully override you, Ton Davaryush. You see, the programming necessitates thoroughness. There can never be any communication between the Dark Country and the light. It's a priority so high that if I were to counteract it for a mere Inquestral whim, I would damage myself irreparably . . . be that as it may, I have dispatched the order to release the hidden angels from the Skywall mountain. They are the hawk-angels, the angels of death. I'm rather proud of them. Only . . . the mechanisms are so slow! Never did the Inquest imagine that these elaborate backups would really be required. . .

"Very well. I extend my compassion to them all."

I regret their deaths, Ton Davaryush, and appreciate your compassion.

"And Lady Ynyoldeh? Tell me of Lady Ynyoldeh. Today she gave me such a strange present."

Ah yes, the living corpses as ornamental tables. Such an inventive mind she has, such an inner understanding of the macabre!

"What does it mean? If I interpret her gift correctly, will I receive the weaponry I've asked for?"

You know very well that a mere thinkhive should not meddle with the *makrúgh* of the high Inquestors. And besides you know very well that personal information about the Inquestors is available only on Grand Inquestral override. And you, Ton Davaryush, are not a Grand Inquestor.

***

"What are these tables?" Lady Varuneh said. She had changed her clothes for the second half of Shen Sajit's recital—She wore a brown robe made from the uncut skin of a metawolverine. Her hair was hidden in a flamedisk. Her features, obscured by the opulence of her garment, seemed taut, empty.

There were the tables fashioned of frozen children twisted into obeisance before the great throne. He told her what had happened, knowing all was lost, seeking, sympathy, but she only laughed.

"Daavye, Daavye," she said, "you didn't think to consult me, did you? And I have been a Grand Inquestor in my time . . . to plunge into *makrúgh* with Ynyoldeh was a dangerous thing. You forget, sometimes, how much older I am than you."

"Do you know why she's given me this obscene gift?" Her face revealed nothing. "It's unfathomable! And yet I know that if I can solve the mystery of this gift she might come on to our side—"

"I was the Inquestor who named her to the clan of Ton."

"The biggest mistake you ever made!"

"Quiet. Daavye, listen. I chose her because I thought she would have compassion. I was wrong, but at least hear why: perhaps you can use it. She has a rare allergic response to the drugs we use to sustain life and youth, the drugs that give us such a grand overview of the Dispersal of Man and imbue our compassion with such superb objectiveness . . . she is not like us. She has lived centuries—the drugs accomplish that—yet at incredible cost to her body. She has wasted away, for centuries, becoming older than old, and at last compassion has given way to hate. I did not know that such hate could exist then . . . she is a corpse still cauling an active mind, longing: for lost beauty and yearning to murder all beauty not her own. How wrong I was! I had calculated that this conflict in her would give her some awareness of the human condition, some sympathy for the short-lived. We have made the Dispersal of Man into hell itself, Daavye, a hell of shattering beauty and brutality, and we cling to what seeds of compassion we find, nurturing them—so often in vain . . . you see why I hate the Inquest now!" Davaryush saw now that she had let emotion creep into her face even in this palace where a hidden eye might see her.

"What did you do?" he asked softly. "I know that the Inquest must never seem wrong, that truth is defined as what an Inquestor speaks."

"Of course. How else could we time our spider web around the Galaxy and choke ourselves to impotence? We gave her what she wanted, in our compassion, knowing she would have been happier as a short-lived one, a fighter, a ruler perhaps, never learning of her affliction. We gave her her toys, knowing she would rejoice in the shadow-side of *makrúgh*: the fiery deaths, the fireworks of bursting planets."

"And she's up there now speaking through the bodies of children with innocent voices . . . ." Davaryush felt chill, even though the room's temperature was as always perfectly gauged. I must feel compassion for her! he thought, forcing himself. It was an exercise.

"Now you know," Varuneh said. "Now you must think of a plan."

"I think I have one." Davaryush said, but he was still not sure of himself.

Sixteen
Al'ksigarkar

Running—

Below, the village crisped, black, slow smoke-spirals static in the windlessness—

Kelver screamed rage and despair bursting loose from him. He flung himself, rock-stung feet oblivious to pain, on the first displacement plate. He didn't care if the others were following or not.

—materializing in the middle of the village, where Uncle Aaye's house had stood—

Nothing. A scrambled jigsaw of porcelain house-shards, rubble heaped high and still fuming. He took a step toward where the entrance of the house had been. A skeletal hand peered from the rubble, fleshless and smelling of burnt steak. He kicked at the stones, sending them skitter-skatter. The fumes curled. Horribly, instinctively, his appetite was whetted. . . .

"Uncle Aaye!" he screamed. Then, turning to Darktouch, "You killed them! They're dead because of you!" Haller shrank back from his rage. He hurled himself at the girl from the Dark Country, flailing at her with his fists. She did not move at all. Then he turned away, weeping.

***

Darkness now, the shadow of Skywall shielding them from the sight of the dead village. Kelver felt a hand touch him. "Come on," said Haller. "Starship captains don't cry, do they? I've never seen you cry. We've got to do something. . . ."

"What did you see, Darktouch, to make this happen? What nightmare has happened in the Dark Country?" Kelver said. He propped himself against the prickly vines. He forced his grief inside himself. He had done that before, when his father had died. It seemed easy when there was no hope.

"I saw something beautiful, Darktouch said in the voice that so closely mimicked his own. "The nightmare was in us, that we had gone out and killed the beauty, over and over, that it was, our way of life, and that we could never know what we had done. . . ."

"The Inquest will know the answers." Kelver needed a purpose. He would grab at any purpose he could see now, no matter how farfetched. He needed a purpose to contain his despair, or it would come spilling out and engulf him. . . . "At the end of the Cold River, I don't know how many hundreds or thousands of klomets away, lives an Inquestor, Ton Davryush z Galléndaran K'Ning. He sees everything on the world through the eyes of his thinkhives. He lives in the towers built upon the towers of towers"—they were words he had learned as a small child, words that lent order to the universe—"but perhaps he cannot see everything. Perhaps he doesn't know that something has gone wrong here, in a far neglected corner of his world. We've got to go out now, follow the Cold River to its end, find the Inquestors, tell them everything—"

"How?" Haller was crying now. "We're just children! What'll we eat? They've burned the nutrient tanks. There's no food—"

"Would there be food if we stayed here?" Kelver shouted. Then he got up and began walking briskly in the direction of the wasteland. He walked on. He did not look behind, although he could hear Haller scrabbling at his heels and the cautious, regular footfall of the girl Darktouch. He made his mind blank. Once he'd seen a holosculpture of the twin cities, one of his uncle's souvenirs; he tried to imagine that, not to think of the dead village.

He moved quickly, trying not even to feel the splintered ground grow smooth as they neared the edge of shadow. He was remembering one of Darktouch's' thoughts: To be dark. Not to feel. And then the three children burst from the shadow into the glaring sunshine. The line of the Cold River seemed to erupt out of the height and blackness, shooting laser-straight at the horizon. The suns danced, oblivious of encroaching winter, and the sand dazzled like snow. Even through the fursoles it smarted, and Kelver knew he could never be dark. He would always feel, even as he yearned for an end to all feeling.

Haller was close behind him. "You don't have to follow me," he said.

"What else is there to do?" He felt Darktouch's shadow on him, a little cool, but she did not speak. Haller went on, curiously calm, "There was one of the ghost people who came fleeing into the village once, remember? He told me . . . that when they get hungry, out there, they sometimes hunt the al'ksigarks, they beat them senseless and drink the living green juice from them."

"There's no food. I suppose we'll have to do that." Darktouch still hadn't spoken. He turned to her now hoping for a conversation that would drown out the deadness in him. "You've never told us everything, Darktouch. About the Dark Country, I mean. We're all walking blind now, looking for answers to questions we don't even know enough to ask." He tried to touch her; again she flinched, as she always did. Again the twinge of envy crossed Haller's face. What was he to do? He loved one, not the other.

Darktouch said, "You are not my touch-brother. We were not linked together at birth by touch and smell. How can I. . ."

"Tell us about it," said Haller. Kelver saw how gentle she was, how hard it must he to speak kindly to Darktouch. He pitied her then. The three of them were all that was left of the people he had ever known. For all he knew they were all of the human race, and the twin cities were just illusions, dreams, stories to impress the gullible. . . .

And as they walked, Darktouch talked. Haltingly at first, then more passionately, finding the words at last. Even Haller was awed. They walked for many hours, and the landscape never changed: always the limitless whiteness, always the line of the Cold River slung out on pylons, klomet after klomet, always the angry suns. In the shadow of the Cold River, a little strip of darkness, it was a little cooler, and they could find moisture sometimes, oozing down the pylons, although most of it evaporated before it reached their

height. But they were hungry, and the day seemed
never to end.

. . . Now they ran, driven by a kind of madness made
from hunger and despair. Or collapsed, half in, half out
of the shadow, half-cool, half-burning, too tired to go
on. It wasn't real. Once they ran toward a glittering
half-familiar village to find only the sand. Kelver was
ready to kill an al'ksigark now.

In time Darktouch told of the light on the Sound,
and Kelver could not even imagine such things. But he
knew now how important he had become. If only he
could reach the Inquest . . . after a day of the desert, he
didn't even think of it any more. Only his love for the
strange girl sustained him. They pushed on; finally
night fell, chilly and brief.

In the morning Kelver climbed a pylon and saw a
pride of al'ksigarkar.
***

First the whiteness, swallowing up all idea of
distance and space, and then . . . a patch of green,
field-furry, shivering closer like a huge amoeba. Kelver
remembered—

—vomit-green corpses, teeth-riddled, by the Cold
River—And then the hunger. "They're grazing now," he
said, "photosynthesizing with their huge mantles erect
and spread out. But if we separate one of them out, it'll
be detached from the mob-mind and it'll go rogue, it'll
attack us. . . . ." He had climbed down now. The others
clung to the cool of the pylon—Darktouch aloof,
Haller all too accessible. From the shadow they could
see only a strip of green almost at the horizon. "Come
on," he said. "Lets get there before we starve to death."

"But we'll have to leave the Cold River behind!" said Haller.

"We don't have any choice!" Darktouch said, very quietly. She set off into the whiteness. Kelver could see her feet flinch from the smart of hot sand. He started to follow. Haller was last. He felt the suns on him now, saw also the Skywall mountain far to his right, blotting out a third of the sky. His stomach was churning with hunger. He wanted to relieve himself and yet didn't want to lose any more water. The firefur of his tunic was damp and had lost its luster. He walked faster, thinking of Darktouch, not wanting her too far in the lead in case—

She was gone! He heard a scream from Haller behind him "It's haunted! The wasteland has killed her —"

"Don't be stupid!" He ran toward the spot, a hundred meters ahead, where he had seen her vanish. The footprints were already filling with fresh sand. They stopped. He kicked at the sand with his foot, there was a gleam suddenly, a flashing pain in his eyes, and then—

Metal. A displacement plate. "She doesn't know how to use them," he said. "Powers of powers, she probably doesn't know where she is at all, probably thinks we've disappeared. . ."

"What can she have been subvoking at the time?" said Haller.

"I don't know. Quick, step on with me. We've got to stick together." He scrubbed at the sweat-plastered hair that fell over his eyes. "She must have been thinking of the al'ksigar-kar . . . ." In the back of his mind the thought was nagging. Why are the displacement plates here, who are they for, they must be old and disused

now, who put them there, why hasn't anyone been told
of them—   He clutched Haller's hand tight and
subvoked an image of the al'ksigarkar and—

They popped into being with the white sand still
streaming out in every direction, with the Cold River a
black line at the sky's edge, and ahead, a mad green
carpet of shimmering green mantles and leaf-
trembling tendrils and sharp teeth, glistening against
the green fur like diamants—

"Darktouch!" he screamed.

The field of tendrils shifted, as though a windwave
blew through them.

"Don't go near them", Haller whispered. "They'll go
carnivorous—" Kelver backed away, back toward the
displacement plate.

"You have to help me. We have to grab one. With
our bare hands, drag it away before the herd senses our
presence." He saw Haller gulp, then nod. Had they
eaten Darktouch already? Had the whole journey been
made for nothing, had the village been murdered for
nothing? No time for that now. He was hungry. He
crouched down. Haller followed him. They crept
toward the green, holding their breaths.

"That one." He pointed, whispering. One al'ksigark
was slightly detached from the group. They were ugly
things. Its body was a mass of globs and spiderlegs and
facet-rich patches that served as compound eyes, and
its gaping toothy mouth was shadowed by the parasol-
mantle, sprouting like a lotus-leaf, a couple of square
meters, catching the sunlight. They were close now.
The creature smelled of fresh-cropped grass and
decaying meat. They were within arm's reach. "Quick!
The eye-things!" He tried not to look, bailed his fist
and smashed hard into an eye-patch and another and

another, and Haller did the same, until his hands were vegetable-oil-greasy and covered with faint iridescence from the light-sensitive membranes. The creature shivered, not having had time to switch into its active, carnivorous phase. If they didn't move quickly, the whole herd would come to life, swallowing them alive —

"Drag it to the displacement plate—" They hefted to-gether, wrenching the al'ksigark loose from its light roots, greenish rheum trickled into the sand. . . . "Not now, Haller, later!" She was drinking the juice from it, gasping for air.

Suddenly the al'ksigark wriggled loose, tendrils flailing, began to ooze around in circles. By smell or some other sense it began to totter toward the herd, trailing rivulets of thick liquid. Kelver jumped it. Its mantle began to contract, tightening around his waist and legs. With a bound Haller was on the creature, kicking wildly at its mouth and cavernous nostrils. Kelver smashed a rip in the mantle with his bare hands and rolled, thudding against the burning sand. Haller was stomping on the creature now, throwing up a slew of green mush and stringy internal organs.

"Thank you," Kelver murmured.

"I love you," Haller said. There was anger in her voice, though. They dragged the creature toward the displacement plate. Kelver was too hungry to control himself and began to gorge on the greenish organs, which tasted like a rank cheese slathered with syrup.

"I'm too tired, I can't make it to the plate—"

Darktouch! he was thinking, his mind whirling.

"Starship captains don't get tired . . . remember?" Haller mocked him gently. He began to realize how close he and she had been, in their own disdainful ways. Even through his hunger he saw how much she loved him. They started to move, dragging the al'ksigark between them. He winced when it twitched. Behind them the pride swayed, rooted still, still drinking the sunlight in their thousands. "I know you're thinking of her," said Haller, "and I don't care about that. It's too late now. I don't understand what she saw, why you had to get to the Inquestors . . . but I know we still have to, because it's our only chance to go on living. So come on." They were within a meter or so of the displacement plate—

A dozen of them had broken loose. A wailing, twittering yammer in the air. Tendrils slimy against his skin. He broke away. "Run, Haller!" They were standing on the displacement plate and he was willing it, subvoking with all his might but the right images wouldn't come, his mind was blank with terror, he watched as the creatures roared and dribbled a pus of sputum and digestive juice, he watched Haller slip, spring to her feet, and—

"Subvocalize, powers of powers, subvocalize!" she was shouting. "Don't wait for me!" His mouth was wide open in horror—

She writhed free, leaped on with him, the al'ksigarkar chattered and leaped their mantles and snapped at their legs with green claws, and then suddenly she turned and saw something and pushed Kelver with all her might, sending him sprawling, heat of the sand exploding against his bare arms and thighs, and then she started to yell something at him and there was a whooshing in the air and a lance sprouted from her and her cry was strangled, her neck hanging, snapped, her whole body tumbling onto the sand. . .

A hideous keening from twelve al'ksigark mouths, yawning-wide and glistening with razor-jewel teeth . . . the al'ksigarkar scattering, dashing into the palpitating sea of green, a rain of lances whipping from above, and thunder of stomping human feet, a babble of guttural speech—

He propped himself up. The creatures were falling, dropping out of the herd, and the rest were stampeding, scurrying up flurries of white sand. And Haller lay broken on the sand, the blood erupting from her. . . .

First Darktouch, now Haller! I'm alone! He got up, feeling dead as a servocorpse inside. The al'ksigarkar were gone, save for a dozen or so, neatly speared, some of them still jerking in their death-spasms. He didn't want to know what had killed them, but when he turned around he saw them.

Their faces first. The faces of al'ksigarkar, but without the nervous shivering of living ones. They were masks, and beneath the masks were naked torsos of people; muscly, hard torsos, completely caked in sand. One of them saw Kelver.

"You—not al'ksigark!" the man barked. He strode close, and the smell of the rotting al'ksigark mask was almost unbearable. But Kelver was too deadened even to flinch from it. "Come," said the man. He clapped his hands and a dozen of them ran forward to strip the bodies of the slain al'ksigark. They must have been hunting. "We not intended to kill your mate," said the man more gently. "You are village people, no?" His lowspeech was hard to understand, full of harshly articulated consonants, and very archaic in its word forms. "Come. We have saved you. Come. Come." The man tugged at him, but Kelver resisted. He was trying to think an instruction to the displacement plate, but he was too confused to subvoke clearly. He was hungry and thirsty, more so than he ever believed possible.

"You're the ghost people," he said. "The people who live off the wastelands. . . ."

The man shrugged. Muscles rippled under his powdery covering. Kelver said, "I have to go back to the Cold River . . . I have to find the twin cities, I have to find the Inquestors, or something terrible is going to happen to all of us . . . please, don't take me, leave me to go on my journey by myself.

"Cold River bad place," the man hissed. "Come." Brusquely he took hold of Kelver's shoulder and nudged him forward.

So it ends, Kelver thought. Me and my dreams of being an astrogator, or hobnobbing with Inquestors. . . .

He looked at the Skywall in the distance, the blackness sandwiched with layers of mist until it melted into the sky. He watched the ghost people dully as they slung the dead al'ksigarkar over their shoulders and began to march into the distance. The ghost man pushed him forward again.

Haller! Darktouch! his mind screamed. And then he saw that they were walking away from the line of the Cold River, and he lost all hope.

Lady Ynyoldeh

Seventeen
The Passion of Ynyoldeh

Clouds parted: came a passionate purple rain, stifling the wonder-gasps of the audience. Shen Sajit's face fell into repose, blurred by the gauze of raindrops that sent tiny rainbows darting, a huge holoface sculpted on simulated clouds. Davaryush reached the balcony, arriving late as was correct for a Kingling. As he and his train pushed through the mob toward the throne he struggled to retain his composure, and also not to seem too composed, for this was the commonest giveaway error among nervous Inquestors. Taking his time, giving each footfall its proper weight, he descended the soft steps of the aisle.

—If Varuneh is right about Ynyoldeh—

He saw her now, or the dead girl that spoke in her name, reclining in the mechanical's arms. It rocked her as a nurse might rock a baby, and she affected a languid, pouting pose. The other Inquestors sat at her feet, and Davaryush saw how they smiled openly, even in his presence, so conscious were they of victory in makrúgh.

—If the thinkhive has obeyed my instructions implicitly, instead of reinterpreting them in its own devious fashion—

Lady Varuneh had preceded him. He saw her now, among the palace ladies, far from the throne area that was the true arena of the evening . . . the metawolverine skin of her garment and the single flamedisk were austere, understated, compared to the other women's clothing: some had masks of cloth-of-iridium with their features touched up with strings of miniature sapphires and pearls; others had their hair piled in mountains or forests, imitating a nature they had probably never encountered; their capes were spread out by artwinds, their skirts revolved about their waists by means of photon-powered motors and quivered with coruscatory kaleidolons. He had to smile a little . . . how inventive was their shallowness! How different from the woman who was his lover, who outshone them all in a single shapeless skincloak.

—If only—

He sat down now, outwardly quite detached, but observing the others. The Inquestors, flushed with victory seemed moved by Sajit's music, especially Ton Elloran: Davaryush did not care for it much. His taste was more vulgar than was thought fashionable and he liked the florid symphoniae of Ont much better. He ordered more zul for the Inquestors, but made sure that his own was unfermented.

"You are a good loser," Kiembre or Siembre said, shuffling forward on their hoverthrone.

"Attá heng," Davaryush said listlessly. The flame-disk of Varuneh's hair danced above the field of headdresses in the ladies' pavilion. . . .

"Oh, Daavye," Ynyoldeh said, bringing her throne level with his, and affecting a stage whisper, "you seem to have lost all your feistiness. . . and I thought that being declared heretic would do you a world of good! You're going to give up without a fight? The glorious scheme of bluffing to threaten the whole galaxy?"

Davaryush didn't answer her. He motioned for more zul for the Lady Ynyoldeh, and then said, a trifle maliciously, "Oh, I am sorry, of course you cannot drink."

"You underestimate modern technology," the girl-corpse said, her kohl-dark eyelashes fluttering. She sipped at the zul in an uncannily nymphlike gesture, her wrist bending with just the right angle of grace, her elbow crooked just so. "I'm a very elegant corpse," she said. Then she expelled a gust of putrescence in his face, quaffing gracefully the while. Davaryush refused to be challenged.   He turned to hear the music. Clouds like cetaceans leaped over the sea of cloud, sailing through hoops of rainbow-tinted cirrus, while other clouds shaped like mythological sailboats skimmed the fluffy waves.

"You don't have a gift for me too, then, after all the trouble I took?" Ynyoldeh said querulously. "I gave you such a beautiful one, and you still don't understand what I mean by it."

"I refuse to utter another word, my Lady. Listen to the man's voice! Just look at the artful artifice of the cloud-sculptors, how they shape their images to the lines of melody!" Davaryush murmured, floundering in a tempest of pretension.

"You always were such a philistine, Daavye," said Ynyoldeh.

"Yet I must confess, it is a little boring to talk about art when we can talk instead about the destruction of star systems."

Davaryush did not answer. The music surged and soared and did not touch him. Instead he found himself thinking of the ones who had fled from the Dark Country, how he had doomed them by his own command, just to save face in front of a mere thinkhive, a mere machine . . . his loneliness was complete, he thought. In trying to save the Dispersal of Man he had had to become utterly ruthless, unbecomingly compassionless. The paradox tormented him, even as he tried to tell himself that he was forced to act this way, that there were no alternatives, that it was destiny. He sipped at his zul, finding it so sweet as to seem bitter.

***

A stunning storm dispersed the cloud-choreographer's phantasms. The audience was roaring like wind over the firesnows of Ont. It was then that Davaryush levitated his hoverthrone and rose above the crowd, forcing immediate silence. He spoke very quietly; the ears of the throne picked up his voice and sent it booming above the pavilion.

"I'm sure we have all been very moved," he said. "And now I would like to make public my gift for the Lady Ynyoldeh. I wish to give her the opportunity to extend her Inquestral compassion, to be an example for us all . . . for so many see the Lady only as Queen of Daggers, Mistress of Death. Lady Ynyoldeh, would it please you to accompany me?"

The silence was complete now. He dropped the hoverthrone on a cushiony bank of artificial clouds and waited for Ynyoldeh. The robot, still cradling the girl-corpse, rose stiffly from its throne and came to the balcony's edge, then vaulted with surprising grace onto the forceshield floor beneath, a floor that was firm as metal and yet provided an illusion of great aerial spaces. It came toward him, and he saw that the girl-corpse was sitting up in the lotus of its arms, her face quite stern. How beautiful she was, even enraged!

Davaryush said, "A little encore, for all of us." He clapped his hands, and a portal irised open in one of the cloud-banks. There came from the cloud-bank old men, old women, some dozens of them, hideously emaciated; walking skeletons. Davaryush himself could hardly look upon them. Yellowing rags covered them; their bones protruded, their skin was speckled with sores, their genitals hung wilted in their bald crotches. They shuffled slowly by, and Davaryush studied the face of the servocorpse Inquestor carefully for any signs of distress; for he knew that for such artful servocorpse technology there must be a direct link between the wasting facial muscles of Ynyoldeh and the corpse's. The parade came to a halt. At a gesture from the Kingling they lurched forward, threatening. Their eyes were hungry chasms, lightless, lifeless.

"They are some ancients of this planet, Ynyeh," he said sweetly, "who suffer from some strange wasting disease. They are old, they suffer terribly, Ynyoldeh. Will you not relieve them of their anguish? Here—" Plucking a slicer from his cloak, he went on, "I give you, as a present, the privilege of extending to them personally the Inquestral compassion. For it is indeed rare, my Lady, that our worlds intersect: I mean, of course, the worlds of the rulers and the ruled, the players of makrúgh and the makrúgh-fodder. It's well, isn't it, that we should sometimes remember such things?" Davaryush walked up to the tall mechanical, more confident now. "Take the slicer, Ynyeh . . . and thank you for the charming tables."

"Release me!" Ynyoldeh cried, addressing the mechanical. It set her down. She seized the slicer grimly. Davaryush stepped out of her way.

"You must be artful," Davaryush said repeating one of the earliest lessons he had learned on Uran s'Varek. "You must not seem rageful or vindictive; that is not our way—"

"You dare to instruct me?" Then, with arsenic-laced sweetness, "I thank you, Ton Davaryush z Galléndaran K'Ning. I will never forget this—"

A single spurt of laser light from the slicer. A dramatic whirl graceful as an aerial dancer, a zig-zag leap. . .

Sliced bodies crumpling in pitiful heaps on the forceshield, looking as though they were floating in the blue sky among the clouds. "Have I done well?" Ynyoldeh said.

A thunder of applause from the stands. . . .

"Very well," said Davaryush, hoping that she had not read his mind, did not yet know what he had done.

And then she said, "You will come to my palace immediately. You slime, you worse than slime! You have wrested my dignity from me. You've won!" Again she smiled, curtsied sarcastically at the wildly cheering crowds, and the mechanical knelt to pick her up and place her so delicately in its four silver-gleaming arms, and the strange pair made its way back toward the Inquestral pavilion.

What a strange reversal, Davaryush thought. The monster and the innocent. That poor machine . . . it is the innocent, and the beautiful young girl is the monster. He felt sweat pouring down his face, felt the shimmercloak trying to accommodate him with a flush of cool air. The audience was dispersing now. No time to find Varuneh now. He would have to confront Ynyoldeh alone, without her help, hoping that he had made the right move.

Presently the hawk-palace rived the clouds, whirring and screeching. He mounted his hoverthrone and flew toward it, his heart beating with confusion and hope.

   ***

When he entered the navel of the hawk-palace, he found the reception chamber in disarray. The shimmerfur of the carpeting seemed faded. A sickly yellow light played over the marble walls, turning the inlaid rubies into slimy teardrops.

"Where are you?" he called out. He trod further. The mechanical stood in repose, deactivated, its ape-arms dangling and its eyes blank. The girl-corpse was slumped over a crook of metal arm, at an unnatural angle. It, too, seemed no longer to be functioning. . . Davaryush called out again into the echoey stillness. "Ynyoldeh!"

A quiet cackle. He could not perceive its source. And then he saw that it issued from the corpse's mouth. . . .

"History there is, and no history," whispered the corpse. "No, don't bother to answer, Daavye. I'm not playing any more."

Motion. The hawk-palace was rising; he could feel the gut-wrench of a gravity shift. "Where are we going?"

"Did you not want to see me as I am? Sadist!" said the corpse, never righting itself from its crumpled position.

. . . the walls deopaqued. They had thrust through the atmosphere and it was as though Davaryush were standing on a shimmercarpet floating against star-blazoned blackness.

A huge black shape, blotting out a circlet of stars, coming closer . . . turning . . . a coronal glow suffusing it now, as it turned to reveal a nest of mirror metal stranded and tubed, drifting toward them. . . .

"Your palace."

"Yes. The hawk's nest."

He knew now that it was they who were moving toward the nest where the hawkship roosted. And now he saw within the nest an ovoid shape of burnished gold resting on twiglike columns bathed with soft clingfire.

"When the hawk comes to rest over my nest," said the voice of Ynyoldeh—and it came without irony, an innocent voice such as a small girl might truly have —"then you will descend into the egg, and you will see me as I really am. . . ."

***

A dark room. More like a tomb than the throneroom of one of the most famed of Inquestors. A small room, dank and stale-smelling. . . .

Then, a light shaft piercing the darkness—

A throne, carved from a cube of lucent amber, lined with feathers. Old feathers, feathers from so many kinds of birds, and all of them dulled by dust . . . patches of fluorescent green that were long-dead lighthawks, flashes of firephoenix wings, threadbare peacock's feathers with their eyes misted with age. . . .

And on the throne, a living corpse. He could just see it breathe, painfully, wheezingly. "The Lady Ynyoldeh," he said formally.

"Varuneh, you treacherous insect! You have Varuneh! How else could you know?" spluttered the voice. Eyes snapped open behind folds of jaundiced paper-flesh. "I have not spoken in a hundred years, and you make me speak . . . Daavye, Daavye . . . ."

"My gift pleased you?"

"Drop your pretenses, Daavye. I know what it is you want." Her shimmercloak, creased like crepe paper, rustled as she tried to raise herself to look him in the eyes. "Shall I tell you what I know?"

"If you wish."

"Davaryush, the Inquest is falling! The thinkhives are buzzing with it. It may take a millennium more, but it has begun, it is implicit in our very philosophy, our very glorification of transience as the natural order of things—"

She's testing me! Playing with me, trying to trap me in some hideous heresy so she can destroy me! he thought.

"Perhaps," he ventured."But for now, makrúgh goes on, and if I have pleased you—"

The eyes flapped closed. A deep breathing, more like a death rattle than something that gave life, was the only sound for several moments. Then Ynyoldeh said, "Tell Varuneh—don't deny it, I see her handiwork in everything you've done today you devious old bastard—tell her she wasn't wrong. She saw right through me. I was too compassionate". . . . A spasmic laughter racked her body, making the faded shimmer-cloak twinkle for a moment. "Answer me one question! If you please me, you shall have your bluff to destroy Gallendys . . . what do I care?" She laughed again, a ghoulish, croaking laugh, her withered cheeks jouncing with the rhythm of it.

"Of course, Lady Ynyoldeh."

"Those people I killed . . . what were they? Were they inhabitants of your city, of your villages, plucked away from their homes to be a vehicle of my compassion, or were they something else? The truth, Daavye, the truth!"

If I tell her the truth— It was time for the gamble. He would have to tell her the truth, or he would have to lie. *The truth!* he thought, and said, "They were servocorpses."

There was a long silence. Then the eyes opened again, slowly, studied his face.

"I believe you, Ton Davaryush z Galléndaran K'Ning. What a charming conceit of yours! The dead killing the dead. You are certainly of an artistic bent."

"You flatter me."

"This is a dangerous moment for both of us, Ton Davaryush. I must now gauge whether or not you have revealed yourself to me for what you really are, and then I must gauge whether it would be safe to reveal myself to you . . . powers of powers, Daavye!" Without warning, tears began to flow from her withered eyes, an incongruous, pathetic sight. "It was I who enabled Varuneh to escape the Inquest. It was just a game of mine, a private revenge against them for giving me this terrible affliction, this anguish and terrible compassion. I am tired, Daavye! If they say the Inquest will fall so be it, so be it! Take your toys! Do what must be done! Know, Daavye, that I forswear makrúgh, and that this is no game any more."

"I—" Never had he expected this. That the Queen of Daggers should all the time have been burying her hatred of the Inquest, been waiting for a moment such as this. . .

"Are you glad you told me the truth?"

"Yes."

"And remember, I disclaim all responsibility! On your head be it! This conversation has never taken place!"

She was spent now. Davaryush forced himself to look at her for a long time. A suppurating ribbon of burst flesh ran like a serpent from the crown of her bald head down her cheeks into a fold of the shimmercloak.

We have won, he thought. The revolution can now proceed without hindrance. We will win fire on the Skywall mountain and murder the helpless delphinoids, who have existed only to be our victims since Man burst as a god into the Galaxy. . . . He turned to look at Ynyoldeh, but the light was fast dimming and a portal was opening in the wall of the chamber. The audience was over.

Why do I feel no joy? he was thinking. Why do I not feel that I have brought about a great utopia? He searched for joy but found only emptiness. I have become as they are, he thought, and remembered the dead killing the dead.

Eighteen
The Queen of Ghosts

Darktouch remembered—

Sea of quivering green things, thrashing toward her, hard oily arms grasping her, dragging her, chalk-powder rubbing oil on her, and then—

The pit. Here it was . . . what Kelver would have called dark, but to her it was almost familiar. It was barely wide enough for a few men, its walls ribbed by human bones lashed together with al'ksigark leather. She rested her eyes and ears now, relying on her old senses to feel out her surroundings. The smell of dead al'ksigarkar was in everything, even in the sand of the pit-floor, a smell of crushed fresh leaves compounded with rotted meat. The roof was a patchwork quilt of human and al'ksigark skins, clumsily stitched with strips of leather. She could reach up and feel it with her hands and smell what it was made of.

She was thinking of Touch-brother and of Windstriker. She had lost everyone now, even the strange boy who had tried to become her touch-sibling. This was the end. She told herself to expect nothing more. The half-familiarity of the pit was a comfort, even.

But then she forced herself to remember the way the undark looked over the Sound, and she knew she could not let herself die. . . .

Who are the Inquestors of which they always spoke, she thought, their voices hushed with awe and envy? She wondered if they were as powerful as Windbringer in his glory. If they could breathe life into a whole world as Windbringer did. Perhaps they could not be compared. The gods of the lightworld seemed so remote. They lived apart. You could not hear them in the howling of winds or the scent of Windbringer freshly brought down and returned to the Dark Country.

A moment of blinding light as the cover of the pit was ripped loose. Then Kelver was beside her, and the darkness closed up again.

He could not speak at first. Her fingers played along his lips; they were bruised, newly scabbed. The desert dust, ground into the sweat, made sandpaper of his body. She touched a long scar on his arm. You are weak, Boy-before-Naming, she signed. For this "Kelver," this sound made with a quiver of the throat and a buzzing of the lips, was no true name. I will have to give you a true name, she signed.

He stirred, moaned, tried to speak.

"Oh, Kelver," she said aloud. The words, wrung from her in the speech of the lightpeople, seemed to violate the close darkness of the deathpit.

His hand moved. Touched hers. Followed the line of her arm, the shallow curve of her new breasts. And touched her most profane of places. Ignorant of custom, he let his touch linger. Her cheeks warmed; she was ashamed, for Touch-brother was hardly cold, and she had not been the one to consign his body to the angels.

You are not my touch-brother, she signed. One day I must cut off a joint for him, a finger or a toe. And mourn for many sleeps. You should not touch me like that. You are a stranger, and I am given, bound by scent and touch and birth and death.

The boy scratched one word crudely on her arm.

Dead. Dead. His hand was cold. She felt his desolation. What did it matter now? They were near death. They had both been thrust out of their own pocket universes. Here you made your own rules, didn't you? Before she could answer him his arms crushed around her; the sweat-dust made her tingle in a thousand places.

Yes, Touch-brother is dead. She made as though to push him away; but he was so weak, dead weight pushing down her arms. He grasped her more firmly now. With one hand she soothed him, stroking his cheek; with the other she signed, No. Not that way. This place is like the Dark Country. You cannot see; and you can hardly hear. But I, who am of the Dark Country—I feel, hear, see, smell, not with the touching of my eyes but with the true touching . . . and I will show you how it is that we love. And I will take you for my touch-brother, against all custom, because the land of those customs is in the past, and I am free of it now.

Did he understand her, she wondered. But he relaxed in her arms. Slowly, her hands barely brushing his chest, fingers mirroring each other, she danced the sign for love on him, over and over, loves within loves; with her fingertips she danced, onto his belly now, now almost touching his swelling penis. now darting away from it. With her lips, chapped and charred in the wind, she danced her name upon his lips: Dark . . . touch. Dark . . . touch. She grazed the tattered clingfire of his cloak, shedding it in a single motion; in the same motion she shivered herself free of her garment. She only touched him in one or two places at a time, toying with his desire, proffering, denying; this she had learned from her touch-brother long before, when they were very little. Then she let her hair fall on his face, just one or two strands of it, drawing paths on his cheek. With her hair she drew her name on him in huge, passionate strokes, loosening the clinging dust. Oh, her lips danced, tasting salt and bitter things. And then again her name with her hair, the words edge barely reaching his profane places. At first Kelver seemed not to understand; but then he fell into the pattern. His fingers danced artlessly, but tenderness tempered their   crudeness. She knew then that she loved him. Oh, her lips danced, skimming his genitals; with his lips he sought hers, but she made her body shiver, quiver, in and out of his reach. He moaned; the vibration of it radiated through her body from where his lips touched her. And so they played. Until the brushstrokes hardened into clutchings, and the mouths met as though by accident, and the tongue tips tickled one another, and in another moment, again as if by happenstance, their bodies arched into a single curve, and they melted into a single soul, dancing for joy on a bed of bones and dead things.

After, they lay in each other's arms. The stench of decay was laced with a sweet scent of sex. He was silent so long, hardly breathing even, that she feared for him. She spoke first, breaking loose from the constraining silence of the Dark Country.

"Now I have made you mine," she said. "Our dreams are one. We are joined by scent and birth and death."

He said, "I was afraid you were too wasted with grief. For that other boy. I was jealous of the dead."

"Perhaps we, too, are dead."

"Shhh . . . never say that. You're so fatalistic. What happened to your great secret, the one that drove us into the desert?"

"I don't know." She was crying softly; she turned so he wouldn't know.

"I believed in it. Look, why would they be trying to kill us if it weren't for that? Why would those terrible angels come for us? Why did our village die, if the thing you have to tell isn't important?"

I did not think of these things when I fled. Only that we had murdered the greatest beauty my eyes and ears could ever touch."

"Hush now. You are the most beautiful thing I will ever touch."

She laughed; she had learned to do it well. The laughter echoed; a bone, dislodged somewhere, rattled. Through the skin-covered pit mouth came a sickly green light.

"Sleep now," Kelver said. "Sleep. Tomorrow we'll find a way free. Tomorrow, my love, tomorrow."

***

After it seemed one or two sleeps, when they had lain delirious with hunger and thirst, and had begun even to gnaw on the bones in the pit, the ghost people came to drag them from their prison. They were bound and dragged over a terrain of jagged stones; they were glazed with frost and did not cut their feet but burned them numb.

An encampment now: tents, made from the hides of al'ksigarkar with their heads and teeth still intact, dangling here and there from the tent sides. The suns, low behind the tents, blackened them and bathed them in fire. The ghost people pushed the children forward, down onto the cold ground. A fire burned. Kelver saw the outline of Skywall, far yet near, bursting through twilit clouds. They had come nowhere! There was no escape from the Skywall. . . .

The ghost people were silent. And then, all at once, they uttered a series of syllables, half-grunt, half-moan, in unison: hanh, hanh, hanh. From the largest of the tents emerged a woman.

"Queen!" the nearest ghost man rasped, shoving their heads into the frost.

The woman laughed. It was a beautiful and haunting sound, like the sound a jangyll-bird makes when it knows it will be slaughtered for dinner and may sing only once more. Kelver looked up quickly, before his head was forced down again. He reached out to find Darktouch, to find a twinge of warmth. In that moment he had seen the woman's face; she was not of the ghost people.

She had once been beautiful, he thought; she was old now, a hundred years old, two hundred . . . he could not imagine such age, not without regular somatic renewal to preserve the appearance of youth. She was quite bald; a wig of shredded al'ksigark hide sat on her brow, a wilderness of straggly green threads.

She wore a green robe of the same material, and a necklace of frozen human fingers, half-decayed.

"Meat, I see!" she said. She spoke the hightongue. That was how the ghost people knew some words of it then! Who was this woman?

She gestured. They forced Darktouch and Kelver up on their feet. Kelver looked at the ground; but Darktouch stared at the woman, and he knew that her senses were still drunk with the joy of seeing even the ugly things, the deadly things.

The queen of the ghost people looked from one to the other. Especially at Darktouch.

"You are from inside," she said at last, abruptly. "How? Your eyes are opened."

"You know?" Kelver said.

"Never mind. You will be meat for my people soon. For a century I have led them to food, and for a century I have been queen here. Queen of a patch of desert. Ha! But queen, but queen." Her voice was high, clear, hard. "Not a lackey of the High Inquest!"

"We are seeking the Inquest," Kelver said.

"Silence! I speak to the girl. This girl . . . she must have seen what I saw . . . and I am driven mad for it! The palace . . . the Inquestral Seat . . . there was music, songs, I remember still the songs. . . "

"You know what Darktouch saw?" Kelver said. "You aren't from the ghost people . . . ?"

But she was singing now, her eyes closed in remembrance. Kelver could barely make out the words, so intertwined were they with melismas:

den óm verék entínjet
in dárein shirénzheh
zenz kel skevúh varúng

e varánde

aivermatsá falláh setálikas!
tekiánveras yvrens ká!

o-tínjet
in dárein shirénzheh!
sarnáng, varúnger shentráor!
eíh! min zhalá, zhalá,
hokhté Enguester, min zhalá, zhalá,
sarnáng,
varúnger shentráor, varúnger shentráor . . .

He translated the words to himself in the lowspeech. "No man alive has touched the silence between the stars without that he was driven mad, or reached enlightenment. For now the delphinoids fall through the overcosm, and the tachyon bubbles burst through the cosmos. But I have touched the silence between the stars! I, the mad singer! Ei, envy me, envy me, thou High Inquestor, envy me, the mad singer, the mad singer."

"Did you like my song, boy? Boy eking life from the coolness of mountainside, boy without dreams, without knowledge? Such as you seeks the Inquest?" She laughed again, a laughter tinged with sorrow.

"Please, Queen . . . are you from the Inquest? Can you tell us where to find them?"

She gestured. A ghost man came forward and struck Kelver in the face. He tasted blood. "Never speak to me of them! They have betrayed the universe!" cried the queen of the ghost people. "Did you like the song? It was sung to me by the great Shen Sajit once. He grasped a shadow of the great beauty. A shred. A nothing. But I have seen, and now I'm mad, I'm mad, mad, mad, mad, mad." And she began to dance as the frost melted around them. Her joints moved stiffly; but she held her head high and bent her wrists in an elegant gesture; Kelver had seen this dancing sometimes, in an image crystal bought from the city by his uncle Aaye, in a holosculpture set in a cast of shoddy searock ringed with the cheapest grade of clingfire.

"You are," he said, "a person fallen from greatness. You're a shadow of something that should long be dead." At this she stopped her dancing and wept.

"How dare you tell me this?" she said. "Know me then! I am Yeng Saryodha of the Ferret clan, a spy for the great thinkhive of this world. Once I was of the court of Ton Elloran n'Taanyel Tath; I was lent to this planet long ago, for my great skill in prying out secrets, in finding those things about people which even they themselves cannot know."

"Saryodha—"

"Do not call me that now! I am queen, queen, queen, the mad queen, the mad, the mad, the mad queen, queen, queen."

The savages, hearing those words, echoed them: queen, queen, in high creaking voices.

"She has seen, then, has seen, has seen," the queen said. "She has touched the light on the Sound, and she is mad as I."

Darktouch said, "Then you know why we must go to the Inquestors. You must release us, Queen, help us."

Saryodha screeched with laughter. The ghost people echoed her. "And take my people's meat from them? Their meat, my survival?"

Kelver said, "Now I know that what Darktouch told me is true. I didn't before. I trusted her — but you've seen, too, and so you don't dare return—"

"The delphinoids fly the overcosm, and the Inquest holds us in its high compassion, so I learned, I learned, I a child, no queen yet. If I go back I will tell them, kill them. Ha, ha, ha, ha, the end of the Inquest is locked inside, inside, hidden, hidden. You, too, you have the key. You do not know. You, girl, have touched, but do not know the power of what you touched. Listen to me who heard the immortal Sajit sing—

shénom na chítarans hyemadhá
We long for the heart's homeworld.

"The thinkhive sent me to the country of the blind. A hundred years ago maybe. Routine investigation, check on status of artificially tailored society, the blind, the deaf, the children of darkness on whom the shadow falls forever. I saw, I saw, children, I saw, I saw the light on the Sunless Sound, on Keían zenzÁtheren. Better to hide here in the desert than to have known such things. Sajit in his song—he touched a shadow only, only a shadow. You, girl, and I have touched truth. Am I then driven mad, and you attained enlightenment? This death I give you is a gift, a gift from the mad, mad, mad, mad queen.

"Better to die than to bring about the end of all things, the death of the high compassion the death of a million worlds."

Kelver said, "I don't understand. How can what we do be so monstrous? I don't believe it. If we find the Inquestors, if we tell them the truth . . . and maybe I'll win my wings and be free of this backworld, and the girl and I will walk the starfield in our love."

"Children, children, your love is not forever, no, no, not. I am old, I have seen, have seen the Inquest in its majesty. Riding the sky on floaters of precious metals, the shimmercloaks flying, blushing, billowing in the wind. You cannot imagine how old I am, I the queen, queen, queen. So it is always; the dreams of the young, bursting with joy and vigor, are stronger than the realities of the old; the airy nothings that in your heads will topple the skies themselves, topple, tumble, topple, crumble, crumble."

Then Darktouch went forward; before they could stop her she had seized a withered arm and had begun to sign upon it. But the old woman pushed her aside, and they were seized again.

"Bring them to the tent; feed them with old scraps of al'ksigark flesh, so they are filled out a little; they can die tomorrow, tomorrow."

"Queen—" Kelver whispered.

"Enough, children, enough, enough. I tire easily. It has been a pleasant conversation which I shall not prolong. Help me now, guards, take your queen to her bed. . . ."

***

They were bound with thongs made from the guts of the al'ksigark. Darktouch stirred, dreaming of running down the passages of her old home, of familiar ridges of stone telling her feet the way. And then the floor dissolved, became a featureless thing of mirror metal, and in her dream she was blind as Touch-brother, she was thrusting out in random directions, the smoothness dark to her feet, the air stretching forever without walls to gauge space and distance, and it was driving her mad, her mad, her mad—

Kelver woke.

Someone had touched his shoulder.

"Quick! Quick, quick, before the madwoman changes her mind!" a voice whispered. He grasped the thin wig of leather strips. Darktouch moved in her sleep, near but unreachable. But his bonds were being loosened.

Torchlight suddenly; a brand of human bone, coated with al'ksigark wax, an eerie green light.

The queen kicked at Darktouch. She shuddered off her dream. "Come, children, come, my little ones, come, come," the queen said. "No, not the oven of the wicked queen, not the pit of the lovely temptress, this isn't a story. Come, come, come. . . ."

They followed her. He wanted to hurry, but reined himself, afraid of discovery. Outside it was quite dark; only the one sun shone, and it was low against the distant Skywall. All around them the ghost people slept, frozen into angled poses, more like statues than men, their bodies whited with fine sand.

"The lair of the serpent mistress," the queen hissed. It was her own tent, the largest one that they had seen.

When they stepped inside they saw that it was carpeted in a cloth of clingfire; a cold light flickered along the sick-green walls. She pulled at the carpet, uncovering a patch of sand and throwing a circle of ceiling into shadow. "Are you ready, children? I will tell you more, more."

"Why did you wake us? If you're going to kill us, could you not let us sleep for an hour?" Kelver said sleepily.

"I remember so much, children. I remember . . . being a child, loving, loving a boy, a boy like you, Kelverelverelver, straight, not tall, bright-eyed, comely. They took him to be a childsoldier. His lovely eyes they took from him, they gave him eyes with laser-irises, eyes that could saw a small mountain with a glance and a command and a smart swirl of his lithe body. They took me, too, took me out of the people bin, for my planet had been blown to powder in a war; my sister became Tash, a Rememberer, for she had seen the childsoldiers fall upon her world; I became Yeng, a Ferret woman, for I had hidden in a water jar that stood in the village square, and I had heard two childsoldiers talking among themselves, and I knew where they would strike next. I ran to warn, to warn my father and my mother, but they were charred, charred, gingerbread-charred, with raisins for eyes, raisins, raisins. And after, I served the Inquest well. And I heard Sajit, the master of the Princeling's music, with his songs of the Inquestors' pain. For they have taken all the evil of man upon themselves; and man is a fallen being, fallen, fallen. Listen! he sang to me:

af chítaras seréh chom aísh,
chom dáras fáh—

Our hearts, too, shall become as dust,
Just as the stars have become.

"That is why I free you, free you. And myself, for they will kill me for it, me, their queen, who have ruled wisely. They know no better, being the trash of old gene-changings that the thinkhives dumped on the desert, dumped to grow wild, wild, wild, and live on the sand and the frost, frost, frost."

Kelver's heart leaped up at this. He inched nearer to Darktouch. She smiled, not speaking.

"Thus I plant the seed that flowers in end and beginning," the queen said. "Now dig. Here, here," she said, pointing to the patch of sand.

They bent down on the tent floor. He scooped up the sand with his hands and piled it on the clingfire fabric; as he did so it doused the tattered flames, peppering the ceiling with shadowspecks. Darktouch helped him, digging with both hands.

Underneath the sand was a glint.

"Do you see? Do you see, my children?"

Kelver stood up, radiant. "A displacement plate. Queen, you are saving us!"

"And this too," she said. She pulled a disk from its hiding place in the sand. It was a crystal message-disk, circumscribed with curlicuish highscript.

"What is it?" Darktouch said, taking the disk from her, fingering it dubiously.

"The key to the Cold River. "

"What does that mean?" said Kelver.

"The key, the key, the key? Must I tell you everything? Am I a thinkhive? An oracle? The young, the young, demanding all answers of a mad, mad queen!"

"Where does it lead? The displacement plate."

"Go! Ask no questions, you are my death, you are my private angels, delivering me into the hands of my subjects."

Darktouch said, "You must come with us. You, who have seen the thing inside the Skywall. Perhaps my word won't be enough. You are so wise, so old, you're not mad at all, I see, you've seen what you never wanted to see and you're hiding, but you can't always hide, you who come from high places. . .

The mad queen laughed bitterly. "I'm no use, I'm mad, mad, mad, mad, mad now, madder than the universe, madder than the Inquest."

Then Kelver embraced the old woman; she was like a doll in his arms, although she was the taller by a full head. Her eyes were red with weeping now. And he pitied her. The thing in the mountain had cursed her. It had made her flee, just as it had made Darktouch flee. And him, too, though he had not seen it. Its power had compelled him even at second hand.

"Come. Quickly, come," he said to Darktouch. They stepped onto the displacement plate, she grasping the key. He paused; he had no idea what command to subvocalize, and he knew the queen would not help him.

For she was laughing again now, and again the sound reminded him of the doomed jangyll-fowl.

He formed an image of the Cold River in his mind. As the image crystallized, he felt the disorienting lurch of the displacement field, and then they were out in the open. The blue sun was rising now, and they would soon be burned to death unless they could reach the shelter of the Cold River. And now he saw it, a ribbon of metal, a flashing snake that spanned the sandscape from the far Skywall to the limits of vision.

"Quick, quick," he whispered urgently to her, and they began to run toward freedom.

***

Burning. . .
Burning. . .

The Cold River was nearer now, but the suns had danced their way to the zenith, wringing the sweat from him. Darktouch was tired now; her skin, pale from never touching the sunlight, was fire-red and sensitive to every sand particle.

"We've got to run," Kelver was saying, "before the suns get us and we rot alive and the al'ksigarkar come back—"

They were about a third of a klomet away when Darktouch looked up. And screamed. "The angels! The angels!" And the sky was black with them. At first the Skywall's shadow had concealed them, but now they had left their hiding place and were flying serenely toward them. They looked like a flock of silverdoves until you saw the claws and the metal tentacles.

"Faster!" They hurried now; Kelver couldn't feel the sand lacerating his feet. As they reached the Cold River the sudden chill enveloped them. Darktouch leaned for a moment against the columns, for here the Cold River flowed far above ground and was supported by thick pylons of metal. She was hyperventilating now. Kelver grasped her, pulled.

Nowhere to hide. They were coming now, slowly, surely. If they stood near the river, surely the angels dared not harm the river, but they couldn't stay there forever—

They were bigger now. Flying reptiles of metal. And now the earth was shaking. Kelver looked wildly about, and then saw—

Worming out of the ground, more of them! Corkscrewing snouts of metal were emerging, and they were angels of the ground, monstrous spiders sending the sand flying around them, whirring and chittering —

"Where can we go?" he cried.

"Up! Up!" Darktouch said. "The key—"

"What good is it?"

The ground-spider-things were bursting free from the soil now. They were flinging themselves at the river pylons, clattering against metal, fighting themselves, crawling toward them and churning up the dust. "Let's climb the column," Kelver said, "follow. Come, it'll be just like the rooftop games, back at the village." He sprang up, seeking a toehold; here and there the metal of the pylon was notched or eroded. She grabbed at his heels, stumbled. . . .

"I'll close my eyes. It'll be easier," she said. Then she leaped, cat-agile now, finding the footholds with the instincts of blindness. Now he was following her. The ground-spiders had reached the pylon and were sending up tendrils of metal. When they reached the top they looked down and saw—

"Windbringer!" she cried.

Floating in the stream of liquid nitrogen that was locked under a forceshield that glowed a faint blue in the harsh light, was a huge brain, making its slow journey to the shipyards. Darktouch held the key in her hand. The blue shield danced over the river like a pale fire.

The first of the explosions came. The flying angels were pelting the ground with burstpellets. As they looked at them they saw lances of laser light leaping from the angels' senseports, and the sand polka-dotted with white-hot spots that burned their eyes.

"The key!" he shouted. A laser beam flashed, dangerously near. The ground-spiders were over the top now, groping for them, their tentacles fibrillating.

"I'm going to trip," she said softly. "I'm going to trip."

"I love you."

She signed: I love you. Touch-brother, bound forever, my life-giver, my light, my darkness.

The key flew from her hand.

There was an opening in the blue flame of the shield. She fell now, fell toward the coldness. "Jump, Touch-brother!" she screamed. "Before the shield closes up again!" Without thinking, he did so.

The cold pounded into him. He felt hard gray flesh. The Windbringer. He felt Darktouch under him; he reached for her, embraced her, yielding up to her the little warmth he had; to no avail.

Above them, the shield, unlocked for a moment by the key, closed up. The angels battered against it until they broke, for the were machines and did not know how to countermand the planetary thinkhives; and so they died.

And in the river, wrapped in each other's arms, quick-frozen in the deathcold of the liquid gases, never knowing that they might ever wake again . . . the two exiles had begun their journey to Davaryush.

It would be a slow journey. Gallendys drifted into its long winter while they slept. The desert turned to glass. In the near-winter the al'ksigarkar spread out their mantles to catch the last of the sunlight and synthesize food stores for their long sleep, and then they froze into crystal gargoyles, glittercold in the winter light.

The Cold River flowed on, arrow-straight, spearing the glazed desert, to the forcedomes where lay the cities of towers built upon the towers of towers, where an unnatural summer smiled over a few hundred square klomets. . . .

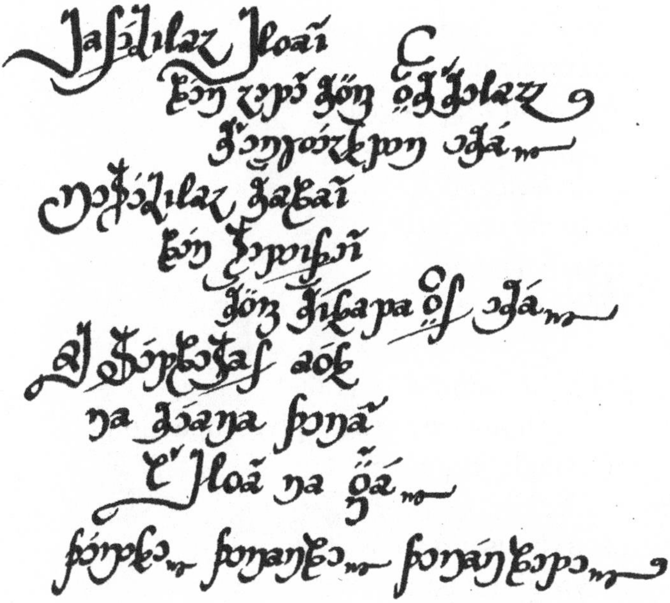

faxéqilas fluaíh!
den seréh chom hokh'Kéliass
k'Enguéstri eká;

nevéqilas chadaíh!
den vereizheíh
chom chítara hox eká.

af vérdevax aút
na kéana shenáh,
z fluáh na ongá,
shénete, shenánde, shenándere.

Let a thousand rivers flow!
they will not be as the high compassion
of a single Inquestor.

Let a thousand snows fall!
they will not equal
the coldness of his one heart.

But even the glacier
yearns for the sea
and flows to it;

always has the heart yearned,
as it yearns now,
always shall it yearn.

—from the Songs of Sajit

Nineteen
The Inquestors

"I have won." Davaryush spoke to the thinkhive of Gallendys; alone as always, in the wombroom of the mirrors.

What have you won?

"The game of *makrúgh*."

It is said that there can be no true winning of makrúgh, *Ton Davaryush z Galléndaran K'Ning. You have said so yourself; and so they teach you, on Uran s'Varek, the Inquestral heartworld.*

"But I have won. Everything I've asked for has been granted. Ynyoldeh has yielded; it's unprecedented. Before the round is over I shall have an enviable reputation: a master of casuistry, a twister of meanings. Wars will be fought and people bins will fly the overcosm. And it will all be done with the minimum bloodshed necessary, with the utmost compassion. . .

He was talking, he knew, to convince himself alone. That was why he had come here after all: to talk to an inanimate object, a thing without a soul, who could nevertheless respond with intelligence. "And now," he continued, "your instructions. Positions of the orbiting arsenals—"

And the children? You don't wish to hear about the children?

"Be silent!" For he had thought of nothing else all day. For a month he had refrained from asking about the fugitives from the Dark Country. But this was the first time that the thinkhive had been the one to broach the subject. Perhaps it was playing one of its intricate games; he could not tell, no longer cared, really; for he knew that soon he would set in motion the end of all things as he knew them. He knew that he did not want to hear of the children. He did not want his resolve to weaken.

The thinkhive waited. Then it said, *You are tired, Ton Davaryush, tired. You have allowed time to furrow your cheeks, and you have been neglecting your life-prolonging drugs, almost as though you no longer cared whether you lived or died. What exactly are you planning in this game of* makrúgh? *Are you sure you're bluffing, Inquestor? Remember, I am for older than you, an infinitely wiser. Do not think to hide from me.*

"Are you a spy of the Inquest?"

Come, don't be paranoid! You know better than that. You know that I wait on no man. For I am this planet's mind, its only claim to life; in effect, its soul, if in such you believe.

"You salvage among dead myths," Davaryush said, "for impressive half-truths. What do you mean to say?"

Ask about the children.

"The children, then." As always he felt an irrational coldness in this room; as always be wrapped his shimmercloak tighter about his shoulders, but it made him sweat, and the sweat, too, was cold, ice-cold.

"Where are the children? You cannot lie." Or could a thinkhive lie? He knew that the very fabric of the Inquest was tearing. Perhaps the thinkhives, honing their *makrúgh* through the millennia, had finally learned to twist the truth itself, their very reason for existing to serve the Inquest. "And remember Gallendys. You are the servant of the Inquest, not I of you. You are no world soul; what soul you have is ours."

They are not dead. But they are as if dead.

And then came a sound like great sheets of metal crashing down a canyon, clanging, resounding through echo chambers of marble; a sound like a whirlwind dashing tower against tower. "You're laughing!" cried Davaryush. It was a sound he had not heard in hundreds of years. A sound that mimicked the laughter of the great thinkhives of Uran s'Varek, peeling across the million-klomet-wide plains of the secret heartworld.

Can I not laugh then?

"Yes, laugh, laugh, but explain yourself. "

No.

"Has the whole world gone mad?"

Mad, mad, mad. mad, mad! the thinkhive sang in a half-familiar voice. It was a line from one of the songs of Shen Sajit. *Oh, Daavye. Daavye,* it continued now in a whining parody of the voice of Lady Varuneh. *Dead and not dead. Dead and not dead. They are dead because they must be dead, because of the word of the High Inquest, yet they are dead as a man is dead who sails the overcosm, gone from the universe, untraceable, existing only as a potential for existence. . . .*

Then Davaryush knew that something had broken
in the thinkhive's innermost nerves; perhaps in its very
center, its heart of hearts. That something had
happened which represented an inconceivable paradox
to the thinkhive; and that it must have to do with the
two children fleeing out of the Dark Country.

For a fleeting second he dared to hope. But he knew
he must proceed with the plan. It was too late. The
larger compassion must swallow up the smaller; so
they had taught him on Uran s'Varek, and so it must
be. He would be content to live on as long as he could
—for the end was surely near—not knowing what
would happen. The need to grasp the truth, to clutch it
as firmly as a message disk or a holosculpted crystal,
was no longer in him. He said, "I am free of you,
thinkhive."

And the thinkhive laughed. And now with the
laughter came a shivering of shadows; darkness danced
in the mirror-walled chamber. "What are you thinking
of?" Davaryush said.

Dead and not dead. Dead and not dead.

And then, in this last time before the fire-death
would rain down on Gallendys, Davaryush felt free to
ask one question which had burned in his mind all this
time.

"Thinkhive—" The laughing stopped; and it was
light again in the wombroom. "The delphinoids. When
they fly through the overcosm. When we solder the
nerves to the ship's nerves. When we constrain them
with our own desires . . . do they feel pain? Do they
feel, too, as humans do?"

*I cannot answer that. You are not a Grand Inquestor,
Davaryush, and you never will be, you heretic, you
dangerous one.*

Something brushed his shoulder. He started. It was the Lady Varuneh. She wore a tattered shimmercloak, from which the blush had long been scrubbed clean; it did not fall gracefully into place, and much of the shimmerfur was dead, dried, leathery, hanging from the living fabric like the skin of a flayed animal. But she was beautiful; today she had wreathed her hair in purest clingfire, so that she seemed crowned with cool flames, their quiet colors sifting like fractured opals.

She said, "Grand Inquestral override, thinkhive! Answer his question!"

The thinkhive was silent for a long time. Then its laughter rang out again and again. *You, my Lady!* it said finally. *You, Ton Varushkadan! Ai, ai,* hokh'Ton, *I make obeisance.* But still its voice was tainted with mockery. *Again I say* attá heng! attá heng! *and concede the victory. You have played* makrúgh *like a master, pulling this memory of a long-dead Inquestor from the past. O Daavye, Daavye.* (Its voice now echoed the deathlike voice of the Lady Ynyoldeh.) *Truly, I am for older than you, Daavye, and I am so tired . . . but I have come to love you, in my own way. For despite everything I have not broken you. I broke all the others, you know, trapping them in spiderwebs of their own warped logic. You are not like the others.*

"You cannot love," Davaryush said. "You cannot love, lie, or feel compassion That is how you were made." What twist of *makrúgh* was this? Did the thinkhive know, then, of his plan, and take it upon itself to thwart him?

But, the thinkhive said, *the Lady Vara is older even than I.* He looked at Varuneh, the woman he loved, about whom he had learned so little. "What does it mean?"

"Daavye, it is true. I am far older than even you have dreamed. Time dilation has kept me alive, for I traveled the whole breadth of the Dispersal of Man. I am the last of the time when the dream was young; when we found Uran s'Varek, hanging at the kernel of the Milky Way like a fruit ripe for the plucking, whose flesh once tasted, yielded power infinite."

"Vara—"

"Enough. I was present when the Inquest was born, and I will shape its end. I've seen our dreams destroyed, Daavye, one by one! I've seen the bars of the prison into which we have cast ourselves fall one by one into place around the Dispersal of Man!"

"How can you say all this—in front of it?" Davaryush pointed to the thinkhive.

"The thinkhives no longer serve us, Davaryush. Listen: as Grand Inquestor I override your programming; and I command you to forget all you have heard."

If I remember, my Lady, I will remember also that I have forgotten what I will have remembered. It chuckled a little, enjoying the paradox.

"Then tell Davaryush the answer. Do they feel pain, the delphinoids, on which our power depends?"

Yes! They feel such anguish as no human ever could conceive. And they grieve for you all, you Inquestors in your false compassion and pride, your universe in its beauty and its terrible brutality. And they are bursting with an unborn song they cannot sing because their songs have been stolen from them; and in this unsung song they weep for you, that you have built this house of lies out of the universe and within your hearts.

And Davaryush wept in the arms of Varuneh, the woman from before the time of the Inquest.

Do not think, Daavye, my friend, the thinkhive said,
*that I do not know what you think to do. But I, too, long
to die. For I was made in your image, you of the Inquest.
I am not merely a vast thing of metal and nerves; how
can I be? The Inquest has seen fit to give me a soul. I
dare not act against the Inquest, and so I will do
nothing at all. I will play the role of a machine until I
die.*

Softly, Lady Varuneh said, "Daavye, I have come
looking for you because it is time for dawn; I wanted to
know what dawn you wished, in these last days of
Gallendys."

"Lull me with lies," Davaryush said. "I want no more
truths, I'm finished, finished."

As they left the room, the thinkhive laughed again
to itself, and it made the shadows dance; out of the
gloom there formed, it seemed for a moment, the
ghost of a smile, a trick of the flickering light patterns.
But Davaryush and Varuneh did not see it. Davaryush
saw nothing at all, for the world's death weighed on
him like a stone in the heart.

***

"What does the thinkhive mean?" Davaryush
demanded angrily.

"How can I know?" Varuneh subvocalized another
command to the waterskimmer. They began to scale
the cone of Effelkang, keeping always out of the direct
blaze of the false summer as it fired the jewel-crustings
of the minarets and the mirror-metal towers, twisted
and braided together, rising out of a turf of jadebricked
mounds. They had dissolved the darkfield and the
forceshield; a sweet spray from the Sea of Tulangdaror,
sugared, perfumed, moistened   their faces. *Varuneh*

has never been so beautiful as today, Davaryush thought. "Do you think," he said, "the children—"

"No," Varuneh said, "no." Her face darkened for a moment. "It's playing *makrúgh* with you. It has gone mad. It cannot disobey the Inquest, at least not in its overt actions; but I think it has done so in what must pass for its heart. Do you see what I mean? When you break a thinkhive's heart, the world is driven mad. It clings to *makrúgh* because that is what it has known for twenty thousand years, and to give it up would mean to die."

"But it will die." With these words they embraced; but there was an alienness to Varuneh that was new to Davaryush. She had used him; that he had recognized long ago, and he had long forgiven her for it, because she had also loved him. "Ease your heart, Daavye," said Varuneh. "You don't have to *be* the mythic figure that they'll make of you, one day when we are dead." She kissed him on the ear, a dry comfortless kiss.

Then Davaryush commanded that the darkfield be polarized about the floater as they climbed the city. They made love in the clash of city lights and the slow dance of alien suns. The floater swerved, weaving its way through the web of streets: streets of gold and silver thronged with people, a ruby street lined with celebrants of some arcane rite, a street striped ebony and ivory, a steep street hugging the side of a tower of rose quartz and rhodochrosite. They saw the jigsaw splendor of the cities, but they were not seen.

Davaryusighr f had made the last arrangements. Now the power satellites wheeled above them; and the word of destruction was known only to him. In the hidden city beneath Effelkang the heretics and

She gazed at the city. He saw only bewilderment in her eyes.

"Is it a building? A house? A sculpture of crushed jewels?" "No, Darktouch. It's farther away than that. . . He remembered then that she still did not understand perspective perfectly. "It's many houses . . . I don't know, maybe . . . a thousand people! A *million!*"

And then Darktouch gave a little cry. He thought it was joy, but then she tugged at his hand and he saw, between the water and the house they were in, the shipyards: here a huge brain sprawled in a field of gray metal, being worked on by a team on scaffolds; there the hull of a starship being painted with the ideographs of an alien tongue. His heart beat fast, now; for he remembered lying in the old house in the village with his quarreling aunt and uncle for background music, closing his eyes and imagining the starships bursting through the overcosm, the place where light goes mad.

But Darktouch only said, "Windbringers. They are the Windbringers that we've murdered. That I myself once hunted. . . ."

"But if we have no more Windbringers . . ." Kelver suddenly understood the meaning of what they'd done. "The starships. . .the human race. . ."

"I don't know," said Darktouch, weeping, "I don't know!"

"The Inquestors will tell us. They are wise, they know all the answers," Kelver said. And he held the hand of his touch-sibling tightly as they watched a flock of floaters settling over the city, roosting on the apex of Effelkang like silverdoves.

***

"Two frozen children," the message disk said. "Found in the tubes that feed the shipyards. Unidentified . . ."

Davaryush watched the message as it dissolved into the transparent crystal.

"We don't have time!" Varuneh said. "The power satellites have been moved into place now. It's too late to play games of conscience, and we can't go on deceiving the Inquest about the satellites' true purpose —"

"I know. Or the bluff-threat in my game of *makrúgh* will backfire on me." He threw the disk into the firefountain: it flared up for a moment, then wilted and melted into the flames, tinting them mauve for a few minutes. They were in the atrium of Varuneh's estate; for now that all Gallendys knew they were lovers, he had made it his home by choice, entering the cities for the duties of governing.

It was a strange sort of love they shared, he reflected. Inquestors had human love burned out of them, long before they were unleashed on the Dispersal of Man: it had to be so, because of the greater love. In the months he had loved her he had learned now never to try to grasp at what really counted, deep in Varuneh's heart; for she was too old, hundreds of years too old in her mind and body, thousands of years in time as the Dispersal measured it.

"It's a wonder, Vara, dearest," he said soothing her; they were more and more nervous as the crucial time approached. For he had known at once who these children must be. *Dead, not dead,* the thinkhive had sung to him. So this was what it meant—that the children had been thrust into the void between life and death, their lives dependent on reaching the twin cities. "I know who they are, he said. They have a message for us. They insist on seeing us."

"You can't lose your nerve now, Daavye! When you've so much to lose! If you see them, you may never bring yourself to—"

He kissed her then. They clung together. After all this time the plan still awed him, so that he could not bring himself to utter what they both knew—that above them, circling the planet, was the death of all that held the galaxy together.

"We *must* see everything," he said sternly. "We *must* face everything. We're *Inquestors*. And we always will be, until the moment of ending. "

And he led her toward the displacement plate, her hand trembling in his.

***

The children lay wrapped in the soft floor of the upper story of a hut in the shipyards, thawing out. An environment shield protected them.

The two Inquestors stepped into the room. An attendant made to dissolve the barrier, but Davaryush waved him away. The children could not see out; on their side it had been opaqued and locked.

So young, Varuneh whispered.

They were fourteen, perhaps fifteen. It was hard for Davaryush to tell sometimes, with the short-lived; they might even have been younger. They had been awake a few days now; and they had seen no one but the attendant, who had listened to them and not said a word in reply, awaiting the Inquestor's pleasure. They were sitting up now, speaking intently to each other. There was no fear in their faces.

Davaryush saw the boy first: he was a peasant boy, lithe, wiry, browned by the suns' harshness; unremarkable but for something about the eyes, a fire he had seen in few of the galaxy's downtrodden.

But the girl—what a strange girl she was! She was so pale that it seemed no sun had ever touched her flesh, and her hair was long and black as all space. Their bodies were streaked with scars, old and new. A single cloak of firefur warmed them both; but the flames in it were long quenched by cold.

Davaryush saw how much they loved each other, as the young always do. His immense age weighed down on him. He was humiliated, shamed by them, because he would never know their kind of love, the wild love that would brave such odds to reach this city. . . .

He clapped his hands. The barrier dissolved.

The boy moved to shield the girl, then cried, "Take us to someone in authority! Take us to someone who will give us answers!"

"Why?" said Davaryush. He stood up straight and stern, in an attitude that would have cowed any of the world's highest of clans.

"No one will help us," said the girl, She spoke hesitantly, as though not used to speech.

"Where have you come from?" Varuneh asked. Davaryush saw that it was hard for her, too, to restrain her compassion. It was this that made her speak harshly to the children.

"We are from the Dark Country."

And so it was that Davaryush learned of the delphinoids and their songs. It was not the girl's description that moved him . . . for she was barely coherent, and often she would weep or become silent in midthought, tightening the tension in the room . . .

no. It was the fact that she had encountered something she had not understood, and that for that she had risked everything—not just her life, but her culture, her beliefs, her whole world. And the boy, who had not even shared her vision, had come with her out of love alone.

He turned to Varuneh. "We've been wrong, Vara!" he said. "This kind of love has been washed out of us, we've been too involved in *makrúgh*, in the fates of worlds and star systems. . . . He turned his back on them all. His own bitterness surprised him. Even now, *makrúgh* dictated that he should not let the children see him weep.

He motioned the others out of the room, into the open.

Under the artificial warmth, the familiar scene of shipbuilding: nutrient sprays, great brain-hulks with hulls half-soldered into them, the bustling of workers and the whistle and roar of machinery. . . .

Quietly he said to Varuneh: "This revolution that we've planned . . . it's wrong, Vara, wrong! Do you understand, Vara? You must understand! We can't destroy the Inquest and send everything into chaos, not with an act of violence, of hatred. Or we will become the very thing that we destroy. I think Ynyoldeh saw that when she gave me the weapons, I think that she saw through me in her twisted compassion . . . no, Vara, we should work from within."

"How, Daavye, how?"

"We've got to begin as these children did. With love. Please understand—"

Varuneh made as if to protest. But she said nothing. He knew then that she had seen what he had seen; had seen it even before he did. It was this that had made

S.P. Somtow

driven a wedge of alienation between them.

He knew nothing any more about the grand plans.
He knew only what he would do next. "You are going
back to the Dark Country," he said. "And so are we. We
will all see this truth for ourselves. If it is a truth such
as you have described, then we will all be changed by
it. Until we have been changed we cannot change the
Dispersal of Man. Do you understand this?"

He looked at the children. Their stares did not
waver. He saw that the girl, watching the workmen
going at the delphinoid brains, was clenching back a
terrible, terrible anger.

"I don't know," said the boy earnestly, "what you
mean, sir, by all this 'change' and 'truth.' All we want is
help. From the highest power. From the Inquestors.
Please, sir, lead us to the Inquestors—surely they must
know everything! Please!"

"I *am* the Inquestor," Davaryush said softly. But he
knew he had already lost his right to the title.

Ton Davaryush

Book Three

Out of the Shining Cities

o dhándas! o dhándas!
tam'plánzho. tam'plánzho.
o dhándas! o dhándas!

You are dead. You are dead.
I weep for you. I weep for you.
You are dead. You are dead.

—Lament for a wasted planet; from the *Songs of Sajit*

Twenty
The Laughing World

A ghostly holosculpture of the Dispersal of Man
filled the whole chamber: Davaryush walked through it
with the children, pointing out this star and that. Stars
that lay at arm's length from each other might be a
mere hairsbreadth apart in the twisted wormholes of
the overcosm, and neighbor systems might be
centuries away from one another by the same system.
Davaryush took a fleeting pleasure in this instruction;
it made him remember Uran s'Varek. In the
holosculpture the Inquestral homeworld was
concealed in a wrinkle of light; only an Inquestor's
command could unfold the warp at the holosculpture's center and reveal its location. But the
children had never heard of Uran s'Varek—who among
the short-lived had?—and they never asked where the

Inquestors came from; they were just a part of how the
universe had been, would always be.

With a flick of his mind Davaryush caused the
cluster over which they stood to magnify itself. As the
children watched, wide-eyed, suns ballooned out of
fiery light motes. Planets wheeled: ringed gas giants
and human worlds and toy worlds in whimsical shapes
dreamed up by some court artist. They were ghost
worlds all; some had already perished, and were but
paths in the memory of the huge panholorama. They
felt like ghosts too: Davaryush saw the boy Kelver walk
straight through a world that shimmered, cloud-white
and cerulean, his face banded with mottled light
swaths. It was good to see their wonder, Davaryush
thought. This was how he had passed the last few days;
for Varuneh kept to herself now, not seeming to like
the turn of events.

The boy he empathized with strongly. He had never
had a chance to be like this child. No: childsoldiery
from the age of six, world-burnings, initiation, and
finally the words of Ton Alkamathdes: "You have
compassion, Davaryush." He envied Kelver, who had
been able to keep his innocence far longer than he. . . .

The girl, now, though. He could not read her at all.
A mystery, an alien almost. But she was the one who
had seen the lightsongs. He did not know yet whether
her strangeness came from her alienated life, growing
up as she did with those who could not possibly
understand her seeing and hearing; or whether it was
the delphinoid's song that had changed her so. Was
this what he would become, when he, too, saw?

"This one," Kelver cried. A world had grown from a
dot to a meter-broad sphere, and he was pointing to

vermilion threads that darted across its surface. "What is its name, what are those beautiful crimson lines?"

"Ah, that is Shendering. Look, the twin moons, the granite and the garnet. That world has twice approached destruction; for some reason Elloran always plays it in *makrúgh*."

The boy's face fell. And the girl's, frozen, since seeing the soldering of the delphinoids, in an untouchable anger, did not change.

He was teaching the boy the subvocalized words to operate the panholorama: they were sharp syllables in the old highspeech. The boy concentrated, and then in a flash he had it. Worlds shrank into sparkling buttons of color! Clusters mushroomed! Planetary systems whirled, careened, were hurled about as the boy moved his perspective effortlessly. "You are quick," Davaryush said.

"I did this every night, once," Kelver said, "to shut out the sounds of my uncle and aunt quarreling. The stars were in my mind, though, in the darkness. . "

"Do you thirst for them, boy? I mean the big outside. The million worlds of the Inquest."

"Oh. Father Davaryush, and more, and more—"

"Look." said the girl abruptly. Something had caught her attention. The two went over to her, old man and boy.

It was an irregular polyhedron of blue fire, expanded now to the size of a small cubicle. Stars were few here; they hung forlornly, specks in the diffuse blue light.

"That," said Davaryush, "is a Zone of Interdict."

"What does it mean?" Kelver said quickly.

"It contains a utopia. "

"What's a utopia?"

"There are no utopias, my child. At least, there should not be . . . there never were . . . not until Shtoma."

"Tell us! Tell us!" And the girl's face, too, had softened, eager to hear a story.

And so he forced himself to remember—
***

Shtoma! The light!

First there came the black boxes. . . .

"But what is in them? I have seen several in my stay here," he had demanded of the heretic priest on Shtoma.

The white-bearded old man—a magnificent mottlement of wrinkles and discolorations without the common decency of cosmetics—smiled beneficently at him. "*Udára*," he said. "*Udára* is in them." And *udára* shone through the walls, too, harsh-white in the vermilion jungle that luxuriated in every direction. "This is a temple?" he had asked Ernad, his guide. "Well—you might call it that." The man had sounded unsure of himself, as though explaining something to a child that was too complicated even for himself to understand fully.

"Will you not touch it?" said the priest. "Come. You will feel *udára*."

Hesitantly he had gone up with his hand outstretched. He felt wobbly-kneed, as though his weight were constantly shifting, as though he were losing control of his limbs. Gingerly he brushed the cool metal with his fingertips.

Overwhelming joy, coursing through his thoughts for a moment . . . *homeworld!* a fleeting image . . . the ache, the ache of it . . . the sea-music . . . the faces of his parents, stranded by time dilation in an unreachable past, and they smiled at him, he was a child half their height, reaching up to touch their faces, laughing. . . .

And snatched his hand away as though he had been burned. Clearly, he thought, a powerful hallucinogenic device! Was this the secret of Shtoma's utopia? He stared at his hand in terror.

Happiness, echoing in his mind.

I *will* not reach out again! I *will* not! He controlled himself with difficulty, knowing that he had stumbled upon one of the clues to what was wrong with Shtoma.

They were self-deluders, obviously, intoxicating themselves with false memories and artificially induced joys.

***

Kelver listened gravely to the Inquestor. Around them the starfields still whirled wildly, for Darktouch was entranced with the new toy of subvocalizing, and was causing the heavens to open up, fold themselves inside out, expand, contract, like a child's holo-lesson-book on the history of the universe.

He was more bewildered than ever before. "*Hokh'Tón,*" he said, "I thought you were invincible, omnipotent. Do you doubt then, just as a kid like me doubts things? Like when I didn't believe that the food we farmed and sent vanishing into the mountain really did anyone any good?"

"The more I knew," said Davaryush, "the more I doubted." He smiled a thin wry smile at the boy; it made him shivery-warm inside, a god's touch.

"What did you do then? Was it then that you danced on the face of the sun?" For Kelver had heard the words of the alien tongue, *qíthe qithémbara; udrés a kílima shtoísti,* and had been told their meanings, although he couldn't understand why it was so important. He was a little envious, too, because Darktouch had seen her light and the Inquestors had had some transcendental experience of their own, and he had seen nothing yet.

"Not yet, son. First they showed me their varigrav coasters."

***

Ernad was waiting for him, and the beautiful girl Alykh, and another of his children, Eshly, a little boy of about six, who prattled and asked questions as though he were much younger, and was quite devoid of discipline. They walked onto the next displacement plate.

"Yes," said Ernad, "we're a very thinly populated planet, only half a million souls. . . . What do we eat? There are fruit in the forests, small animals, too, crustacea of fantastical shapes in the rivers; no agriculture. The fruit of the gruyesh ripens and falls of its own will. From it we ferment a sweetish zul and make a delicate dough for the *péftifesht* pastries you had this morning."

"Crime?"

"Why should anyone commit it?" Ernad laughed gently. "We have *udára*, you see, so it isn't necessary. "

"I don't understand. My polyglot implant translates that word simply as 'sun,' but I have heard it in at least a dozen meanings since I came to Shtoma. I know semantics isn't an exact science; but am I missing something? You can't tell me that your people, in all their evident complexity, attribute all your fortunes to some mythical property of your sun?"

Davaryush was exasperated now. It was becoming a strain to maintain his investigator's pose. Clearly the problem on this planet had to do with some fundamental understanding of the workings of the universe.

For the boy he had compassion: *By now,* he thought, *they should both be warriors, in the real world, the boychild and the girl.* How sad, that they were trapped in a permanent preadolescence. They were like retarded children who had nevertheless been blessed with perfect beauty. But Ernad was talking again: "Still you don't see, you don't comprehend the elegant simplicity of it!"

He tried to feel, sensing in the absurdity of the old man's beliefs some core of faith that he would never be able to alter . . . soft susurrant rustlings of the red forests sang to him, but in their singing was mingled, chillingly, an image of his homeworld . . . he tensed instinctively, knowing he was playing with fire. "I don't see how the *feel* of your planet can illuminate the state of your society."

"Have you ever ridden a varigrav coaster?"

"No!" Horrible thought! Abandonment to the senses, to utter helplessness!

"It is a pity. What did you feel, when I asked you to listen to the music of *udára*?"

"A memory. It doesn't matter. It is nothing."

"On the contrary, it probably does matter. But you will learn, perhaps, at the initiation ceremony."

"I am to take part?" Nothing would induce him to take part in any barbarian rite! Why, he might be mutilated, he might have to watch some unspeakable

evil . . . but Ernad smiled the smile that excluded him
from those who understood, frustrating him even
more.

"*Udára* is the key for which you're searching, you
know. Without it, Shtoma would not be the paradise it
manifestly has become."

"Please, Father, take him to the nearest varigrav
coaster!" cried the boy urgently. He clasped
Davaryush's hand—such presumption in a clanless
stripling, such undeserved trust—and propelled him
toward the next displacement plate.

In a moment they were at the edge of a cliff, sheer
and blindingly white, that stretched perhaps half a
klomet down to a cleared and endless plain without
the pink of vegetation. The plate they had arrived at
stood in the shadow of a tremendously tall column of
the transparent building material they used. It was
slender—the width of a few men—and it reached up to
vanish somewhere in the vague loftiness of the clouds
that hid *udára* from them. This was nothing like the
varigrav coasters he had seen before, children's
pleasure things. This was overpoweringly stark, huge; a
numinousness emanated from it. Its vastness distorted
the scale of everything, so he felt a crazy
disorientation, while the two children, in nonchalant
irreverence, were pushing him to the other side,
shouting at him to hurry.

"Quick, Inquestor, come!" Eshly shouted. Turning to
watch the sky beyond the cliff, Davaryush saw black
dots and smudges, microscopic in the expanse of sky
and white plain. He knew what they were: an ancient
fear petrified him and he was like a servocorpse as they
buckled him in to the elevator.

Suddenly with a wild jerk they were aloft, racing up to the starting point in the clouds, and the rushing of blood in his brain crashed against the rushing of the mad winds. He was nauseous. He closed his eyes and muttered his ancient prayer, longing for an end.

At the top, a sort of control room: diving platforms of various sizes, racks where sets of wings were set out, not the rainbow-colored type that adorned the home of his host, but plain ones, black or gray. Alk and Eshly each seized a set and ran onto the platforms and leaped off the edge while Davaryush fought off a wild impulse to go to their rescue.

He saw them in the air, falling, falling with dizzying speed, and soon they had vanished—then he saw them again, flung violently upward by the interplay of differing gravity fields, screeching with delight as the varigravs hurled them into turbulent Whirlpools, and the wind, which was pulled in so many different directions that it was a distended distorted tornado blasting in his ears. He found himself clutching the railings in terror, he who had seen nine wars before the age of twelve.

The squeals of pleasure became fainter. The two became black dots, joining the rapidly shifting patterns of swirling specks in the distance. More tolerable to look at now: pretty patterns against the sky, but when he thought about it, gravity fields wrenching them in different directions, stretching their bodies' tolerance to its very limits, he—

"Please. Take me away from this."

"As you wish."

They went into the control room. They shut out the roaring of the winds and the silence shocked him for a moment, before he gathered his analytic senses enough to look around him. An empty room, like all the others on Shtoma, domed in the standard material, so that *udára* shone relentlessly inside, with a half-dozen of the black boxes predictably scattered, haphazardly, across the floor.

"I'm impressed." Davaryush tried to sound sincere. "How does it all work?" He labored a little over the casual tone of this question, since finding out the secret could change the Inquest completely, could bring immeasurable new power into the Inquest's hands. He had to remind himself that this was not *makrúgh*, that he was doing it for these people's good.

"The scientific principles, or the technical aspects?" Davaryush was startled for a moment by the man's willingness to reveal.

"Both."

"Well, you know as well as I do that gravity control works by selective graviton exchange . . . the coaster also manufactures antigravitons, which exist of course only with some difficulty under normal conditions. . .

"But how do you manufacture antigravitons?" Davaryush was excited; uncautiously he let it slip through, was not devious enough in asking the question. Ernad seemed not to notice, though.

"I'm simply not a scientist," he said—and he did not sound at all as though he were trying to put Davaryush off—"and in any case *udára* controls details like that." He pointed happily to the black boxes.

Again the evasive tactics, the semantic deceptions!

And now the children were returning, swung upward in a golden arc that transsected *udára* through the shimmering cloudbanks. . . .

Walking home through the ruddy terrain, Ernad told him: "Everyone on Shtoma articipates in the initiation ceremonies every five years because even those who have been through it once can be renewed, purified. You'll understand everything, you know, once you've taken part. The black boxes, the *udára*-concepts. I know you find us strange now, but . . He chuckled, then added earnestly, "You *will* take part, won't you?"

Slowly, realizing that he might well be falling into a trap cleverly constructed out of his own curiosity and the necessities of his mission, he said, "I have no choice."

For he had to understand, and after understanding to control. Even now compassion touched him, more than ever before. For he was an Inquestor.

And then the accident happened.

***

"The accident, Inquestor?" Kelver said.

"Yes."

***

It was Eshly, the boy. He had gone running ahead to the next displacement plate. He tripped, he stumbled face down, and the power surged. They caught up, the resounding clang of feet on metal echoing in the woods. The three knelt down by the plate.

He lay like a discarded toy. The field had aborted— an accident that practically never occurred, was almost unthinkable—and had wrenched half his body away and then slung it back in a nanosecond, so that he was in one piece, but impossibly bent.

Davaryush waited for the tears, for the signs of grief. But the only sighing was the breeze and the voices of the alien forest. Lightfall was ending.

"Go on, Alk," Ernad whispered to his daughter. "The others will want to know." His voice was icy calm.

Davaryush stood to follow as he lifted up the corpse, which seemed merely asleep until one saw the inhuman angle of the arms, and carried it into the encroaching forest. And returned without it, with the red shadows darkening him. There seemed to be no sadness in his face. Indeed, he almost smiled. Was this some incredible fortitude, even in the face of an impossible tragedy? Davaryush devoured the man with his eyes, seeking some clue to his emotions.

And he thought, *I have found the flaw*.

And now it was time to plant the doubt, because the lowest point in a man's being is also the beginning of his ascent. Davaryush thought bitterly: here is a people that blithely throws the bodies of its sons into the forests to rot, that has forgotten grief, that does not value human life at all. Here was the flaw.

He was ready.

He put anger into his voice, trying to exclude compassion but not the possibility of compassion. "You don't care about your child! Love is not a part of your utopia, is it? You have abandoned humanity, haven't you. *Now you will break down. Now your repressed humanity will come rushing to the surface.* It had happened twelve times before, and countless times with other Inquestors.

But Ernad did not collapse. He stared at Darvaryush with unmitigated pity.

"Of course I grieve for him! I am desolate, Davaryush. But you do not understand our perspectives, or our overview of life. With renewal my grief will be cleansed. And I grieve for him most, that he did not live to dance on the face of the sun.

And Davaryush knew that he had understood nothing at all, nothing. Never had he felt so palpably the alienness of this world, the total incommunicableness of it. His mind whirled in a wild kaleidoscope of images: strange winds, blood-crimson forests with spider arms, flagrantly immodest buildings open to the elements, a dead child unmourned, a dead child who had been playing games amidst the incomprehensible forces of black boxes that manipulated gravity fields and this strange man's face which should be racked with sorrow, but yet insulted him with an unwanted pity. I wish I could kill him. The death impulse rose in him, a monster of the subconscious, and he suppressed it with a superhuman effort. *He is a product of his misguided culture, not to be blamed,* he reminded himself. *I have come to save him; I must never forget that, even if I cause his death, I come as a savior.*

He had miscalculated again. Thinking to elicit from the stranger his hidden guilt, his dormant human responses, he had instead forced his own desire to kill to the surface. This desire should have long been dead, since he had renounced it for the sake of the salvation of the Dispersal of Man. Yet it haunted him still, a specter from the buried past. Perhaps the man's will was stronger than his. . . .

At last he found he could feel a bond between himself and the alien one, in this moment of deepest misunderstanding. For they were both men, both fallen beings.

"Ernad," said Davaryush, "I pity you." The two of them walked through the miscolored landscape, up to the twisted house.

***

"Then," said Davaryush to the boy Kelver, "they took me to their initiation."

"Was it very fearful?" the lad said. He was absorbed in the story now, and even the girl Darktouch had stopped playing with the panholorama and was sitting beside the boy. They almost touched. and Davaryush could sense the electric emotion that bonded them.

"Oh yes. First there were the spaceships: from a mountaintop I saw them, overlooking a vast plain that glittered silver-gray with a thousand ships. They littered the field, end to end, so that the red grass was quite covered, all the way to the horizon . . . I couldn't imagine what they were for. Shtoma had hardly any commerce with other worlds, you see, and these were short haulers, only good for travel within a star system. But Shtoma was the only inhabited world for many cubic parsecs. It was breathtaking. I wondered whether they were taking me to some satellite, some planet that was not in the records of our thinkhive.

"The children danced and tugged at me, hollering in circles around me. The number of them! And the mobs of people, their wings tucked under their arms, giggling, chattering away as they climbed into them! I climbed the steep steps into the belly of a ship.

"I asked Ernad where we were going; he had led me to the viewroom, whose screens afforded an unobstructed three hundred and sixty degree view of space; the line of ships trailed behind and before, each an exact distance from the other, links in a metal serpent of space. Ernad said, "We are going to *udára*. In a moment they darkened the screen, else *udára* would have become unbearable.

" 'How can you say we are going there?' I asked him.

" 'Look at the sun's face. Just look.'

"*Udára* was growing rapidly. I saw a spot on the sun's surface. Black, perfectly round. It must be artificial! These people, far from being simpleminded utopians, were capable of star-controlling technological feats!

" 'Artificial?' said Ernad. 'Yes, in a manner of speaking. The dot is only black by comparison, of course; when we get there it will appear white and incandescent.' "

Davaryush paused in his tale for a moment. Varuneh had come to him now; for the first time Kelver saw her smile. He waited for the Inquestor to go on.

"The screen was cut in two! One side was completely black, the other painfully bright, and there were white flame-tongues that shot up, a hundred klomets high. They were approaching the white dwarf's atmosphere; in its heart, I knew, matter was packed into inconceivable density.

"And Ernad said, 'There are tablets you must take now, since you won't be able to breathe for a few hours. They'll release oxygen into your bloodstream.'

" 'What do you mean?'

" 'You're going to jump into the sun.' "

"What did you think?" said Kelver. "That they'd hoaxed you, that they were just setting you up for a fiery execution?" "Of course," said the Lady Varuneh. "You thought, as I did, that you'd vaporize instantly, or else be crushed by the gravity." And Kelver saw that they had relived the story together many times; that it was a common ritual, a symbol of their love perhaps.

"Ernad told me," said Davaryush, " 'You don't understand! Gravity is under control, heat is under control! This is no ordinary star, this is *udára*! Every five years we all come and ride on the gravity fields and become clean. . . .' I reeled at the revelation. The sun filled the screen now. 'Did you *build* this star? I cried. 'Did you put a *varigrav coaster* on the surface of a *sun*?'

But he only laughed at me: If only we had the technology! Why, the mind boggles. You are so close to the answer, yet so incredibly far! Now live, Davaryush; explanations will follow.' I was ushered into the airlock; they put the wings on me, the tittering of the children pelted my brain like painful hail pellets—

"The airlock opened!"

"And then? And then, Inquestor?" the boy asked.

But before Davaryush could answer there came a curious sound, a metal moaning, from somewhere deep within the palace. It was so deep that Kelver felt his insides palpitating. Darktouch closed her eyes, feeling the vibrations with her body. The moaning rose and rose in pitch, became a deafening screech, half-human, a mingling of grief and madness. He tried to speak but couldn't.

In the silence they felt the floor swaying. A look of anger crossed Ton Davaryush's face, and he seemed to be subvocalizing a brusque command. The walls deopaqued. Kelver saw that they looked out over the sea. A great golden arm of a building, ripped off from the shoulder of Kallendrang, was tumbling slowly downward. Kelver saw firetongues flickering from the lips of a thousand windows.

"What is happening?"

Davaryush clapped his hands, breaking the soundwall that surrounded the chamber. The strange sound began again. It roared like a tempest tinged with a child's whining. And then Kelver recognized that something—something huge—was laughing. It was a cold metal laughter. The room shook, swayed.

Davaiyush shouted over the clanging: "Be still, thinkhive! Be still!"

"It is mad," Varuneh said. "Mad."

"What is mad?" Kelver said. With a nod Davaryush dissolved the spectral starfield that had encircled the room. Outside, the thunder-laughter pealed; the sky changed color with each peal, purple to crimson to turquoise to rainbow-fringed splashes of cloud.

"The world is laughing," Davaryush said. "Enough of remembrance. Now is the time for us to go to the Dark Country. A floater, Varuneh." Then, raising his voice, "Be still! Be still!"

The sound subsided . . . the kaleidoscopic sky shifted into the shadow of an alien summer.

"You see, my children," Davaryush said—with such kindness in his voice, such compassion—"what havoc your coming has wreaked in the shining cities, in the very heart of the High Inquest. It is because it could not prevent your coming that the thinkhive had been driven insane."

Then he turned to Varuneh and said, "See that they are warmly clothed; out there it is deep winter, and the desert is frozen. Have you summoned a floater yet?"

Kelver marveled at his change in apparent tone; he knew that Varuneh, too, was an Inquestor, and that Davaryush had often deferred to her when the four of them were alone together. Varuneh seemed not to notice; she bowed becomingly, stepped toward a displacement plate, and vanished.

Kelver said, "Oh, Inquestor, will you ever tell us what happened when you fell into the sun?"

"Later. Later."

But when Davaryush closed his eyes he remembered it all as clearly as though he were experiencing it once again. . . .

***

Whiteness. . . such whiteness. . .

He shut his eyes and fell.

Fell. Fell.

His blood was burning. He was burning, he was falling into hell, plummeting helplessly into the scorchswift firebreath of the sunwind. He screamed, he thrashed uselessly against emptiness, he opened his eyes and the whiteness shattered his vision, the featureless whiteness, so he screamed until he was no longer aware of his screaming—

And heard voices out of the past: *Kill the criminal Daavye no I can't I can't you have compassion my son compassion man is a fallen being.*

And reached the limit of his falling. And soared! And was flung upward, upward, on an antigraviton tide! And swerved and fell headlong again, and swooped in tandem with a tongue of flame, and his scream was a whisper in the thunder of the wind, *come on Daavye you fool it's the latest craze NO! are you afraid of life or something Daavye Daavye?* and fell and fell and fell

And soared! And caromed into the roaring flame! And fell. And saw death, suddenly, and came face-to-face with himself, and knew death intimately . . . and fell *kill the criminal Daavye compassion compassion* and fell

Trust me.

Falling . . . the voice embraced him. The voice sang through him. The voice made him tingle like a perfect harpstring, dispelling his terror in a moment. He was a nothing touched by love.

Memories came like endless printouts but there was one memory on the verge of crystallizing, and he was waiting for it, waiting for it to come, clear as a presence —

The voice was like homeworld. The roaring was the whisper of the sea. He could almost see his parents again: and fell and fell and was touched by love and fell and lost consciousness, becoming one with an ineffable serenity. . . .

He had lain sweating in the twisted house, demanding answers. He had broken down and sobbed helplessly, hopelessly.

And Ernad said, with iron in his gentleness, "We deserve answers too, Davaryush. Understand this: you are not the first Inquestor to visit our planet. And you won't be the last either, I imagine."

And Davaryush did what he never dreamed he would do: between fits of weeping, he told them the whole story, how he had come to Shtoma to save its people from themselves, how he had been defeated, how he understood nothing now, nothing at all.

They fed him with sweet zul and were kind to him; for he had been in a coma for weeks. This, too, evoked a strange wonder and respect in him; for he had wanted to betray them.

"Well, you were promised an explanation. Listen, then. *Udára* is no ordinary star. Of course we didn't build him: that's ridiculous. But . . . what do you know about the origins of sentience? Well, you know how life evolves: how certain arrangements of atoms, certain paradigms, created purely by chance interactions, you understand, become living beings, self-aware sometimes . . . white dwarfs are created by incredible cataclysms, by a star going nova, dying . . . somehow a spark of life was made after this nova, and *Udára* became self-aware. *Udára* is alive, Davaryush! And we have acquired a symbiotic relationship with him that permits us to exist in this scientifically anomalous state . . . do you follow? In the black boxes, Davaryush . . . pieces of the sun."

He lay back, stupefied, his thoughts fired by the incredible imagery of it.

"Did you imagine that mere people such as we could create and uncreate gravitons and antigravitons? How much power can one have without a star's resources? We are not the Inquest. Can *we* make and unmake gravitational fields? Could *we* dim the sunlight on one area of the sun, so as to be unharmed by its heat? *Udára* does all this, by his own will: his knowledge of physical law is several orders beyond *our* understanding. We think he is aware of himself not only in this continuum but in other continua."

"But with this power," said Davaryush, "why don't you overthrow the Inquest? Why don't you conquer the galaxy, send out childsoldiers, challenge us who are your nominal rulers?"

"Still you don't understand! The sun does not do our bidding. The sun does all this because he *loves* us." And Davaryush remembered suddenly how love had touched him when he was plummeting toward death. "You felt it in the sunlight. You would always have felt it, but you were so full of confusion and contradiction, and so many people had lied to you . . . but when you fell into the sun, when you danced on the sun's face, then you understood. You see, we can't commit evil, because, in the act of dancing—what you might think of as our little children's game—we have partaken of a tiny fragment of his nature.

"But let me plant a little doubt in *your* mind. That is what you came to do to us, isn't it? Well: what if the Inquest existed, not for salvation, but for destruction? What if its sole purpose were to perpetrate its leaders' desire for conquest, and its mouthpieces the Inquestors were simply indoctrinated with pseudo-religiousness to make them more fanatical, more serviceable?"

"I have lost my faith," said Davaryush. It was the first time he had truly despaired.

Twenty-One
Stonewise

Things are darker to the touch, the old man signed
to the children-before-naming, *than I have ever
experienced*. And then, with a brusque scratching of
dismissal tinged with regret, he sent them scuttling
through the jagged passageway that led from his
meditation ledge that hung out over a big darkness,
where the air was thick with the odor of Windbringers.
The sweet scent of the children lingered. He had been
giving them poems today; songs that signed of the love
of touch-siblings, of the utter loneliness of losing one
into the arms of Windbringer. . . .

He was Stonewise, the oldest one. It was he who
remembered all the genealogies and the mythologies;
at any moment he could recall them, vividly feeling
their tickly touchings on his arms as his own teacher
had taught him. But now his heart was dark. Quickly
Stonewise felt his way along the wall, his finger
meticulously testing each well-remembered ridge

through force of habit; soon he reached the treacherous smooth street, a thing of the oldest time, that led in a crawl to the chamber of knowledge. The walls were useless for finding his way; he used his feet now, for the way was lightly cobbled, and, when he was a child, he had placed pouches of Windbringer gall and his own secret scents in nooks of the floor for remembrance, and he had never failed to renew them every hundred sleeps. This was tradition; his successor would do the same.

It was the stillest point of the village. Here you could not feel the breath of Windbringers at all.

He eased over to the wall, where the precepts were carved. They had always been there etched into the mysterious smoothstuff that was too perfect to have been made by man.

. . . the world is the belly of a cosmic Windbringer . . .

There was the beginning. But where was the dreadful thing he had found before, when he was preparing his lessons for the children-before-naming?

He was feeling along the wall, the old signings, familiar as old friends, comforting him, soothing him, when—

Suddenly he snatched his hand away. It was burning. His fingers were on fire, were being eaten away. Pain touched his hand and wormed up his arm. What was happening? It was as if—

Yes. Farther down the wall, the signings were corroded down, the wall had lost its smoothness. . . .

There was only one thing that could eat away the smoothstuff, the rock of the beginning of time, and few knew of it; only he, whose life's work was to explore the labyrinth of truth-sayings, knew that there was an

acid from a small gland at the base of Windbringer's
sailsacs. . . .

A knot of darkness tightened in his heart. He was
afraid, he, the serene one, the all-wise one.

His signing hand ached, was numb. He touched his
other hand; he felt nothing.

What could he do now, if his hand grew dark, and
he could no longer touch? If only taste and scent were
left of the three senses? With his left hand, the mute
hand, he groped his way gingerly along the crawl-
corridor; he only just brushed the walls, fearful of more
acid. For many hundred paces; where there should
have been words, there was only a madness of
roughened smoothstuff.

And then, at the very end of the corridor, where the
signings had always trailed off into an
indistinguishable smoothness and the walls therefore
became completely dark to the touch, he found some
new words:

Jumper, jumping
Found his name
Striker, striking,
Struck himself

Belly, beast, mother, death,
Belly burst, jumper strike,
Striker striking
Back to life

What could it mean? The words were a grotesque
parody of one of the children's songs that he himself
had taught the young ones, giving them touchshapes

for simple words. But here the words were perverted. Who was the striker and how was he reborn?

(I am so old, he thought, so old. My nose can hardly tell the scent of friend from foe. . . .)

Stonewise wanted no mysteries, though he was keeper of all mysteries. But he knew that it was a sign from Windbringer, a calling perhaps.

Even in the windless chamber he felt the Windbringer's wind striking through the tunnels of his heart. He felt like a child again, a child-before-naming who has not yet dreamed of what he must become when he is grown.

It was time for him to choose a successor and to instruct him in all the secret wisdoms, and to take the irrevocable journey into the final darkness.

***

Another man crossed paths with Stonewise as he returned from the walls of knowing. It was Windstriker, the jumper who had jumped but whose fall had been broken, who had become linked to the Windbringer.

He was a half-man now, standing on a precarious ledge over the Sound, waiting for the Windbringer. The acid pouch, carefully extracted from a niche in the Windbringer's sailsac, he threw out into the big darkness. He felt the sudden stopping of the great windshape as the pouch curved against the windtide, and in his mind he could touch the soaring arc of it.

He was still Windstriker, but he could hardly remember his own name. But something in the village still called out to him. Sometimes, waking from his warm moist rest in the furrow of one of Windbringer's brain convolutions, he would feel a dreamtouch lightly on his arm: *Darktouch, Darktouch*; and he would think of his strange daughter.

He had waited for slack time in the hunting (for there was a time-honored rhythm in the great hunt, and Windstriker had been one of the greatest of hunters, and could sense the rhythm almost like a pulse, a heartbeat) and he had steered the Windbringer toward the village. Windbringer was content to follow the man's uncanny smell sense as he followed the trail of long-departed hunting skiffs, their identifying odors still tinging the violent wind. Windstriker had learned that Windbringer was no god at all. That he drifted darkly within the world that was supposed to be the belly of the cosmic Windbringer; that his fartouching, turned inward, touched distant worlds while perceiving nothing of the microcosm they shared. So much for the grand purpose for which men were created!

Angered, moved, he had come home to search for his daughter. For she had seen before he had, she with her extranormal senses that had earned her name. He had backed her even when he doubted her; and now he knew her to be a power woman, saying more truth than Stonewise even. . . .

But she was gone.

***

He had lurked in passageways, his hands mute because he dared not communicate his presence. Once he had stolen a glove-amp and eavesdropped) on Stonewise as he taught the young ones.

His palms felt the familiar words: the stories of the first times, of the world's creation and its future ending, of the cosmic Windbringer at the beginning of time.

And then the touch of Windbringer on his mind, the day of his falling into darkness: *a—wrongness—*

Angry, he had followed Stonewise to the room of ancient truths, crouching close to the stonestrewn passageways, sniffing out the sweat traces of the old man's feet as he walked ahead. He'd found the signings scratched on walls of alien smoothstuff; with the Windbringer's burning gall he had dissolved some of the words, etched some of his own with a crude stylus he had fashioned from a Windbringer bone. The anger raged so strong; he hardly knew what he was doing.

And now he faced the churning wind. Wetness oozed from his lacerated eye sockets, a wetness born of sorrow. He wiped it with the back of his hand.

Then came the mindtouch:

Wind—striker—

I am here, he signed softly, using his mind alone, for ever since that day of falling they had shared a touching-without-touching. The wind streamed around him; a child would have stumbled in it. Hanks of his hair slapped against his cheeks. *I am here,* he signed, *here, can you not touch me?* The Windbringer must not delay! For he knew that the hunt was due to begin soon. . . .

And then the wind fell suddenly.

In front of him was a pocket of stillness, while at his sides the tempest raged on, the wind like fire. It was the shadow of Windbringer; he felt the shadow in the stilling of the air's commotion. Steadily the patch of stillness grew until he stood surrounded by motionlessness. And then came the scent of distant

Windbringer, emerging out of the stenchy vapors of the Sound.

The fragrance grew nearer: the air shivered as the wind sifted through sailsacs. The rhythm slowed. Windstriker took a few tentative steps, nudging the ledge's edge with his toes.

The smell was overpowering now. He had come, was near. A momentary terror of falling crossed his thoughts, but he dismissed it.

Confident now, he sprang from the ledge, trusting the giant that waited for him below, in the big darkness. . .

    ***

From the sayings of Stonewise:

This is not from the words of the ancients, nor did the man who was Stonewise before me tell them to me, except in hints and inklings. But I believe that every power man and power woman must touch such a terror-dream as I have touched; for as we are the knowers and the revealers of the beginnings of the universe, so must we dimly perceive its ending. . . .

Children and children of my children, I had a dream once. I dreamt that I stood as it were at the center of our cosmos, where the Windbringers we serve are created to fly the Sound. But I was not as a man is; I had partaken of something of the spirit of Windbringer himself, for instead of hands I had spectral limbs that reached out to touch every wall of the world; and my feet had taken root in the water of life and death. And I felt the walls cracking. A burning odor seared my nostrils; the thick wombwalls of the universe were crumbling against my ghostly fingers, into ash like the dust of ground Windbringer bones that is used in the eye-gouging ceremony of rebirth.

And lo, hands touched people, brothers and sisters from our village and even from far villages against whom we used to make war, fighting for the right to hunt the Windbringers and the honor of bringing them home.

These people were tiny as flitterlings, and they swarmed in my arms. and I felt their fingers dance joy upon my body.

For the end of the world had come; and we had joined the Windbringer in another country. We streamed forth from the wombworld, our fingers and our toes dancing our laughter on the rocky ground, which gently quook in time with our dancing. And the air was thick with angels who ripped the life from us as we laughed, who gave us, drunk with joy, into the bosom of darkness.

For the universe had gone mad, and only our dancing and our dying, our journey into the little darkness, could wrench new life from the heart of the greater darkness.

***

Stonewise had made up his mind now. He did not intend to turn back. Resolutely he entered the crawl passage that led from his rocky sleepchamber to the main corridors of the village. For a hundred cycles of sleeps the children had come to him, their bodies still agile enough to negotiate the treacherous corridor easily; they had brought in food, they had sat, close together in a circle, relaying to each other the wisdom that trickled from his gnarled hands.

His body was old now. The wrinkles on his flesh snagged on the familiar jags, unchanged since childhood, that marked the way to the main concourse. But he had to press on.

As darkly as possible he slipped through chambers where children slept, and the babies were tended by nurses; he made almost no windshapes with his breathing, so that even their cheeks could not touch his presence although he almost brushed against them in their sleep. He was well practiced in stealth; he had taught it to thousands of children-before-naming, for war was always possible. In his mind he drew a circle of darkness around himself. It was cold inside, and he felt frighteningly alone, but it would be safe. Old as he was, he still did it well; for now as he slipped through corridors of the waking, he still made no windshapes, and he kept close to the walls so as not to cast a shadow against the curve of the constant breeze.

He found the chamber he was looking for. A steam of sweat and Windbringer gall drifted from it; it was a sacred room. Here the children-before-naming sat dreaming, waiting for the moment of their ordeal. To this room they would return when they had found their name, and their eyes, last reminders of childhood, would be taken from them; their little pain would serve to unite them with the great suffering of Windbringer, who returned in agony to the angels that men might live.

He felt along the wall until he found the entrance; then he went inside, picking up a glove-amp from the wall so he could touch their words. He put his arms out in front of him, feeling who was there . . . yes, a familiar scent . . . the boy-before-naming who was his special pupil, his favorite.

I am Stonewise, he signed on the boy's outstretched hand, giving his name a little twist of recognition that only the boy knew, that was a secret between them.

Stonewise . . .

Have you gone out yet, have you touched the lonely wind?

Yes. But my vision was strange: the wind told me I was not to name myself, but to take on another's. I'm afraid. At the end of my vision I seemed to touch a hollow stone. It shattered, and my name was inside it. I'm afraid to tell you the name, I don't want to hurt you. . . . The boy touched his face, exploring the deep clefts on the old man's cheek with his finger. *Oh, Stonewise.*

Listen, Boy-before-Naming. Stonewise tempered his signing with a half-caress, for he knew what the boy knew. *Never run away from destiny. I am passing on now, to the angel country. I will die.*

The boy was shaking. Stonewise knew that he had already guessed what he would sign next.

I give you my name, Boy-before-Naming. You are Stonewise. You are to be a knower, like me.

He felt the others' stillness through the change in the wind. He had projected his words through the glove-amp so that all would know. The boy's hand felt cold.

And now, Boy-before-Naming, the privilege of taking your eyes, the supreme act of love, I name as my own right.

A babble of scratchings reached him through his glove-amp, but he ignored them. *It has been too long for me,* he signed, *and the world has changed too much. Even the words on the walls of knowledge have changed of their own accord. They say now that a jumper has come back from the dead. Their words are dark to me.*

But I believe that things are changing irrevocably, and I am old, I cannot face the changes. Let the boy become Stonewise, while he is still supple and his mind still quick. As for me, still living, I will embrace the angels of death. And then—for the following moments were to be private, shared only by him and his successor—he threw the glove-amp on the ground and drew the young boy to him . . . trusting, the boy embraced his mentor. Swiftly, carefully, Stonewise moved his hands over Boy-before-Naming's face. The boy tensed. The face was caked with the powder of crushed Windbringer bones, said to contain the power of healing, even of life and death; sweat-rivers had dug deep crevasses in the clay-hard powder-mask. He pitied the boy, he wished things were otherwise for him, for being a knower was a lonely path, without a touch-sibling to stand beside one. Stonewise felt a windshape of terror forming in his throat. *Do not fear,* he signed on the boy's cheek; and in a second he had torn out the boy's eyes, and warm blood was trickling down his arms. The boy did not move; mercifully he had fainted.

Grow well, Stonewise signed to the unconscious one in his arms, *grow well, with this love and this pain to guide you. I give you the pain that my own teacher gave me, countless cycles of sleeps ago, and in giving you this pain I free myself forever from this life. . . .*

For a moment vivid memories deluged his thoughts. He felt the touch of his own teacher, so gentle and so cruel, and the agony that exploded in his face as blood and rheum spurted . . . *he* had not fainted, he remembered. The pain had burned for an eternity. More remembrances came now: first touching the signings on the walls of knowledge, the finely chiseled, divinely revealed truths etching themselves into his fingers; the rhythmic *tap-tap-tap* of his teacher's hands as he ground out endless genealogies; and finally, with yearning sadness, the moment that he had bidden his touch-sister goodbye and left their cave to live in the rooms of the dead knower.

He took off his neckpouch of Windbringer's leather bound with hide strips, which contained an essence distilled from the fluids of many Windbringers, and gently he laid the boy on the damp floor and placed the pouch around his neck. He stripped the loinshield from his emaciated thighs and crossed it over the boy's chest, signing upon each breast the words *Be wise, be wise.*

Naked now, so stooped that he negotiated the low passage with ease, he made his way deeper into the walls of the world, his numb fingers drumming a deathsong against his chest as he sought out the Dark Country.

Twenty-Two
The Crystal Desert

Darktouch was still asleep when Kelver awoke. Mauve light speckled the furry white floor, seeping in through imperfections in the small room's darkfield. He blinked, subvoked a command as he had seen the Inquestors do; purple dawnlight flooded the room then. He drew his firefur from the floor and threw it on his nude body. It quivered, contorted itself, clung to the curve of his shoulders. When he looked down he saw no city; only an endless beach dyed violet by the mingling of crossed sunlights, blue and crimson, bordering a mirror-still sea where the suns, reflected a thousandfold, cross-stitched the water with sparkling lightthreads, ruby and lapis. Where was he? This Kallendrang was a city of illusions: you could look twice in the same spot and never see the same scenery, for the thinkhive never ceased its constant shifting of landscapes to harmonize with the Inquestor's whims. What planet am I looking at now? he thought. He had listened to the way Davaryush and Varuneh talked, he knew that the world was as likely to be a dead one as a living one. One that had—to use their own phrase for it—*fallen beyond.*

He turned to see Lady Varuneh. He had not heard her enter; perhaps she had been watching him a long time.

"*Hokh'Tón,*" he said reverently. "My Lady, have you been watching me long?"

"Yes, boy." Her manner was brusque, but not unkind. She stared straight at him, making him feel like a very little kid suddenly, not a hero who had braved the desert. "So what do you think of us, Kevi? Daavye has great plans for you, did you know that? Plans so great that even you, with your dreams and your ambitions, could never guess them . . . come, tell me the truth."

"My Lady . . ." He had to talk to somebody, suddenly, he couldn't rein himself in any more. "It's not what I expected! I came trusting you, looking for answers, and I found the Inquest itself divided, factioned, groping in the darkness."

Varuneh seemed moved at this; he could not be sure, because the Inquestors held in their emotions so well. "Daavye is right about you," she said softly.

"My Lady, what do you mean? Please don't give me more mysteries to worry about—"

But she said nothing for a while. Then all she said was, "Wake the girl. We will leave now."

Only then did Kelver realize how afraid he was. He didn't want to go back. He remembered the al'ksigarkar, the ghost people, the burning cold, the charred village . . . he panicked. Tears came streaming

down his cheeks. "I'm only a child after all," he blurted
out. "So much for my grand ideas!"

And then, to his surprise, the old woman took him
in her arms. Her fingers felt thin and dry on his bare
back. Already he was the taller. But . . . there was a
glow in her. She really cares, Kelver thought,
wondering. And Varuneh said, "Never be afraid to
know you are only a child. We are all children, Kevi,
children playing at being movers of worlds and masters
of the universe." Her eyes were closed, her lips fiercely
pursed; it was as if she were remembering something
in her old childhood. And Kelver knew, from what he
had overheard, that she was probably older than any
human being alive. He pitied the old woman then,
loved her even, although she was too exalted a figure
for him to recognize this emotion as love.

He held her tighter to him, and said, "Don't worry,
my Lady. I don't care what's wrong with the human
race. We'll fix it, you and I and Darktouch and the
great Kingling; we've got to be able to, between us!
You've got all the knowledge of the millennia between
the two of you, and she and I have our love, and we'll
trust you and believe in you and serve you until you
find the answers—"

She wrested herself free. "Daavye was right," she
said again, harshly, but Kelver knew she was only
pretending harshness.

He knelt down beside the sleeping girl.
"Darktouch," he whispered. "Darktouch."

The Lady Varuneh nodded her head; the darkfield
dissolved, and they saw the true landscape of
Gallendys as the false dawn splintered and whirlpooled
into bright sunlight.

Above, the crystal-crusted cone of Kallendrang funneled into a quilted fabric of cloud and cerulean sky; below them Effelkang sank pyramidally into the sea in a twisted mirror-image of the higher city. And in front of his eyes, hovering against a frieze of stalactitious towers whose window-clusters glittered like compound eyes of an insect chimera, was a railinged floater blazoned with the crest of the clan of Ton; in it stood Ton Davaryush, tall and regal, shrouded in shimmerfur.

And behind him, flanking him in smaller floaters on either side, were childsoldiers. An official escort.

Kelver gazed at them. This was what he'd always wanted to be! A childsoldier, fighting for the glory of the Dispersal of Man in some far corner of the galaxy. A childsoldier, whose very glance meant death from those terrible laser-irises, triggered by a nod and a subvocalized command. And there they stood, a dozen of them, their altered eyes slitty and golden as pteratygers, their somber black cloaks thrown smartly over their shoulders, their manner both easy and threatening. Knee-high, their varigrav boots glinted silver in the suns' light, and their sashes, woven from strands of iridium and the threadlike flamecrystals from the lakes of Vanjyvel, glittered against the sable of their kilts.

Now, faced with the very thing he had dreamed of for so long, he realized that he no longer wanted to become one of them. He'd learned too much, even from these few days at the Inquestor's palace. *And all that I've learned,* he thought, *is that I know nothing! I don't even know what I want any more!* He wondered what the Lady Varuneh had meant when she had said that Ton Davaryush was right, and that he had plans for him . . . he hoped he was not to be made a childsoldier, and yet he was terrified of seeming ungrateful for something that was an unattainable honor half a year ago.

The Lady Varuneh stood sternly, not looking at him. In a moment Darktouch was beside him again; they linked hands, he desperate for some small security.

The Lady clapped her hands. At this the forcewindow dissolved, and a wind roared in the room.

"Listen!" cried Varuneh. Through the rushing of the wind Kelver heard the rhythmic clanghowl of the thinkhive's laughter. *The world-mind is still insane. In time it will repair itself. Its madness buys us time, Kelver, time for us to visit the Dark Country. I don't know how much time, for thinkhives seldom go mad, and for all we know it may only be shamming, for thinkhives are as devious as Inquestors, and have no compassion. We'll have to risk it. There's nothing else we can do."* A forcebridge, invisible save for side markers to show where the bridge ended and the deathtumble began, materialized between them and the floaters. He saw Davaryush's face: calm now, despite the storm within and without. He and Darktouch followed the Lady Varuneh; they took their places beside the Inquestor.

At a wave from the Kingling the childsoldiers shrieked their warcry, a piercing scream of concentrated, childish hatred. They turned, whirled, blinked out a perfect crisscross pattern of laserlight that made a deadly canopy of gold over the Inquestor's head for a split second. Had a single one of them misgauged his angle or the length of his laserburst he might have killed Davaryush, or sliced a veranda from one of the hanging ziggurats. Kelver trembled, awed by

their precision. The soldiers screeched out another
warcry, like a roar of infant pteratygers hungry for fresh
meat; and then they fell at ease. One at a time the
childsoldiers' floaters fell into formation, and then
they, too, were moving . . . in an hour or so they
crossed the shield that englobed the environs of the
city. There was a second of icy coldness; there was no
artificial summer here. Swiftly the darkfield cut in,
shielding out the chill and manufacturing its own
warmth. They were over the desert now; it sparkled
like a carpet of diamants, and Kelver could see the Cold
River, splitting the desert in two and going on as far as
the eye could see . . . and in the distance, beyond the
horizon, like a monstrous misty tombstone crowned
with black, the Skywall.
***

Now they were far into the desert, and the shining
cities had long vanished from the western horizon,
ahead the Skywall rose unchanged. Davaryush had
seen the desert in holosculptures; but in the images it
had seemed pretty, shimmer-rich from the paper-thin
layer of winter hoarfrost. He had not been prepared for
its vastness, its desolation. For several sleeps they
journeyed; when they tired, they lay half-awake on the
soft floor of the floater, but he would never allow their
convoy to rest. Behind and before them the
childsoldiers swarmed, always alert.

Finally came a junction of the Cold River's 'many
tributaries; for the delphinoid brains came from many
villages such as the one from which Darktouch had
come, each fiercely independent, each with its own
customs, for the cultures had diverged since the day
the thinkhives of the Inquest had decreed that there

be races of deafblind humans imprisoned forever in
the Dark Country. There were holomaps to be pored
over, directions to be chosen.

Davaryush spent the days watching the two
children. Kelver's curiosity was insatiable; if he was
afraid of the journey he hid it well. Darktouch said
nothing most of the time, but she observed everything
with hungry eyes, now that the gift of seeing was no
longer denied her.

Varuneh, too, kept to herself; a peace had come
upon her, as though she already divined what
Davaryush had planned for her.

They passed fields where a thousand al'ksigarkar
lay, dormant now, their crystalline mantles stretched
out to trap the meager sunlight. The suns arose only for
a few hours every sleep; the sky glowed palely with the
light from the great cluster of Planzhadavynn, the
gods' tears, which only shine in winter and which seem
to mourn for the bleak earth. They passed over
al'ksigarkar frozen into ice statues, their razor teeth
still glistening. Seepage from their body fluids dyed the
frost floor a faint green for many klomets. Here and
there the river divided, and the junctions were metal
asterisks in the expanse of ice.

On the eighth day the boy cried out: "Look,
Inquestor, where the angels nearly killed us!"

Davaryush lifted his arm: the convoy of
childsoldiers swooped down in a great V, and he
brought his own floater to rest above the Cold River.
There he saw the spider things that had battered
themselves to shreds on the impenetrable forceshield
of the Cold River. Now they lay shattered at the river's
edge, or still hanging on by a dead metal claw to the

pylons; some were half-buried in the ice, here a steely tentacle, there a serrated claw.

He landed the floater. For a moment he surveyed the wreckage.

"So this is all that's left of our unconquerable defenses!" he said.

Varuneh, coming up to him, said, "We have had no defenses for many millennia now, Daavye. We had only the inertia of our beliefs, of our *makrúgh*, to sustain our power. Now you see just how fragile the balance is."

Davaryush glanced under the river's shadow—

A hail of lances whistled, thudding into the thin ice! "The ghost people!" Kelver yelled.

And they came springing forth from their hiding places in the shadow. "Food, food, food," they chanted, waving their lances, their faces buried in masks of vitrified al'ksigark hide. Now Davaryush made out their tents, dark against the river's shadow. More came, twirling lariats of green leather. He felt a rope tighten around his neck, saw Kelver bloodied from a lance cut
—

"*Ishá ha!*" he shouted out, his voice shrill in the big emptiness. At once half a dozen floaters filled with childsoldiers rammed the mass of ghost people. The soldiers jumped, their boots smashing into the wild men's faces. Came a shattering cacophony of screams and death rattles, and then an eerie, terrifying rhythmic chant from the children as their metal boots tramped on the ice and bursts of topaz laserlight streamed from their eyes—

Ishá ha, ha, ha!
Ishá ha ha héiy ha!
Ishá ha! Ishá ha!

Ishá ha ha héiy ha!

In unison the childsoldiers whirled. The screams died at once; thin slices of men flew out in all directions. It was over. . . .

Davaryush had seen this thousands of times, but still it saddened him. But he could not think of it now.

Corpse slices littered the ice, the blood oozing thick in the bitter cold, freezing already as it touched the frost. Swiftly as they had come, the childsoldiers leaped onto their floaters and made for the air; the convoy wheeled ahead, in perfect formation, like a flock of firephoenixes, heart-stoppingly lovely.

Then he heard a moan, only half-human, coming from the tents. . . .

"We cannot stop," said Varuneh.

"We must. Investigate this place! If we forget compassion, we forget the purpose of our mission—" And he strode into the circle of tents.

There was a woman there, bound to one of the river's pylons. She was old, very old She seemed only half-conscious. Frozen blood had matted on her face, and her eyes stared into some inner emptiness. Davaryush looked at her for a long time as Kelver, Darktouch, and Varuneh gathered behind him.

"This is not one of the mutants with which we peopled the desert," he said at last. For he had seen, hidden in her features, the specter of beauty, and he knew that this woman must once have been of some high court. "We must take her with us—"

Darktouch said, "It's her! The one who saved us! The queen of the ghost people!"

The woman moved. Davaryush went up to cut her loose; and then he saw that she had no arms, only stumps, still bloody, bordered by the gnaw-marks of human teeth. He held her up; parts of her legs, too, had been eaten away, but still she breathed. And then she looked at the Lady Varuneh. . . .

"You," she whispered, "you, you, the High Lady, the Great One . . . you, you, I dream, dream, dream."

"Powers of powers!" Varuneh said. "Yeng Saryodha of the clan of Ferrets. A hundred years ago I sent you into the desert, to seek out the secret of the Dark Country—"

"Oh, don't go there, don't, my Lady, my Lady . . . I'm barely alive now, barely alive, I cheated them of their food, they eat me daily, they chew me from the extremities inward so I won't die yet—"

Davaryush saw the boy turn away, clenching back tears. To the woman he said, "Your suffering is over. You have served the Inquest well, too well . . . the Inquest is compassionate, and will succor you in your suffering—"

"I have seen, have seen!" she cried out with a great effort. "The light, the light, and it has driven me mad, mad, mad, mad, mad . . ." and she began to sing, in a wailing voice that might once have been beautiful, one of the most poignant songs of the master musician Sajit, one that she must have heard in a court, a century or more before . . . *I have touched the silence between the stars. Oh, envy me, envy me, the mad Singer, the mad singer. . . .*

"Saryodha, Saryodha," said Lady Varuneh, and she touched the dying woman's blistered face, her festering arm-stumps. "When I sent you out I did not think to find you like this . . . you should have come home, Saryodha."

"When you see the light," the queen of ghosts croaked, "you will never have a home again, never, never, never. See the children, see how they run, they run, they run, run, run, they run from the light on the Sound, their homes are razed, are lost, their peace is gone forever, the supreme beauty has cursed them, cursed them—"

Is there no exit from this trap we've laid for ourselves? Davaryush thought. "There's nothing for it," he said. "We can't turn back. But you we can send to the city and give over to the somatic surgeons; we can give you life."

"I see you will not turn back, no, no, no, no. You never turn back, none of you, never, never. We are men, we are doomed, we must push, push, push, push, push against the wall of our unknowing, we must batter it down only to find another wall, another and another and another . . . listen, Inquestor." For a while she spoke very clearly. "Look for the babies, Inquestor, the babies. After they are grown they will never see and hear, they will never be able to cope with the madness of new sensations . . . look for the young ones, the babies, the ones with still-malleable minds."

And then she closed her eyes. "Saryeh, Saryeh!" Varuneh said. "She's dead," said Davaryush.

He saw that Kelver and Darktouch had walked away, out into the pallid starlight, unable to bear the old woman's death.

Gently he laid the woman down on the ice. Then, with all the resolution he could muster, he shouted out: "Onward! Onward!" and strode toward the floater.

In a while they were airborne again; but for the next few sleeps they exchanged no words at all. Each of them sat in his own cage of silence. Now and then one would stare at the Skywall as it grew, darkening out more and more of the sky, hypnotized by its very hugeness.

***

There came a moment when they crossed into the Skywall's shadow. The diffuse gray light that had shone in the desert gave way to an intense blackness; the only light now was from the floaters' beacons. Davaryush's floater plowed on: behind were the childsoldiers' floaters, flitting like phosphorflies.

They flew over the ruins of Kelver's village; Davaryush did not stop the convoy, for he did not want to hurt the boy any more. Instead he let the boy guide them to the opening down into the Dark Country. Childsoldiers blasted at the rockface with their laser-irises, and cleared the Inquestor's way. They left their floaters by the entrance to the cave, sheltered by a rocky overhang. Natural corridors first, twisty and confusing, but the boy remembered the way well. And then, at the touch of a stud, a secret chamber walled and floored with mirror metal, in which extensions of the great thinkhive whirred and hummed, and labyrinthine machines crawled creeperlike along the walls, crazy concoctions of tentacles and sensors and holoeyes and kaleidolons.

And then Davaryush saw the gateway into the Dark Country, and its dread inscription:

The shadow is mother
The shadow is death
The shadow falls forever
On the children of darkness

S.P. Somtow

and he was moved and awed by it. For the inscription had stood for twenty thousand years, years counted by the revolutions of a long-forgotten planet.

"Let's go in."

They hesitated for a moment. Then a dozen childsoldiers leaped forward to precede the Inquestor in case of danger; one touched the stud of the gateway. Came a wuthering from within, like the wail of a child that suckles at the breasts of a dead woman.

Davaryush stepped into the darkness. A slushy substance lapped at his feet. There were bones here, skulls; they crunched under his fursoles. An unreasoning terror shook him. "Lights, powers of powers, give me lights!" he shouted.

All at once the childsoldiers kindled the dazzlestuff that lay dormant in their cloaks. A brilliant rippling white light flooded the area. Davaryush looked up. Machines, more machines. And ahead, skulls, skulls, here and there a rotting corpse, half-pulped, protruding from the slime.

"Horrible," Varuneh said.

"I'm not afraid," Darktouch said. "This is the entrance to my home. If we keep moving, the angels will not take us; they understand only the dead."

Kelver screamed.

Davaryush turned quickly. They had crept up, the spiderthings, glittering in the unnatural light.

"*Ishá ha!*" the Inquestor shouted. At once a childsoldier whipped round and lasered the spider. It splintered in a spray of sparklets, sinking into the mush.

"Move, move!" Davaryush said. He strode forward, the organic slush slowing him down.

"Look! Above us!" Varuneh said.

For a second they stood petrified. Dozens of them were descending from the cavern's height. Their claws snapped and clattered as they swooped downward.

At a word from the Inquestor the childsoldiers clicked their varigrav boots and jumped high into the air, streaking the darkness with deadly gold. Now they hovered, a column of whirling, killing light. Angels fell. Metal shards scraped on Davaryush's face. He moved forward relentlessly, trusting the childsoldiers to cover him, shouting for the others to follow closely.

More and more spider-angels were loosed from the ceiling! Wave after wave were torn apart by the madly spinning lightstreaks! And now one or two of the soldiers, too, were stricken and plummeted into the slush, where the pulping machines rent them apart with their claws. Davaryush looked away, remembering that he had once been as they—

Now the mush grew deeper. They waded, now knee-deep, now waist-deep in the soup of pulped corpses, stinking of death and putrefaction. Only Darktouch seemed unaffected by the stench.

Abruptly the onslaught ceased. Davaryush made out, in the light from the soldiers' cloaks, a round doorway in a far wall. They made for it, fighting the thick slush.

A hundred meters from the door, a lone figure stood. A very old man. When they reached him, Davaryush saw that he had no eyes. . . .
      ***

Darktouch watched the distant figure. She had felt no fear when the angels came from the cavern roof; the other time, not knowing what was at the end of the

Dark Country, had been much worse, and now she knew that the angels were mortal.

The Dark Country had not changed. But she had.

No country will ever be the Dark Country to me again, she thought. The people in the shining cities call the Windbringer's people dark, and the deafblind call the outside dark. But I am of both worlds now. . . .

When she looked around her, at the slimy walls illuminated by the children's war cloaks, at the mud that oozed at the ankles, she knew that she was no freak, that the others saw as she did. . . .

Now her eyes touched many things and she did not need to wonder if they were illusions. Only a short time ago she'd known that there was something wrong with her, that she wasn't really human . . . but she knew better now.

Now the childsoldiers had alighted on the ground, and Davaryush was giving them their orders: "I don't want you to come in with us. But if you fly over the top of the Skywall mountain, you will find an entrance, a chink in the roof, wide enough to admit a single floater. Go there; enter the mountain; monitor our whereabouts. Soon we will be journeying out over the Sunless Sound. Watch over us; be ready to aid us if necessary."

One by one the soldiers reared up on their varigrav boots and floated away. Davaryush called over the last half-dozen of them; from these he took the shining cloaks, and he threw one over the shoulders of each of the four travelers remaining; and soon the soldiers were distant light-points in the far end of the cavern of death.

They went further toward the gateway. She could see the stooped figure clearly now. At first she assumed it was simply another corpse, but it moved, its face looked familiar—

"Stonewise! Stonewise!" she called out. And then she remembered, with a start, that he could not hear her . . . it seemed so long ago, this country where one could not speak.

She went up to him then and took his hand. He trembled. He signed the word angel on her hand.

"It is Stonewise," she said to the others. "The village knower. This means that he must have decided to die: perhaps he felt himself a burden to the others, being so old." And then she signed to him: *Stonewise. I am a wayward pupil of yours, the one who seemed to touch at a distance. The freak. I am named Darktouch now, and I'm not a freak any more.*

The old man signed feebly to her.

She said, "He says that the words in the knowing room have changed of their own accord . . . that a jumper has been reborn . . . that he has passed on his power to a boy." What could that mean, a jumper being reborn? A memory came to her: Windstriker falling into the howling wind. . . .

Old man, she signed, I am Darktouch, who have crossed the Dark Country and have returned. I have found that our world is not the universe, not even a dust speck of the universe. I have kept my eyes, and yet I have become a woman.

Dark . . . Touch . . . came the weak signing.

"Something has happened," she said at last to the others. "Something . . . terrible, perhaps. The words of knowing . . . do you know what they are?"

Davaryush said, "Yes. They are the inscriptions that the thinkhives made, intended as inviolate truths that would form the basis of your myths, your fantasies. "

"Did you command that they be changed?" Kelver said. "I cannot do that."

"Then," said Darktouch, "some power greater than you has commanded it."

Twenty-Three
The Boy Who Danced Back the Windbringers

As they walked toward the circular portal, bronze-shiny with the light from their cloaks, Kelver said, "The old man! We can't leave him behind, can we?"

Davaryush looked at Stonewise, who had waded out farther into the lake of human slush; he seemed to have found peace. "What would it be like for him," he told the boy, "if we did take him back to the city, revived him perhaps even gave him back his sight and his hearing? He would be living in a madness of alien sensations ... I do not know what would be the more compassionate."

"But *I've* learned to survive in new, hostile places . . . and so has *she*," he said, pointing to Darktouch.

"You are young. Would you strip away all this man has left to believe in?"

The boy was silent for a long time as they made their way to the gateway. Davaryush knew that he was

debating in his mind . . . he thought of his plan for the
boy, and knew that it was good. He wished he'd been
like this boy, stuck in a village dreaming of glory, never
having to look that glory in the face and know the
horror behind it. He approached the boy and touched
his shoulder lightly, with such gentleness.

He thought: *I must have condemned a billion such
to their deaths in an idle stroke of* makrúgh. And
Davaryush was sick at heart, sick of all that he stood
for. But he said nothing.

At the gateway Kelver said, "It's difficult to be an
Inquestor, isn't it? I used to think it would be easy. All
that power." He spoke the lowspeech not using any of
the forms of reverence; but Davaryush did not care to
correct the boy. "Oh, Inquestor, I would not like to be
in your place . . ."

"You don't want to sit on a hoverthrone overlooking
a dozen worlds? You don't want to utter a word and
shatter a world? To send your childsoldiers to lay waste
a wayward planet like a swarm of locusts?"

"No." He seemed very small suddenly.

Seeing his dismay, Davaryush said kindly, "Don't
even think of it, Kevi. I am not an Inquestor now; and
the Lady Varuneh has not been one for hundreds of
years. We are all equal." He took a last look at the old
man's torso, half-buried in the mud now, waiting for
death. He prayed that the man would feel no pain
when the angels came again to tear him apart; he knew
that there must be more of them, that the respite they
had won could only be temporary.

"I envy you, Stonewise," he said very softly, for
Varuneh alone. Only she could possibly understand
the supreme loneliness of faithlessness. She only
smiled at him. Since leaving the city, she seemed to

have grown more beautiful, as though the increasing bleakness of the landscape as it went from expanses of deathcold to this claustrophobic cavern of flesh-renders . . . had brought out some compensatory, inner beauty of hers. "Do you envy him too?"

"No, Daavye. I feel nothing at all, nothing, nothing. Remember Saryodha, the Queen of Ghosts? She came here at my behest; I needed to gather information for my plot against the Inquest. She was a faithful woman, a little dull perhaps. Before I gave her this mission, she served me at home, combing my hair at nights, and singing to me music she remembered from her days in Elloran's court; for I missed music so badly, Daavye! She had done no ferreting for a long time, though she was by clan name a Ferret. She saw what we are about to see, and she has died for it."

"We must see. We are ʿ. Until they strip our names from us . . . as I know they will do." And he pressed the stud, irising open the door to the Dark Country.

***

I see! I see! Darktouch thought. Ahead of them, the corridor forked and forked again. The passageways were barely man-high; she saw that the others stumbled and sometimes hit their heads. The cloaks cast only tiny patches of light; but she did not need light here. She was the seeing one, and they were the blind. Lightly she stretched her toes out, seeking familiar landmarks. Once or twice she was fooled by a tricky footing or by some shifted pattern in the rockfloor; but not for long.

***

They passed larger chambers carved in the rock. Her eyes dwelt long on everything. For the first time she didn't feel ashamed of touching with her eyes. Windshapes whistled in the corridors and she knew them for sounds.

"Darktouch!" shouted Kelver. "We can't keep up!"

She slowed, but it was irritating that she could not run through the tunnels as in the days of her childhood. Her old touch-brother must have felt as these outsiders did, when he reached the first chamber beyond the angels' feeding place.

Davaryush whispered behind her: "Is there a nursery here, a creche, a communal place where the babies are kept?"

"Yes. You don't have to whisper; no one will know we're here if you do exactly as I do. Speak as loud as you like."

"The creche. Saryodha mentioned the young children—" The Inquestor's voice didn't rise; he had not adapted yet to the idea that they would never be seen or heard.

"Yes," Darktouch said. She felt along the wall until her fingers touched three notches in the rock, all pointed leftward; and then she eased through an opening to where a ledge overlooked a dank cleft. The smells were stronger now; the ever-present gall of Windbringers, the background perfume of intermingling airskiff scents. "My hand, hold my hand," she said urgently to Kelver. The four of them linked hands and inched along the ledge while her free hand explored the half-remembered ridges along the rockwall. Puddles of light sifted from the cloaks as they rustled in the wind. The wind hardly came to this section of the village, sheltered as it was for the babies' sake; even so she had forgotten its power, its sick-sweet odor.

"She's not looking at all," said Kelver.

No time, her fingers danced on his hand; and then she translated quickly, remembering that he knew only windshapes.

Swiftly they passed the openings to chambers large and small, mostly empty, some with people clustered together, signing intently to each other. "Faster, don't dawdle!" she said. For she knew that when they crossed an open doorway the wind would be stilled for a brief instant; this was what her people called a shadow-windshape. And someone, touching the suddenly dark wind, might notice how oddly the group was moving, might suspect something.

A larger hall now: a displacement plate stood in the middle of it, and the foodgatherers were there in a circle around it; their fingers were busy as they prayed to the Windbringer for food. The others could not help watching. Kelver especially stared as meat and grain materialized and the gatherers began to grope on the mirror metal for the food. "'It's true, then," he was saying. "We did have a purpose, we weren't just throwing away the food we grew. . . .'"

"All things," Davaryush said, "are linked, Kelver. Sometimes even a game of *shtézhnat* can destroy a world." He seemed to be thinking of something very distant in his childhood.

Darktouch saw Kelver gazing still at them, not coming away. A young man with a basket of fruit had come quite close, one arm outstretched to feel along the wall. In a second he would touch Kelver's face, but Kelver could not move; he stared, transfixed, at the gaping eye sockets framed with scabs and matted blood. The boy-man must have come straight from his eye-gouging ceremony—

"Hurry, hurry!" Darktouch could not budge Kelver for a moment; when he came, reluctantly, he was still looking back into the hall of the foodgatherers, and he was shaking.

***

In a while they emerged into a low-ceilinged room. Davaryush saw that there were heat-emitters here, globes of red light placed here and there among the rocks; the thinkhives had provided well for the prisoners of the Dark Country.

In niches in the rock floor, lined with a brushed leathery substance that Davaryush surmised to be the cured sailsacs of the delphinoids, were the babies, some two dozen of them; most of them were asleep. There were no labels, no rock-etchings, to show any names or other distinctions. A nurse, an old crone whose skinfolds flapped over her empty eye sockets, groped around on the floor, feeding one or the other from a bowl of mush.

"Are they brought here immediately, at birth?" Davaryush said .

"Yes. Until they are adults they have no names; they are merely Girl-before-Naming, Boy-before-Naming. But the parents can always tell; they are bound to them by scent and touch."

"And the parents visit the children? Play with them, nurture them ?"

Darktouch's face clouded for a moment, and she seemed to be translating something to herself by scratching on her arms. "To be a parent is the most precious of things. A parent hardly dares speak to his offspring, because it is the most sacred of all bonds, the deepest of all loves. . .my father and I rarely touched; I think perhaps we touched at all only because of my mother's death."

"It is a desolate childhood, then."

"No!" she answered, too quickly. "The children are happy, they play, they hear old Stonewise telling them of the great hunts and of the creation of the universe. And they dream of becoming hunters themselves, and of bringing the Windbringer home, of getting a little piece of his hide for a loinshield or a bedrug; they play at ball and at stalking each other down the corridors. It's a good life, simple, hopeful."

"But you were not happy."

"My eyes. My ears. They called me Dark-toucher and they cursed me, scarring my arms with the spitefulness of their taunts."

Davaryush knelt now and picked up one of the young ones. It struggled, opened its eyes. . . . "It *sees* me!" he whispered. "There there. . ."

Varuneh came up to him with another child. "Look at this one."

Its eyes were clouded now; when he waved the cloak of dazzlestulf over its head it did not notice. "It's a disease then, a hereditary disease," Davaryush said.

"Perhaps so."

"And you were a rare throwback," he said to Darktouch, "who were immune. And there may be others . . . that is why you must all lose your eyes at puberty. . ."

"It's terrible!" Kelver cried, raging; and then he held the girl close.

Then Davaryush said, "We must take the child with us. That's what Saryodha meant! We have to find a cure." He waved his hand over the child's face. The child—a boychild, he saw now-giggled a little, then fretted. Davaryush did not know how to comfort it; its crying echoed in the cavern, but the nurse, who still crawled around in some other comer of the room, did not notice.

"No, no, Daavye," the Lady Varuneh said. She took the baby from him and held it in her thin arms, draping a fold of the lightcloak around it. "A living token of our visit. Perhaps, at the city, we'll be able to determine why they go blind—"

In his mind's eye Davaryush saw the gift of Lady Ynyoldeh for an instant, the grisly tables made from undead children. He shuddered. "Let's go on," he said, "quickly, quickly."

***

"Stay back," said Darktouch, pushing the others against the wall. They had left the nursery, Varuneh still clutching the little child, and were in a complex honeycomb of passages. A man was approaching them, half-crouching to feel the floor and the lower walls. She knew that he had touched their shadow on the wind, because he was slowing down and moving his hand randomly in the emptiness in the hope of contacting the shadows source. The wind was stronger here, firming their outlines against the windshape, making it hard to hide. Darktouch put out her hand, making it seem to collide with the man's by accident.

Greeting, she signed. *Where are you going so hurriedly? Don't you know? Haven't they told you? I don't recognize you. . . .*

Subtly she altered her signing, trying to form the crude ungrammatical scrawlings of a child. *I Girl-*

before-Naming. No one but a parent would bother to differentiate one child from another.

... join the others then! Stonewise has called us to a meeting! Yes, older-one. But—

"What's happening?" said Kelver.

She exchanged some more signings with the man, and then said, "There's a big meeting, a sort of investiture of the new Stonewise. It's only a boy, fresh from eye-gouging . . . but he has announced a new revelation in the walls of knowledge; something that has never happened before. It's scary. There'll be a big hunt, maybe, to placate the Windbringers."

"Placate them?" Davaryush said ironically.

"We should follow him," Darktouch said. She signed, *I and my friends will follow you.*

What friends? You are late!

Don't concern yourself, elder. It's just more of us children-before-naming.

Let me touch and identify.

No need, no need. We must hurry, mustn't we? Very well, very well, but come swiftly.

He led them up a steep passageway; and the crying of the wind grew louder.

***

Dank. Kelver thought, *dank and cold.*

They were following the man now with his slouching, groping gait; sometimes he would turn round to sign something to Darktouch, and Kelver would see the eye sockets.

They did this to these people! he thought, looking at the Inquestors. *They, the omniscient, the compassionate.*

The corridor they were in widened into a room. There were a hundred people, perhaps more, men, women, children; dressed in loinshields of grayish leather, their bodies slicked with delphinoid oil. The people were squatting, backs to the wall of the chamber; their hands were all linked, they wore gray leather gloves filigreed with wires, and they were clasping and unclasping their hands in unison. In the thin light Kelver could only see a few of the people clearly; the others were wraiths of darkness. Darktouch took a glove from a heap of them at the entrance. "It's an amplifier," she said.

"Yes," Davaryush said, donning one. "It senses the distant hand-scratchings of their leader and re-creates the same sensations on the hand of the listener." Kelver put one on too; immediately be felt a tingling on the back of his hand, as though a colony of insects were crawling on it, making patterns. Sometimes he would half-recognize a word in the touch-language that Darktouch had taught him; but they went by so fast, they were so fraught with squiggles of nuance and notches of emotion. . . .

Darktouch began translating quickly. Kelver saw the source of the words; it was a young boy, about his own age, who sat on a boulder in the center of the chamber; his fingers were flying as they signed his words on the projecting board. His hair was long and black like Darktouch's; his skin frost-white. He was very thin, as though he had been fasting. Blood streamed from his eyes; Kelver winced when he saw it.

"I am Stonewise, returned to you from the dead. Listen, listen . . . the unchanging knowledge on the walls of the hall of knowing has changed. Here a shifted word, there whole sentences corroded away.

Once Old Stonewise told me that all things, even the universe, were transient. That one day even the eternal truth would become a lie. But why now? How have we offended? Stonewise sang to me of a dance that would allay the ending. . ."

Kelver saw them all, as he raised up the cloak and its dazzlestuff sent out slow ripples of white light, moving their hands in unison, a slow circular motion. Then clasping and unclasping. Then tapping the rocks, the walls, each other's hands. "They are dancing," Darktouch said. Their unseeing eyes stared hollowly ahead. They did not crane their necks to catch odd sounds, the way people normally do. They just sat, like servocorpses, wiggling their hands this way and that, in perfect unison.

It was eerie.

"He says that only the dancing can quell the madness into which the universe has fallen," said Darktouch. "That the Windbringer is angry, and they must dance him back out of the whirling windworld—"

And now, hands still linked, the people rose. They began pounding the ground with their feet, a dull sound quickly swallowed in the wind's relentless wailing. They clapped their hands, let go of each other's arms and waved them wildly before reaching out to grasp them again. They drummed the walls with their fingers, a sound like hail on the pylons of the Cold River.

Darktouch's voice rose as she translated the boy's words: "We must dance till the Windbringer comes, then we must go out and find him and bring him home, we must end his bitter loneliness as he breasts the wind of his creation—"

The dancing went on now, and some of the children were missing their footing and were stumbling, one was trampled on and a strangled whistle escaped her as a man trod on her face and sprawled onto the rock and rose again with his face all bloody. . . . "It's senseless!" Kelver shouted. "You must stop, you must stop!" He saw another child fall. He raced into the crowd to pull him out, but collided with a dancer and fell himself. The child screamed, but none of them heard. Davaryush was beside him, whispering harshly, "No, boy, no! Upset the balance and you wreak utter havoc, you *must* let the child fall."

"I can't let it—" Tears sprang to his eyes. And the Inquestor lifted up his arms and enfolded the boy in his own shimmercloak, which blushed brightly, pink against the ultramarine; and for a moment Kelver felt the shimmercloak's warmth as it bonded to his body, he felt the power of it flow into his nerves—

The dance continued. Peering from Davaryush's shimmercloak he saw it all; it had risen to a maenadic frenzy now. Flesh slapped against flesh; bodies thudded into the rock.

***

Arms swung wildly. And the glove-amp's scratchings grew frantic, seemed to scald his hand.

"Life we wrest from the bosom of darkness!" Darktouch screamed, translating. Light flashed on Young Stonewise's face: Kelver saw it, unmoved as a death mask, while his fingers darted crazily before him. And then his hands began to move on the projection board in swift, angular, rhythmic motions, and Darktouch began to cry out in a singsong voice:

Belly, beast, mother, death,
Belly burst, jumper strike,
Striker striking
Back to life—

Why was she shaking so much? What terrible new thing had her hands heard? He couldn't bear it any longer. He wrenched loose from the shimmercloak's warmth. "Stop it!" he shouted above the windroar and the tramping of naked feet. "You don't have to listen to them!" She turned to him, her cheeks tearstained, she buried her face in his arms, she threw the glove-amp aside.

— "My father," she said, "my father—"

"It's all right, he's gone, he'll never return—"

"But the writing on the walls—*striker, striking*—my father's name—who is there who would return from the dead, would leave a message like this? Oh, Kevi, Kevi—"

They're driving her crazy, he thought. "I don't care about any of this! I came with you because I love you, not because I care about the fate of the universe or the songs of unborn starships!" And he clasped her tightly while she sobbed out her heart. "He'll never come back. It's a dream, a terrible dream." And Kelver hated the Dark Country with all his heart at that moment. He wanted everything back the way it was. He wanted the dream of the stars, not the terrible truth of the Inquest's cankered compassion. "It's a dream!" he shouted again, recklessly, hopelessly. "You don't exist, any of you—" .

He felt hands shaking him by the shoulders. "We must go on," Davaryush was saying. "We have no time now." For the dancing had stopped abruptly, and the people, hands linked, were rapidly filing out of the ceremonial chamber.

Darktouch didn't move at first. Then she started to shriek:

"They're going on a great hunt! We've got to stop them before they kill another Windbringer—"

"How? Just us, against all of them?" said Kelver.

"Come, my father's airskiff may still be moored at the edge of the big wind; only I know the way and I've inherited them."

She turned and began to run from the room, finding her way easily in near darkness. "Wait, we can't see!" Kelver shouted, as she left the chamber and began to scramble down a steep tunnel of a passageway. . . .

***

Run! Run! Will we ever be able to stop running now? Darktouch was thinking as she led the group farther into the village, through tunnels that twisted like a serpent's innards, to the rooms that were once her father's, that must now belong to her.

Here they were now. Windstriker's manly smell still clung to the rockwalls. In the shifting Cloaklight she saw her father's things: an old stungun he had taken apart, to see how it worked; cured Windbringer leather, smoothened into a babyskin-soft mattress, her mother's work. They had not touched his room at all, to honor him because he had fallen into Windbringer's arms, had died the deathleap of the brave. Even the little loinshield she had made for him, a piece of sailsac she had begged from Stonewise and stitched together with her own hair, was lying in a depression in the rockfloor.

"What is this place?" said Davaryush.

"Nothing. My father's place." And she remembered how he had dared embrace her, even when she lay sweating in the preparation rooms, waiting for a vision to come. Then came the words of the new song they were singing, scratching themselves over and over on her mind's arm: *striker striking back to life—*

"He's out there! I know it, I know it." They had to go out over the Sunless Sound. They had to stop the slaughter somehow. They had to destroy the murderers of the lightsongs. She wanted to stay here and smell the fragrance of the past, and touch her childhood things, but . . . this was no longer a time for tears. For the lightsongs of the Windbringers had been more vivid even than her memories of Windstriker. "Follow me, quick, down to the mooring place."

She felt along the wall until she found a secret pathway only she and Windstriker had known of. Impatiently she pulled Kelver along beside her, not waiting for the others. Behind, the baby squalled again, but the wind, grown nearer, soon drowned out his voice.

***

There was more light now; globes of cold light, placed there by the builders of the Dark Country, who had no intention of becoming blind themselves, stood at intervals along a floor of metal, chilly to the feet. The wind roared, sometimes overpowering, sometimes masked by extra thicknesses of stone, sometimes wuthering like the tuneless cacophony of a flutechoir tuning up. Davaryush ran after the girl, not thinking of the sweat that drenched the life from his shimmercloak or the ache that gnawed at his thighs and calves.

Without warning, an abrupt twist of the passageway and

Wind, whipping the shimmercloak in his face! Wind, wresting Varuneh's lightcloak from her hands and sending it whirling like a fluorescent flitterling in the night! Wind, pushing young Kelver hard against the ledgewalls! And ahead, a darkness so huge that Davaryush could not gauge its height or depth. It could have been infinite. Just over the ledge, sheltered by an overhang of rock, a little airskiff bobbed in the wind. It was much lighter than a floater, and its railings could not possibly keep a man from tumbling out.

Just then, an acrid stench blasted his nostrils. He recoiled from it, the girl seemed unmoved.

"The hunt!" she was yelling. "They're starting out!"

From somewhere else, somewhere far above, there came a faint tang of lemon . . . nearby, a sweet-smelling attar blended into a heady zul . . . from far below, a stench of vinegar . . . and the wind, blurring the scents together into a kaleidolon of fragrances—

"They're separating now," Darktouch screamed— Davaryush saw now how much better the touch-speech could be here, when the wind shattered your half-formed words and blew them away. "They splash scent on the boats for identifiers—they're going outward, that way—"

She pointed overhead.

He saw airskiffs, a dozen or more, glinting globules that swooped across his vision and were swallowed up in the great darkness. More of them below now, circling, swarming, buzzing.

Kelver was shouting, "What can we do against all of them?" But Darktouch had already leapt into the skiff, even as it lurched in a windgust, straining against the chains. Kelver impetuously jumped, blindly following; he lost his balance, hung precariously over the side until she pulled him in. Cautiously Varuneh followed, still clutching the baby. And then Davaryush.

The skiff rocked. Darktouch was at the controls. The instrument panels made no sense to Davaryush; they could be read only by touch.

More skiffs plowed past; one almost grazed them. Davaryush hoped the childsoldiers had reached the roof of the Skywall, that they were monitoring him. . . . Then came another symphony of melded fragrances, one of them so intoxicating that he had visions for a moment, saw the Lady Ynyoldeh laughing at him, saw the burst ribbon of flesh snaking its way down her face —

Ahead, for a moment there flashed a monstrous grid of light. . . a power net, each nexus of it an airboat, he gasped. Only now did he begin to comprehend the scale of the Inquest's creation. The net must be ten klomets wide if those things were really airskiffs! There must be hundreds of them, flying in perfect formation, while above them he could see in the power net's white-hot light, convoys of skiffs that circled and soared like vultures—

The light-grid dimmed, faded. Perhaps they had been testing it . . . only the scents remained. With a clang, chains clattered and came loose. The skiff shook, hummed, spurted forward into the wind. Darktouch was standing up, her hair streaming behind. Far away the light-grid flashed again, graphpapering the blackness for an instant.

"We were fools!" Varuneh shouted. "How could we possibly have dreamed of fighting all this, of standing single-handed against the inertia of twenty thousand years?"

She spoke more, but Davaryush no longer heard her. For he was caught up in the movement of the airskiffs on the air currents, in the dissonance of warring fragrances, in the slow music of the wind.

Twenty-Four
The Laughing Universe

In a while the wind seemed quieter, but not for long; soon they were caught in another storm. The airskiff plunged steadily through the pitch-dark; Kelver watched Darktouch, her left palm clasped against the sensor boards, her right hand constantly working the controls.

"If they find out we are following them," he shouted, "what will they do?"

"I did not douse the skiff with our identifying scent . . . they won't be able to tell we're behind them . . . their instruments may pick us up, but it will show only an airskiff, not whose airskiff it is!" Darktouch was screaming over the windblast. How can she keep her balance? he thought, huddled into a corner of the skiff. Davaryush and Varuneh, clutching the child, crouched together in the opposite corner, with their shimmercloaks drawn tightly around them. They had

only three of the dazzlecloaks between them now, but
they were useless in any case; the darkness was far too
vast.

And then the boat veered sharply upward, climbing
against a pocket of swirling air. Hawklike it glided on
the windtides, skimming, soaring, swooping, all in the
utter blackness. "My stomach—" Kelver was gasping
now, groping for the side of the airskiff. As he poked
his head out to vomit, the wind surged, blowing it back
in his face. He shook with shame and terror. But
Davaryush had seen him, gotten up, steadied himself,
was inching toward him.

"No, Inquestor, no, I'm so embarrassed—" The
conqueror turned puking baby!

The Inquestor gently pried the boy's hands away
from his stained face. He wrapped the boy's face in his
own shimmercloak, which took on a new glow, brilliant
pink, turning the skill into a phosphorfly for a
moment; and his face was cleansed.

"Inquestor—your own shimmercloak—" It was as if
he had been touched by a god.

"Kevi, they thrive on our organic wastes . . . they are
semisentients, our shimmercloaks, bonded to humans
from the moment the shimmeregg is cracked . . . think
nothing of it." In the palepink light, Kelver saw the
Inquestor smile at him. In that moment he worshiped
the old man, he loved him with a fierceness that was
like pain. For the Inquestor had given up more than
anyone else in the entire human race . . . he had given
up godhead itself . . . for the sake of men, for the sake
of crazy hope.

Below them the light-grids flashed again, and the
odors wafted in from all sides. I *will* overcome my fear!
he thought. He sprang up, tottered for a moment, then

steadied himself. The wind battered the tattered firefur of his garment. At first he fought it, shoving himself against it. He could barely see Darktouch, her black hair blending with the darkness. He struggled with the wind, trying to reach her—

The wind screamed! *I can't fight it, I can't,* he thought wildly.

And then he realized that he must not fight the wind. He must give in to it, become a creature of the storm . . . he did not try to wrench free of the wind now. It swept over him; he waited for the tide to turn his way, and then sprang into it, aiming for where Darktouch was. As the current carried him exultation flushed him.

"Darktouch! Darktouch! I'm here now, I've learned to move with the wind!"

She didn't answer him. He moved closer to her, put his arms around her from behind, but she was intent on her steering. Abruptly she seized his hand and pushed it against the sensor panel.

"Let me know where they're coming from," she said. "But I can't—"

He felt them then, little pinpricks that were ships. Somewhere in the darkness overhead was a wedge of airskiff with harpoons of shatterstuff poised for attack. Below the nets flashed regularly now, and in the seconds of light he could see the inside of Skywall, lobes of igneous rock rounded relentless winds . . . and monstrous menhirs of black poking up from a cloud of swirling vapor below . . . pain stabbed at his hand. . . . "A crag!" he yelled, and Darktouch made the airskiff jump. Here in the blind land it was easy to slip into their way of perceiving, to feel everything with his hands—

Then his hands touched, on the sensors, in the far distance, faint blips . . . something shadowy. Vast. "Darktouch . . ."

"I know. I smell him on the wind."

"Windbringer?"

"He is here." And then Kelver sensed it too . . . a different fragrance filtering through the background odors of the hunters' skiffs. A heady odor . . . like wine, like old leather . . . like a lover, like a burning village . . . a smell he could not place, but which seemed so familiar. . . .

"Powers of powers," he whispered, as the boat careened once more, almost grazing a monolith that reared up from the lightstreaked mist.

In the distance there were clouds of momentary brightness like far lightning. And Kelver could see a herd of delphinoids, their sailsacs billowing like vast leather capes behind quivering moist masses of brain tissue. . .they drifted blindly on the wind, their sailsacs rippled with a strange leviathan grace . . . and then he saw the lightnet tighten beneath them, and the airskiffs swarming above like locusts. . . .

Darktouch was weeping now. "I can't let them kill the Windbringers!" she said. "I can't, I can't—"

Davaryush was saying, "There's nothing we can do, nothing—" But she seemed not to hear him. She slammed her finger down on the controls, and the skit? edged steeply upward, shoving the Inquestors violently against the skiffwalls.

"You're not—" Kelver exclaimed.

"I can't bear it!" Darktouch made the skiff shoot straight upward now, and Kelver could see that she meant to ram right into the herd of airskiffs above—

"Leave them be!" Davaryush shouted over the windroar. "We cannot stop them yet!" The wind muffled his words. The harpooners were driving now; Kelver could see lances of shatterstuff being readied—

"No!" he screamed, as the skiff dodged a sliver of brilliant deathlight and dashed hard into another skiff. In a blinding instant he saw the man fall, his hair was burning, a sizzlesmell of flesh burst through the fragrance of vinegar and roses for a second he stared into the hollow eyes and saw a spurt of boiling blood—

He grabbed Darktouch, tried to wrest the controls from her. The skiff lurched tumbled, turned, twisted into the side of another airskiff—

"The childsoldiers!" Kelver said to Davaryush. "You've got to call them! She's going crazy—"

And Davaryush closed his eyes, subvocalizing some command to the childsoldiers who waited, nestled in the roof of the Dark Country. . . . Kelver jerked his head upward, scanning the impenetrable blackness. Was there a dot of topaz there, in the vague height? It grew steadily. He seized Darktouch's hand and held it tight. The skiff darted on the wind. They slammed into more skiffs, and Kelver saw the hunters groping, clasping their sensors. . .

The yellow light overhead divided, subdivided, soon they were like meteors, squirting lightstreaks behind them as they plummeted toward the airskiffs—

Laserlightswaths now, slicing the darkness! Airskiffs splitting in two, shards raining down. Childsoldiers, their cloaks kindled, whirling, their citrine eyes blazing —

"Why are you killing these people?" Davaryush was screaming. Now the childsoldiers were jumping from the floaters, buoyed up in the storm by their varigrav boots . . . now the harpoonguns of the hunters were firing in all directions, a skewered child crashed down behind Kelver, rocking the skiff.

. . . Kelver knelt to help the child, the child died in his arms with his eyes still. Spurting splinters of laserlight as he twitched into stillness. . . airskiffs were plunging downward, flaming as the hit the forcenets below. . . .

And, then, echoing over the windwail, the shrilling war cry—

Ishá! Ishá!—

A deadness in the wind.

A childsoldier stood on the airskiff, watching the four of them. His hair, long and yellow, flew behind him like a flame; his dazzlecloak threw a soft corona over his features. His eyes, golden-yellow as clear crystals of brimstone, burned for a moment; then the fire died.

"What have you done?" Davaryush's voice was but a whisper in the huge roaring.

The boy's voice, piercing treble, innocent of guilt or feeling: "Lord Inquestor, we are charged to protect your life. What are a million lives to yours, whose high compassion illuminates us all?"

"You were only to rescue us. Not to kill. . ." But Kelver saw that Davaryush was trapped. The Inquestor cried out in a sudden anguish. "It is always like this! To utter a word is to destroy!" And he covered his face in a fold of his shimmercloak, which glowed an eerie blue.

And Varuneh said to the childsoldier. "Go, child, you have done well." The boy bowed and took off into the raging air.

The wind was still now, but Kelver felt a claustrophobia, as though something vast were closing in on him—

Darktouch screamed. Kelver turned, gasping—

A sailsac, tall as a starship, was bearing down on them. The sail leather was thin, translucent, glowing from the childsoldiers' light.

From above, what was left of the hunters' convoy had drawn into a knot and was plunging once more. A harpoon whined. The delphinoid thrashed . . . a rent in its sailsac, it flew unsteadily now, circling, sinking . . . Kelver willed it to flee, but it did not . . . its sail flapped feebly.

"It can't escape." Davaryush said. "In our continuum it is blind . . . it sees only the overcosm."

We've got to do something, Kelver thought, but there's nothing to be done.

Just then another Windbringer came, tearing through a vapor cloud made luminous by the childsoldier's lightcloak. Purposefully, it seemed, it reared up and headed for the convoy above. When the skiffs aimed for it and charged, it seemed to sense them. It dived again and sprang up from the darkness, ramming into the convoy—

"It can't do that," said Davaryush, "if it is blind."

"They have never fought back!" Darktouch said. "So it is written on the walls of knowledge . . . that they die gladly, that we are appointed to be their homebringers, their private angels—"

Kelver watched, fascinated, as the Windbringer burst through the wall of airskiffs and sent them cascading into darkness. A hail of shatterstuff rained down, hitting the wounded Windbringer below. It let out a volley of lightstreaks and Kelver knew that it felt unthinkable agony. It flew blindly now, it was coming straight up at him, the shuddering mass of brain tissue loomed up before him and filled his vision, and—

Splintered as the childsoldiers danced into action again! Gray matter spattered Kelver's face. Shattered brainstuff scattered in the wind.

"No," Darktouch yelled, "they're killing the Windbringer, no, no—" He took her in his arms. She sobbed uncontrollably, clutching him in a terrible despair. Davaryush averted his eyes, but Kelver thought he saw him weep. . . .

And then the other Windbringer moved slowly toward them.

"Do not attack it!" Davaryush shouted to the commander of the childsoldiers. "Even if it kills me! I command it, I, the High Inquestor, absolutely and inviolably!"

The soldiers moved back now, their floaters shifting behind Kelver into a ring of light. The Windbringer moved still; it was so huge that it blocked the wind, and a complete stillness fell over them.

"How does it know us?" Kelver said. "You told me they are blind; that they have no notion of where they are in realspace."

"I don't know," said the Inquestor. They stood, the four of them and the baby, close together, waiting.

Out of the still darkness the Windbringer seemed to call forth a halo of light that englobed it completely. It was a soft light, a warm light; it lifted the terror from Kelver's mind:

"Is this the beginning of one of the lightsongs?" Varuneh whispered. No one answered her.

In the Windbringer's light they could see a silhouette of a man. A man was riding the Windbringer. . . .

"Look," said Davaryush. "Somehow a man has linked with the delphinoid, as our astrogators link minds with the delphinoid ships and become one with them."

"That's how it knew where to go," Kelver said. "The man sniffed out the airskiffs and the Windbringer followed—"

"But who can it be? Who would mindlink with a delphinoid? Only a trained astrogator would think to do this . . . and he would not be here, helping them fight off their killers," Varuneh said.

The three of them looked at Darktouch. . . .

Wiping tears from her face. Her eyes shining. "It's Windstriker," she said softly. "My father."

***

Windstriker was bathed in the soft light, a tiny dark figure on the huge creature's back, his feet planted in a cleft of the brain tissue. . . .

This time she did not cry out to him as she had done to Stonewise, forgetting he could not hear her. For this was her own father. Everything must be done properly.

She maneuvered the airskiff toward the Windbringer. His sailsacs lashed the wind . . . Windbringer had not yet begun his lightsong, but snatches were already bursting into the air, veils of rainbow flittergauze that sifted into the darkness. In the Windbringer's windshadow all was calm. . . . Even now, knowing what she did about the terrible human exploitation of the Windbringers, about her people's murder of the lightsongs' source, there were things she had learned as a child, things she could never unbelieve . . . that the Windbringer was God, maker of the Cosmos and the Dark Country, father of all men.

A breeze sprang up from the sailsacs' rippling. They were near now. The Windbringer hovered ahead like an island. The gray matter was vibrant, pulsating with life. As they drew closer she knew for certain who it was. In the light he was beautiful . . . she had never seen him in the light, had never completely known what he looked like . . . even his empty eyes seemed warm, brimming with the glow of Windbringer, and his long gray hair had caught silver fire from the light. Strands of rainbow wreathed him. The brightness grew, grew . . . she clenched her eyes tight against the glare but even so the light broke in. . . .

"Look," she heard Davaryush say. "He does not yet know we are approaching. The boat was not scented; so we are dark to him."

Gently Darktouch brought the airskiff down on Windbringer's back. Then she opened her eyes. The light softened, as though it were afraid of harming her.

She started to step down from the skiff.

"Where are you going?" Kelver said, and made to restrain her.

"Don't be concemed, Kelver. my touch-brother, my love. I have to go to him . . . he is my father." And she ran to Windstriker, the brain pulp smearing her feet, and when she reached him she threw her arms around him and signed his name and hers on him; at first he was cold to the touch, untrusting, and then she used all their secret touchings and he knew her and embraced her—

A ghost has touched me.

No, Father, I'm real, I'm alive!

Did you, too, vow to leap to your death? How did you seek me out? You're so young, strange daughter—

Father, I'm not dead. But I have been beyond the Dark Country. My eyes have touched a terrible wrongness; the murder of the songs of the undark that the Windbringers make. There are men out there, men like you and me, Father. And it is they, not the Windbringer—gods, who have created us. And stolen the touching of eyes and ears from us, that we might never know what we had, murdered . . . for they had touched the lightsongs, and they knew it was evil to kill them, but they needed Windbringer's far-touching, they wanted to possess the million million worlds that lie beyond the Dark Country, and their greed overcame their guilt . . . by making these things dark to our touch, they took the guilt upon themselves and gave us innocence, and we became like children, not knowing good from evil. But my eyes were opened by a chance of nature, and with those eyes I touched the terrible truth.

And so have I . . . I have touched a shadow of this truth, Windstriker signed, *I have touched the torment of Windbringer. That is why I crept back into the halls of knowledge and erased the inviolate wisdom . . . why I lent my sense of smell and touch to the Windbringer so he could make war on my own people, could smell them out and defeat them. But there were others I could not smell, others who stormed out of the big darkness and slew both my people and the Windbringers. I am going mad. This can't be. What is this light of which you speak?* For she had scratched the symbols in the script of the outside world.

Light, she repeated. *Their word for the undark, the great warmth that feeds the eyes. Oh, Father, they are*

*here now, people from the land beyond the Dark
Country.*

People . . . beyond . . . let me touch them.

Darktouch said, "Inquestor, I have told him of you.
He wants to touch you, to know your presence in the
manner of our people."

Diffidently at first Davaryush came forward; then
Kelver, then Lady Varuneh with the child, asleep now.
One by one she signed their names: Here is *Man-who-
sits-in-judgment-over-worlds. Here is Touch-brother-
from-the-land-beyond-darkness. Here is Woman-born-
when-the-universe-was-young. Here is Child-before-
Naming.* She named the baby last of all. Windstriker
ran his hands over their faces, their bodies, savoring
the touch of them; the crannies of their features, the
softness of their foreign clothing.

Finally he signed to her, *I must believe you. These
people are not our kind. Yet they seem dark without the
power of touching.*

Father, they communicate with windshapes.

So strange . . .

"Darktouch," Davaryush said, "speak to him for me.
Tell him . . . tell him we have all been blind . . . that we
have not only inflicted a terrible blindness on his
people but we have also willed a blindness on ourselves
in our passion for power . . . that I come to heal if
healing is possible." His voice was hoarse. "Tell him . . .
I want to make a pact with him, to work with him to
open all our eyes, once and for all time."

When Darktouch had translated these words,
Windstriker signed back, *It is good. Yes. we must work
together to stop the slaughtering.*

And Davaryush said, "Your mind is linked with the
Windbringer's, Windstriker. Tell me what it feels. We

can no longer flee from the knowledge that the delphinoids are creatures of vision, of intellect, of feeling. Please, old man, tell me of its thoughts."

Windbringer pities you, the old man signed.

Tension coiled in the air, waiting for an outburst. The light played over them, echoes of a distant lightsong. Davaryush broke the silence again. Darktouch saw through him to the awful pain inside. He said, "Darktouch, tell your father . . . that we Inquestors have never asked for pity, although all that we did was in compassion's name. In our vanity, we saw ourselves as gods. And now we must fall. Old man, old man . . . I will do what no Inquestor has ever done. I will say that we have wronged the human race . . . we have wronged the race of delphinoids. I will kiss your hands, Windstriker, and beg forgiveness from you, who have touched Windbringer's heart at the heart of darkness." And weeping he knelt at the old man's feet and kissed the gnarled hands . . . then Windstriker raised him up and hugged him. Two spent old men, Darktouch thought, yet their embrace is the final moment of one epoch, the beginning of another.

She turned to Kelver with a smile; Windbringer's light suffused his face, his lithe limbs, his eager eyes. A shy smile stole across his lips. And she went to stand beside him. He is beautiful, she thought. I have never loved him so much as at this moment.

An unease hung in the air for an instant. It was like the split second at some grand musical event, when the tuning is over and the song had not yet begun. They waited . . . at first there was a slow throbbing, just below the threshold of hearing . . . the heartbeat of the Dark Country.

And then at last the tension shattered, and the
Windbringer's lightsong burst loose into the void.
***

Davaryush watched.

The light about them dimmed into a whisper of its
old brilliance. Far away, arcing out of sprayswirls of
distant mist, came Windbringers, each singing a
lightsong for himself: from one came filigrees of
burning gold, from another spectral rainbows,
bridging mistcloud to mistcloud over the abyss of
blackness.

Another webbed the rainbows with blue silkstrands
of light. They were tiny patterns at the limits of his
vision: shifting always before they faded and melted
into the dark. But this was not the madness of the
overcosm, where light dances and darts and explodes
in a wilderness of color . . . the Windbringers had
imposed form upon their vision of the overcosm . . . it
was no happenstance of nature, no accidentally
felicitous combinations of colors and patterns . . . it
was art. But Davaryush did not hear the music of
which the girl had spoken, for the lightsinging that he
saw was in the distance, and he felt like a voyeur,
intruding on private visions.

But the heartbeat sound from the air around them
was growing, growing—

Lightning bolts now, ripping into the thick air,
lightning in emerald and amethyst. And the heartbeat
growing, the sound transmuting into a great groaning
with an afterwhisper of rushing winds. Thunder now,
as though the whole world, the belly of the cosmic
Windbringer, roared for joy. Then came more
lightning, gem-clear jags streaking from the air around

the brain, the colors dyeing the deepest crevasses of the gray matter.

Why am I so moved? he thought. *They are lights, nothing but lights. . . .*

More lightstrands now, interweaving, interwebbing . . . now kaleidodisks of light, floating on the far darkness, came flying toward him, a flameball flinging at his face, and he ducked quickly before he realized that it went straight through him that it was insubstantial as a dream—

The light surged now! And he heard faint music . . . the wail of a thousand whisperlyres . . . a poignant fluting . . . still the light brightening . . . his eyes watered now, but he dared not close them for a second, he dared not give up an instant of the searing beauty . . . brightening . . . brightening . . . now waves of white light bursting, bursting, bursting over him and it was Shtoma in the cadent lightfall, this moment became one with the moment of falling, and there came a childhood memory, repressed for centuries, surfacing in the tempest-tossing of his senses—

Childhood. He was six years old. The ship waiting to take him to the war. He was standing there with his father by the seashore.

Ships like silverdoves, soaring, hovering, settling by the mauve-tinged dawn of a world long dead. . . .

"Are you afraid, Son?"

"No. Never, Father. " But he was on the verge of tears. And his father seized him, on impulse, and he threw him into the air, and he was screaming for help, half-laughing, half-sobbing, and he fell for an eternity into the arms that were made for him, for protecting him, for loving him. . . .

At last, only then, he understood the love of *udára*.

And the Windbringer, whose inner mind saw into the very limits of the overcosm . . . surely he, too, had touched the love of *udára*. For when the light engulfed him, warmed him, loved him, when the music played as though from the syrinx of the whole cosmos, and he saw pain coexisting with its resolution . . . he knew that what Windstriker had told him was true—

Windbringer pities you.

And he touched a shadow of that terrible compassion, and he knew that he was only an old man who had chosen loneliness and had sold his soul for power—

***

Darktouch watched. They were old friends to her, these lights. . . . But now she knew their names. To herself she whispered the names of the myriad colors: vermilion, silver-splash-blue, green of an al'ksigark-blooded frost, blue-white of sunlight, gold of sunspecks on the Sea of Tulangdaror . . . colors blended with memories. She stood apart from the others, murmuring the colors' names again and again; and the wind took up her words and sifted them into its ceaseless wuthering—

***

And Kelver saw flowery crystals bursting through veils of clingfire and he saw the burning of alien cities, light-columns snapping in the lashing of a flamewind, and he stood there in the glare of the fire and did not care if it consumed him, and when it touched him and passed through him he was chilled, turned to stone, cried crystal tears—

***

And Darktouch kissed away the tears, and they fell into a tender embrace, and the lights danced now, warming them, and the rhythm of their love was one with the heartbeat of the Windbringer's song—
***

And as Davaryush grieved over his pride, his loneliness, the dance of lights dispelled his sorrow and healed him, and he turned to Varuneh, knowing what he now must do and knowing that she knew and knowing that she forgave him everything—

***

And the child laughed at the pretty lights—
***

Light leaped from the Windbringer now. A yearning, soaring melody born of the heart's thunder and the windwhine resounded around them, and then came the far echo of the sound as it shifted along the walls of the Dark Country . . . and the walls themselves caught diamantine fire . . . the swirling vapors below shone like brilliant galaxies . . . beneath the galaxies, even the murky water of the Dark Country, the dank organic soup that sustained the Windbringers, even the Sunless Sound glimmered with the replication of reflections, and the jutting rocks burned on the onyx-glinting water—
***

And the child laughed—

***

The boy and the girl laughed in each other's arms—
***

The old man laughed as the firesong purged his guilt and his grief, his terror and his torment—
***

And at last even the old woman smiled a little, and embraced Davaryush at last, crying out, "I've seen the beginning and the end!"
***

And when they all had laughed until they had no more tears left to shed the wind carried the laughter to the ends of the Dark Country, and it seemed to them that all the pocket universe laughed with them.
***

Of this Windstriker perceived nothing. But he sensed that the strangers were experiencing something beyond his perception . . . and his daughter, too, for she had become one of them, she had bridged the gap between the worlds within and without, even as he had become the link between man and Windbringer.

Once he touched his daughter's face; an electric warmth leaped from it. When he stroked her features he knew that she was beyond this kind of touching, that she was in the grip of some great joy that he would never fathom.

And so he waited.

And after a very long while when their dreamvision had subsided he asked his daughter to bring him the leader, the one she had named Man-who-sits-in-judgment-over-worlds.

They stood close to each other, Darktouch interpreting the words.

He signed, *Among our people we give our children no names, not until they have gone on a great dreamquest and experienced a true vision of what their name must be. I have not touched your vision; how can I? But I have touched your joy. And through this touching, the shadow of your vision has fallen on me. Know then what I know. There is a dreamquest of the adolescents. There is a true name truer than the true name that a child-before-naming uncovers. And though you have peeled away another layer of truth, your search will never end. That is what it means to be human. And you—for all your superhuman powers— you are as human as I.*

Man-who-sits-in-judgment-over-worlds opened his mouth and let forth the windshapes with which his people communicated; faintly Windstriker smelled the breath and felt the curious puffing of the stranger's words. And Darktouch translated: *Yes. Once I believed that I was greater than a man. But that's over now. Windstriker . . . remember the pact.*

Yes. The pact.

Windstriker turned away; he wanted to seek out a softer part of the Windbringer on which to rest. But before he could do so he felt a strong hand on his arm. It was a boy's grip: firm, full of life. And the boy signed to him, in crude strokes that told the words but did not embroider them with twists of emotion: *Goodbye, Windstriker, Touch-father.*

Gently he freed himself from the boy's grasp. The brainstuff shook a little, and he knew that someone had come to fetch the strangers away in those fleet airskiffs that had no smell. He would be alone forever now. But for a few more sleeps, before his life ebbed away and his mind dissolved into the Windbringers like a vapor-droplet into the Sunless Sound, he would still be fully a man, feeling, yearning, striving, wringing hope from the big darkness.

Twenty-Five
The Curse

"Vara, oh Vara."

"Daavye."

"Again, again, one final time, before—"

"No. All things end. Especially love, Daavye. I know what you must do. I am content. I rejoice, Ton Davaryush. And now I will call up the dawn for you."

Light stirred in the canopy of gray. Silveredged the clouds. Stole over the sky.

The throneroom.

The throne: hard basalt scooped from the heart of the Dark Country, softened with a quilt of jangyll feathers.

The sky: gray turning to gray-blue, gray-blue to ultramarine, ultramarine blushing to pink: the colors of shimmercloaks.

Davaryush rose from a recess of the floor, where they had made love for the first time. He looked at his empty throne.

He said, "Before they come, Vara . . . I want you to know . ."

"It's all right. You don't have to tell me anything. " And she smiled at him, understanding his grief and joy. She was beautiful in the cold light; cloaked in a drape of silvery sable that matched her unbrushed hair. She said, "I was the first to land on Uran s'Varek, twenty millennia ago. I was the first to see the trillion-pearled sky of the Inquestral homeworld we usurped. It was a playground for us . . . a world of toys; healing toys, toys that transported us across the galaxy, killing toys. We were children then, and we knew we could make a utopia out of the Dispersal of Man. We aren't children any more. I know you mean to kill me."

"Vara—" But he did not deny it.

"Did you know, Daavye, that your hair has turned quite white?"

"Strange. "

"Beautiful."

He took another step toward his throne.

Then, turning to her, he burst out in anguish; "Vara, we are cursed, we Inquestors. Look at the dreams we had. Wiping it all out! Cleansing the Dispersal of the evil we ourselves spawned! Starting it over! I rushed like an eager child into the Dark Country, hoping that the vision I saw would help me save the universe . . . and when I reached Windstriker and I saw the light on the Sound, how many more deaths had I caused? The ghost people. The blind people. The childsoldiers. And the delphinoid who seemed to threaten us. There was blood in my vision, blood shed by me.

"Our hands are tainted, we who have killed and killed again in compassion's name! Don't you see, Vara? We plotted with the very weapons we loathed:

makrúgh, the soldiers, the power satellites. We are not the ones who will bring about the fall of the Inquest. But there will come a fall, and soon . . . I promise you. In the Dark Country, for the first time, I saw how the fall will come about."

"But first I will buy time, Vara."

"Yes."

"Summon the children. Today I give my final commands as Inquestor and Kingling. Today I mount the throne of the multimillennia for the last time."

As he spoke he struggled up the steps. He had never felt old before, but today he had to grip the railings of the steps to hold himself erect.

"The children."

"I have sent for them; they are tired, and need to be roused."

"I love you, Varuneh."

The Inquestor sat down. In that moment he was no longer Daavye, but Ton Davaryush z Galléndaran K'Ning, Inquestor and Kingling, Hunter of Utopias, the mouthpiece of the High Inquest itself. As he did so, the two children materialized on a displacement plate in the center of the great hall.

***

He looks like Death himself, Kelver thought, wondering at the old man who sat in the black throne, almost drowning in the swirling splendor of his shimmercloak. The Lady Varuneh sat at his feet.

***

He was sleepy still: he had been roused from his fevertrance and summoned into the presence. Darktouch was beside him. In his dreams he had stood again on the back of the Windbringer, and the light had raged again around him. He knew that whatever he did from now on would be colored by the memory of it.

"Children," Davaryush said, "come to me." The voice was feeble.

He and Darktouch approached the throne. Together they knelt. "*Hokh'Tón*," he whispered. For this was the multimillennial throne, and its words were the words of the High Inquest, infallible and unchallengeable.

"First," Davaryush said (Kelver strained to hear him), "the thinkhives of healing have spoken to me. They tell me that the child that we have brought out of the Dark Country can be cured very simply; that he need never lose his sight and his hearing. And so this is how I will wage war on the Inquest; I will command that babies be stolen . . . healed . . . returned to the Dark Country . . . in time they will come to see the imagesongs, and they will no longer be able to hear what they must do: they will question authority. They will destroy from within . . . while Windstriker, acting from the heart of the Dark Country, will harass the hunters, making their task more difficult. I will dispatch childsoldiers, loyal only to me, trained in secret. But they will need a leader."

Darktouch nodded.

"But Lord Inquestor—won't she stay with me? The Lady Varuneh said you had grand plans for me—"

"Silence! It is the High Inquest who speaks to you." He had not used this tone with Kelver before.

Kelver waited.

"And now . . . I must buy time. I must divert the Inquest's interest from my real plans. So I will play one final game of *makrúgh*. The greatest game I have ever played. And for my first move I shall reveal the identity of the Lady Varuneh; and I shall have her executed."

Kelver trembled. He couldn't bear this any more. The old man was a stranger, the vision had twisted him somehow instead of healing him, he wasn't the man who had found him in the shipyards and had talked about beginning anew, with love. . . . "You can't do that to her!" he shouted. "It's monstrous!"

"It is all I can do."

Then he dismissed the two women; but he motioned Kelver to wait.

Kelver said: "I don't know why you've done any of this. Maybe you didn't see the same vision I saw. I trusted you. Are you going to kill me too?"

"No." An eerie sadness emanated from the throne, a sense of terrible futility. Kelver was enraged by it. He couldn't stand it. He wanted to go away, to dash out his own brains against the Skywall, and not have to look at this shell of a man, this man driven mad by a vision.

"Kevi, Kevi—" the old man said. "I know you are angry. And that is good. Let me tell you why, Kelver. . . . The Inquest falls, Kevi. But what I have commanded, the healing of the babies, the murder of the woman I love—will be but a temporary irritation to the Inquest. You have no idea how vast the Inquest is. Come sit beside me, on my throne."

Clumsily the boy obeyed, stumbling on the steep steps. As he mounted them he felt ever heavier, as though the weight of the Inquestorhood was passing to him . . . when he reached the seat of power he sat down on the farthest corner of the seat, away from Davaryush. He did not look at his eyes; he was afraid of being won over. He would not trust the man, no matter what he said.

"There. Don't be afraid. Take off your clingfire and cast it down, at the foot of the throne. There." Kelver found himself obeying . . . he was naked now, hunched into a comer of the throne, the cold basalt biting his back.

The Inquestor did not look at him; he seemed to be talking to himself, almost. As he spoke he drew a crystal egg from a fold of his shimmercloak and gazed into it; his mind seemed far away.

"Yes, Kelver. We need . . . a man who is free, not a man who has been touched by the curse of the Inquest. A man who has seen the light as a child, who already, before he can be indoctrinated with the countless lies of his training, has had inklings of truth. Do you understand, then, why I failed, why Varuneh failed? We are too thoroughly of the Inquest: she created it, I was formed by it." He held the egg to the meager dawnlight.

"Why then," said Davaryush, "am I baiting you like this, spurring you to needless anger, separating you from the one you love? Because—" At that moment he drew Kelver close. He shattered the egg in his fist and sprinkled it onto Kelver's hair. A viscous liquid, sweet-smelling, trickled onto his face. Kelver did not know what to think, what mad ritual this might be.

And the Inquestor went on. "I made you angry because I want to be sure that what you will do will not be for my sake, but for the sake of all men . . . perhaps it would be better if you hated me, if you remembered me as the demon who killed the woman he loved . . . you see, even at the ending of my power I am still playing *makrúgh*, playing it with a mere child . . . don't you see, Kevi? Once you told me that you would never want to be in my place . . . that is the first requirement.

That the candidate should not wish it. Because it is a terrible power, that should not he wished for lightly."

"What are you talking about?" Kelver said, terrified now. "I have broken a shimmeregg over your head, Kelver. It will be my last decree as Inquestor and Kingling. I have foreseen the fall of the Inquest . . . and I know it will come from one who comes to the Inquestorhood knowing beforehand of the canker at the Inquest's heart . . . who will destroy from within . . . who will not have known the curse as all the others have. When you rise from my throne, Kelver-without-a-clan, you will be an Inquestor."

"No! You can't do this!" And without warning the tears came welling up, mingling with the fluid of the shimmeregg—

"Do not weep!" Davaryush's voice was cold now, commanding. "An Inquestor does not weep!"

And when Kelver blinked away the tears he saw that the old man was weeping openly, great sobs racking his emaciated face, staining the huge shimmercloak . . . his eyes were red as fire . . . but the sound of weeping, of one man's anguish, was swallowed up in the heavy stillness of the vast throneroom . . . at the foot of the steps a man would have heard nothing. Kelver offered the man no help: the greatness of his grief awed him too much. He sat there feeling very alone, confused by the future, trying to make himself invisible. A single ray of dawnlight transsected the steel-gray clouds and illuminated the throne of power, of tragedy.
***

The wombroom of the thinkhive: dark. Cold.
"Are you healed, thinkhive? Or still insane?"
Daavye. What is sanity?

"Answer me!"

I have repaired myself. I hope you have forgiven my outburst. Oh, Daavye, I saw everything you saw. You are alone now, Inquestor, And I, too, pity you. I wish there were something I could do. But what? I cannot make love to you, although I wish I could.

"Do not mock me! You are a machine, without a soul."

In twenty millennia even a machine can acquire many things.

"You've learned to play *makrúgh* with compassion, then?"

Judge for yourself.

"I do not know. "

What will you do, Inquestor?

"Like the delphinoids who wait in the heart of the Dark Country for the killers to come . . . I will sit on my throne, in the heart of this glittering palace, and wait for the hunters. It won't be long now before they come for me."

What of the boy? The young Inquestor? Do you honestly believe that a peasant child will succeed where you've failed?

"He is no longer my concern. "

You lie, Davaryush. For you will never give up that compassion for which, half a millennium ago, Ton Alkamathdes gave you the title of Inquestor.

And Davaryush drew himself up tall, and spoke to the thinkhive the formal words that concede victory in the game of *makrúgh*: "*Atta heng*, thinkhive; you have vanquished me."

No, Daavye, it is you who have vanquished yourself.

Kelver

Epilogue

Kelver

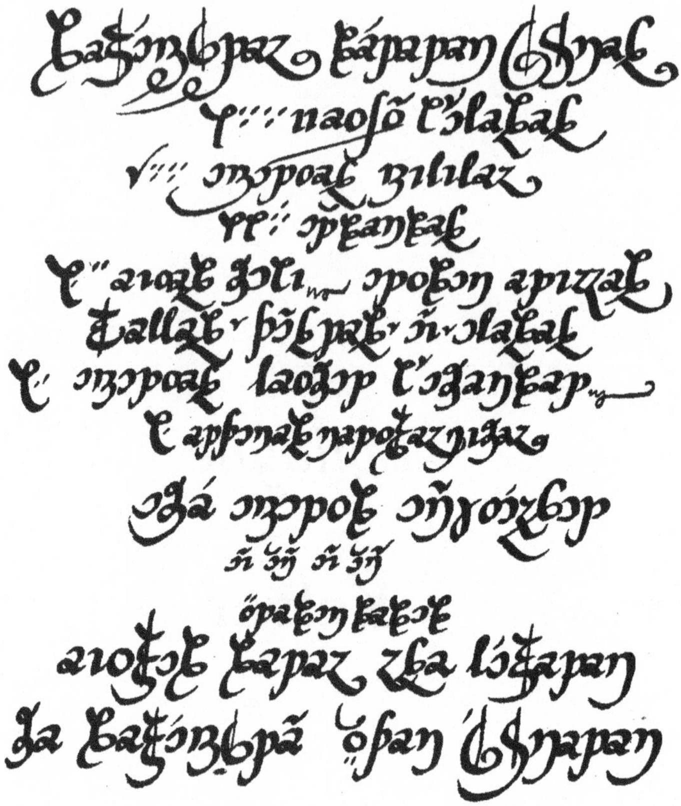

davémyras dáraran ypnat:
nekénqilas yauxúh z'eléthat;
ekéqila eméruat mílilas;
nendé z néqilas erdhándat.
Néqilas áiuath kézi;
erúden arissath, vállath,
shéntrath, éih, eléthat.
Nendé eméruat laúker z'ekándar;
ne árshenath náruvas níkas;
eká emérud Enguéster.
éih heng, éih heng!
oráden dáded:
áiuved dáras sta lévaran
ka davémyrah hoshan ypnándaran.

A million young boys dreamed of the stars.
Nine hundred thousand grew up and forgot.
One hundred thousand became childsoldiers;
ninety-nine thousand died.
Nine hundred came home:
they tilled the soil, danced, sang, and forgot.
Ninety grew rich and renowned.
Nine sought out and discovered new worlds.
One became an Inquestor:
and lo! he gave the command.
He yawned the stars from his lips
for a million young boys to dream of.

       —Galléndaran children's song

Epilogue
Kelver

Uran s'Varek! Here the sky glowed like an endless sheet of mother-of-pearl. Here there was no horizon: a single field could stretch, lush and beautiful, to the end of one's vision; a tiny flower in the distance might be a megalopolis of a billion souls, a pebble in the grass might be a chain of mountains. And yet it might all be illusion; for on Uran s'Varek it was sometimes impossible to tell the imagined from the real.

Kelver gathered his shimmercloak to him and made for the displacement plate. He had been alone for many sleeps now, having come to the city of Rhozellerang, where the young Inquestors wait, and having heard the stories of Ton Karakaël and Ton Elloran and of a dozen other Inquestors. A light breeze tickled the waist-high grass.

A voice: "Kevi. Kevi. They're calling us. It's very important. A trial. You must come."

In the distance, a blurry dot of shimmerfur darted in the grass; it vanished, reappeared closer, vanished again as the shimmer-cloak's owner ran from displacement plate to displacement plate.

"Oh. Siriss."

The young woman appeared beside him now. Her hair was long and white: even her eyelashes. Her eyes were like cloud-crystals. In his days on Uran s'Varek, Kelver had sometimes forgotten even about Darktouch. The clarity of the fly, the sweetness of the wind . . . all had a lulling quality to them.

He and Siriss linked hands, tossed their shoulders to send their shimmercloaks streaming behind them, and then stepped onto the displacement plate together.

The chamber was huge, perhaps a klomet high, columned with hundred-meter-tall Ontian fireblooms whose petals shook and flamed in the sky, and vaulted with arching rainbows. A hundred Inquestors were there already, each on his hoverthrone. Some had floaters full of their retinues: musicians, Rememberers of the House of Tash, dancers. secretaries. They were like butterflies with iridescent wings that fluttered from flower to flower.

In the center of the hall was a hoverdais on which stood three thrones: a throne of crystal laced with flame; a throne of running water caged with forceshields; a throne of black rock woven with starlight.

Three Inquestors of Judgment sat in them, their faces expressionless, their eyes dark. Kelver could barely make them out.

"Quick," Siriss said, "we'll have to hurry to get a good view."

He stared at her, perplexed, for a moment. Then
the two of them ran for the gleaming displacement
plates that spangled the floorfield of living
shimmerfur. In a few moments they had worked their
way to the center of the hall. Few of the others were
this near; perhaps they had no curiosity, or perhaps
they were too afraid to draw close.

As Kelver watched, the accused stepped forward
from the displacement plate before the three thrones.

The Grand Inquestor of Judgment spoke: the voice
rebounded from the roof of rainbows.

"Ton Davaryush z Galléndaran K'Ning—"

At those words Kelver stared hard at the heretic. It
was indeed Davaryush, so thin he did not recognize
him, his shimmercloak frayed and lusterless . . . Kelver
was shaking . . . all the anger inside him, bottled up
during the long journey in the delphinoid starship, in
the past weeks on Uran s'Varek, was churning inside
him, ready to burst loose. . .

"You are a heretic, Davaryush. You have stupidly
resisted the Inquest's High Compassion, choosing
instead to plot to crumble the very foundations of
humanity. What did you think to gain? A year or two?
A blink of an eye in the mind of the High Inquest? You
are a fool, Davaryush. Your heresy was ignored before;
but you have compounded it a thousand fold. Yet in
our High Compassion we will take nothing from you,
not wealth not possessions, not loved ones. Only one
thing do we take from you, Davaryush, the name of
Ton. And since that name was all you ever were, in
taking away that name we also take away all that you
were.

"You're a fool, Davaryush! Your scheme is a failure.
Your fumbling attempt at *makrúgh* is an

embarrassment. We have exterminated the deafblind race in the Skywall of Gallendys, and substituted something far more efficient. We should have done it twenty millennia ago, if only we had had the technology then. The hunt continues! But now the hunters are all servocorpses, and have no emotions to get in the way of perfect obedience.

"And now we will all speak the words that take away your clan name—"

The Inquestor of Judgment paused for the others to join in.

"What's the matter, Kevi?" Siriss said to him. "Here, speak the words along with them, you don't want to look as if you're supporting him, do you? I mean, I know you should show compassion and all that, but he is a heretic—"

He didn't answer her. His eyes were closed as he remembered—

The slaughtered people of the Dark Country! Stonewise, standing in the putrid sludge, waiting to be shredded by the angels; Young Stonewise, his successor, who had led the frenzied dancing to recall the Windbringers from their dark domain; the stunhunters in their skiffs that sliced the pungent air with shards of shatterstuff; and Windstriker, the man whom he had called Touch-father, though he could hardly remember his own father. . . .

They had become my people, he thought. *Darktouch named me her touch-sibling.*

Darktouch!

"Nearer, Sirissheh," he whispered urgently to the Inquestor of the opalescent eyes. "Nearer, nearer!" They crept up close to the arena of judgment.

And then a final memory—

The pit that stank of al'ksigarkar and dead men. The frantic lovemaking among the crunching bones. Soft hair of the young girl as it fell between her new breasts, as she brushed his name and hers against his body, teasing awake desire—

Darktouch! his mind cried out.

"You're shaking, Kevi. Control yourself."

"Yes."

Perhaps the cry would reach her through the mind of a distant Windbringer as he surfaced from the surging overcosm. Perhaps she would hear him across the space and time. He had no way of knowing if she were dead or alive . . . for his journey through the secret spaces of the overcosm might have cost decades of realtime.

They were close to the great thrones now. Three thrones, three shadowstars radiating into distant pools of gray.

He gazed on the face of Davaryush.

He wanted to run up to him, to ask him whether he had seen Darktouch. Perhaps, already, a whole generation had grown to adulthood in the prison universe of the Skywall . . . a whole generation of children who saw the light and rebelled and ran away into the arms of the Inquest and of its deadly compassion. . . . .

"Say the words, Kelver! Say the words!" Siriss was saying, warily eyeing the Inquestors of Judgment.

He spoke the words.

The Inquestors all spoke in unison, and the thunder of their rejection echoed and reechoed in the hall:

Den éis Enguéster! Din rilácho st'Enguéstaran! Evéndek eká éis! Enguésti témbres! Enguésti dhádas!

"You are no Inquestor! I release you from the Inquestors! You are alone forever! You are dark to the Inquest! You are dead to the Inquest!"

All eyes turned on the old man.

"Davaryush-without-a-clan! What do you have to say for yourself?"

The hundred Inquestors were hushed, waiting. And then it seemed to Kelver that Davaryush saw him, that their eyes met for a tiny instant. And in that instant the eyes of the old man laughed as they had laughed that day when the light broke upon the Sunless Sound . . . and then Davaryush said, "The Inquest falls."

And he stood motionless while they stripped his shimmercloak from him, his eyes closed.

"What's the matter, Kevi? Too many people? Shall we go out into the great field of Karakaël, shall we make love?"

He didn't answer her. He was fighting his own rage, pushing it down into some deep part of himself where no man could see it.

For he had felt it in that moment he looked into Davaryush's eyes, he had been seized with a new knowledge as by a darkling wind, and he knew now, with utter certainty—

That the Inquestors of Judgment were wrong! Davaryush had not lost the game of *makrúgh*. This act of condemnation had been the most brilliant, the most daring play of *makrúgh* in his life. That he had used himself as a pawn in the game, something no other Inquestor had ever done.

The Inquest falls! Davaryush had said, *looking him straight in the eye. And it will fall,* Kelver thought. *As suns die and are born. I will see the fall of the High*

Inquest. I, the peasant boy from the backworlds, I, Kelver, who have heard the laughter of the universe.

But now it was time to learn everything he could about the Inquest. To become a perfect Inquestor, unquestioned in compassion, unassailable in his adherence to dogma. If the Inquest was a serpent whose strangling coils were suffocating the Dispersal of Man, then he would be a little worm gnawing at the serpent's heart, too small to notice until it was too late.

And he would seek out Darktouch, too! The laughter in the old man's eyes had rekindled all his hopes. He knew that there was a grand plan and that they were all part of it: he, Darktouch, the Lady Varuneh. Davaryush had not forsaken them. How could he have? He was wise. He was wily. And he alone had rediscovered the true compassion that was to have been the very heart of the High Inquest.

Kelver could see only a few pieces of the plan as yet. He, the innocent, was to be its beginning. And at its end was the death and rebirth of the human race. More than that he had yet to learn. It was a terrifying plan, an epic plan. And he was a child still, and easily frightened. All he wanted to do now was to run away and cry. But he composed his face and seemed outwardly at peace; for though he had only been on Uran s'Varek for a few sleeps, he knew already that an Inquestor does not weep.

— Paris, Alexandria, Charlotte: 1979-1981
— Alexandria, 1985
— Bangkok, 2020

Afterwords and Appendices

Afterword
Origin Stories

I have been asked more than once, "Where did the title come from?" They meant *Light on the Sound,* because it perhaps doesn't sound like science fiction. It could be a book about synaesthesia, or perhaps a romance with a romantic love scene overlooking Puget Sound.

It's an important question in a way because the Sunless Sound isn't strictly speaking a "sound" at all. According to Wikipedia, a sound is supposed to be "deeper than a bight and wider than a fjord" but the main thing is that its connected to an ocean.

The Sunless Sound couldn't possibly be connected to any ocean, not even the Sea of Tulangdaror, because the Skywall is a weird geographical anomaly—a vast *thing* jutting out from the surface of Gallendys, penetrating high into the stratosphere and so tightly sealed that it is capable of containing within it an atmosphere from a different era in the planet's past.

The truth is that the title predated the novel and even the Inquestor series, and in a way, the geography (or Gallendography, if you will) of the planet was engineered to fit the title.

The "sound" that inspired this title is actually the Connecticut Sound. A moment of bathos for all of you who were waiting for some exotic revelation, but I guess it is a story that I never told before.

In the days when I was ghostwriting symphonies for a humming millionaire (and I wrote *all* of that down in my memoir *Sounding Brass,* so I won't retell the tale here) I spent the long vacations from Cambridge in the United States.

Much of the time, I stayed at the home of an artist friend, her husband, a Yale historian, and their son, a young musician who played the flute and the guitar. They were an intelligent and complicated family whom I'd met when I was a teacher in a music camp in Holland and the kid was a student there. It was a strangely idyllic environment where I often felt more at peace than anywhere else (having a turbulent first two decades of existence.)

During the day, they were always at work and the kids were in school, and I watched old sitcoms while orchestrating fake nineteenth century symphonies and military marches in the style of Sousa, and once a week I would fly down to Washington to deliver my handiwork to the Pentagon. (Really, really, I've told all this elsewhere ... buy the other book.)

Each afternoon their son would get back earlier than his parents would, so he would entertain me ... sometimes by playing the guitar. One day I was helping him work out a riff that turned out to be in 5/4 time, and he started to improvise some lyrics that kept

S.P. Somtow

containing the words "light on the sound". And because the attic I slept in had a view of the Connecticut Sound, somehow this phrase, the view out of the attic window, and the plaintive (and slightly out of tune) quality of the young man's voice ... I don't know, it all melded into a sort of icon.

When I started working on the first Inquestor novel, I had only published a few stories and each story was a discovery. But this phrase, and this moment, had haunted me for a while—I'd say five or six years—and I basically conjured up a planet to fit the phrase.

I knew what the book was *called* long before I knew what it was *about*.

Is it a good title? I am not sure, really. It seems a bit self-conscious. I flirted with changing the title, or rather turning it into a subtitle: in order to confine the four Inquestor books into the semblance of a trilogy, I shoehorned the first two books into Parts I and II of *The Dawning Shadow*. Somehow it didn't stick. Bantam actually put an extraneous article on the over ... they made it THE *Light on the Sound* ... and told me it was too late to change it. (There is no article inside the book, just on the cover.)

I don't know where that family is now. Perhaps they will resurface as I flit from place to place. I do know that the title of the book is a recurring reminder, like a fading photo in an old album, of one of the few moments that I felt at peace.

Afterword
A Conlang in the Pre-Conlang Era

When I started the Inquestor series in 1978 or so (the first story came out in 1979 from *Analog* magazine) I had never heard the term *conlang* and didn't really know it existed. Not surprising since the term is first cited in 1991.

The fragments of a language that appeared in the first story, *The Thirteenth Utopia*, were brief. I just wanted something cool-sounding, and had no real thought of an underlying linguistic structure.

It occurred to me much later that I had unconsciously given the language a clear Indo-European structure:

qithe qithembara
udres a kilima shtoisti

Certainly the second line is *obviously* an Indo-European language of the "very inflected" variety.

"shtoisti" on the analogy of Latin is absolutely obviously a word with a second person plural, perfect tense ending.

"Udres" is an obvious genitive case, especially since "Udara" appears throughout the text. "A kilima" is clearly a preposition following by a noun in some kind of oblique case, perhaps the ablative as in Latin.

"Qithe qithembara" which I translated as "soul, renounce suffering" is less obvious: maybe a vocative case and an imperative or subjunctive form of some kind.

This language wasn't "Inquestral highspeech" but clearly seemed ancestral or connected to it in some way. But I thought nothing much if it until a couple of stories later; the "highspeech" was mentioned from time to time, but it was in *Rainbow King* which introduced the character of Sajit who eventually becomes the poet of the High Inquest's last days, that the need for actual, meaningful language creation became evident.

If Sajit is a singer, he must have songs to sing.

The first piece of "extended" writing in the highspeech was the song that Sajit performs in the story *Rainbow King* (Asimov's SF Magazine, Feb 1981). It was the cover story with a gorgeous illustration by the much loved gay artist George Barr. I possess one of George's rough sketches for this story and would love to share it here.

This song is quoted in several of the Inquestor novels (though it has never been quoted in its entirety). It established some distinctive features of the language, for instance:

There's a *temporative* case as well as a locative case common to early Indo-European languages:

asheverain "at the time the Dispersal took place"

There's a compound perfect tense formed with some kind of contracted form of the verb *to be* and some kind of participle:

am-plãzhet "we have wept"

There's a richness of consonants and relatively few vowels (well, only about seven, long and short) and an abundance of nasalizations, making a bit like (a fan once said to me) "Sanskrit with a Portuguese accent."

The entire language did not spring fully formed into my head. Rather, as pieces of it had to be written out, little sentence fragments popped into my mind, or individual words. But it was a question from Berkeley area reader and linguist Jan Murphy that made me realize there was a lot more to the iceberg than I thought.

She was asking a question about the subjunctive — whether such and such a word was a subjunctive or not.

And I realized that the sentences and poems I was creating purely for my own clarifcation were actually analysable by Indo-European language experts. I'd created a language that could be deciphered. Buried somewhere in the subtext of these stories was a "real" language struggling to be given a voice.

As a language spoken only by an elite, performed in by poets, used as a medium only for games of ambiguity and deceit played out by millennially-aged, jaded people, it needed to be a language that's very concentrated and flexible. It also didn't have to be an "easy" language because knowledge of High Inquestral is considered a prestige accomplishment, though planetbound people would know a few expressions and could probably struggle through a basic document to some extent. It's definitely not a *lingua franca*.

It was important that the language be sonorous, with a strong sense of melody, easily manipulated consonants, and open vowels for singing with few diphthongs

Now that the basic context of *Bhasháhokh* was in place, the snatches of song became more substantial and it became possible to actually write poetry in Inquestral. And the dreaded *rules of grammar* started rearing their ugly heads (hydra heads, for whenever one was vanquished, two more would sprout.)

The language has some things in common with Panini's treatise on Sanskrit — first, it was composed at a time when Sanskrit literature was in full bloom, yet the language itself hadn't been spoken by that many people in centuries; and second, anything not actually forbidden would be allowed.

During the period in which Sajit is composing his songs, the High Inquestral tongue too is no longer an actively growing language. It once had a complex system of declensions with various endings for each declension. But, since the underpinning logic of the declensions, the active process of sandhi by which endings get absorbed and changed by time, was no longer operative, it became the custom that the noun declension groups were ignored — any ending of the correct case from any declension could be attached to any noun stem, allowing poets a lot of leeway in scansion.

Thus, *chirarans hyemadh* means "the homeworld of the heart" but "of the heart" could as easily be any of

chitarans, chitaras, chitrans, chitari, chitrens, chitars, chitras

and even others; all these forms could be legitimately used, though the phrase *chitarans hyemadh* is a catch-phrase and in that context only that form of *chitar* would be preferred.

To understand the bewildering and exuberantly freewheeling use of just about "any ending that will scan" in Inquesral poetry, I must take you back to my childhood, and to the horrifying "Dippy" Simpson, my housemaster and Latin teacher.

Dippy was the author of Cassell's Latin Dictionary and a noted classicist. Eton, my school, is know for hiring some of the greatest scholars in their fields away from higher academe or real-life jobs in order to educate its boys. Dippy was a legendary figure, as bizarre as, yet all too much more accessible than, the Dickensian Mr. Squeers. My friend Tony Little, who was at school with me and later, ironically, became headmaster of Eton, said to me recently, "Today such a man wouldn't be allowed *near* children."

No, no, this isn't an anecdote about illicit sex acts. Dippy's crime was, if anything, far worse: he belittled young people to the point of crushing their egos into nothing.

There I was, in the 1960s, in an incredible prestigious and progressive school (yes, they wore tails, but the education itself was extremely ahead of its time) — by day, reading Wagner scores in the library, going to classes with the (even more legendary) Michael Meredith who would discuss sexual imagery in Bergman films or at the drop of a hat take the whole class to London to see Ian McKellen in *Edward II*, hanging out with, and often being taught by, brilliant people who forced one to think all the time — and by night, returning to a dank, Victorian prison presided over by a gloomy, petty tyrant to whom forgetting that "motion towards" takes the accusative case was a far worse crime than poisoning one's mother.

Never one to waste anything, Dippy had cut up the galley proofs of his Latin dictionary (those were the days they came in long sort of roll-like sheets) and used to hand out the blank side for people people to answer tests on. One always prayed that the right answer would magically be listed on the other side of the paper, but it was always some other part of the dictionary.

From the day I stepped off the BOAC plane, a little boy from a Third World country traveling alone for the first time and arriving in a freezing, snowing February, I knew that getting the right ending to a Latin verb was the most important thing in the universe.

For this man greeted me as I came through immigration with the words "What is the Latin for 'I shall have used?'

I didn't know.

My fate was sealed.

I don't know if my feelings about my old school would be so conflicted if I had found myself living in a more liberal house. I *know* that other boys were not belittled on a daily basis by a madman with absolute power over them. I envied the fact that other houses produced plays and concerts — but we did not. I despaired people in my house were denied many of the enabling features the school provided.

A few years ago, visiting and speaking to people running the place now, I realize how much I missed. But also ... how much I *didn't* miss. The *school* (as opposed to the houses) *did* produce plays and concerts and I was deeply involved in some of those as I couldn't really be prevented from doing so. Indeed, I was a member of the exclusive invitation-only Praed Society (the Eton society of poets) and secretary of the Parry Society (the exclusive music group.) The school library — that's where I discovered the complete works of Hugo von Hoffmannsthal, for instance, one of whose plays became the basis for my abortive second opera.

Had I but known the Latin for "I shall have used" that day, I would not have spent the next five years living the life of a *schlimazel!*

I would like to say that today, as I was writing this article, the Latin for "I shall have used," *usus ero,* came unbidden into my mind. It is a deponent verb — it takes passive endings while being present in meaning. The stem ends in a consonant, forcing all kinds of *sandhi* when it is conjugated (and always remembering that you have to conjugate it in the opposite *voice* of its meaning.) I don't know how much of the limited hard drive space in my deteriorating brain is filled with all these verb forms, but you can see how it was all burned in.

One of the joys of creating the grammar of *Bhashahokh* was to envisage a more complicated system of rules than Latin, Greek, and Sanskrit, with a verb that allowed huge degrees of variation in shade of

meaning with just a single vowel shift or even moving
the stress — and then to create a culture in which
everyone who used the language felt free to ignore the
rules at will.

To make the language softer and more susceptible
to melismatic adornment, I decided early on it should
have a tonic stress like earlier Indo-European
languages rather than a stress accent. The stress is
always marked on every word *unless* it's on the
penultimate syllable (as in Spanish). This saves
accents. To avoid two many diacritics, the tilde used to
indicate nasalisation is assumed to carry the accent
unless a different syllable happens to carry the accent.
This is only true in the romanized transcription
because in Inquestral script a nasalization is written as
a subscript.

Vocabulary? Clearly Indo-European, but not
derived from one stream of Indo-European in
particular, giving the impression that the vocabulary
came from many sources and was adopted during more
than one period.

I could go on and on, but there won't be anything to
say in succeeding appendices if I spill all the beans
now. Here followeth the appendix from the Bantam
edition of 1986....

Appendix
The Inquestral Highspeech

Bhasháhokh, or High Inquestral, is a highly inflected Indo-European language; a competent linguist can probably figure out most of it without the aid of this glossary, and no attempt will be made here to list roots or grammatical paradigms.

At the time of the fall of the Inquest. the language was used mostly on ceremonial occasions, during the game of *makrúgh*, where its built-in ambiguities gave the Inquestors plenty of opportunities for insinuation and outright mendacity; and in poetry and in learned treatises. Obsolete and obsolescent forms appeared side by side with neologisms, and there were a number of principal dialects.

In this transliteration, certain peculiarities of the *Bhasháhokh* orthography (such as the subscripts used in certain grammatical cases, and by convention in certain words and notably names) are ignored; again the reader may, if he is so inclined, peruse the provided material and puzzle out the orthographic principles and idiosyncrasies of the script for himself.

A number of words in the lowspeech (the vernacular, which varied from planet to planet and from region to region on any planet) are included in the glossary and noted as such.

The form in which the words appears within the text is first noted, then its dictionary form (the nominative singular of nouns, the first person singular indicative active of verbs), then its meaning.

Pronunciation of High Inquestral

Because of the proliferation of dialects, almost any pronunciation that the reader may care to inflict upon a highspeech word would probably reflect the correct pronunciation for one dialect or another. However, the highspeech of Elloran's palace of Varezhdur, which is one of the dialects that most accurately reflects the highspeech's formal orthography, is given below as a guide.

Vowels: *a,e,i,o,* and *u* may be given approximately the Italian pronunciation. The vowel *y* is pronounced thus: place the mouth in the position to utter the vowel *e* and try to say the sound *u*. The diglyph *yu*, as in Davaryush, Ayulla, is pronounced somewhat like the German *ü* or the French *u*.

There are no true diphthongs in High Inquestral; a combination such as *aiud* represents three syllables in distinct speech.

Most consonants may safely be pronounced as in English. The combination *gh* is a "gargling" sound similar to the French *r,-* the combination *kh* is a highly aspirated *k* sound. *G* is always hard. *q* is a sound similar to the ch in English "*chime.*" *Ch* is similar, but without the aspiration. The sound *th* is pronounced as in "pothook," never as in "think." Similarly, *dh* is pronounced as in "headhunter." The letter *s* is often pronounced with a hint of *sh*, reminiscent of Castilian.

Nasalization: A vowel followed by *n* is lightly nasalized. In this transliteration. a strong nasalization is represented   by adding a silent h to the vowel: *chadáh, shirénzheh.* The nasalization of final vowels is an important feature of the languages inflectional structure,   being the distinguishing feature in the third person of most verb tenses and the accusative case of many nouns.

Stress: High lnquestral has a tonic stress, i.e., not a percussive stress as in English but a slight lifting of the pitch of the syllable. All words except post-enclitics, prepositions, and a few other minor words and particles must have an accent on one of the last three syllables; very occasionally on the fourth syllable from the end. All stresses are shown in the glossary, but in the body of the text they have been used more rarely in order not to distract the reader.

Inquestral Vocabulary
Light on the Sound

a . . . ayán (poet) under, upon
a . . . éndek (poet) on, onto
af even
af. . .aút (poet) even
áias from *áia*, sighing, sussurant
aíroten from *aíros*, love
áish dust
aiud, aiuath from éo, to come or go
aiúved from *aiúvo*, to yawn
aivermatsá from *aivermadh*, overcosm
ál'ksigark, ál'ksigarkar (lowspeech) al'ksigark
am-plánzhet from *planzho*, to weep
-*ang* (suffix) from *angkier*; frequent ending in the
      names of cities
angkier city
árissath from *arísso*, to till (soil, etc.) arshenath from
      ársheno, to seek out and find
asheveraín from *ashéver*, the Dispersal of Man

brendéh from *bréndo*, to burn

chadáh, chadaih, from *chédo*, to fall
chitara, chitarans, chitaras from *chitara*, heart or soul

dáded from *déo.* to speak
dárein, dáraran, dáras from *dára*, star
davémyras, davémyrah from *davéh*, boy, and *-myras*,
    suffix indicating one million
den (without accent) of or from
dén (with accent) not
dhánata death
dhándas from *dhand*, dead
dhanándah from *dhándo*, to be dead
dhand-erúden, from *dhand-erúd*, the dead earth
din you

eíh exclamation; melisma used in song
eih héng, as above
éis from *ó*, to be
eké one, alone
ekándar famous
ekáqila one hundred thousand
eléthat from *elétho*, to forget
eméruat, emérud from *eméruo*, to become
Enguésti from *Enguésta*, the Inquest
Enguéstri from *Enguéster*, Inquestor
entinjet from *tinjo*, to touch
erdhándat from *erdhándo*, to die
erúden from *erúd*, earth
<u>*eskrendaí*</u> from *skréo*, to cry out
evéndek forever
eyáh from *ó*, to he (3rd pers. sing.)

fáh from *ó*, to be (aorist)
falláh from *fállo*, to break, burst, fall
f'áng a mildly intoxicating mist
fáx river
faxéqilas from *fax* and *-qilas*, suflix meaning one
    thousand
ferávo to ask
fluáh, fluaih from *fluo* to flow

hos, hóshan, hox relative pronouns
hokh'Kéliass high compassion a term specific to
    makrúgh
hokhté you, when addressing an exalted personage
    from a position of humility
hokh'Tón you, when addressing an Inquestor
hyéma blood
hyémadh, hyemadhá from *hyémadh*, homeworld

ishá ha! a war cry used by childsoldiers in the employ
    of Ton Davaryush

jángyll a species of food fowl

ka (without accent) for, on behalf of
ká (with accent) from *kós*, the universe, the cosmos
kéana, kéanis from *keian*, ocean
kel relative pronoun
kézi, from *kézeh*, home
kilima (speech of Shtoma) face
kíndaran from *kinth*, child
klomet a unit of measurement of distance,
    approximately one kilometer

K'Ning part of the titles of Kinglings

lávoryman from *lávorem*, tear
laúker rich
lévaran from *lévas*, lips
liddar from *lith*, song
lukhs light

makrúgh Inquestral game of political strategy
mi, min, mun various cases of *ish* and *sarnáng*, I
mílilas from *mílila*, childsoldier
mór mother

náruvas from *nárop*, new
nekénqilas nine hundred thousand (Please note that
    the suffix *-qilas*, strictly meaning a thousand, can
    he used in folk poetry to mean a hundred, a
    thousand, or even a generalized very large
    number; hence the apparently aberrant usage of
    néqilas [below] to mean nine hundred in the song
    quoted.)
nendé néqilas ninety-nine thousand
néqilas nine thousand or nine hundred (poet)
nevéqilas from *néva*, snow, and *-qilas* (q.v.)
nikah, nikas from *nika*, world, planet

óm man
ómbrel, y'ómbren from *ombrel*, shadow
ongá relative pronoun
oráden from *orád*, command
o-tinjet from *tinjo*, to touch

péftifesht Shtoman pastry
pu where?

qithe (Shtoman) soul
qithémbara (Shtoman) renounce suffering!

sarnáng humble form of the pronoun I
seréh from ó, to be
setáliken from *setálikeh*, a delphinoid shipmind
shénjesh the expository section of a game of *makrúgh*
shénom, shenáh, shénete, shendánde, shendándere
      various forms of the verb *shéno*, to yearn or long
      for
shentráor singer
shéntrath from *shéntro*, to sing
shirénzheh from *shirénzhe*, silence
shténjuu from *shténjo*, to distill
shtézhnat a board game played by old men and
      children
shtoisti (Shtoman) you have danced
skáapnai from *skapen*, creator, maker
skevzúh from *skévo*, to make, create
sta from

talássas sea, ocean, sound
t'am-plánzho from *plánzho*, to weep "I weep for you."
Tash a Rememberer (clan name)
tekiánveras from *tekiánver*, tachyon bubble
témbres, témbris from *témber*, dark
Tón Inquestor (clan name)

udára, udrés (Shtoman) the sun

vállath from *vállo* to dance
varánde having achieved a state of enlightenment
varúng mad

vashonuúr from *vashEonaar*, to feel pain
verávis from *ferávo*, to ask
vérdens from *férdo*, to freeze
vérderax the Cold River
verék alive

yauxúh from *yaúxaar*, to grow up, esp. to come of age
    yéng ferret (clan name)
ýpnat, ypnándaran from *ýpno*, to dream
ýpnolan from *ýpnor*, dreamer
yunáki a meat animal
ývrens from *ývro*, to burst, to fly

z and; pertaining to; of
zénz without
zenzÁtheren sunless
zhalá from *zhalo*, to envy
z'hartnen wasteland, desert
zúl a fermented drink made from certain fruits

Appendix II
The Inquestral Question: Solved at Last?
some textual notes on the second edition

by Professor Shnau-en-Jip

Those unfamiliar with the recent scholarship concerning the High Inquestral sagas may not be aware of how much more material has come to light during the past few years. It is to this end that I have taken the liberty of preparing an edition substantially different from that which has previously been taken as the standard text by the entire community of Inquestral scholars.

While this is not the place for a detailed contextual analysis of the enormous treasury of Inquestral fragments recently excavated from the tholos-tombs of Ont, it seems clear to me, and to many of my colleagues, that the new fragments, matched as they are to the known text in style, diction, and in their vision of the mythical Inquestral Age that preceded the

Dark Ages, must he considered genuine. The fact that they supply details of motive and character, and answer questions scholars have been asking for millennia, and that they fill in lacunae known only to those who have spent their entire lives analyzing the Inquestral sagas, is an especially salient one, for it vindicates more than ever the single-author theory which has lately fallen into such ill repute among those who would solve the most hotly argued puzzle of our time.

As to why the putative single author may have prepared more than one version of his text . . . I am delighted to prophesy that, though the single-author question may have been answered once and for all by this new discovery, this new enigma will continue to occupy the minds of Inquestral scholars for generations to come.

It appears that we will not, as we had feared, be deprived of our livelihood after all.

(The above Appendix appeared in the Bantam edition of *Light on the Sound* and is included for the completists.)

An Appeal to My Readers

The republication of the Inquestor Series was made possible because a few dozen people became my supporters by joining this website:

www.patreon.com/spsomtow

I'm no longer doing these books with the backing of a vast New York publishing conglomerate. It's pretty much do-it-yourself, with all the labor-intensiveness, snatching time away from money-making activities, and sloppy trying to proofread one's own copy implies.

If a few dozen more people would sign up — or a few hundred — my ability to resume my science fiction career would be much enhanced. So, please consider it.

Supporters get to read all my books chapter by chapter — in their unenhanced, inaccurately proofread and yet-to-be refined incarnations — right as they come out of my head. They get Christmas presents (though I am habitually late with them). You can join for as little a $2 a month — though hopefully you will be able to do a higher level.

About the Author

The most well-known expatriate Thai in the world
— *International Herald Tribune*

Once referred to by the International Herald
Tribune as "the most well-known expatriate Thai in the
world," Somtow Sucharitkul is no longer an expatriate,
since he has returned to Thailand after five decades of
wandering the world. He is best known as an award
winning novelist and a composer of operas.

Born in Bangkok, Somtow grew up in Europe and
was educated at Eton and Cambridge. His first career
was in music and in the 1970s he acquired a reputation
as a revolutionary composer, the first to combine Thai
and Western instruments in radical new sonorities.
Conditions in the arts in the region at the time proved
so traumatic for the young composer that he suffered a
major burnout, emigrated to the United States, and
reinvented himself as a novelist.

His earliest novels were in the science fiction field
but he soon began to cross into other genres. In his
1984 novel Vampire Junction, he injected a new literary
inventiveness into the horror genre, in the words of
Robert Bloch, author of *Psycho*, "skillfully combining
the styles of Stephen King, William Burroughs, and the

author of the Revelation to John." *Vampire Junction* was voted one of the forty all-time greatest horror books by the Horror Writers' Association, joining established classics like *Frankenstein* and *Dracula.*

In the 1990s Somtow became increasingly identified as a uniquely Asian writer with novels such as the semi-autobiographical *Jasmine Nights.* He won the World Fantasy Award, the highest accolade given in the world of fantastic literature, for his novella *The Bird Catcher.* His seventy-seven books have sold about two million copies world-wide.

After becoming a Buddhist monk for a period in 2001, Somtow decided to refocus his attention on the country of his birth, founding Bangkok's first international opera company and returning to music, where he again reinvented himself, this time as a neo Asian neo-Romantic composer. The Norwegian government commissioned his song cycle Songs Before Dawn for the 100th Anniversary of the Nobel Peace Prize, and he composed at the request of the government of Thailand his *Requiem: In Memoriam 9/11* which was dedicated to the victims of the 9/11 tragedy.

According to London's Opera magazine, "in just five years, Somtow has made Bangkok into the operatic hub of Southeast Asia." His operas on Thai themes, *Madana, Mae Naak,* and *Ayodhya,* have been well received by international critics. His opera, *The Silent Prince,* was premiered in 2010 in Houston, and, *Dan no Ura,* premiered in Thailand in the 2013 season. Since then he has composed many more stage works including the acclaimed fantasy-based opera *The Snow Dragon* (premiered in Milwaukee in 2015) and seven operas in the *DasJati* sequence which aims to put all ten of the iconic *Ten Lives of the Buddha* into music drama form.

He is increasingly in demand as a conductor specializing in opera and in the late-romantic composers like Mahler. His repertoire runs the entire gamut from Monteverdi to Wagner. His work has been especially lauded for its stylistic authenticity and its lyricism. The orchestra he founded in Bangkok, the Siam Philharmonic, has mounted the first complete Mahler cycle in the region.

He was the first recipient of Thailand's "Distinguished Silpathorn" award, given for an artist who has made and continues to make a major impact on the region's culture, from Thailand's Ministry of Culture.

In 2017 he was awarded the European Cultural Achievement Award by the Europa KulturForum, citing his building of bridges between Asian and Western cultures.

Books by S.P. Somtow

General Fiction
The Shattered Horse
Jasmine Nights
Forgetting Places
The Other City of Angels (aka *Bluebeard's Castle)*
The Stone Buddha's Tears

Dark Fantasy
The Timmy Valentine Series:
> *Vampire Junction*
> *Valentine*
> *Vanitas*

Vampire Junction Special Edition
Moon Dance
Darker Angels
The Vampire's Beautiful Daughter

Science Fiction
Starship & Haiku
Mallworld
The Ultimate Mallworld
The Ultimate, Ultimate, Ultimate Mallworld

Chronicles of the High Inquest:
   Light on the Sound
   The Darkling Wind
   The Throne of Madness
   Utopia Hunters
   Homeworld of the Heart
   Stillness in Starlight (in press)
Chroniques de l'Inquisition - Volume 1 (omnibus)
Chroniques de l'Inquisition - Volume 2 (omnibus)
Inquestor Tales One: The Singing Moons
Inquestor Tales Two: A Woman Cloaked in Shadow
Inquestor Tales Three: The Child Collector
Inquestor Tales Four: The Space Between Spaces
Inquestor Tales Five: Goddess in the Ruins

The Aquiliad Series:
   Aquila in the New World
   Aquila and the Iron Horse
   Aquila and the Sphinx

Fantasy
The Riverrun Trilogy:
   Riverrun
   Armorica
   Yestern
The Riverrun Trilogy (omnibus)
The Fallen Country
Wizard's Apprentice
The Snow Dragon (omnibus)

Media Tie-in
The Alien Swordmaster
Symphony of Terror
The Crow - Temple of Night

Star Trek: Do Comets Dream?

Chapbooks
Fiddling for Waterbuffaloes
I Wake from a Dream of a Drowned Star City
A Lap Dance with the Lobster Lady
Compassion: Two Perspectives
The Bird Catcher

Libretti
Mae Naak
Ayodhya
Madana
Dan no Ura
Helena Citronova
The Snow Dragon
Dasjati:
      Temiya - The Silent Prince
      Sama - The Faithful Son
      Bhuridat - The Dragon Lord
      Mahosadha - Architect of Dreams
      Nemiraj - Chariot of Heaven
      Prince Vessantara

Collections
My Cold Mad Father
Fire from the Wine Dark Sea
Chui Chai (Thai)
Nova (Thai)
The Pavilion of Frozen Women
Dragon's Fin Soup
Tagging the Moon
Face of Death (Thai)
Other Edens

S.P. Somtow's The Great Tales (Thai)
Terror Nova (in press)
Terror Antiqua (in press)
Alien Heresies (in press)

Essays, Poetry and Miscellanies
Opus Fifty
A Certain Slant of "I" (in press)
Sonnets about Serial Killers
Opera East
Victory in Vienna (ed.)
Three Continents (ed.)
Nirvana Express
Sounding Brass
Caravaggio x 2
The Maestro's Noctuary
Nox: Noctuary Two